Summer of '69

ALSO BY ELIN HILDERBRAND

The Beach Club

Nantucket Nights

Summer People

The Blue Bistro

The Love Season

Barefoot

A Summer Affair

The Castaways

The Island

Silver Girl

Summerland

Beautiful Day

The Matchmaker

Winter Street

The Rumor

Winter Stroll

Here's to Us

Winter Storms

The Identicals

Winter Solstice

The Perfect Couple

Winter in Paradise

Summer of '69

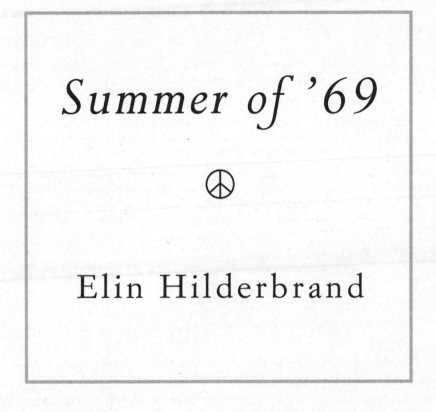

Elin Hilderbrand

Little, Brown and Company

New York   Boston   London

Little, Brown and Company
Hachette Book Group
1290 Avenue of the Americas, New York, NY 10104
littlebrown.com

First Edition: June 2019

Little, Brown and Company is a division of Hachette Book Group, Inc. The Little, Brown name and logo are trademarks of Hachette Book Group, Inc.

The publisher is not responsible for websites (or their content) that are not owned by the publisher.

The Hachette Speakers Bureau provides a wide range of authors for speaking events. To find out more, go to hachettespeakersbureau.com or call (866) 376-6591.

ISBN 978-0-316-42001-3 (hardcover) / 978-0-316-45416-2 (large print) / 978-0-316-49281-2 (Canadian) / 978-0-316-45799-6 (Target) / 978-0-316-45801-6 (Barnes and Noble) / 978-0-316-45803-0 (signed)
LCCN 2018967263

10 9 8 7 6 5 4 3 2 1

LSC-C

Printed in the United States of America

*This book is for the three people who were
with me in the early-morning hours of
July 17, 1969:*

*My mother, Sally Hilderbrand, who went into
labor four weeks before her due date;*

*My maternal grandmother, Ruth Huling, who
"ran every red light" to get my mother to the
Boston Hospital for Women;*

*My twin brother, Eric Hilderbrand, who I
imagine turned to me and said,
"Are you ready for this?"*

Summer of '69

Prologue

Fortunate Son

When the Selective Service notice comes for Tiger, Kate's first instinct is to throw it away. Surely this is every American mother's first instinct? Pretend it got lost in the mail, buy Tiger a few more weeks of freedom before the U.S. Army sends another letter— by which time, this god-awful war in Vietnam might be over. Nixon has promised to end it. There are peace talks going on right now in Paris. Le Duan will succumb to the allure of capitalism or Thieu will be assassinated and someone with better sense will take over. Frankly, Kate doesn't *care* if Vietnam succumbs to the Communists. She just wants to keep her son safe.

When Tiger gets home from his job at the driving school, Kate says, "There's a letter for you on the kitchen table." Tiger seems unconcerned about what it might be. He's whistling, wearing the polyester uniform shirt issued by Walden Pond Driving Academy with his name stitched on the pocket: *Richard*. The letter uses that first name too—it's addressed to Richard Foley—though no one ever calls him anything but Tiger.

Tiger says, "I taught a real cutie today, Ma. Name was Magee, that was her *first* name, which I thought was far out. She's nineteen, like me, studying to be a dental hygienist. I flashed her my pearly whites and then I asked her out to dinner for tonight and she said yes. You'll like her, I bet."

Kate busies herself at the sink arranging daffodils in a vase. She closes her eyes and thinks, *These are the last easy thoughts he'll ever have.*

And sure enough, a second later, he says, "Oh jeez, oh wow..." He clears his throat. "Ma?"

Kate spins around, clutching a handful of daffodils in front of her like a cross to ward off a vampire. The expression on Tiger's face is part shock, part excitement, part terror.

"I got called up," he says. "I'm to report to the army recruitment office in South Boston on April twenty-first."

April 21 is Kate's birthday. She'll be forty-eight years old. In forty-eight years, she has been married twice and had four children, three daughters and a son. She would never say she loves the son the most; she will say only that she loves him differently. It's the fierce, all-consuming love that any mother feels for her child, but with a dash of extra indulgence. Her handsome son—so much like his father, but kind. And good.

Kate opens her wallet and sets twenty dollars on the table in front of Tiger. "For your date tonight," she says. "Go someplace nice."

On April 21, it's Kate who takes Tiger from Brookline to South Boston. David offered to drive, but Kate wanted to do it alone. "He's my son," she said, and a flicker of astonished pain crossed David's face—they never speak in those terms, *her* children, meaning *not* his—and Kate berated herself while at the same time thinking that if David wanted to know what real pain was, he should try being her. Tiger said goodbye to David and his three sisters in the driveway. Kate had instructed the girls not to cry. "We don't want him to think he's never coming back," she said.

And yet it's this exact fear that's holding Kate hostage: That Tiger will die on foreign soil. He will be shot in the stomach or the head; he will be killed by a grenade. He will drown in a rice paddy; he will burn in a helicopter crash. Kate has seen it night after night on the news. American boys are dying, and what have Kennedy and Johnson and, now, Nixon done? Sent more boys.

At the recruitment office, Kate pulls into a line of cars. Ahead of them, kids just like Tiger are hugging their parents, some of them for the last time. Right? It's indisputable that a percentage of the boys right here in South Boston are headed to their deaths.

Kate puts the car in park. It's obvious from watching everyone else that this is going to be quick. Tiger grabs his rucksack from the back seat and Kate gets out of the car and hurries around. She takes a moment to fix Tiger in her eyes. He's nineteen years old, six foot two, a hundred and eighty pounds, and he has let his blond hair grow over the collar of his shirt, much to the dismay of Kate's mother, Exalta, but the U.S. Army will take care of that pronto. He has clear green eyes, one of them with an elongated pupil like honey dripping off a spoon; someone said it looked like a tiger eye, which was how he got his nickname.

Tiger has a high-school diploma and one semester of college at Framingham State. He listens to Led Zeppelin and the Who; he loves fast cars. He dreams of someday racing in the Indy 500.

And then, without warning, Kate is sucked back in time. Tiger was born a week past his due date and weighed nine pounds, twelve ounces. He took his first steps at ten months old, which is very early, but he was intent on chasing after Blair and Kirby. At age seven, he could name every player on the Red Sox lineup; Ted Williams was his favorite. At age twelve, Tiger hit three consecutive home runs in his final game of Little League. He was voted class president in eighth grade and then quickly and wisely lost interest in politics. He took up bowling as a rainy-day pastime in Nantucket and won his first tournament soon after. Then, in high school, there was football. Tiger Foley holds every receiving record at Brookline High School, including total receiving yards, a record Coach Bevilacqua predicts will never be broken. He was recruited to play at Penn State, but Tiger didn't want to travel that far from home, and UMass's team wasn't exciting enough— or at least that's what Tiger claimed. Kate suspects that Tiger just ran out of enthusiasm for the game or preferred to go out on top or just really, really disliked the idea of four more years of school. Kate would have liked to point out that if Tiger had gone to college, any college, or if he had stayed at Framingham State part-time, he would not be in this position right now.

"Don't forget, you promised to check in on Magee," Tiger says.

Magee; he's worried about Magee. Tiger and Magee went on their first date the day Tiger got the letter and they've been insepa- rable ever since. Privately, Kate thought it was unwise to jump into a relationship only two weeks before going to war, but it might have been the distraction he needed. Kate has agreed to check in on Magee, who Tiger says will be very upset that he's gone, but there is no way a girlfriend of two weeks will be as upset as the soldier's own mother.

A tour of duty is thirteen months, not a lifetime, but some of the mothers here outside the recruitment office are unknowingly say- ing a permanent goodbye, and Kate feels certain she's one of them. The other mothers didn't do the terrible thing that she did. She deserves to be punished; she has enjoyed every happy day of the past sixteen years like it was something she borrowed, and now, fi- nally, the time for payback has arrived. Kate had thought it would be a cancer diagnosis or a car accident or a house fire. She never considered that she would lose her son. But here she is. This is her fault.

"I love you, Ma," Tiger says.

The obvious response to Tiger is *I love you too,* but instead Kate says, "I'm sorry." She hugs Tiger so tightly that she feels his ribs beneath his spring jacket. "I'm so sorry, baby."

Tiger kisses her forehead and doesn't let go of her hand until the last possible second. When he finally goes in, Kate hurriedly gets back into the car. Out the window, she sees Tiger heading for the open door. A gentleman in a brown uniform barks something at him and Tiger stands up straighter and squares his shoulders. Kate stares at her fingers gripping the steering wheel. She can't bear to watch him disappear.

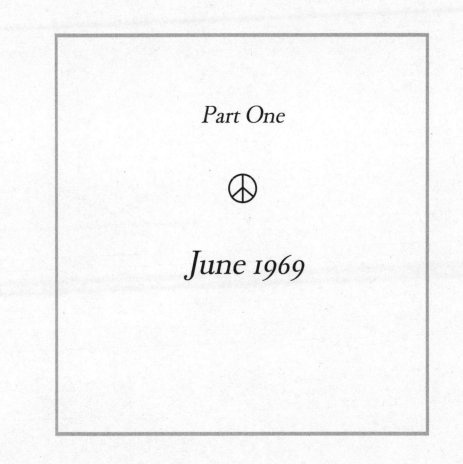

Part One

June 1969

Both Sides Now

They are leaving for Nantucket on the third Monday in June, just as they always do. Jessie's maternal grandmother, Exalta Nichols, is a stickler for tradition, and this is especially true when it comes to the routines and rituals of summer.

The third Monday in June is Jessie's thirteenth birthday, which will now be overlooked. That's fine with Jessie. Nothing can be properly celebrated without Tiger anyway.

Jessica Levin ("Rhymes with 'heaven,'" she tells people) is the youngest of her mother's four children. Jessie's sister Blair is twenty-four years old and lives on Commonwealth Avenue. Blair is married to an MIT professor named Angus Whalen. They're expecting their first baby in August, which means that Jessie's mother, Kate, will be returning to Boston to help, leaving Jessie alone with her grandmother on Nantucket. Exalta isn't a warm and fuzzy grandmother who bakes cookies and pinches cheeks. For Jessie, every interaction with Exalta is like falling headlong into a pricker bush; it's not a question of whether she will be stuck, only where and how badly. Jessie has floated the possibility of returning to Boston with Kate, but her mother's response was "You shouldn't have to interrupt your summer."

"It wouldn't be interrupting," Jessie insisted. The truth is, coming back early would mean *saving* her summer. Jessie's friends

Leslie and Doris stay in Brookline and swim at the country club using Leslie's family's membership. Last summer, Leslie and Doris grew closer in Jessie's absence. Their bond made up the sturdiest side of the triangle, leaving Jessie on shaky ground. Leslie is the queen bee among them because she's blond and pretty and her parents are occasionally dinner guests of Teddy and Joan Kennedy. Leslie sometimes gives Jessie and Doris the impression that she thinks she's doing them a favor by remaining their friend. She has enough social currency to hang with Pammy Pope and the really popular girls if she wants. With Jessie gone all summer, Leslie might disappear from her life for good.

Jessie's next older sister, Kirby, is a junior at Simmons College. Kirby's arguments with their parents are loud and fascinating. Years of eavesdropping on her parents' conversations have led Jessie to understand the main problem: Kirby is a "free spirit" who "doesn't know what's good for her." Kirby changed her major twice at Simmons, then she tried to create her own major, Gender and Racial Studies, but it was rejected by the dean. And so Kirby decided she would be the first student ever to graduate from Simmons *without* a major. Again, the dean said no.

"He said graduating without a major would be like attending the commencement ceremony in the nude," Kirby told Jessie. "And I said he shouldn't tempt me."

Jessie can easily imagine her sister striding across the stage to accept her diploma in just her birthday suit. Kirby started participating in political protests while she was still in high school. She marched with Dr. Martin Luther King Jr. from Roxbury through the slums and dangerous neighborhoods to Boston Common, where Jessie's father picked Kirby up and took her home. This past year, Kirby marched in two antiwar protests and got arrested both times.

Arrested!

Jessie's parents are running out of patience with Kirby—Jessie overheard her mother saying, "We aren't giving that girl *another dime* until she learns to color inside the lines!"—but Kirby is no longer their biggest concern.

Their biggest concern is Jessie's brother, Richard, known to one and all as Tiger, who was drafted into the U.S. Army in April. After basic training, Tiger was deployed to the Central Highlands of Vietnam with Charlie Company of the Twelfth Regiment of the Third Brigade of the Fourth Infantry. This situation has rocked the foundation of the family. They'd all believed that only working-class boys went to war, not star receivers from Brookline High School.

Everyone at school treated Jessie differently after Tiger was deployed. Pammy Pope invited Jessie to her family's annual Memorial Day picnic—Jessie declined out of loyalty to Leslie and Doris, who hadn't been included—and the guidance counselor Miss Flowers pulled Jessie out of class one Monday in early June to see how she was doing. The class was home economics, and Jessie's leaving inspired enormous envy in all the other girls, who were battling with their sewing machines in an attempt to finish their navy corduroy vests before the end of the term. Miss Flowers brought Jessie to her office, closed the door, and made Jessie a cup of hot tea using an electric kettle. Jessie didn't drink hot tea, although she liked coffee—Exalta permitted Jessie one cup of milky coffee at Sunday brunch, despite Kate's protests that it would stunt Jessie's growth—but Jessie enjoyed the escape to the cozy confines of Miss Flowers's office. Miss Flowers had a wooden box filled with exotic teas—chamomile, chicory, jasmine—and Jessie chose a flavor as if her life depended on picking the right one. She decided on hibiscus. The tea was a pale orange color even after the tea bag had steeped for several minutes. Jessie added three cubes of sugar, fearing the tea would have no taste otherwise. And she was right; it tasted like orange sugar water.

"So," Miss Flowers said. "I understand your brother is overseas. Have you heard from him yet?"

"Two letters," Jessie said. One of the letters had been addressed to the entire family and included details of basic training, which Tiger said was "not at all as hard as you read about; for me it was a piece of cake." The other letter had been for Jessie alone. She wasn't sure if Blair and Kirby had gotten their own letters, but Jessie kind of doubted it. Blair, Kirby, and Tiger were all full biological siblings—they were the children of Kate and her first husband, Lieutenant Wilder Foley, who had served along the thirty-eighth parallel in Korea and then come home and accidentally shot himself in the head with his Beretta—but Tiger was closest to his half sister, Jessie. Actually, they weren't allowed to use the terms *half sister, half brother,* and *stepfather*—Kate flat-out forbade it—but whether or not anyone chose to acknowledge it, the family had a fault line. They were two families stitched together. But the relationship between Tiger and Jessie felt real and whole and good, and what he had said in the letter proved that. The first line, *Dear Messie,* made tears stand in Jessie's eyes.

"Letters are the only thing that make it easier," Miss Flowers said, and at that point, her eyes had been brimming as well. Miss Flowers's fiancé, Rex Rothman, had been killed in the Tet Offensive the year before. Miss Flowers had taken a full week off from school and Jessie saw a photograph of her in the *Boston Globe* standing next to a casket draped with the American flag. But when the new school year started in September, a romance seemed to blossom between Miss Flowers and Eric Barstow, the gym teacher.

Mr. Barstow was as muscle-bound as Jack LaLanne. The boys both hated and respected Mr. Barstow, and Jessie and the other girls at school had been wary of him—until he started dating Miss Flowers, when he suddenly became a romantic hero. That spring, they spotted him bringing Miss Flowers a delicate bouquet of lilies of the valley wrapped in a wet paper towel, and after school each day, he carried her books and files out to the parking lot. Jessie had seen them together by Miss Flowers's Volkswagen Bug, which was painted the color of a Florida orange, Mr. Barstow leaning an elbow on the roof while they talked. She once saw them kissing as the school bus drove away.

Some people—Leslie, for example—are unhappy that Miss Flowers saw fit to replace her dead fiancé *within a year*. But Jessie understands how losing someone tragically leaves a vacuum, and as they learned in science class, nature abhors a vacuum. Jessie knows that after Wilder died, her mother had hired a lawyer to fight the insurance company's claim that his death was a suicide; the lawyer argued that Wilder had been cleaning the Beretta in his garage workshop and it had discharged accidentally. This distinction was important not only for life insurance purposes but also for the peace of mind of Kate's three young children—Blair had been eight, Kirby five, and Tiger only three.

The lawyer Kate hired—who *was* successful in convincing the court that the death was accidental—was none other than David Levin. Six months after the case was settled, Kate and David started dating. They got married, despite Exalta's vehement objections, and a few short months after the courthouse wedding, Kate became pregnant with Jessie.

Jessie hadn't wanted to talk to Miss Flowers about Tiger and Vietnam, so to change the subject, she said, "This tea is delicious."

Miss Flowers nodded vaguely and dabbed her eyes with the

handkerchief she kept tucked into the belt of her dress to offer her students (she was, after all, a guidance counselor for adolescents, and their hormones and feelings ran amok on an hourly basis). She said, "I just want you to know that if you have any dark thoughts during the school day, you can come to talk to me here."

Jessie had glanced down into her cup. She knew she would never be able to take Miss Flowers up on this offer. How could Jessie talk about her dark thoughts regarding her brother—who was, as far as she knew, still alive—when Miss Flowers had actually *lost* Rex Rothman, her fiancé?

Jessie was tormented each night by thoughts of Tiger getting killed by mortar shells or grenades or being captured and marched a hundred miles through the jungle without any food or water, but she stayed away from Miss Flowers's office. She managed to avoid seeing the guidance counselor alone until the last day of school, when Miss Flowers stopped Jessie on her way out the door and said in her ear, "When I see you in September, your brother will be home safe, and I'll be engaged to Mr. Barstow."

Jessie had nodded her head against the rough linen of Miss Flowers's jumper and when she looked into Miss Flowers's eyes, she saw that she truly believed those words—and for one sterling moment, Jessie believed them too.

June 7, 1969

Dear Messie,

I'm writing a letter now to make sure it reaches you in time for your birthday. They say it only takes a week for mail to reach the States but when I think about the distance it has to travel, I figured better safe than sorry.

Happy birthday, Messie!

Thirteen years old, I can't believe it. I remember when you were born. Actually, all I remember is Gramps taking us for ice cream at Brigham's. I got a double scoop of butter brickle in a sugar cone and the damn thing fell over and Gramps said, Aw, hell, then got me another one. I don't know how much you remember about Gramps, you were pretty young when he croaked, but he was a hell of a guy. Before I shipped over, Nonny gave me his class ring from Harvard, but we aren't allowed to wear rings, so I keep it in the front pocket of my flak jacket, which isn't that smart because if I get blown to bits, the ring will be lost forever, but I like to have it next to my heart. It makes me feel safe somehow, which may sound corny but Messie, you would not believe what counts for a good-luck charm around here—some guys wear crosses or Stars of David, some carry rabbit feet, one dude has the key to his girlfriend's bicycle lock, another guy has an ace of spades that won him a big hand of poker the night before he shipped out. And I have Gramps's class ring from Harvard, which I don't advertise because the guys might think I'm trying to boast about my pedigree. But what I guess I'm trying to tell you is that the guys carry things they think have magic powers or things that remind them why they might like to stay alive.

There are a few of us who have proven to be natural-born survivors, which is good because our company has been dropped right into the action. I've made two real friends here in Charlie Company—Frog and Puppy (properly Francis and John). The other guys call us the Zoo because we all have

17

animal nicknames but they're jealous of how tough we are. The three of us have stupid contests, like who can do the most pull-ups on a tree branch and who can learn the most curse words in Vietnamese and who can smoke an entire cigarette without taking the damn thing out of his mouth the fastest. Frog is a Negro (gasp—what would Nonny think?) from Mississippi, and Puppy is so blond and pale he's nearly albino. We should have called him Casper or Ghost, but those nicknames were already taken by other guys in our regiment, and since he's the youngest in the platoon, he's Puppy. Puppy is from Lynden, Washington, all the way up by the Canadian border—raspberry country, he says, bushes as far as you can see, all of them growing fat, juicy raspberries. Puppy misses those raspberries and Frog misses his mama's vinegar coleslaw and I miss Brigham's butter brickle. So we are a mixed bag, a cross-section of our great country, if you will. I love these guys with all my heart, even though I've known them only a few weeks. The three of us feel invincible, we feel strong—and Messie, I hate to say it, but I know I'm the strongest of the three of us. At first, I thought that was because of Coach Bevilacqua making the team do so many wind sprints and climb all the stairs in the stadium, but that only makes you tough on the outside, and to survive here, you also have to be tough on the inside. When it's your turn to take point when you're charging a position, you have to be brave, and I mean brave, *because chances are good you're going to be the first one to encounter Charlie. If you meet up with enemy fire, you're taking the bullet. The first time I led my company, we were headed down this jungle path, the mosquitoes were roaring like lions, it was the dead of night, and a group of VC sneaked up behind us and slit the throat of Ricci, who was bringing up the rear. We engaged in a firefight and a couple others were shot, Acosta and Keltz. I made it out with nothing but two dozen mosquito bites.*

I hear other units have gotten shrinks to come in and help them deal with the way this stuff messes up your head. When we go out on a mission, it's almost certain that at least one of us is going to die. Which one of us is only a question of luck, like which ducks are you going to hit with your water pistol in a carnival game. When I was teaching kids to drive in Brookline, I knew the war was going on, I watched it on TV with you and Mom and Dad, I heard the body counts, but that didn't feel real. Now I'm here, and it's too real. Every day requires fortitude, which wasn't a word I knew the definition of until I got here.

At night when I'm on watch or I'm trying to fall asleep while also staying alert, I wonder who in the family I'm most like. Whose DNA is going to keep me alive? At first I thought it must be Gramps's, because he was a successful banker, or my father's, because he was a lieutenant in Korea. But then you know what I realized? The toughest person in our family is Nonny. She's probably the toughest person in the entire world. I'd put our grandmother up against any Vietcong or any one of my commanding officers. You know that way she looks at you when you've disappointed her, like you're not good enough to lick her shoe? Or when she uses that voice and says, "What am I to think of you now, Richard?" Yes, I know you know, and that's why you're dreading going to Nantucket, so if it helps you be less miserable, remember that the qualities of Nonny that are making you unhappy are also the qualities that are keeping your favorite brother alive.

I love you, Messie. Happy birthday.

Tiger

The night before they leave for Nantucket, Jessie and her parents are sitting at the kitchen table sharing pizza out of a delivery box—Kate has been too busy packing to cook—when there's a knock on the front door. Jessie, Kate, and David all freeze like they're in a game of statues. An unexpected knock on the door at seven thirty in the evening means…all Jessie can picture is two officers standing outside on the step, holding their hats, about to deliver the news that will shatter the family. Kate will never recover; Blair might well go into preterm labor; Kirby will be the most histrionic, and she will loudly blame Robert McNamara, Lyndon Johnson, and her particular nemesis, Richard Milhous Nixon. And Jessie—what will Jessie do? She can only imagine dissolving like the Alka-Seltzer tablet her father drops in water at night when he's working on a stressful case. She will turn into a fine dust and then she will blow away.

David stands up from the table, his face grim. He isn't Tiger's biological father, but he has filled the role since Tiger was a small boy and, in Jessie's opinion, has done a good job. David is slender (tennis is his game, which is his only saving grace as far as Exalta is concerned), whereas Tiger is tall with broad shoulders, the image of Lieutenant Wilder Foley. David is a lawyer, though not the kind who shouts in courtrooms. He's calm and measured; he always encourages Jessie to think before she speaks. David and Tiger have a close, nearly tender, relationship, so Jessie bets David feels sick as he goes to answer the door.

Kate reaches for Jessie's hand and squeezes. Jessie stares at the half a pizza remaining in the box and thinks that if Tiger is dead, none of them will ever be able to eat pizza again, which is too bad because it's Jessie's favorite food. Then she has an even *more* inappropriate thought: If Tiger is dead, she won't have to go to

Nantucket with her mother and Exalta. Her life will be ruined, but her summer will, in one sense, be saved.

"Jessie!" her father calls. He sounds irritated. She stands up from the table and scurries to the front door.

David is holding the screen open. Outside, illuminated by the porch light, are Leslie and Doris.

"I told your friends we were eating," David says. "But since you're leaving tomorrow, I'll give you five minutes. They came to say goodbye."

Jessie nods. "Thank you," she whispers. She sees the relief on her father's face. Being disrupted during the dinner hour is not good, but the reason for it is far, far better than what they had all privately feared.

Jessie steps out onto the porch. "Five minutes," David says, and he shuts the screen door behind her.

Jessie waits for her heart rate to return to normal. "You guys walked?" she asks. Leslie lives six blocks away, Doris nearly ten.

Doris nods. She looks glum, as usual. Her Coke-bottle glasses slide to the end of her nose. She's wearing her bell-bottom jeans with the embroidered flowers on the front pockets, of course. Doris lives in those jeans. But as a concession to the heat, she's paired them with a white-eyelet halter top that would be pretty if it weren't for the ketchup stain on the front. Doris's father owns two McDonald's franchises; she eats a lot of hamburgers.

The air is balmy, and among the trees bordering the road, Jessie sees the flash of fireflies. Oh, how she longs to stay in Brookline through the summer! She can ride her bike to the country club with Leslie and Doris, and in the late afternoons they can buy bomb pops from the Good Humor man. They can hang out at the shops in Coolidge Corner and pretend they're just bumping into boys from school. Kirby told Jessie that this is the summer boys her age will finally start getting taller.

"We came to say *bon voyage,*" Leslie says. She peers behind Jessie to make sure no one is lingering on the other side of the screen door and then lowers her voice. "Also, I have news."

"Two pieces of news," Doris says.

"First of all," Leslie says, "it came."

"It," Jessie repeats, though she knows Leslie means her period.

Doris wraps an arm across her own midsection. "I've been feeling crampy," she says. "So I suppose I'll be next."

Jessie isn't sure what to say. How should she greet the news that one of her best friends has taken the first step into womanhood while she, Jessie, remains resolutely a child? Jessie is envious, fiendishly so, because ever since "the talk" led by the school nurse last month, the topic of menstruation has consumed their private conversations. Jessie assumed Leslie would be first among them to get her period because Leslie is the most developed. She already has small, firm breasts and wears a training bra, whereas Jessie and Doris are as flat as ironing boards. Jessie's envy and longing and, on some days, anxiety—she heard a story about a girl who never got her period *at all*—is foolish, she knows. Both of Jessie's older sisters moan about their periods; Kirby calls it "the curse," which is a fairly apt term in Kirby's case, as the monthly onset gives her migraine headaches and debilitating cramps and puts her in a foul temper. Blair is slightly more delicate when referring to her own cycle, although it's not an issue at the moment because she's pregnant.

Leslie can get pregnant now, Jessie thinks, a notion that is almost laughable. She's ready to stop talking about all of this; she wants to go back inside and finish her pizza.

"What's the second piece of news?" Jessie asks.

"This," Leslie says, and she produces a flat, square, wrapped present from behind her back. "Happy birthday."

"Oh," Jessie says, stunned. Like everyone else with a summer birthday, she has given up hoping that it will ever be properly celebrated by her classmates. She accepts the gift; it is, quite obviously, a record album. "Thank you." She beams at Leslie, then at Doris, who is still clutching her abdomen against imaginary cramps, and then she rips the wrapping paper off. It's *Clouds,* by Joni Mitchell, as Jessie hoped it would be. She is obsessed with the song "Both Sides Now." It's the most beautiful song in the world. Jessie could listen to it every single second of every day between now and the time she died and she still wouldn't be sick of it.

She hugs Leslie, then Doris, who says, "We split the cost." This statement seems meant to elicit a second thank-you, which Jessie delivers more specifically to Doris. Jessie is happy to hear they actually *bought* the album because, in the two weeks since school let out, the three of them have engaged in a spate of shoplifting. Leslie stole two pink pencil erasers and one package of crayons from Irving's, Doris stole a day-old egg bagel from the kosher bakery, and Jessie, under extreme pressure from the other two, stole a Maybelline mascara from the Woolworths in Coolidge Corner, which was a far riskier crime because Woolworths was said to be wired with hidden cameras. Jessie knows that stealing is wrong, but Leslie turned it into a challenge, and Jessie felt her honor was at stake. When Jessie walked into Woolworths on the day of her turn, she had been afraid, indeed terrified, and was already framing the apology to her parents, already deciding to blame her bad decision-making on the stress of her brother's deployment, but when she walked out of Woolworths with the mascara tucked safely in the pocket of her orange windbreaker, she felt a rush of adrenaline that she thought must be similar to getting high. She felt *great!* She felt *powerful!* She had been so intoxicated that she stopped at the gas station near the corner of Beacon and Harvard, went into the ladies' room, and applied the mascara right then and there in the dingy mirror.

The less thrilling part of the story was that Kate detected the mascara the second Jessie walked into the house, and the Spanish Inquisition had followed. What was on Jessie's eyes? Was it mascara? Where did she get *mascara?* Jessie had given Kate the only believable answer: it was Leslie's. Jessie hoped and prayed that Kate wouldn't call Leslie's mother, because if Leslie's mother asked Leslie about it, it was fifty-fifty whether Leslie would cover for Jessie or not.

All in all, Jessie is relieved not to be receiving a stolen record album. If her mother ever found out about the shoplifting, she would pluck Jessie from Leslie's sphere of influence permanently.

"When are you coming back?" Leslie asks.

"Labor Day," Jessie says. It seems like an eternity from now. "Write me. You still have the address, right?"

"Yup," Doris says. "I already sent you a postcard."

"You did?" Jessie says. She's touched by this unexpected act of kindness from grouchy old Doris.

"We're gonna miss you," Leslie says.

Jessie hugs the record album to her chest as she waves goodbye and then goes back into the house. She wasn't the first to get her period, she might not even be the second, but that doesn't matter. Her friends love her—they bought her something they knew she wanted—and, more important, her brother is still alive. For one brief moment at the tail end of her twelfth year, Jessie Levin is happy.

Early in the morning, there is a light rapping on Jessie's bedroom door. Her father pokes his head in.

"You up?" he asks.

"No," she says. She pulls the covers over her head. The floaty feeling from last night has disappeared. Jessie doesn't want to go to Nantucket. It isn't even possible to look at *both sides now.* There is only one side, which is that without her siblings—and, eventually, without her mother—Nantucket is going to stink.

David eases down onto the bed next to her. He's dressed in his navy summer-weight suit, a white shirt, and a wide orange-and-blue-striped tie. His curly dark hair is tamed, and he smells like work, meaning Old Spice aftershave.

"Hey," he says, pulling the covers back. "Happy birthday."

"Can't I just stay here with you and go on the weekends?" Jessie says.

"Honey."

"Please?"

"You'll be fine," David says. "You'll be better than fine. Big summer for you. Thirteen years old. You're finally a teenager, stepping out from the shadow of your siblings..."

"I like their shadow," Jessie says. The summer before, Kate had enlisted each of Jessie's siblings to entertain her every third day. Blair always took Jessie to Cliffside Beach. They got hot dogs and frappes at the Galley and then worked diligently on their Coppertone tans while Blair turned the pages of John Updike's wife-swapping novel *Couples,* reading the scandalous sections out loud to Jessie. Updike was fond of the word *tumescence,* and the first time Blair read the word, she eyed Jessie over the pages and said, "You know what that means, right?"

"Right," Jessie said, though she hadn't the foggiest.

Blair had lowered the book and said, "There's no reason to be grossed out by sex. It's perfectly natural. Angus and I have sex every single day, sometimes twice."

Jessie had been both intrigued and repulsed by this information, and she hadn't been able to look at Angus the same way after. He was ten years older than Blair and had dark hair that he never had time to comb because he was too busy thinking. He was always working on math problems and Nonny liked him so much that, while they were staying at All's Fair, she let him sit in Gramps's leather chair at Gramps's antique desk. Angus rarely went to the beach because he hated sand and he burned easily. Jessie didn't relish the thought of Angus's voracious sexual appetite. Blair was beautiful and smart enough to have any man she wanted, but she'd married Angus and given up teaching English at Winsor in order to keep house for him. Now she worshipped Julia Child and wore Lilly Pulitzer patio dresses—but on the beach, she was more like a naughty aunt than a matronly older sister. She smoked Kents, lighting up with a silver lighter from Tiffany that was engraved with a love note from Angus's younger brother, Joey, who had been Blair's boyfriend before Angus. She reapplied her lipstick every time she came out of the water, and she shamelessly flirted with the Cliffside lifeguard Marco, who hailed from Rio de Janeiro. Blair spoke a few select phrases in Portuguese. She was glamorous.

Kirby also took Jessie to the beach, but she opted for the south shore, where the surfers and the hippies hung out. Kirby would let some air out of the tires of the fire-engine-red International Harvester Scout that their grandmother had bought for island driving, and they would cruise right onto Madequecham Beach, where every single sunny day was cause for celebration. People played volleyball and plucked cans of Schlitz out of galvanized tubs of ice, and the air smelled like marijuana smoke. Someone always brought a transistor radio, so they listened to the Beatles and Creedence and Kirby's favorite band, Steppenwolf.

In Jessie's opinion, Kirby was even prettier than Blair. Kirby's hair was long and straight, and while Blair was voluptuous, Kirby was thin as a rail. Surfers with wet suits hanging off their torsos like shed skin would throw Kirby over their shoulders and toss her into the waves. She would scream in protest, but secretly, Jessie knew, she loved it, and unlike Blair, Kirby didn't care what she looked like when she climbed out of the water. She wore no makeup and she let her blond hair dry in the sun, uncombed. She smoked weed instead of cigarettes, but two tokes only when she was watching Jessie; that was her rule. Two tokes mellowed her out, she said, and the effects had always worn off by the time they stepped back into All's Fair.

Jessie's days with Tiger were adventures. They rode their bikes to Miacomet Pond to fish; they hiked to Altar Rock, the highest point on Nantucket, and shot off Tiger's potato gun. But their favorite activity was bowling. Tiger was a legend at Mid-Island Bowl and had been since he was twelve years old. All of the locals knew him and spotted him games and bought birch beers for Jessie, which she savored because Exalta didn't tolerate any soda except for ginger ale mixed with grenadine at the club, and even then, Jessie was allowed only one.

Tiger's prowess at bowling was surprising because they played the game only on Nantucket and only when it rained. Exalta didn't believe in children staying indoors on beautiful summer days. Once Tiger was old enough to drive, of course, he could bowl whenever he wanted. On days when he minded Jessie, he took her with him, but they kept it from Exalta, which made it an even bigger thrill. When Tiger lined the ball up with the pins and then let the ball sail from his fingers as his back leg lifted behind him, it was like he was dancing. He was graceful, he was strong, and he was accurate. Most of the time he swept away the pins in their entirety like he was clearing a table. Jessie had hoped and prayed that his God-given talent would prove to be a genetic trait she shared, but no such luck; Jessie's balls veered to the right or the left, and at least half the time, they dropped into the gutter.

Jessie tries to imagine a Nantucket summer without her siblings. She will rattle around All's Fair with her summer-reading book, *Anne Frank: The Diary of a Young Girl*—that is, when she's not at tennis lessons, which her grandmother is insisting on even though Jessie has less than no interest. Jessie isn't spoiled enough to call the prospect of a summer on Nantucket *dreary,* but why, oh why, can't she just stay home?

Her father, sitting on her bed, pulls a small box out of his jacket pocket. "Turning thirteen is a very big deal in the Jewish tradition," he says. "I had a bar mitzvah, but since we haven't raised you Jewish, we won't be having that kind of ceremony for you." He pauses, looks away for a moment. "But I want to acknowledge how important this age is."

Jessie sits up in bed and opens the box. It's a silver chain with a round pendant the size of a quarter. Engraved on the pendant is a tree.

"Tree of Life," David says. "In the kabbalah, the Tree of Life is a symbol of responsibility and maturity."

The necklace is pretty. And Jessie loves her father more than she loves anyone, even Tiger, though she knows love can't be quantified. She feels protective of her father because, while Jessie is related to everyone in the family, David is related by blood to no one but her. She wonders if he ever thinks about this and feels like an outsider. She loves that her father has chosen to acknowledge this bond between them. She has heard that to be considered a "real" Jew, one's mother must be Jewish, and if that was true, Jessie wouldn't qualify, but she feels a connection to her father—something spiritual, something bigger than just regular love—when she secures the clasp and lets the cool weight of the charm rest against her breastbone. She wonders if Anne Frank owned a Tree of Life necklace, then decides that if she did, she probably hid it with the rest of her family's valuables so the Nazis wouldn't take it.

"Thank you, Daddy," she says.

He smiles. "I'm going to miss you, kiddo. But I'll see you on weekends."

"I guess since I'm supposed to be responsible and mature now, I have to stop complaining about going away," Jessie says.

"Yes, please," David says. "And I'll tell you what. When I come to the island, we'll walk to the Sweet Shoppe, get you a double scoop of malachite chip, and you can complain about your grandmother for as long as you want. Deal?"

"Deal," Jessie says, and for one brief moment at the beginning of her thirteenth year, Jessie Levin is happy.

Born to Be Wild

The conversation isn't going well, but that's hardly unusual for a twenty-one-year-old woman talking to her parents in the summer of 1969.

"I need some space to breathe," Kirby says. "I need some air under my wings. I'm an adult. I should be able to make my own choices."

"You can call yourself an adult and make your own choices when you're paying to support yourself," David says.

"I told you," Kirby says. "I found a job. And I won't be far. One island away."

"Absolutely not," Kate says. "You've been arrested twice. *Arrested,* Katharine."

Kirby cringes. Her mother only breaks out Kirby's first name when she wants to sound stern. "But not thrown in jail."

"But fined," David says.

"For no reason!" Kirby says. "It's like the Boston police never heard of freedom of assembly."

"You must have done something to provoke the officer," David says. "Something you're not telling us."

Well, yes, Kirby thinks. *Obviously.*

"And we've had to lie to your grandmother," Kate says. "If she finds out you've been arrested—twice—she'll..."

"Take away my trust fund?" Kirby says. "I think we all know she can't do that." Kirby will be given control of her trust fund when she graduates from college or when she turns twenty-five, whichever comes first. This has been her sole motivation for staying enrolled at Simmons.

David sighs. "What's the job?"

Kirby gives them a victorious smile. "I'll be working as a chambermaid at the Shiretown Inn in Edgartown."

"A *chambermaid?*" Kate says.

"You can't even clean your *own* room," David says.

"Now you're exaggerating," Kirby says. She decides to stick with eagerness and enthusiasm because she knows this will be more persuasive than anger and indignation. "Listen, I realize I've never held a job before. But that's because I've spent all my spare time on my causes."

"We've spent all *our* spare time on your causes," Kate says with a barely concealed eye roll.

"Dad has," Kirby says. "Remember when I was in high school? You didn't even want me to march with Dr. King. You told me I was too young!"

"You *were* too young!" Kate says.

"What you meant was that I was too white," Kirby says.

"Don't put words in my mouth, young lady."

"No one will ever march with Dr. King again," Kirby says. "So that memory is officially priceless and you nearly kept me from having it. I was with Miss Carpenter the entire time, nothing bad was going to happen; it was a *peaceful* protest, that was the point! The antiwar protests this spring were different because the country is different now. Students like me are the enemy of the establishment—but you should both be happy I'm thinking for myself and not just falling in line!" Kirby pauses. She sees David softening a bit, but her mother remains rigid. "I want to get a job this summer, and after I graduate, I'm going to pursue a career. I want to be more than just a wife and mother. I don't want to end up like...Blair."

"Watch it," Kate says. "Being a mother is a blessing."

"But you have to admit—" Kirby stops herself before she shares an ungenerous opinion about her older sister. Blair and Kirby have long been described as the overachiever and the underachiever, respectively. (Okay, no one has ever said that out loud, but Kirby knows people think it.) Blair scored straight As all through high school and went to Wellesley College, where she made the dean's list every single term. She won the English department's award for outstanding student, and her thesis about Edith Wharton received some sort of special distinction from a panel made up of professors from all the Seven Sister schools. Blair had gotten a job teaching the top-tier senior girls at the Winsor School, a position that opened up approximately once every fifty years. From there it would have been a short hop to a graduate degree and becoming a professor. But what had Blair done? Married Angus, quit the job, and gotten pregnant.

"Admit *what?*" Kate asks.

That Blair's a disappointment, Kirby thinks. But that's not true. The person who's a disappointment is Kirby herself.

Kirby is tempted to come clean with her parents, to tell them she has just endured the worst three months of her life, both physically and emotionally. She needs to wipe away the memory of the protests, the arrests, her love affair with Officer Scott Turbo, the trip to Lake Winnipesaukee. She had been dealt a losing hand of fear, anxiety, heartbreak, and shame.

She needs a fresh start.

She appeals to David, who has always been more compassionate than her mother. "I'm bombing in my classes at Simmons because they're *boring.* I don't want to study library science and I don't want to teach nursery school."

"You want to clean hotel rooms?" he asks.

"I want to *work,*" Kirby says. "And that was the job I happened to nail down." Here, she casts her eyes to the floor because she's not being 100 percent truthful.

"You don't know anyone on Martha's Vineyard," Kate says. "We're Nantucket people. You, me, Nonny, Nonny's mother, Nonny's grandmother. You're a fifth-generation Nantucketer, Katharine."

"It's that kind of us-and-them attitude that's destroying our country," Kirby says. When David laughs, Kirby realizes she's going to get her way. "Spending the summer somewhere else will be educational. Do you remember my friend Rajani from school? Her parents have a house in Oak Bluffs and they said I can stay with them."

"Stay with Rajani's family all summer?" David says. "That sounds excessive." He turns to Kate. "Doesn't it? Rajani's family shouldn't have to shelter and feed our daughter."

"Correct," Kate says. "She should come to Nantucket, where she belongs."

"There's also a house a few blocks from Rajani's that I found in the classifieds. Six bedrooms to let, college girls preferred. A hundred and fifty dollars for the summer."

"That makes more sense," David says. "We can pay the rent, but your day-to-day living expenses will be up to you."

"Oh, thank you!" Kirby says.

Kate throws up her hands.

Kirby and her best friend from Simmons, Rajani Patel, drive to Woods Hole in Rajani's maroon MG with the top down. Kirby secured a room in the house on Narragansett Avenue for the summer. She gave her parents the phone number and the name of the proprietress, Miss Alice O'Rourke.

I suppose she's Irish Catholic, David had remarked. *Let's hope she runs a tight ship.*

When Rajani and Kirby drive the MG off the ferry into Oak Bluffs, Kirby brings her palms together in front of her heart in a gesture of gratitude. She is starting over on her own somewhere completely new.

Well, okay, maybe not *completely* new. She's still on an island off the coast of Cape Cod; as the crow flies, she's only eleven miles away from Nantucket. She could have gone to inner-city Philadelphia to work with disadvantaged youth. She could be driving around rural Alabama, registering people to vote. So this is just a first step, but it will be good for her.

Rajani is excited to play tour guide. "There's Ocean Park," she says about a large expanse of green lawn with a white gazebo at its navel. "And to the left are the Flying Horses Carousel and the Strand movie theater."

Kirby swivels her head, trying to take it all in. The town has a carnival feel; it's a bit more honky-tonk than Kirby expected. She eyes the carousel—which Rajani has informed Kirby is the nation's oldest operating platform carousel—and then turns her attention to the people on the sidewalks eating fried clams out of red-and-white-checkered cardboard boats and swirling their tongues around soft-serve ice cream cones. The town does offer the diversity Rajani promised, which is refreshing. A black teenager glides by on a unicycle. Somewhere, there's a radio playing the Fifth Dimension: *This is the dawning of the age of Aquarius.* Kirby bobs her head along to the music. This is the dawning of something for Kirby as well. But what?

"We live in the Methodist Campground," Rajani says, and Kirby tries not to grimace. The only thing she can think of that's less appealing than living in a campground is living in a *religious* campground. But the "campground" turns out to be a neighborhood of homes painted the colors of Easter eggs, each house decorated with elaborate gingerbread trim. "That one's mine." Rajani points to a lavender home with a sharp triangular gable over the front door; the white fretwork drips from the eaves like icing on a fancy cake. The house is straight out of a fairy tale, especially when compared with the architecture of downtown Nantucket, where every house resembles a Quaker widow.

"Look at that blue one," Kirby says. The blue house down the street is a showstopper. It's nearly twice as big as Rajani's, with two gables over a gracious front porch that has a bench swing and a row of ferns in hanging baskets. There are blue hydrangea bushes on either side of the front walk, and the gingerbread trim all around is fashioned to look like icicles—or at least that's how it seems to Kirby.

"That's my friend Darren's house," Rajani says. "He's going to be a senior at Harvard. Do you want to go see if he's home?"

"We don't have to," Kirby says.

"Come on," Rajani says. "You want to meet people, right? I don't see his car but it might be in the garage. His parents are really nice. His mother is a doctor and his father's a judge."

A doctor and a judge. Harvard. All Kirby can think is how happy both Nonny and her mother would be. She's meeting the right kind of people, just like on Nantucket, where everyone is a judge or a doctor or holds an Endowed Chair of Effortless Superiority at Well-Bred University.

"Okay," Kirby says. She'll write her mother a postcard later, she decides, and mention all the esteemed people she's met on Martha's Vineyard. "Let's go say hi."

Rajani strides up the walk and jabs the doorbell. Kirby wonders about Darren from Harvard. It would be nice to have a summer romance, a romance where she, Kirby, calls the shots instead of being an emotional wreck. It would be nice to stop thinking about Officer Scottie Turbo, with his devastating green eyes and his geisha-girl tattoo and his powerful hands that could pin both her wrists over her head as he kissed the spot just below her left ear.

A black woman in a white tennis dress opens the door. Her arms have sculpted muscles and there's a sheen of perspiration on her forehead. Her hair is in a ponytail and she's wearing diamond earrings. She looks at both girls—women!—but her gaze settles on Rajani and she smiles.

"Rajani!" she says. "Now the summer can officially begin!"

Kirby is initially confused. She thinks, *Maid? Housekeeper? In a tennis dress and diamond earrings?* And then, one instant later, she's mortified by her own obtuseness and—let's just say it— *bigotry*. This woman must be Darren's mother, the doctor.

Darren's mother holds open the screen door. Rajani steps inside and Kirby follows. The house is bright, summery, and modern. A peek in the living room to the right reveals a navy-and-white-striped divan with bright yellow throw pillows and a white coffee table shaped like a kidney bean. Kirby loves it. There isn't a piece of furniture in Nonny's house that's less than a hundred years old.

"Dr. Frazier," Rajani says. "Meet my friend Kirby Foley."

Dr. Frazier offers her hand. "Nice to meet you, Kirby." She studies Kirby for a second longer than she might have—or is Kirby just being paranoid? Kirby looks respectable, she thinks, in a strawberry-print wrap skirt, a white scoop-neck tee, and a pair of Dr. Scholl's. She abandoned her usual minidresses, peasant blouses, and cutoff jeans in favor of this outfit because she wanted to make a good impression with her landlady, Miss O'Rourke. She senses hesitation on Dr. Frazier's face. Is it because Kirby is white? Should Kirby inform Dr. Frazier that she's a civil rights activist and a feminist, that she marched with Dr. Martin Luther King Jr. next to her beloved high-school civics teacher, Miss Carpenter, and that she personally defended Miss Carpenter against the racial slurs of the ignorant boys in her class? Should she show Dr. Frazier her National Organization for Women membership card? Should she mention that she's read Simone de Beauvoir, Aimé Césaire, and Eldridge Cleaver?

All of that would sound like bragging, she fears, or, worse, like she's trying to appropriate African-Americans' struggle for rights and respect when anyone can see that she's as white as Wonder Bread. Besides, it's exaggerating a bit—she *has* read Aimé Césaire, but she barely understood a single word. She decides the best defense is genuine human warmth. She smiles at Dr. Frazier, and as she does, she realizes she has seen this woman before. But where? Dr. Frazier doesn't work at Simmons, and yet somewhere...Kirby has met her somewhere.

"Are you here visiting for a few days?" Dr. Frazier asks. "Or for the summer?"

"The summer," Kirby says, hoping this will be a point in her favor. "I'm renting a room from Alice O'Rourke. I'll be working as a chambermaid at the Shiretown Inn in Edgartown."

"Chambermaid?" Dr. Frazier asks. She gives Kirby the once-over with what appears to be an incredulous eye. "Where are you from, Kirby?"

Kirby clears her throat. "My parents live in Brookline?" She's so nervous she sounds like she's asking the question instead of answering it.

"Kirby normally spends her summers on Nantucket," Rajani announces. "But she's decided to give the Vineyard a whirl."

"Brookline and Nantucket," Dr. Frazier says. "And you're cleaning rooms at the Shiretown Inn? And you've signed on to live in Alice O'Rourke's house? Do your parents know about this?" She sounds either disapproving or amused; Kirby can't tell which. It feels like Darren's mother has the whole situation figured out: Rich white girl trying on a working-class hat for kicks. Kirby doesn't need the chambermaid job; in fact, she's taking it away from someone who *does* need it. Or maybe Dr. Frazier thinks Kirby has been cast out by her family for one transgression or another.

And then Kirby realizes where she knows Dr. Frazier from. Her face grows hot and stiff like she's gotten a bad sunburn, and the back of her throat starts to close. She needs to get out of there pronto. But before Kirby can think of a way to excuse herself, Rajani speaks up. "We came to say hello to Darren. Is he around?"

"He went to Larsen's with his father to pick up lobsters for dinner," Dr. Frazier says. "With all the traffic up-island, I can't say how long they'll be."

"No problem," Rajani says. "We'll come back another time."

"Well," Dr. Frazier says. She hesitates, and Kirby is pretty sure she's debating whether or not to invite them to stay and wait for Darren. If so, she decides against it. "It was good to see you, Rajani. And nice to meet you, Kirby. Enjoy our island." She holds the front screen door open almost as if she's eager for Kirby to get out.

She knows who I am, Kirby thinks, and her dream of a fresh start with a clean slate here on Martha's Vineyard vanishes in a snap.

Fly Me to the Moon

People throw around the phrase married with children *like loose change,* Blair thinks. No one ever talks about the drama that matrimony and parenthood entail. So is it any wonder Blair was taken by surprise?

Blair met Angus Whalen, a professor of astrophysics at MIT, because she was dating his younger brother, Joey. Blair had just graduated from Wellesley, and Joey from Boston College. Blair was teaching honors English and the Art of the Novel to senior girls at the Winsor School. Joey wanted to move to New York City and "get into business," but for the time being, he was captaining one of the Swan Boats in Boston's Public Garden and living in Cambridge with Angus.

"My brother is a crazy genius," Joey told Blair. "He's helping NASA with the moon launch."

Blair's ears had perked up. "He's an *astronaut?*" Blair was obsessed with astronauts. She'd covered her dorm-room corkboard with pictures of Jim Lovell and Pete Conrad and the most handsome astronaut of all, Gordon Cooper.

"Not an astronaut exactly," Joey said. "I mean, he's not going up in the rocket. He just does the calculations that make the rockets fly."

Close enough, Blair thought. If she and Joey ended up getting married, she would have a brother-in-law who was almost an astronaut!

Although Blair considered herself a modern woman, getting married was never far from her mind. Nearly all of Blair's Wellesley classmates were engaged by the time they graduated. The exception was Blair's best friend, Sallie, who, like Blair, wanted a career.

A truly modern woman, Blair thought, could have both.

Blair liked Joey. He was handsome, fun-loving, and easy to be with. If Blair had a complaint, it was that he was maybe *too* easy—but, she reasoned, she was complicated enough for both of them. Joey was head over heels for Blair and she got swept up by the wave of his enthusiasm. He once sent a bouquet of fat red roses to Blair at the Winsor School, and the administration saw fit to deliver it right in the middle of Blair's lecture on Carson McCullers.

Blair's students all swooned, and Frankie from *The Member of the Wedding* was forgotten as the girls buried their noses in the flowers and inhaled what they naively believed to be the scent of true love.

The weekend after the (distracting) arrival of the roses, Joey invited Blair for a private ride on his Swan Boat. It was early October and the leaves in the Boston Public Garden were at their most flamboyant. Joey pedaled to the middle of the pond, produced a bottle of cold duck, and poured it into waxy paper cups. He and Blair drank and talked and laughed until dusk descended. At some point, they started kissing, really kissing, and the Swan Boat tilted first in one direction, then the other. Joey broke away, out of breath. "Will you come to my place?" he asked. "Please?"

Blair didn't want Joey to think she was too easy, but the cold duck had gone right to her head.

"Okay," she said. "But no promises."

Joey's "place" was the entire ground floor of one of the gracious turn-of-the-century mansions on Mt. Auburn Street. Blair had been expecting a bachelor pad—posters of Jayne Mansfield and Marilyn Monroe, piles of dirty laundry, empty beer cans—but when Joey opened the door and ushered Blair inside, she was pleasantly surprised. A framed print of Édouard Manet's *A Bar at the Folies-Bergère* hung in the entryway, and Blair heard Rachmaninoff playing somewhere in the house.

Art? Blair thought. *Classical music?*

"Damn," Joey said. "My brother's home."

When they stepped into the great room, Blair took a quick inventory: Persian rug, leather sofa, mirror-topped cigar table, and, most impressive, a wall of floor-to-ceiling bookshelves. At the far end of the room, a man sat at the head of a long harvest table, working by the light of three pillar candles. This was Joey's brother, Blair realized, Angus, the almost astronaut. He was bent over a notebook, scribbling furiously. He didn't even seem to notice them come in.

Joey was visibly perturbed. "I thought you were going to the faculty potluck."

Angus didn't respond. *He's working!* Blair thought. *Leave him be.* It was clear, however, that it would be rude to withdraw to the bedroom for amorous pursuits.

"Angus!" Joey said. "Get out of here. We'd like some privacy."

Angus held up an index finger as he scribbled something in his notes. "Got it!" He slammed the notebook shut and, with this action, seemed to reenter the present moment. He said, "Who is 'we'?"—and then he noticed Blair and leaped to his feet. "Hello?" he said. He moved toward Blair tentatively, as though she were an exotic bird that might fly away. "Who are you?"

Behind Angus's glasses, Blair noticed, were a pair of tender brown eyes. Her head buzzed with the effects of the cold duck.

"Blair Foley," she said, offering her hand. "It's nice to meet you. I just love your apartment. I noticed the Manet print when I walked in. That painting is a particular favorite of mine."

"Did you study art history, then?" Angus asked.

"I thought you were going to the faculty potluck," Joey said again.

"Literature, actually," Blair said. "Female novelists, to be specific. Edith Wharton, to be specifically specific."

"Edith Wharton," Angus said.

Blair was about to proffer her standard one-line Wharton biography—*American novelist born into the upper echelons of New York society who was the first woman to win the Pulitzer Prize for Literature*—because lots of people, especially men, had no idea who Edith Wharton was. But then Angus said, "I've read all her work."

"Have you?" Blair assumed Angus was making fun of her. "Which novel was your favorite?"

Joey made a loud snoring noise, which was the kind of dismissive attitude Blair expected from men when she discussed Wharton. She ignored him.

"The Age of Innocence," Angus said. "Countess Olenska is positioned as the other against the lily-white backdrop of May Welland."

"You *have* read it!" Blair said.

"Yes," Angus said. "I told you, I've read them all."

"Of course," Blair said. "It's just that…Joey told me you were an astrophysicist."

Angus offered her a wry smile. "And astrophysicists aren't allowed to enjoy Wharton?"

Blair was dazzled. She felt suddenly connected to Angus, as though they had both visited the same far-off country.

Joey snatched up Angus's notebook and held it over the candle flames. "Get out of here, Angus, or this goes up in smoke."

"Joey!" Blair said.

Angus shook his head. "He does this all the time," he said. "Acts like a child to get attention." He took Blair's hand. "Please, can I take you to dinner?" Blair looked into Angus's soft brown eyes and thought, *This date just got very complicated.*

Blair and Angus's wedding had been a small but lavish affair at the Union Club, paid for by Exalta, who had taken a particular shine to Angus. With Exalta, one was considered remarkable or one was barely noticed; those were the only two options. Blair herself fell into the latter category, but then, so did most people.

Blair had suspected Exalta would view Angus's rarefied intellect with disdain, but Exalta thought Angus was just marvelous, and when Blair and Angus got engaged, Exalta's opinion of Blair seemed to improve.

Blair loved being a bride. She loved her dress, a trumpet silhouette with lace overlay, a satin sash under the bustline, and a low dip in the back. It was from Priscilla's of Boston, and Blair had been fitted by Priscilla herself, which made her feel like Grace Kelly. Blair loved licking stamps for the invitations and then checking the mail for the reply cards. Fifty guests were invited; forty-two accepted. Blair asked her sister Kirby to be the maid of honor, her best friend, Sallie, to be the bridesmaid, and her sister Jessie to be the junior bridesmaid. Blair chose peonies and lilies for her flowers, a palette of pink and green, and they were granted a stunning June day. The lamb and the duck at the reception was a welcome change from beef and chicken, and Exalta had agreed to French champagne, Bollinger. Blair and Angus danced to "Fly Me to the Moon," which was a joke about Angus's job; they held hands under the table through Joey Whalen's sweet, funny, and very drunken toast ("We all worried you would never find a wife. And you didn't. *I* found her"). After the reception, Blair changed into a peach silk shift with dyed-to-match pumps and they ran through a shower of rice to the getaway car, Angus's black 1966 Ford Galaxie convertible, which had been festooned with crepe paper and empty tin cans.

The honeymoon was a week in Bermuda at the Hamilton Princess—pink sand, men in knee socks, sex. Angus was an accomplished lover, and Blair figured it must be a natural gift, like his intelligence, because he told her he had never had a real girlfriend before her.

However, it was on their honeymoon that Blair learned that

the nimble, lightning-quick gymnastics of Angus's mind came at a cost. On the third morning of their trip, Angus refused to get out of bed. He wasn't sleeping; he just lay there, his eyes open but vacant. Blair placed a hand on his forehead. His skin was cool.

"Angus," she said. "You're scaring me. What is it?"

He shook his head, then his expression crumpled and he appeared ready to cry.

"What is it, Angus?" Blair asked. But of course, it could be only one thing. He didn't love her; he'd made a mistake in marrying her. "Angus?"

"Please leave," he said. "Just for a little while. I need to be alone."

Blair left. What else could she do? She was relieved that at least it was temporary.

Blair wandered the hotel gardens, filled with June roses and butterflies, then sat pensively with a cup of coffee on the patio until an hour had passed. When she returned to the room, she heard Angus's voice through the door. He was on the phone, she realized, which seemed like a good sign. She knocked, then entered. She heard Angus say, "I have to go now. Goodbye."

Blair crossed the dim bedroom to kiss Angus's forehead. Still cool. "How are you feeling?" she asked.

"A bit better," he said.

She waited for him to tell her who he had been talking to, but he didn't and she decided she wouldn't ask.

"I'm sorry," Angus said. "Some days I wake up and I'm just... paralyzed."

Blair assured him that he didn't have to be sorry. She worried he had gotten too much sun or not enough sleep. She also suspected he was working too hard; even here in Bermuda, he sat at the little round table on their balcony and pored over his calculations, and when he finished, he picked up one of the books he'd brought. He was reading Hermann Hesse's *Siddhartha* in the original German and, "for fun," *The Death of Ivan Ilyich.*

"You're thinking too much," Blair said. "Your mind needs a rest, Angus."

"No, that's not it," he said. "It happens. It's an affliction." He then confessed that he had been visited by these "episodes" since he was an adolescent. The paralysis—mental and emotional—came and went capriciously, like a ghost haunting a house; there was no predicting its cause or its duration. He had been to hospitals, tests had been run, pills prescribed—but nothing made it better.

"I didn't tell you because I didn't want you to think you were marrying damaged goods," Angus said.

"I would never think that, darling," Blair said. She remembered Joey calling Angus a "crazy genius." She'd thought Joey had been jealous.

The rest of that summer passed in a blissful haze. Because the MIT students were on summer break, Angus had been able to join Blair on Nantucket. While she sunned herself on Cliffside Beach, he worked on his research at Blair's grandfather's desk. They often met in the late afternoons in the shaded garden next to the Nantucket Atheneum, stopping at the Island Dairy Bar for one chocolate-and-vanilla soft-serve cone that they shared as they strolled back to All's Fair. In the evenings, they ate with the family, then either drove out to the beach in the Galaxie and made love in the back seat or walked up Main Street and sat side by side on a bench, sharing a cigarette and looking out over the twinkling lights of town. Once a week, they had date night at the Opera House, with its proper European waiters, all of them old and with heavy accents, or the Skipper, where the college-age servers sang show tunes. One day Blair and Angus rode their bikes all the way out to Sankaty Head Lighthouse; another day they puttered Exalta's thirteen-foot Boston Whaler over to Coatue, where they sat on the beach under an umbrella. They were the only people there that day, so Angus untied Blair's bikini top and kissed the length of her spine, then flipped her over and made love to her right out there in the open where passing boaters might see them. Blair had to admit, that only made it more thrilling.

When they arrived back in the city after this extended honey-moon, they had their first argument.

Angus told Blair that he didn't want her to return to Winsor.

"What are you talking about?" Blair said. She had been work-ing on lesson plans since the first of August; she had ordered thirty copies of Flannery O'Connor's *A Good Man Is Hard to Find*. Angus knew this! There were girls who had written to Blair on Nantucket to tell her how excited they were about taking her class. "Of course I'm going back."

"No," Angus said. "I need you to stay home and handle things here."

"Handle *what?*" Blair said, though she knew he meant the house—cleaning, cooking, shopping, laundry, errands. "I'm more than capable of teaching *and* running the household, Angus."

He'd kissed her nose and she nearly swatted him away, the ges-ture was so patronizing. "You *are* more than capable. But you don't *have* to work. I make plenty of money and we have your trust fund."

The trust fund was fifty thousand dollars that Blair had gotten when she graduated from Wellesley. It was now in an account at the Bank of Boston under both her and Angus's names.

"That money isn't meant to be squandered on day-to-day expenses," Blair said. "You know that."

"Blair," Angus said. "I don't want a wife who works. My job is very taxing. Please, I need you at home. I realize every marriage requires compromise, which is why I gave up my place in Cambridge."

"Wait," Blair said. It was true that she had lobbied to live in Boston proper, and now she and Angus were renting a modern two-bedroom on Commonwealth Avenue. But she hadn't realized that decision would put her *job* at risk!

"Blair," Angus said. "Please."

"What am I going to *do* all day?" she asked.

"Do what other women do," Angus said. "And if you have any spare time, you can read."

Blair opened her remaining wedding presents. Some of them she returned (toasters, teacups, an angora blanket that shed like a St. Bernard), and some she placed around the apartment (crystal vases, candy dishes, a Moroccan tagine pot that they would never use but that looked stylish on the open shelves of the dining nook). She wrote thank-you notes on stationery engraved with her new monogram, BFW. She set up accounts at Savenor's on Charles Street, at the liquor store, at the hardware store. She placed the photos from the ceremony and reception in the white album that said *Our Wedding* in foil-pressed letters on the front.

When all of that was completed, Blair found herself at a loss for something to do. Angus had suggested she read, but now that Blair had hours to read, entire days to read, potentially an entire married lifetime to read, books lost their luster, and she grew resentful. Angus said he wanted her home, but for what reason? He worked *all* the time. He had classes to teach and graduate students to oversee but what gobbled up most of his waking hours was the Apollo 11 mission. He was *never* home, and it didn't take long for Blair to wonder if she'd made an error when she'd traded one Whalen brother for the other. Joey Whalen had given Blair a secret wedding present, a slender silver lighter engraved with the words *I loved you first. Eternally yours, Joey.* Every time Blair smoked a cigarette, she felt secretly, deliciously desired. Really, was there any better gift? Blair half wanted Angus to discover the lighter; she started leaving it out, engraved-side up. But Angus couldn't be bothered with the minutiae of Blair's life, so if there was one small secret between them, it was his own fault, she thought.

At the end of September, Angus traveled to Houston, then to Cape Kennedy. Blair stayed home and kept house. She bought *Mastering the Art of French Cooking* and decided that she would become a gourmet cook and host fashionable salons twice a month, evenings of cocktails and delectable bites where the conversation would focus on literature, art, music, history, and travel. Blair clung tight to the vision of these salons for a few feverish days, imagining that they would be in the same vein as gatherings hosted by the Duke and Duchess of Windsor. But then Blair tried and failed to make an edible *poulet au porto* three times, and she realized that Angus would never be able to commit to two nights home per month, and they didn't have any friends anyway.

The middle of October brought the annual faculty potluck, the very same one Angus had famously skipped the year before. This time it was to be held at the home of Dr. Leonard Cushion, professor emeritus of microbiology; he lived on Irving Street, a few doors down from Julia Child herself. Blair was excited for the potluck—finally, a chance to get out of the house and socialize. She slaved over a potato galette made with clarified butter, thyme, and rose-mary that, when cut into slender wedges, would be a sophisticated shared dish. She was eager to meet Angus's colleagues and enjoy some adult interaction. Blair wanted to appear serious and intellectual and so she chose to wear black bell-bottoms with a black turtleneck. She pulled her normally bouncy blond hair into a sleek ponytail and secured it with a black, orange, and pink Pucci scarf that had been a gift from her friend Sallie. Blair considered wearing silver hoop earrings but feared they would make her seem frivolous. She decided the same about makeup; she applied only eyebrow pencil and clear lip gloss.

When she came downstairs, Angus said, "That's what you're wearing?"

Blair picked up the galette with two quilted oven mitts and strode ahead to the car. Angus knew a lot about astrophysics and a little bit about Edith Wharton, but he knew nothing of women's fashion.

Or did he?

Much to Blair's dismay, the other wives at the potluck were wearing sheath dresses or dirndl skirts in fall colors—goldenrod, flame orange, burgundy. They had all had their hair set and were in full makeup, complete with false eyelashes and bright lipstick. Blair was greeted by Mrs. Nancy Cushion, who was a good thirty years younger than the esteemed Professor Cushion. Blair handed Nancy the galette, and the other wives—Judy, Carol, Marion, Joanne, Joanne, and Joanne—gave it sideways glances as they arranged trays of hors d'oeuvres, most of which appeared to be composed of three ingredients: cream cheese, olives, and toothpicks.

By the time Blair finished introducing herself, Angus had disappeared.

"Where did my husband go?" Blair asked Nancy Cushion.

"Men in the den," Nancy said, raising her pencil-line eyebrows. "They drink bourbon, smoke cigars, and talk science."

Blair was offered a glass of Chablis, which she gratefully accepted, and then a celery stick stuffed with salmon cream cheese and topped with paper-thin slices of olive, which she originally declined but then changed her mind and accepted.

She turned to the person next to her, a woman who wore turquoise eye shadow that exactly matched her silk bolero jacket. "Have you read anything interesting lately?" Blair asked. She hoped that this woman—Blair thought she was one of the Joannes— wouldn't mention *Cancer Ward* by Aleksandr Solzhenitsyn because Blair had twice tried to read it but found it too bleak.

Maybe-Joanne said, "Oh, please, the only thing I've read in the past twelve months is *Pat the Bunny*."

The very next day, Blair applied to the graduate English program at Harvard. She didn't say a word to Angus, telling herself it was a lark; she merely wanted to see if she could get in. She received a letter three weeks later—she had been accepted. Classes started in January.

When Angus returned home that night—at quarter to eleven— Blair was awake, waiting for him with a couple of glasses of good scotch that she'd bought to celebrate and the acceptance letter. Angus had been displeased to find Blair still up.

"Whatever it is will have to wait until morning," Angus said. "I feel an episode coming on."

"Just read this quickly, please," Blair said, and she thrust the letter into his hands.

Angus read the letter; there was no change in his expression. "This is lovely news," he said when he finished it, and Blair clasped her hands to her heart. "But you're not going to go."

"What?" Blair said. "But it's Harvard. I got into *Harvard,* Angus."

"Didn't you tell me your grandfather went to Harvard?" Angus said. "That probably helped."

It was all Blair could do not to slap him. "I didn't mention my grandfather," she said in a tight voice. But the arrow had hit its mark: Angus didn't believe Blair could be admitted to Harvard on her own merits. This pointed to a deeper, more disturbing truth: Angus didn't think Blair was as smart as Blair thought Angus was.

"We agreed you wouldn't work," Angus said.

"It's not work," Blair said. "It's *school.* Surely you, of all people—"

"Blair," he said. "We've been over this. Now, good night."

Blair kept the acceptance letter in her lingerie drawer, where she saw it every day. She decided she would revisit the topic with Angus in a few weeks, during the morning hours, on a weekend perhaps, when it was less pressing for Angus to get to the university early. She would make sure he was feeling okay. She would cook corned beef hash with poached eggs, his favorite, and inform him that she was enrolling at Harvard despite his objections. After all, it was 1968; he couldn't tell her what to do.

They spent their first Thanksgiving at Exalta's house in Beacon Hill. Blair made Julia Child's Tarte Normande aux Pommes and presented it proudly to her grandmother, who handed it off to her cook. Exalta then linked her arm through Angus's and escorted him to the library for cocktails and canapés. At Thanksgiving, Exalta always served cherrystones on the half shell, a relish tray with French dressing, and cocktail peanuts. Blair helped herself to a clam and then a few moments later bolted for the bathroom in the back of the house, the commode the servants used, because she was going to vomit.

A week later, it was confirmed: she was pregnant.

Her dream of attending Harvard would be put on hold. Blair wrote the admissions committee a letter explaining that she found herself with child and would like to defer enrollment until the following year or the year after that. She heard nothing back; probably, they felt they didn't need to respond because they accepted as a matter of course what Blair could not: she would never attend Harvard.

Indeed, the pregnancy disrupted even the meager routine Blair had established for herself on Commonwealth Avenue. She was absolutely *flattened.* Entire days slipped past when she didn't even leave the apartment. The nausea set in at five in the afternoon, like clockwork. Blair spent at least an hour on her knees in front of the toilet, retching. The only things that kept the nausea at bay were smoking and a small glass of scotch, which was odd because normally Blair drank gin, but her pregnant body craved brown liquor, the older and more complex, the better.

On the day Blair chose to put up the Christmas tree, her mother came over to help. Between the two of them, they managed to wrangle the tree onto the stand, and then Kate went about stringing the lights while Blair collapsed on the divan with a cigarette and two fingers of Glenlivet, willing the nausea to just leave her alone for once. She had invited her mother and David for dinner and planned to serve cheese fondue; she'd painstakingly cubed a loaf of sourdough and sliced some cured sausage, both provisioned that morning from Savenor's. Angus had called at lunchtime and said he would be working late *again,* and Blair wanted to cancel the dinner altogether, but Kate insisted that Blair needed company, so now Blair could look forward to a lopsided fondue dinner with her parents.

She watched her mother wind the lights around the tree,

infinitely patient, careful, thorough, and competent in her task. She wore a dark green shirtwaist and pumps and had pearls at her throat; her blond hair was in a smooth chignon, her lipstick perfect. Kate was always put together, always impeccable. How did she manage it? Blair knew that her mother had suffered dark times. Blair's father, Wilder Foley, had been fighting in Korea for much of the last years of their early marriage, and then when he came home, there were, as Kate put it, "adjustments" to make. Blair remembered her father's homecoming: They picked him up at the airport; he was wearing his dress uniform. She remembers him at the breakfast table in a white undershirt, smoking and eating eggs, pulling Kate down into his lap and growling at Blair to take her sister and brother upstairs to play. Wilder didn't drive Blair to school or ballet; her mother did. Her mother prepared their food, administered their baths, read them stories, and tucked them in. Blair remembered one night her parents had gone out for dinner. Her mother wore a red sheath and her father his dress uniform, and Janie Beckett from down the street had come to babysit, which had been a matter of great excitement. Kate had bought Coke to offer Janie, and Blair had sneaked peeks at the three exotic green bottles in the icebox; the Foley children weren't allowed soda. That night, Janie gave Blair one sip of the Coke; it had been so crisp and spicy and unexpectedly fizzy that Blair's eyes had teared up and her nose tingled.

She had retained all of those details but relatively little about her own father. And then, suddenly, he was dead. Kate had found Wilder's body in his garage workshop, a gunshot wound to his head.

On that morning, Blair had been taken to the park by her grandfather, which was unusual indeed. When she got home, there had been men at the house, so many men—neighbors, Mr. Beckett

(Janie's father), a swarm of policemen, and, later, bizarrely, Bill Crimmins, the caretaker for the house in Nantucket.

Blair doesn't remember being told that her father was dead; possibly, she overheard something or just intuited it. Nor does Blair remember her mother screaming or even crying. This struck Blair as unusual only when she was older. When Blair was sixteen, she and Kate had an argument about Blair's public displays of affection with her boyfriend, Larry Winter, and Blair turned Kate's composure during this time against her, saying, *You didn't even cry when Daddy died. You didn't shed one tear!*

And Kate had spun on her in an uncharacteristic show of anger. *What do you know about it? Tell me please, Blair Baskett Foley. What. Do. You. Know. About. It.*

Blair had had to admit that she knew nothing about it, really, and that was true to this day. Kate must have been devastated, haunted, and set adrift by her husband's unexpected death. Blair was tempted to ask her mother now what it had been like to find him, how she had coped afterward. Blair wondered if she could learn something about her own marriage by asking Kate those questions. But at that moment, her mother held her hands up to showcase the tree. The lights were evenly hung at different depths on the branches in a way that created a glowing, three-dimensional marvel.

"What do you think?" Kate asked.

Blair admired her mother so much, she couldn't summon words strong enough to praise her. She nodded her approval.

Everyone promised Blair she would feel better during her second trimester, and this proved to be true. The month of April delivered the sweet spot in her pregnancy. The nausea was gone, and the exhaustion had abated somewhat. Blair's hair was long and shiny;

her appetite for both food and sex was prodigious. But Angus was even more distant and remote and he suffered his episodes more frequently. The only days he took off from work, he spent lying in bed, despondent.

On Tuesday, April 8, two days after Easter, Blair woke up and immediately consumed two grilled-cheese sandwiches, a butter-scotch pudding, three chocolate-coconut eggs, and a handful of black jellybeans from the Easter basket that Exalta still prepared for all four of her grandchildren even though three of them were adults. It was a glorious spring day, warm for the first time in months. Blair, energized by the sudden sugar rush, decided to walk from their apartment all the way over to the MIT campus and surprise Angus at work. She wore one of her new mater-nity dresses, a full-term size even though she was only five and a half months pregnant. Her girth was a source of private em-barrassment. She was *so* big. Exalta had commented on it with disapproval at Easter, and Blair had feared that Exalta might even withhold her Easter basket. Blair had no explanation for her size except that everything about her pregnancy had been extreme—she had been *so* sick and *so* tired, and now she was *so* enormous. She assumed it meant that the baby would be a strapping, healthy boy—smart like Angus, handsome like Joey, athletic like Tiger.

Blair wore low, stacked heels, comfortable for walking, but when she reached Marlborough Street a tiny, blue-haired woman stopped her on the sidewalk, told her she had no right to be out in her condition, and implored her to return home.

Blair stared at the woman, aghast. "But I'm only five months along," she said. She immediately regretted giving out this piece of personal information. One thing she had noticed with dismay was that being pregnant made her public property. It meant that old women who had probably given birth at the turn of the century felt they could stop her on the street and tell her to go home.

Blair had moved on, indignant but self-conscious. Her maternity dress was buttercup yellow, which suited the spring day but also made her stand out. She had been looking forward to strolling over the Longfellow Bridge and watching the rowers below, but after she'd walked a few more blocks, a taxicab pulled up alongside her; the driver cranked down the passenger-side window and said, "Lady, where ya going? I'll give you a ride for free."

Blair thought about protesting, but her feet were starting to complain and the bridge was still a ways off and MIT ten to twelve blocks beyond that.

"Thank you," she said and accepted the ride.

When Blair reached the astrophysics department, she was informed by the receptionist, a graduate student who introduced himself as Dobbins, that Angus was out.

"Out?" Blair said. "What does that mean?"

Dobbins was wearing a glen plaid suit with a matching bow tie and pocket square—*Jaunty!* Blair thought—but his expression was dour. The department secretary, Mrs. Himstedt, had retired in January, and Angus and his colleagues had been too busy to find a replacement, so they assigned graduate students the odious tasks that Mrs. Himstedt used to handle. Most of the graduate students felt put-upon, as young Dobbins clearly did. He also seemed to be offended by Blair's pregnant state; he watched her warily, as though he thought she might burst. "Professor Whalen had an appointment at ten."

Blair had started out the day with a strong sense of optimism, but it was rapidly dissolving. "Where is the appointment?"

"I can't tell you that."

"I'm his wife."

"I'm sorry," Dobbins said.

"Please just tell me where he went. Is he somewhere on campus?"

"Actually," Dobbins said, "it was a personal appointment."

"Personal?"

"That's what he said. Personal."

Personal, Blair thought. *Where could he be?* He had his hair cut every other Saturday without deviation and he wasn't scheduled to see the dentist until the following month.

She said, "I'll wait for him to return."

Dobbins pushed his glasses farther up the bridge of his nose and turned his attention to a textbook on the desk before him. Blair took a seat in a straight-backed chair and perched her handbag on what remained of her lap. She eyed Dobbins and caught him glancing up from his studying to inspect her with obvious distaste. He was probably made uncomfortable by her fecundity. So many men were.

She sat for more than thirty minutes and was about to get up and leave—she would take a taxi home, she decided, because the sitting was causing her lower back to ache—when Angus came rushing through the door.

"Angus!" Blair cried out, both relieved and joyful. She struggled to her feet.

The expression on Angus's face wasn't one she remembered seeing before. He looked…*caught*. He looked…*guilty* of something. And then Blair noticed he was in a state of disarray, his tie askew, his suit jacket misbuttoned, and his hair mussed. Blair blinked.

"Where were you?" she asked.

"What are you *doing* here?" he asked. Then an instant later, he added, "I was at a department meeting."

Blair looked to Dobbins, who had wisely fixed his gaze on his textbook again. "This nice young gentleman told me you were at an appointment. A personal appointment. Who was it with?"

"Would you excuse us, please, Dobbins?" Angus said.

Dobbins didn't need to be asked twice. If there was anything worse for Dobbins than being confronted with a pregnant woman, Blair supposed, it was being plopped in the middle of a marital squabble. He darted off down the hall.

"What are you doing here?" Angus asked again.

"I came to surprise you!" Blair said and then she dissolved in tears. She was fat, so fat, filled to bursting with child and fluids. She was an overripe fruit. She was…oozing, unctuous, moist, pungent. Blair had to urinate so badly and had lost so much control over her bladder that she feared she would piss a river right then and there.

"I need the ladies' room," she told Angus. "Right now."

Angus seemed relieved by this distraction; however, finding a ladies' room was a problem. The population of the building was so overwhelmingly male that there was only one ladies' room, and it was on the first floor. This involved an elevator ride and a walk down a hushed hallway past closed doors behind which, Blair assumed, men were busy calculating. All the while, Blair was praying she didn't leak. Also, she was wondering about the identity of Angus's mistress. That Angus had a mistress, she had no doubt.

Most professors would have chosen a student, but all of Angus's students were male, every single one, and his colleagues in his department were men. It could be one of the other wives; maybe the Joanne who wore all the turquoise eye shadow. Or it could be a stewardess from one of the flights Angus had taken the previous fall.

Blair finally reached the ladies' room, and she was so relieved to release her bladder that nothing else mattered. And then when she emerged, Angus announced that her visit was a lovely surprise but that he had to get back to work. He would see her at home.

"But..." Blair said.

Angus kissed her and pressed two dollars into her hand for a taxi. Then he smiled, which was rare these days. She supposed he was saving his smiles for the other woman. "I love you," he said, but the words rang hollow.

Blair moved toward the exit, then stopped. "Angus?" she said.

Angus, about to step into the elevator, held the door and turned around. "Yes, darling?"

She wanted to say something terrible like *I'm sorry I married you instead of Joey* or *I'm attending Harvard the instant this baby is born, no matter what you say.* She would *not* stand idly by while Angus lied to her!

But she couldn't start a fight here, in a public building, his place of employment. She had been raised better than that.

"Fix your jacket," she said. "You missed a button."

Time of the Season

Her mother drives the Grand Wagoneer and her grandmother sits up front. Without Kirby or Tiger along, Jessie has the entire back seat to herself so she's able to lie down, resting her head on one of the duffels. The Wagoneer is jam-packed with trunks and valises, boxes and bags, piled to within an inch of the roof. There is no way to see out the back; there never is on this trip, even though every year David implores Kate to bring less "paraphernalia," and every year Kate promises to bring only the bare necessities. Much of the cargo is clothes, of course—for Exalta, for Kate, for Jessie, for David, and even for Tiger, just in case the war ends at some point over the summer and he is sent home. Their summer wardrobes are completely different from what they wear the rest of the year in Boston. Kate packs Lilly Pulitzer patio dresses, espadrilles, a different bathing suit for every day of the week, clam diggers, Bermuda shorts, boatneck tees, her tennis dresses, and Tretorns. Jessie brings basically the same thing, although on a younger, less sophisticated scale. She has terry-cloth playsuits, a pair of white bell-bottoms, two sundresses for dinners out at restaurants, a crocheted vest, and a Fair Isle sweater for the inevitable rainy days. There's a small trunk filled with foul-weather gear—raincoats, hats, boots, umbrellas. There's a box of cooking implements—Kate's cast-iron pan and her chef's knife and butcher block. There's a cooler of steaks and French cheese from Savenor's because Nantucket is okay for seafood but everything else is subpar compared to the city, according to both Kate and Exalta. Jessie brought her summer reading—*Anne Frank: The Diary of a Young Girl*—and her new record album. There are tennis rackets and clam rakes, new life preservers for the boat, new wicker baskets for the bicycles.

The drive along Route 93 and then Route 3 is dull and Jessie's mind wanders. She isn't sure she'll be brave enough to ask Exalta if she can play Joni Mitchell on the Magnavox. Her grandmother listens to big-band records; Glenn Miller is her favorite. Her mother is a little better—she likes Ricky Nelson and the Beach Boys. Jessie wishes her own taste in music were cooler. Kirby likes Steppenwolf and the Rolling Stones, and Tiger listens to Led Zeppelin and the Who.

Will Tiger remember to send letters to Nantucket? Jessie kind of doubts it, so that means she'll have to wait for David to bring the letters down on the weekends.

She feels a twinge in her abdomen. Is it maybe a cramp? Might her period be coming? She suspects it's simple dread. They will get takeout tonight from Susie's Snack Bar at the end of Straight Wharf like they always do on the first night, and then tomorrow Jessie will start her tennis lessons at the Field and Oar Club, but what will she do with her afternoons? Go to the beach with her *mother?* Her mother likes to drive all the way out to Ram Pasture because there is never anyone there. She can plant her chair and read, sleep, and swim in peace. Ram Pasture is the only beach Exalta will go to as well; sometimes, she and Kate go together. Exalta wears a wide-brimmed straw hat and a bathing suit with a skirt. Jessie envisions herself next to her mother and grandmother. It's a happy picture of three generations enjoying a deserted beach, except nothing could be further from the truth.

"Jessie!" Kate says, startling Jessie.

"What?"

"'Yes, Mother,'" Kate prompts.

"Yes, Mother?" Jessie says, sitting up. Her mother is a stickler for manners when Exalta is around.

"The bridge," Kate says.

The Sagamore Bridge is suddenly before them, distinctive and majestic, an arc of steel girders. Objectively, Jessie supposes, it's quite hideous, but even so, Jessie feels a rush of fondness for it. Seeing the Sagamore means that summer is beginning, and Jessie is surprised to feel something like anticipation. The air smells like salt and pine, and as Kate drives over the crest of the bridge, Jessie sees boats slicing through the water of the Cape Cod Canal.

This optimism lasts all the way to the ferry dock. Driving the Wagoneer into the hold of the *Nobska* is a ritual for the family, and Jessie suddenly feels privileged to be doing it. Blair is stuck at home in Boston with heartburn and swollen ankles; Kirby is on Martha's Vineyard among strangers. Tiger is in the jungle in Vietnam. Tiger would likely give anything to be here right now. Before Jessie complains again, even to herself, she's going to remember that.

They park the car so its front bumper is right up against the back bumper of the ragtop VW Bug in front of them, and Jessie is reminded of Miss Flowers's juicy orange Bug—but school seems very far away. It's the family's tradition to climb to the uppermost deck and "take in the sea air," as Exalta says, so Jessie follows her mother and grandmother up the metal staircase, first to the main deck, where there are the men's and women's toilets, which are filled with a blue chemical instead of water, and a snack bar that sells hot dogs and chowder, and then to the upper deck, where the sun is the brightest and the breeze the strongest.

"Oh, look, there's Bitsy Dunscombe," Kate says. "I'm going to say hello. Want to come, Mother?"

"Heavens, no," Exalta says. "That whole family is tiresome."

Jessie happens to agree. Bitsy Dunscombe is the mother of twins, Helen and Heather, who are Jessie's age. A "friendship" with the Dunscombe twins has been pressed on Jessie since early childhood. The twins are absolutely identical, each with white-blond hair in a pixie cut, freckles across her nose, a slight gap between her two front teeth, and, recently, pierced ears (which Jessie finds scandalous, since she has been taught that the proper age for a girl to get her ears pierced is sixteen). Heather Dunscombe is lovely and kind, while Helen Dunscombe is mean and stinky. (For example, Helen routinely asks Jessie when she's getting a nose job.) Jessie would be okay hanging out with just Heather, but they come as a package, so Jessie keeps her distance whenever she's given a choice.

Kate saunters off, leaving Exalta and Jessie standing at the railing, staring at the water. It looks blue in the distance but green when Jessie gazes down on it directly from above, and she knows that if she were to collect this water in a glass, it would be clear. Water has no color, she learned in science class. What people see is a reflection of light. Jessie thinks about sharing this knowledge with Exalta in order to break the silence, but Exalta is humming as though she's in some kind of meditative state, which makes her seem unlike her normal self.

Finally, she turns to Jessie, tilts her head, and says, "Where did you get that necklace?"

Jessie's hand flies up to touch the pendant. "My father gave it to me this morning. It's the Tree of Life."

Exalta lifts it from Jessie's neck to better inspect it. "Tree of Life, you say? What does *that* mean?"

This feels like a thorny question. "It signals maturity and responsibility," Jessie says. "In the Jewish tradition, thirteen is an important age."

Exalta is wearing very large, round sunglasses in the style of Jackie Kennedy Onassis, so Jessie can't judge her expression.

"Today is my birthday," Jessie says. "My thirteenth birthday."

Again, the glasses make it impossible to say whether this announcement comes as a surprise to her grandmother. It would not be unlike Exalta to forget Jessie's birthday. The only grandchild's birthday Exalta faithfully remembers is Kirby's, September 30, because that also happens to be Exalta's birthday. This is why Kirby is her favorite, or it's one of the reasons.

Exalta rests her handbag on the railing, unsnaps the ball clasp, and pulls out a small velvet box.

"Happy birthday, Jessica," she says.

Jessie is stunned. It takes her a moment to realize that Exalta has not only remembered her birthday but gotten her a present, and this present is most definitely not a savings bond, which is what Jessie usually receives. She accepts the box but waits for Exalta's encouraging nod before she pries it open.

It's a necklace. The gold chain is so fine, it looks like gold dust. Hanging from the chain is a gold filigree knot in which is embedded a diamond the size of the head of a pin.

"Your grandfather gave that to me on our first wedding anniversary, back in 1919," Exalta says. "Try it on."

Jessie can't believe Exalta is giving her a piece of *her* jewelry. When Jessie was younger, she and Kirby used to tiptoe into Exalta's room and paw through the jewels, trying to guess which would be left to whom in Exalta's will. Exalta keeps an array of porcelain ring boxes on her dressing table, and Jessie adored the boxes nearly as much as the treasures they contained. Kirby's favorite ring was a black pearl held in a clawlike platinum setting. Jessie's favorite had been a trio of irregularly shaped opals set in gold. Opals had seemed magical to Jessie when she was younger; in the light, she could see they contained the entire rainbow. Blair, who had been too old to play the game but not too old to critique their choices, said that opals were garish, and Jessie had been secretly happy that Blair felt that way because if Exalta left the ring to Blair, Blair might give it to Jessie if she asked for it.

Jessie had never seen this particular necklace but she knew that some of Exalta's more valuable pieces were kept in a case that locked—her pearls, for example, and a diamond tennis bracelet and Jessie's grandfather's Harvard class ring, the one

Exalta gave to Tiger before he deployed. Jessie had never dreamed that she would receive something out of the locked case.

The problem with this gift, however, is that it requires her to take off the necklace from her father. Jessie sees no alternative, so she unclasps the silver chain and slips the Tree of Life necklace into the front pocket of her shorts. She secures her grandmother's necklace around her neck, and Exalta beams and says, "Exquisite on you, as I knew it would be."

Jessie forces the corners of her mouth up. She is, of course, thrilled about the necklace and about Exalta thinking her worthy of it, but she feels bad about the necklace her father gave her, the Tree of Life, which isn't in the same class as this one. She worries that Exalta somehow schemed to give Jessie the gold knot with the diamond in order to replace the Tree of Life so that Jessie won't be wearing any symbol of her Jewish heritage.

What is she going to do?

"We need to put that back in the box," Exalta says. "It's too precious for everyday wear. Special occasions only. I'll keep it in my room, where it will be safe."

Jessie is relieved. Special occasions only. The rest of the time, she can wear the Tree of Life. For once, things have worked out perfectly.

"Thank you, Nonny," Jessie says, and she kisses her grandmother's cheek.

Part of the appeal of Nantucket is that it never changes, which is especially important now that the rest of the country is going haywire. John F. Kennedy was shot when Jessie was in first grade, though she was too young to understand what that meant. Then last year, when Jessie was in fifth grade, Martin Luther King Jr.

was shot in Memphis, and later that year, Bobby Kennedy was shot in California. Jessie's parents had been deeply unsettled by these assassinations, and Kirby had been inconsolable. "Every man who tries to move the country forward is being murdered in cold blood!"

And, of course, American soldiers were being killed every day in Vietnam.

It's comforting for Jessie to see all the familiar signs as they roll up the cobblestones of Main Street in the Grand Wagoneer. The Charcoal Galley is the greasy spoon; it stays open late to accommodate the patrons of Bosun's Locker, the bar next door. (Jessie has been taught to cross Main Street to avoid passing Bosun's Locker, which only makes it more intriguing.)

Charlie's Market is where her mother does the shopping, and sometimes Jessie goes along. And then there is Buttner's department store. A few summers earlier, a housekeeper had parked her employers' Bonneville in front of the store and gone to run some errands. She returned to the car, started it up, and put it in reverse—or so she thought; she'd actually put it in drive. The curb stopped the car from moving forward, and the housekeeper, not understanding why the car wouldn't back up, hit the gas hard, which sent the vehicle shooting through the front window of Buttner's. As soon as that news reached All's Fair, Tiger and Jessie ran down to view the crash. Jessie had been aghast; in her mind, the destruction caused by the car ramming into a building could never be fixed. Tiger, she remembers, had been delighted. He stood by as one policeman tried to calm the hysterical housekeeper and another policeman tried to calm Miss Timsy, a longtime saleslady at Buttner's, and the photographer from the *Inquirer and Mirror* snapped pictures. The car had practically no damage, and, luckily, no one had been hurt. For two weeks, Buttner's window had been covered with brown paper, but then one day the glass was back in and a man came and painted on the lettering in black and gold, and it was just like nothing had ever happened.

They pass Claire Elaine's Beauty Shop and Mitchell's Book Corner, new last year, and the Sweet Shoppe, where Jessie will go with her father to eat malachite chip ice cream and air her grievances.

After they pass the Pacific Bank, they are on Upper Main Street, where most of Exalta's friends live. Some families come to the island before Memorial Day, but Exalta feels it's still too chilly in May. She has claimed the third Monday in June as "her" arrival day. On Thursday of this week, Jessie knows, the *Inquirer and Mirror* will announce that "Mrs. Pennington (Exalta) Nichols is in residence at her home on Fair Street for the summer after spending the winter at her home on Mt. Vernon Street in Boston."

The entire family believes that Fair Street is the prettiest road on the entire island. It's narrow, and traffic runs one way into town; Fair connects to only small side streets, so there aren't many passing cars. The homes on Fair Street are old but well cared for. Most of them are gray-shingled with trim freshly painted white every few summers. Some of the neighbors engage in unofficial competitions for the best window boxes, which Exalta claims is a "preposterous waste of time," but Jessie and Kirby used to have fun riding their bikes up and down the street, awarding first, second, and third prizes to the geraniums, petunias, pansies, and impatiens. Nearly all the homes have names—Fair and Square, Fairy Tale, Family Affair. Exalta's house, which is distinctive because of its yellow clapboard front, is called All's Fair, taken from the saying "All's fair in love and war." A few houses down on the right is Jessie's favorite, a white Victorian with a turret and fancy fretwork, although she keeps her preference to herself because she knows Exalta would be offended and might even tell Jessie to go knock on the Blackstocks' door and see if she can live with them since she likes that house so much.

They park the Wagoneer on a side street, Plumb Lane. Mr. Crimmins, the caretaker, appears out of nowhere to open Exalta's door and help her out of the car.

"Oh, Bill," Exalta says. "You didn't have to meet us. I know you're busy."

"You look as lovely as ever, Exalta," Mr. Crimmins says. He takes Exalta's hand and gazes at her for a second. "I was sorry to hear about Tiger being sent over."

"He'll be just fine," Exalta says, and she extracts her hand from his.

Mr. Crimmins turns to Jessie's mother. "Katie, how are you?"

"Bill, you got my letter? About the…"

"It's all set," he says. "As it were. In the den, like you asked." Mr. Crimmins winks at Jessie. "It looks like you've grown a whole foot there, Miss Jessica." He pulls a green-apple-flavored Now and Later out of his shirt pocket and hands it to Jessie. This, too, is a tradition. Mr. Crimmins has met Jessie with a green-apple Now and Later for as long as she can remember, though today, for the first time, accepting it feels childish. At thirteen, she is too mature and responsible to be interested in candy, and yet refusing it is unthinkable.

"Thank you," she says.

"And some mail came for you," Mr. Crimmins says. As he reaches into his back pocket, Jessie's heart leaps—a letter from Tiger! Her mother must be thinking the same thing because she steps forward in anticipation, but what Mr. Crimmins produces is a postcard. He hands it to Jessie.

The front shows a picture of Coolidge Corner in Brookline.

Confused, Jessie flips the card over and reads *Dear Jessie, Summer is boring. I miss you so, so, so much! Your friend forever, Doris.*

"It's from Doris," Jessie says. Her mother sighs.

Exalta, Kate, and Jessie go through the wrought-iron gate on the side of the property and walk up the brick steps to the back door; the only people who use the front door are guests. The kitchen runs the entire length of the rear of the house. It has a brick fireplace oven, which makes entering the kitchen feel like stepping back into Colonial times. The first owner of the house was a man named Ebenezer Raymond, who was a blacksmith. Ebenezer's two brothers were carpenters, and they'd built the house for him in 1795. Back then, many people died young, and newborn babies died all the time. Ebenezer got married, but his wife died; he married again, and then, at age thirty-eight, Ebenezer died. His second wife continued living in the house with their child and two of the children from Ebenezer's first marriage. There are so many people who've died in All's Fair that Jessie can't believe the house isn't haunted like some of the other houses on Nantucket. But then again, Jessie can't imagine Exalta tolerating a ghost—or a ghost tolerating Exalta.

The house smells the same, which is to say it smells old and dusty, like a museum. Jessie's grandfather used to smoke a pipe and a hint of his tobacco lingers.

Jessie has *Anne Frank* in one hand and her most important suitcase, the one with the record album, in the other, but she drops both at the bottom of the stairs so she can peek into the front rooms. To the right is the formal living room, which has a mural painted across three of the four walls. It's a scene of Nantucket circa 1845, the year before the Great Fire destroyed downtown, which guests ooh and aah about when they first see it. At the far end of the living room, in an alcove that is almost but not quite a separate room, is Jessie's grandfather's desk and leather armchair.

The oldest antique in the house is a wooden spinning wheel said to have belonged to Ebenezer Raymond's daughter. Years ago, before Jessie was born, Kirby spun the wheel too fast and broke the pedal. Exalta demanded an apology, which Kirby refused to give, and so Exalta punished her by shutting her up in the buttery—a dark little closet under the stairs where in olden times they stored the butter and milk—for ten whole minutes, a prospect that terrifies Jessie. When Kirby emerged from the buttery, she *still* wouldn't apologize and Exalta had famously called her a "little rebel" and then given her a piece of strawberry candy.

To the left of the stairs is the den, which has a fireplace, a console that houses the Magnavox, and a collection of whirligigs and whimmy-diddles, which are one of Exalta's passions. Jessie has always been fascinated by her grandmother's collection and seeing them again each year is nearly like seeing friends. There's the Indian chief with his long feathered headdress sitting upright in his canoe with paddles that move, a blue whale with fins that flip, a farmer bending over to be repeatedly kicked in the rear by his mule, a little Dutch boy and girl kissing next to a windmill with arms that spin, and Exalta's favorite, the mustached man in red-striped pajamas riding an old-fashioned tricycle. Jessie takes stock of the whirligigs and picks some up to maneuver their moving parts, but gently, so as not to break them; the last thing she wants is to be stuffed into the buttery. When she turns to leave, she sees something so surprising that she cries out.

There's a television, a big one, sitting on a stand in the corner.

Jessie approaches tentatively, as though the television is a spaceship that might blast off at any moment—that's how unlikely its presence in this house is. The set is even bigger than the one in

Doris's house, and Doris has the biggest TV of anyone at school because Doris's father likes to watch the commercials for McDonald's. This television is plugged in, and a rabbit-ears antenna sits on top. Gingerly, Jessie turns the knob, and the screen illuminates to show a sea of gray fuzz.

Jessie switches the TV off and hurries back to the kitchen, where Kate is unpacking her cooking implements and Exalta is sitting at the table with a gin and tonic in front of her and her checkbook out. Mr. Crimmins always hands Exalta a stack of bills from the local contractors on her arrival.

"There's a TV in the den," Jessie announces.

Exalta looks up. "What?"

"Mother," Kate says.

Jessie realizes she should have known better: It took her grandmother years to agree to the Magnavox and she has resisted updating to a more modern hi-fi, despite Kirby and Tiger constantly imploring her to do so. There was *no way* Exalta would have sanctioned a television set. This is Jessie's mother's doing.

A tremendous quarrel ensues.

"Get it out," Exalta says.

"I will do no such thing. David and I paid for it."

"I should hope *so!*" Exalta says. "But nevertheless, this is my house. *My* house, Katharine, and I want it out."

"I'm sorry, Mother. I realize I should have asked, but I thought you'd say no."

"Of *course* I would say no. I *am* saying no. No!"

"I absolutely have to watch Walter Cronkite," Kate says. "I'm sorry, Mother, but Tiger is my *son*. He's so far away, and the only way I can know what's going on over there is by watching the evening news."

"Darling," Exalta says. She pauses to throw back the rest of her drink, and when she speaks again, her tone of voice is a degree softer. "If there's anything to know, they'll tell you."

"That's cold, Mother."

"But true. Unless we hear otherwise, we can rest assured he's alive. I don't see how watching Walter Cronkite is going to do anything but make you worry. And the names they come up with for these battles—my goodness. Hamburger Hill? It turns the stomach."

"I need the television for my peace of mind."

"I'm sorry, darling. I'm going to ask Bill to take it back to wherever he got it. You should never have gone behind my back."

"I'm a grown woman, Mother. The television is staying."

"If you're interested in a test of wills," Exalta says, "you've chosen the wrong opponent."

"If the TV goes, I go," Kate says.

"You can't be serious."

"Try me."

Jessie wonders if she's going to have her wish granted so easily. Will Kate leave Nantucket and take Jessie with her? She has never seen her mother and grandmother argue. Usually, Exalta states her wishes and everyone else bends over backward to accommodate her. Jessie knows they did have a battle when Kate announced she was marrying David Levin, but that was about true love versus religious bias. This is about...a television set. Kate must feel more passionately about the news broadcast than Jessie realized. She knows her parents watch Walter Cronkite every weeknight, but the same basic information can be found in the *Boston Globe,* and as far as television news goes, Jessie has to side with her grandmother. She finds it gruesome. She doesn't want to hear the body count every night. Before Tiger left, it was just a number. Now,

Jessie realizes, each body in that count was a person with a name and a family and talents and quirks and likes and dislikes. She also realizes that if Tiger dies, he will shrink to a number, one more body among tens of thousands.

Jessie can't listen to Kate and Exalta another second. She slips out the back door to the cool fresh air of the yard. The yard is composed of a brick patio and a small plot of grass. Along the grass is a flagstone walk that leads to the property's second dwelling, known as Little Fair, which fronts Plumb Lane. Little Fair is where Blair, Kirby, and Tiger stay. Upstairs, there are two bedrooms, one bathroom, and a small living space with a galley kitchen. Downstairs, there's a third bedroom and a half bath. Around the side of Little Fair is an enclosed outdoor shower. According to Exalta, there is no reason to shower indoors during the summer, so although there are three full baths in the main house and a bathroom with a stall shower in this house, Exalta insists that everyone in residence at All's Fair and Little Fair line up for the outdoor shower.

Jessie decides to check on things at Little Fair. She's thirteen years old, and she knows that her siblings stayed by themselves in Little Fair as teenagers, but somehow she doubts she will ever be allowed to make the move to Little Fair. She might be able to use it as a clubhouse, however—a quiet place to read and escape the tensions across the yard.

As Jessie pulls open the screen door—the groan of the door is as familiar to her as her own voice—she wonders why Kate didn't think to hide the TV in Little Fair. Exalta never comes over here.

The inside of Little Fair smells like bacon. *Bacon?* she thinks. *Has someone been cooking in here?* Jessie's stomach growls. She peers in the downstairs bedroom that used to belong to Tiger. The bed is unmade and there's a copy of *The Godfather* on the night-stand. Jessie's eyes flick to the closet. There are clothes inside, a man's clothes.

What?

Jessie suddenly feels like Goldilocks. She tiptoes up the stairs because now she hears a noise, a repetitive *thwack,* and then a softly uttered curse word: "Damn."

"Hello?" Jessie calls out. She pokes her head between the spindles of the railing and sees a boy, probably two or three years older than she is, lounging on the couch with one of those paddles with a ball attached by a rubber string. The boy wears only a pair of mustard-yellow bathing trunks, a choker of what looks like wampum beads, and a white rope bracelet.

He sits up. "Oh, hi. You're Jessie, I bet."

The boy is tan already and his hair has a glint of gold that Jessie knows can only be achieved by swimming in salt water and letting your hair dry in the sun. At least, that's Kirby's claim. Jessie's hair is dark brown, and dark brown it remains all summer long. The boy's rope bracelet is fairly new, Jessie notes; it's still bone-white and loose on his wrist. Jessie has forgotten about rope bracelets. At the start of each summer, she and Kirby and Tiger would walk to the Seven Seas gift shop and each of them would pick out a brand-new clean white rope bracelet that would then shrink and weather with every swim. By the end of summer, the bracelet would be dingy gray and snug around Jessie's wrist, but somehow Kate would wiggle the blade of the scissors between rope and skin to cut the bracelet off before they returned to Brookline.

"Who are you?" Jessie asks.

"Pickford Crimmins," the boy says. "Call me Pick."

"Pick," Jessie says. "Are you related to Mr. Crimmins, then?"

"I'm his grandson."

Grandson? Jessie didn't know Mr. Crimmins even had a child, much less a grandchild.

"I'm Jessie," she says. "Jessie Levin."

"I know," Pick says. "Bill told me about you."

"You call your grandfather Bill?" Jessie calls her grandmother Exalta in her mind only; if she ever called Nonny Exalta to her face, she would be stuffed into the buttery for all eternity.

"That's what he asked me to call him," Pick says. "I met him for the first time at the beginning of May."

"You just met your *grandfather?*" Jessie says.

Pick tosses aside his paddle game, gets up off the couch, and stands at the top of the stairs, where Jessie can get a better look at him. Pick is tall and lean...and cute, Jessie decides. Very cute, cuter than any boy at school, but that only serves to make her self-conscious. She loses her wits for a second, then regains them. What is he doing here?

"What are you doing here?" she asks.

"Making lunch," he says. "Bacon, lettuce, and tomato sandwiches on toasted Portuguese bread that Bill got from this place called Aime's Bakery. You ever heard of it?"

Portuguese bread from Aime's, another summer tradition that Jessie has forgotten about. Portuguese bread is a dense white that makes the world's best toast. Some people buy twenty loaves at the end of the summer, take them home, stick them in the freezer, and enjoy the bread all year, but Exalta and Kate think this is cheating. Portuguese bread, like tomatoes and corn from the farm stand on Hummock Pond Road, is meant to be enjoyed only in the summer.

"Of course I've heard of it," Jessie says. "They make chicken pies on Thursdays and brick-oven beans on Saturdays."

"Good to know!" Pick says. "So, can I fix you a sandwich?"

"Yes, please," Jessie says. She's confused and a little uneasy about what Pick is doing in Little Fair, but her hunger wins out. She sees at least a pound of bacon, crispy and brown, draining on a paper bag. There are two tomatoes and a head of iceberg lettuce on a cutting board, the one that Tiger scorched with a pot long ago.

"Want mayo?" Pick asks.

"Yes, please," Jessie says. She sits down at one of the seats at the table for three and wonders what her siblings would think if they could see this stranger in the kitchen at Little Fair. Technically, he's not a *stranger,* Jessie supposes. He's Mr. Crimmins's grandson and they have known Mr. Crimmins all their lives. But do Blair, Kirby, and Tiger know that Mr. Crimmins has a grandchild? Pick said he only just met Mr. Crimmins in May. What does *that* mean?

Jessie has questions, but she's temporarily mesmerized by the sight of Pick creating the sandwiches. He toasts the precious bread until it's golden brown, spreads it with mayonnaise, layers on the bacon and sliced tomato, then tops it with lettuce that he shreds expertly with the dull chef's knife that has probably been at Little Fair longer than Jessie has been alive. He puts the sandwiches on plates and gets down two glasses from the cabinet. He knows where everything is in this kitchen. How is that possible? He brings a frosty pitcher of lemonade out of the icebox, delivers both sandwiches and drinks to the table, and then reaches into the narrow closet that serves as a pantry and produces a cylindrical tin of Jays potato chips. Jessie's mouth drops open. Potato chips are expressly forbidden in both houses. The only time Kate allows Jessie to have potato chips is with her chicken salad sandwich at the club, and even then, if Exalta happens to be present, Jessie has to ask for carrot sticks instead.

An entire tin of potato chips here, at Little Fair!

Pick raises his glass of lemonade to Jessie. "Nice to meet you," he says.

Jessie stares at him. He has arresting ice-blue eyes, the color of the rarest pieces of sea glass.

"Okay," she says. They touch glasses and Jessie feels embarrassed. She has never touched glasses with a boy before. She has never eaten a meal alone with any boy except for Tiger.

When she finishes half her sandwich and a large handful of chips—it's taking all her willpower not to devour the entire canister in a frenzy—she says, "Are you *living* here?"

"I am," he says. "And my grandfather is living in the room downstairs."

Jessie is so shocked by this news that she is temporarily speechless.

Pick snaps his fingers in front of her face. "Earth to Jessie."

Jessie can't help herself. She smiles at him. "I'm here," she says.

June 16, 1969

Dear Tiger,

Thank you for the birthday wishes. I got a record album and two necklaces, but the best present was the letter from you. There was no cake this year because we drove to Nantucket, but after fried shrimp at Susie's Snack Bar, we walked to the Island Dairy Bar and I got a hot fudge sundae.

There are two things I have to report. One is that Mom and Dad bought a television set and Mom asked Mr. Crimmins to put it in the den at All's Fair without telling Nonny! (Mr. Crimmins sends his best, by the way, but more about him in a minute.) Mom and Nonny had a fight where they raised their voices and Mom threatened to go back to Brookline. I left the house before the end of the fight, but guess what? The TV stayed. Mom later told me that the way she convinced Nonny to keep it was to tell her that, for the first time ever, Wimbledon is going to be shown on television in the United States, so Nonny will get to see her true love, Rod Laver, play.

Jessie stops to think about the time Kirby called Rod Laver "Red Hot Laver" right to Exalta's face and how Exalta had thrown her head back and laughed. Tiger had been there to witness it as well, and later they agreed that Kirby could get away with anything. Exalta had always had quite an affinity for Rod "the Rocket" Laver (Kirby had off-color fun with the nickname as well), and it intensified after Gramps died. Her mother had been smart to bring him up in her battle to keep the TV.

The other thing I have to tell you is that Mr. Crimmins will be spending the summer living in Little Fair with his grandson, whose name is Pickford Crimmins but who goes by "Pick." Pick is fifteen years old and he used to live in California with his mother, whose real name is Lorraine but who goes by "Lavender." Lavender is Mr. Crimmins's daughter but she left Nantucket when she found out she was pregnant. Pick says they lived in towns all over California, including, for the past five years, in a commune near a pear orchard. But one morning Lavender decided she wanted to "do some traveling," so she just up and left without Pick! Someone else at the commune knew how to contact Mr. Crimmins, so he drove out to California in his old truck and brought Pick back to

Nantucket. Now Pick has a kitchen job at the North Shore Restaurant. He works the salad station but he hopes to get promoted to the hot line over the course of the summer. He worked in the kitchen at the commune, which is where he learned to cook. The commune was vegetarian so Pick hadn't had any meat ever in his life until the ride back from California with Mr. Crimmins when they stopped at McDonald's. Now Pick loves meat. His favorite is bacon and I told him that was your favorite too.

Jessie pauses and reads through the letter. She wonders if she has talked too much about Pick. Will Tiger be able to tell that she has a crush on Pick? She never understood the term *crush* before, but now it makes sense because every cell in Jessie's body feels like it's being squeezed; her heart is like an orange pressed into the knuckle of the juicer until all of the emotion oozes out.

I start my tennis lessons tomorrow morning. I would say I'm dreading it but I know you are facing a lot worse things than two hours on hot clay smacking balls over a net. I miss you, Tiger. Please stay safe.

Love, Messie

Magic Carpet Ride

Kirby is the last girl to arrive at the house on Narragansett Avenue for the summer, Evan O'Rourke informs her. Evan is Alice O'Rourke's bachelor nephew, a balding forty-year-old with a paunch who's wearing white shirtsleeves, brown pants, and brown oxford loafers despite the June heat.

Kirby is still smarting from her interaction with Dr. Frazier. She has been replaying the conversation again and again, trying to interpret Dr. Frazier's facial expression and tone of voice. *Do your parents know about this?*

Dr. Frazier had asked Kirby the exact same question the first time they met.

Evan tells Kirby that he lives in the basement apartment of the house and manages things for his aunt Alice, who is almost completely deaf and has cataracts.

Kirby decides it might not be a bad idea to give Evan a glimpse of her charming side. "Well, your aunt certainly is lucky to have you."

Evan turns scarlet. He follows Kirby up two flights of stairs—which allows him to glimpse more than just Kirby's charm—and she can see that this job probably affords Evan all the excitement he can handle. By the time they reach the attic room, he's flushed.

"You're in luck," he says. "The girl who was living here didn't like being on a floor by herself, so she moved down to the room that was supposed to be yours, which is the size of a telephone booth. So now you get this room, which has a double bed. And your own sink."

"It's grand," Kirby announces. The attic room is, as one might expect, spacious and dusty. The sides of the room slant with the roof, but there is still sufficient space for a double bed, a dresser, a wardrobe, a standing fan whose steel blades create a welcome breeze, and the promised sink with a tiny round mirror nailed above it. There's also one window that looks like it opens onto a lower portion of the roof. Magnificent.

"I love it," Kirby says. Evan sets down her big suitcase and Kirby puts down her duffel and places her prize possession—a portable Silvertone record player—on the bed. "My father has paid the rent, correct?"

"Correct," Evan says. "You also get breakfast every day except for Sunday. The shower and toilet are on the second floor, shared by three other girls."

"Women," Kirby says.

"Are you a feminist, then?" Evan asks. Suddenly, he looks intrigued. Maybe he's wondering if Kirby is into free love, if she ever goes without a bra, if she has shed the sexual inhibitions that shackled girls who grew up in the 1950s.

Of *course* Kirby is a feminist! She has been somewhat promiscuous in the past (before Officer Scottie Turbo, she had two other lovers), though after what happened this spring, she has vowed to wait for love before jumping in the sack with someone again. She will never, ever sleep with Evan O'Rourke. But she can have some fun with him, maybe.

"Do you smoke grass, Evan?" she asks.

He looks startled and Kirby wonders if she misread him. Maybe he'll ask Kirby to leave the house before she unpacks a single miniskirt. She will have to ask Rajani for a place to stay after all. Or she will be forced to spend the summer on Nantucket with Exalta, Kate, and Jessie. Unthinkable. When, when, *when* will she learn to keep her mouth shut?

Suddenly, Evan breaks out into a lopsided grin. "On occasion," he says. "Though *technically,* smoking in the house is forbidden. Also forbidden are alcohol consumption and guests of the opposite sex."

"All of that *forbidden?*" Kirby asks. No wonder David wrote the check so readily; he must have confirmed this place was a convent. "Really, Evan?" She reaches out to touch Evan's hand, which is as pale as pudding. He jumps and Kirby pulls back; the last thing she wants is to give poor Evan an erection.

"Well, *technically,*" Evan says.

"What about music?" Kirby asks. "Is music allowed?"

"As long as it's not too loud," Evan says.

Kirby purses her lips. She'll break Evan in slowly. She unzips her duffel. "I brought only six records," she says. It took Kirby hours to choose the six, which were all that would fit in her bag; in the end, she decided it was most important to have albums for different moods: jubilance, anger (personal and political), hope (personal and political), heartbreak, mellow introspection, and rainy day/Sunday. Optimistic, she pulls out *The Second*. "How do you feel about Steppenwolf?"

A few minutes later, Kirby and Evan O'Rourke are on the roof, lying back and propping themselves up on their elbows, stoned out of their minds; John Kay wails in the background. The roof has a tremendous view of Circuit Avenue, Ocean Park, Vineyard Sound. Evan is far more tolerable to Kirby in her present condition.

"I've got a job cleaning rooms at the Shiretown Inn," Kirby says.

"That's in Edgartown," Evan says. "Do you have a car?"

"No car," Kirby says.

"A bike?"

"No bike," Kirby says. "And no money to buy a bike, even secondhand."

"So how will you go back and forth to Edgartown?" Evan asks.

"I thought maybe I'd walk?" Kirby says.

Evan breaks out in a fit of giggles. If Kirby closed her eyes, she would swear he was a ten-year-old girl.

"It's too far to walk," Evan says. "Three miles, at least."

"Three miles isn't that far," Kirby says, though her heart sinks. She's used to Nantucket, where there is only one town. On Martha's Vineyard, there are six towns, some of them quite distant from here. She vaguely knew this, but she hadn't given any thought to the reality of her commute. "What will I do?"

"You'll have to hitchhike," Evan says. "Pretty girl like you shouldn't have any trouble."

The next morning finds Kirby up early and one of the first women at breakfast, which is porridge with fresh blueberries, brown sugar, and milk as well as a platter of brown bread with butter and apricot preserves. Kirby isn't usually a breakfast person and she certainly isn't a porridge-and-brown-bread person but she decides that, since the food is free, she will eat, and eat lavishly.

When all of the women are assembled around the table, Kirby sees that she chose a good seat. The only person who looks even remotely promising is the woman sitting next to her. She's plump with a pretty face, big blue eyes, long dark hair, rosy lips, and a cheerful attitude.

"Patricia O'Callahan," she says, offering a hand. "Call me Patty."

"Katharine Foley," Kirby says. "Call me Kirby."

"You took the attic room?" Patty asks.

"Yes, I love it," Kirby says.

A thin-lipped girl across the table snorts. "It's hot," she says. "And there's a mouse."

"I kept the fan on," Kirby says. "And I'm not scared of anything."

"So there, Barb," Patty says.

Barb scowls at Kirby, and Kirby regrets her display of bravado. The fact is, she *is* scared of certain things—hitchhiking, for one, and the prospect of unemployment, for another. She lied to her parents, Dr. Frazier, and Evan O'Rourke when she said she had a job. The woman she'd spoken to at the Shiretown Inn had said only that they had openings for chambermaids. She couldn't offer Kirby a job without an in-person interview.

During breakfast, Patty talks about herself: She's the youngest of nine children, her parents live in South Boston, and she came to the Vineyard because her brother Tommy is the manager of the Strand movie theater and he got Patty a job working the ticket window for matinees and some evening shows. Patty wants to be an actress; she applied to the Lee Strasberg school for acting in New York but was rejected, and she doesn't have the money to attend Yale. She figures if she sees as many movies as possible, she might learn by osmosis. Plus she gets free popcorn.

"My brother lives with two other guys out in Chilmark," Patty says. "I'll introduce you."

"Do you have a car?" Kirby asks hopefully.

"Bike," Patty says. She casts a longing look at the butter and apricot preserves. "My goal is to lose twenty-five pounds this summer."

* * *

84

After breakfast, Patty shows Kirby her room. She's on the first floor to the left of the front entrance (which is good, she says, because it makes it easy to sneak out after curfew) and she has to share the downstairs bathroom with only one other person—Barb, who traded the attic for the broom closet. Barb is odious, Patty confides. She's always sullen and she was judgmental when Patty slept through church this past Sunday.

"Church?" Kirby says. "No one goes to church in the summertime."

"You must be Episcopalian," Patty says.

"Guilty as charged," Kirby says. The Episcopal church on Nantucket, St. Paul's, is located on Fair Street a scant block and a half from Exalta's house, but she and the family normally go only once a summer, usually for an evensong service. Although they might attend more often this year, with Tiger overseas. Kirby wonders if she should go to Mass with Patty so she can light a candle for her brother.

"The other three girls live on the second floor and they're Irish, from County Cork. I call them the Ms, for Miranda, Maureen, and Michaela. They're square—don't drink, don't smoke, don't sleep around."

Kirby decides then and there that she loves Patty. "How dull," she says.

On Patty's advice, Kirby dresses in a knee-length skirt and a proper blouse for her interview at the Shiretown Inn. She brushes her hair, collects it in a ponytail, then coils the ponytail into a bun. Then she walks to Seaview Avenue and sticks out her thumb.

A bunch of vehicles pass her by, including a laundry-service truck and an open-top Jeep filled with college boys. One of the boys whistles and another one holds up two fingers in a peace sign, but the Jeep doesn't slow down and there's no room for Kirby anyway. Kirby walks along the water. It's serene and seems completely safe, but she still wonders what her mother and—God forbid—her *grandmother* would think if they saw her *hitch-hiking*. They would think she had a death wish. Why else would she get into a car with a complete stranger? Anything could happen—abduction, dismemberment, rape, murder.

A cherry-red Chevy Corvair slows down, and Kirby sees that the driver is black. She knows this shouldn't influence her decision about whether or not to accept the ride; how can she claim to be a progressive if she displays the very prejudice she's seeking to change? The car stops and a young man cranks down the window. He's good-looking, she notes. He wears a spotless white T-shirt and Ray-Ban Wayfarers. "Where you headed?" he asks.

"Edgartown?" she says. "The Shiretown Inn?"

"Know it well," he says. "Hop in."

Kirby hesitates, but only for a second. This is how hitchhiking works, right? When someone offers you a ride, you take it.

Kirby hurries around and hops in the passenger side. The car is clean—there's no trash, no dust, and no sand. Kirby feels a pang for the International Harvester Scout that she drives on Nantucket. She was almost proud of how, by Labor Day weekend, the Scout contained the souvenirs of a summer well spent: her Bing Pintail surfboard, a handful of bikini bottoms, sand dollars and slipper shells, wadded-up takeout wrappers from the Seagull in Madaket, half a dozen damp beach towels, a few crushed Schlitz cans, the random horseshoe crab carapace, a swollen, rippled paperback of *Valley of the Dolls,* and approximately half a ton of sand.

This car looks like it just came from the dealer.

"I'm going to a job interview," she says.

"Nice," he says. "Did you just arrive for the summer?"

"Yesterday," Kirby says. "I go to Simmons, in Boston."

The guy laughs. "I go to Harvard," he says. "In Cambridge."

"Wait a minute," Kirby says. "Are you...Darren?"

"I am," he says. He shifts his Ray-Ban Wayfarers to the top of his head, then breaks into a truly radiant smile and snaps his fingers a few times. "You must be Rajani's friend. Is it...Kathy? Kitty?"

"Kirby," she says. "My real name is Katharine but everyone calls me Kirby."

"Didn't Rajani tell me your family has a house on Nantucket?" Darren asks.

"Afraid so," Kirby says.

"So why the switch?" Darren asks. "Don't get me wrong, we'll take as many pretty girls as we can get on the Vineyard, but I thought Nantucketers kept to their own island."

"I needed a change," Kirby says. She gazes out the window as they cross a wooden bridge; to the right is a large, placid pond edged with reeds. "I had a trying year." She closes her eyes and shakes her head. She had *not* meant to say that. "My brother was deployed to Vietnam in May."

"Man," Darren says, "that sucks."

"I tried to convince him to go to Canada, but he said Canada was for people who were afraid of getting shot at. He agrees the war is wrong—"

"Really wrong," Darren says.

"But he felt a sense of duty. Our father"—Kirby swallows—"was in Korea. He was a big hero, I guess. I don't know. He died a few months after he got home so I never really knew him, but...I mean, we'd always been taught he was a war hero. I think Tiger took that legacy pretty seriously."

"I can see that," Darren says. "I have friends from Boston Latin who were drafted, and then my freshman-year roommate at Harvard enlisted. He was killed in the Battle of Dak To."

"I heard about that one on the news," Kirby says. "I'm sorry. That's one of the reasons I'm against the war. Westmoreland sent American soldiers in to take that hill at any cost, and then a couple weeks later, the army abandoned it."

"People say Abrams is better," Darren says. "I'm sure your brother will be fine."

"He has to be fine," Kirby says. That was what she told Tiger before he left. He *had* to come back alive. Other families might be strong enough to bear the loss of their sons and brothers, but the Foley-Levins weren't. They just weren't. Or maybe it was only Kirby who wouldn't be able to survive. She had been pretty messed up in her own life when Tiger left; her heartbreak over Scottie had been at its most acute. She had, in fact, told Tiger that she would move to Canada *with* him. They could get a flat in Montreal, learn to speak French, learn to like hockey. They would emigrate and never look back.

She desperately needs to change the subject. "What do you do for work?"

"I'm a lifeguard at Inkwell Beach," Darren says. "I was headed there when I saw you."

"I took you out of your way!" Kirby says. "I'm so sorry. But thank you. This would have been one heck of a walk."

They pass a sign announcing that they're entering Edgartown, and Kirby takes in the leafy streets lined with charming white clapboard homes. It's even more picturesque than downtown Nantucket, which Kirby didn't think was possible. They cruise by the whaling church, an exquisite pocket garden with stone benches in the shade, a white-columned building called Preservation Hall.

"I don't have to be at work until ten," Darren says. "I just like to get there early. Lead by example, you know." He grins and Kirby can't help herself—she practically swoons. Darren is so good-looking and so cool. Kirby has never had a black friend before, though she's on good terms with the black women at Simmons, especially Tracy from her English class, who introduced her to the poetry of Gwendolyn Brooks. Rajani is Indian, and she and Kirby have spent countless hours discussing racially charged issues, so Kirby *feels* like she's had her eyes opened; she wants nothing more than to live in a country that's free from prejudice.

She wonders what it would be like to date Darren. Of course, he isn't asking her out. He's just giving her a ride.

Darren drops Kirby off in front of the Shiretown Inn just as a woman with bright red hair wearing a green dress is walking up the steps. Darren calls out, "Hey, Mrs. Bennie!"

The red-haired woman holds a hand over her eyes to shade them as Kirby climbs out of the car, careful to gather her skirt around her legs. Mrs. Bennie is the woman she spoke to on the phone, and Kirby wonders how it will look, her climbing out of Darren's car.

"Hey there, Darren!" Mrs. Bennie says. "Please tell your parents how much I enjoyed myself the other night. There's nothing like steamers at the Frazier house."

"Will do," Darren says.

Mrs. Bennie waves and disappears inside.

"Thanks for the ride," Kirby says. "You're a lifesaver."

"Good luck with your interview," Darren says. "Where are you living?"

Kirby tells him the address.

"Miss O'Rourke's house," Darren says.

"You know it?"

"The prettiest girls live there each summer," Darren says. "And I can see this year is no exception."

"Aw, thanks," Kirby says. She executes a quick curtsy.

"Just watch out for Evan," Darren says.

"I can handle the likes of Evan," Kirby says. "Putty in my hands."

"I'm sure he is," Darren says. "So, hey, why don't you swing by Inkwell Beach sometime? I'm always there, and it's an easy walk from your house."

"Okay," Kirby says. "I'll do that."

"I mean it," Darren says. "Come by."

Kirby's heart somersaults. "*I* mean it," she says. "I will."

Darren waves and drives off, and Kirby stands on the sidewalk staring at the car until it disappears from view.

Hitchhiking is the best thing she's ever done.

It turns out Mrs. Bennie is the general manager of the Shiretown Inn. She invites Kirby into a small office behind the front desk.

"How do you know Darren?" Mrs. Bennie asks.

Kirby nearly says she just met him hitchhiking but she worries how that will make her sound. "From school," she says.

Mrs. Bennie looks at Kirby's résumé, which is on the desk before her. "But you go to Simmons," she says. "That's a girls' school."

Women's school, Kirby thinks. "I met him through a friend of mine at Simmons," Kirby says. "She and Darren grew up here together in the summers."

"Well, you know, Darren's family has lived here forever," Mrs. Bennie says. "I've known that boy since he was an itty-bitty baby."

Kirby loves hearing this. Martha's Vineyard is a place where racial harmony exists!

Mrs. Bennie points to a handwritten note in the margin of Kirby's résumé. Kirby spent hours on her sister's Underwood typing and retyping until the thing was perfect, and yet someone has scribbled all over it. "It says here that you're interested in a chambermaid position," Mrs. Bennie says. "But I'm sorry to say, those jobs have all been taken. The Irish girls, you know, they get here in May."

Kirby's spirits fall. The Irish girls—like Miranda, Maureen, and Michaela on the second floor—arrived in May and snapped up all the jobs. If the cleaning jobs are gone, what will be left for her? Pumping gas? Bagging groceries?

"I wanted to get here earlier," Kirby says. "But I had to finish up the semester."

Mrs. Bennie raises her head and seems to see Kirby for the first time. "You're a pretty girl," she says. "And you have three years of college." She leans over so that Kirby has a view of her matronly cleavage. "How would you feel about a position on the front desk?"

It's too good to be true. Speechless, Kirby nods.

"I've just had to fire a girl," Mrs. Bennie says. "For being indiscreet."

Kirby knows not to ask, but she naturally wonders: What did this girl do?

Mrs. Bennie seems to read Kirby's mind. "We had a guest staying with us, a gentleman guest, and Veronica gave this gentleman's *wife* a key to his room without checking with him or with me. It led to a very unfortunate situation."

Gentleman guest caught with a co-ed, Kirby guesses. Or his secretary. Or someone else's wife. She pushes away thoughts of Scottie Turbo.

"Before you accept, I need to make certain aspects of the job clear. You are to be on time. You are to be neatly dressed with your hair coiffed. No pants or culottes. No bare arms. We have distinguished guests at this inn, Wall Street types, business executives. In fact, I just booked a room for Senator Edward Kennedy. He's coming to stay with us next month."

Teddy Kennedy! Kirby can't believe it.

Mrs. Bennie continues. "Our priority here at the inn is our guests' comfort and their privacy. Is that clear?"

"Crystal," Kirby says. She's glad she tied her hair back for this interview, though she worries about a wardrobe. She'll have to see if the Vineyard has a store like Buttner's where she can buy some appropriate outfits. Teddy Kennedy! She can't wait to tell Rajani about that. Except no...she has to be discreet.

"The shift that's available is eleven p.m. to seven a.m. Is that going to be a problem?"

It takes Kirby a moment to process this—eleven at night until seven in the morning. Mrs. Bennie is offering her the graveyard shift. *Is* that going to be a problem? Kirby quickly calculates. She will get back to Narragansett Avenue in time to eat breakfast with the girls, and then she'll go to sleep. If she sleeps from eight to two, she'll still have afternoons to go to the beach and her evenings free. It's not optimal, but she knows better than to turn this offer down.

"Weekends off?" she asks hopefully.

"Mondays and Tuesdays off," Mrs. Bennie says. "You'll leave here Monday morning at seven and return Wednesday night at eleven. The job pays ninety dollars a week."

Ninety dollars a week! Kirby is appalled at herself for bending to the power of the American dollar, but there's no denying its allure. She has to give up her weekends, but considering her troubled past, this might not be a bad thing. She has to prove herself worthy; she has to develop a work ethic. Mrs. Bennie is offering Kirby a chance to demonstrate that she's a responsible adult. Also, with this schedule, she'll avoid the log jam for the second-floor bathroom, and her parents will have no reason to complain.

Kirby is going to be a front-desk clerk!

"I'll take it," she says.

Those Were the Days

She has made a deal with the devil.

She had no choice.

Kate is no stranger to military sacrifice. Wilder died when he was back home on American soil, but Kate knows he never returned from Korea, not really. However, sending a son into battle is different, and Vietnam is a different war. The jungle is nearly impenetrable, the heat murderous, the insects predatory, the swamps thick and green with murk. It's hard enough to battle the country itself, never mind the ruthlessly immoral Vietcong. They set savage booby traps—punji sticks, snake pits, grenades in a can.

Kate and David had been quietly antiwar since 1965. A paralegal from David's firm enlisted, and this young man—twenty-two years old—was killed in the Battle of Ia Drang after only a week in-country. Kate had feared that Tiger would enlist as soon as he graduated from high school but he'd halfheartedly enrolled at Framingham State. Now she wishes that he had enlisted; then, at least, he might have had choices. He might have been able to train for a job that kept him off the front lines.

But Tiger took his chances and now he is a grunt, one of thousands. He is expendable.

Kate's only hope for getting Tiger home quickly—possibly as soon as September—rests with Mr. Crimmins. When Kate wrote to Bill Crimmins to let him know that Tiger had been drafted and wouldn't be coming to Nantucket that summer, Bill had written back to say that his brother-in-law had served with Creighton W. Abrams in the Battle of the Bulge and that he still corresponded with the general weekly about matters both military and personal. Bill said he would ask his brother-in-law to use his influence with the general to get Tiger out.

But Bill requested a favor in return.

The drama about the television served as a good cover for the drama about the boy. Kate glimpses Pick from her bedroom window as she unpacks her suitcase. He's getting on his bicycle. Kate notes the shape of his shoulders and the golden glint of his hair. She finds she's trembling.

Kate thought Exalta would prove to be an obstacle to the plan, but that wasn't the case. Kate had explained the situation to her a few weeks ago—Mr. Crimmins had discovered that Lorraine had a son out in California; Lorraine (now called Lavender) had vanished, and Mr. Crimmins had gone out to fetch the child, but he had no room in his efficiency on Pine Street to house the boy— and Exalta had easily been led to the solution: Bill Crimmins and his grandson would both live in Little Fair.

"It'll be nice for us to have a man around," Exalta said. Kate didn't bother pointing out that David would be coming every weekend; she was simply relieved that Exalta didn't oppose this new arrangement. In fact, Exalta proceeded to act as though inviting Bill Crimmins and his grandson to stay in Little Fair had been *her* idea.

Everything will be okay, Kate tells herself. Bill Crimmins wrote to his brother-in-law last week, just before he and the boy moved in, and he would likely hear back this week or next. Tiger would be plucked from danger as suddenly as he had been dropped into it. He would come home.

Following the boy out of Little Fair is someone else, a young woman. It's *Jessie,* Kate realizes. The way Jessie stands as she talks to the boy, with her hand on her waist and her hip cocked, looks very mature. Well, Kate thinks, she *is* thirteen…today. Poor, sweet Jessie has had to sacrifice her birthday to the task of arriving and settling in. Kate is too addled to do anything more than take everyone to Susie's for dinner, and that isn't a birthday ritual but a first-night-on-Nantucket ritual. However, she supposes they can stop at the Island Dairy Bar on the way home for a sundae.

It's a pathetic effort to celebrate the beginning of her youngest child's teenage years. Kate decides she'll make it up to Jessie next week, once things have calmed down. They'll have dinner, just the two of them, at the Mad Hatter, Jessie's favorite.

Kate shoves her suitcase to the back of the closet the way she always does, an attempt to avoid thinking about the reality that she will have to pack it up again. She then takes stock of the room, her summer bedroom for as long as she has been alive. She lived here as a little girl, back when America was happy and prosperous; she lived here as a teenager during the Depression, when men from around the island would knock on the door to see if Kate's parents needed any work done on the house. It was in this era, Kate recalls, that they hired Bill Crimmins to do odd jobs and Lorraine, his daughter, to serve as maid and cook. The Crimminses had moved to Nantucket year-round after Bill lost his job at the textile mill up in Lowell, Mass. Bill's wife died when Lorraine was a baby.

Kate had lived here as a young wife to Wilder Foley with his manic-depressive disorder, his pathological lies, and his undeniable magnetism. She can remember sitting in the window seat waiting for Wilder to come home on one of the many nights he insisted on staying late at Bosun's Locker. She'd lived here as the bereft mother of three fatherless children during the awful summer of 1953. Lorraine Crimmins had run off to California, and Kate spent the better part of July and August without anyone to mind the children. She cut out paper dolls with Blair and Kirby; she taught Blair to ride a bicycle on Plumb Lane; she dug holes in the sand at Steps Beach with Tiger, crying behind her giant sunglasses. Next, she had lived here as the wife of David Levin, the Jewish attorney whom Exalta had never accepted despite the fact that he was a good, kind, stable man—as sane and calm as Wilder had been reckless and unpredictable—willing to take on three children not his own and treat them the same way that he treated his own daughter, Jessica. And now Kate is forty-eight years old, an age she only properly feels when she's in a place that holds all of her different lives together, as this room does.

On the dresser, there's a photograph of the family taken in the dunes of Steps Beach: Kate and David in the center back row, Blair and Angus on their left, Kirby on their right, and Tiger and Jessie sitting in front. They're all smiling and glowing with their summer coloring—lighter hair, darker skin. Exalta had enjoyed too many Hendrick's and tonics that day at lunch and had fallen asleep, missing this excursion to Steps Beach. Kate, frankly, is glad she wasn't there. This is *her* family; *she* is the matriarch. She studies her own face and feels heartbroken at her own naive sense of security.

Those were the days, my friend, we thought they'd never end.

Tiger's absence is only temporary, Kate tells herself. She will have faith in Bill Crimmins. She will do her best to make the boy feel welcome, and she will be duly rewarded. Mr. Crimmins will find a way to get Tiger home. They will be a family again.

Suspicious Minds

In Boston, the temperature hits eighty degrees, and Blair, just entering her third trimester, has outgrown all of her maternity clothes. She has only one dress that still fits. It looks like a yellow circus tent and yet she has no choice but to wear it every time she leaves the house, which she now does as infrequently as possible. Angus agreed to pay extra to have Savenor's deliver the groceries and he has held his tongue about the skyrocketing electric bill; Blair keeps the air-conditioning unit running twenty-four hours a day. The apartment feels like the North Pole and still Blair perspires as she sits in front of the television watching *That Girl* and eating grilled-cheese sandwiches followed by Hunt's Snack Pack butterscotch puddings, one after the other.

Instead of seeing Angus's acquiescence about the extra expenses as kind, Blair understands them as a manifestation of his guilty conscience. He's unwilling to tell Blair the truth about where he was the day she surprised him at the office; he resolutely maintains he was at a meeting, although the nature of that meeting has changed three times, and he can't explain why his hair was mussed or his jacket misbuttoned.

Blair also noted a suspicious phone call. She answered the

phone in their apartment, and a woman's cool, melodious voice asked for Mr. Whalen—this when everyone at MIT calls Angus Dr. Whalen or Professor Whalen. Blair acted on her hunch and said, "I'm sorry, he's not home at the moment. Is this Joanne?" The woman hung up.

One evening in early June, the phone rings and Angus answers the kitchen phone at the same time that Blair picks up the extension next to the bed. She's lying there in her underwear beneath one thin sheet, morosely waiting for Angus to warm up a TV dinner and deliver it like room service.

"Hello," Angus says, "Whalen residence."

"Mr. Whalen?" the silvery voice says. "This is Trixie."

It takes Blair only an instant to realize that Angus doesn't know she's on the line.

"Trixie," Angus says. "Listen, I'm sorry about today. Something came up at work, but...I'd like to see you tomorrow."

"That's fine, but I'm going to have to charge you for today."

"Yes," Angus says. "I understand, of course." Blair barely manages to stifle a gasp. Angus clears his throat and says, "Darling, are you on the phone?" He pauses. "Blair?"

Blair presses the plastic button to disconnect, then carefully sets the receiver down and lies back in what she hopes is a believable imitation of pregnant slumber.

A second later, Angus taps on the door and Blair smells the commingled scents of Salisbury steak, peas, and apple cobbler. "Darling?"

Blair keeps her eyes shut. Angus has been seeing a call girl, a prostitute. On the one hand, this is a relief because it's not Joanne of the turquoise eye shadow and *Pat the Bunny,* and it eliminates Blair's other suspicion, that Angus is involved romantically with one of the male students at the university.

On the other hand, the idea of Angus with a prostitute is sickening. It's so *seedy,* so beneath him. He's *paying* for sex! It's possible he's been paying for sex all along. This would explain how he became so skilled in the bedroom. But what about disease? Does Angus really have so little regard for Blair and for their unborn baby?

Trixie, Blair thinks. It's gratifying to have a name to pin on her rival. The prostitute's name is Trixie.

As Blair waits for the next mysterious phone call, the days grow hotter. Kirby swings by the apartment to say goodbye. She's spending the summer on Martha's Vineyard instead of Nantucket, something Blair doesn't quite understand.

"I need to get Mom's foot off my neck," Kirby says. "It's time for me to grow up."

This, Blair wholeheartedly agrees with. Kirby lacks discipline and seems content to go whichever way the wind blows her. Blair decides not to tell Kirby that being a grown-up is overrated.

"You're working in housekeeping?" Blair says. "Was that the best job you could find?"

"At least I *have* a job," Kirby says. She rakes her eyes across Blair's bed—food wrappers, empty pudding cups, the *TV Guide,* and a copy of *The Love Machine* by Jacqueline Susann, which is what passes for literature these days.

Blair nearly snaps back but she can see that her situation *is* pathetic and she doesn't have the energy to match wits with her sister. Her brain has turned to consommé.

The role reversal is disheartening. Back in the dark days when Blair and Kirby's father died—Blair was eight, Kirby five—Kirby used to climb, whimpering, into Blair's bed. She was old enough to know something was very wrong but not old enough to be told exactly what, and Kate had been focused on caring for Tiger, who was only three and still a handful. Blair remembers someone— her grandmother, maybe, or Janie Beckett—telling Blair that Kirby was lucky to have her as an older sister. She could serve as a role model. Blair had taken this very seriously. Her entire life has been a master class in How to Lead by Example.

But now Kirby must be looking at Blair and thinking, *I do* not *want to end up that way.*

"I shouldn't have quit my job," Blair says. "I should have spent the past year teaching, but Angus wanted me home."

"Why didn't you stand up for yourself?" Kirby asks. "You know what Betty Friedan would say—"

"Betty *Friedan* isn't married to an astronaut!" Blair nearly laughs because that statement is so absurd, and no doubt, Kirby's next point will be that Blair isn't married to an astronaut either— not really. "And now I'm good and stuck, aren't I? Barefoot and pregnant. I'm bored out of my mind. I'm so bored that my imagination comes up with all of these conspiracy theories..."

"Have you figured out who killed the Kennedys?" Kirby asks.

Blair can't bring herself to smile. She longs to tell her sister about Angus and Trixie, but she doesn't want to admit to another failure. Not only is Blair not working but the husband she quit her job for is cheating on her.

"Enjoy your time on the Vineyard," Blair says. "Cleaning is honest work. I'm proud of you."

"Awww, Blair," Kirby says. She puts her hand on Blair's belly and the baby kicks.

"That's your aunt Kirby," Blair says.

"Hey, kid," Kirby says. "Get ready for 1969. I have some protest songs to teach you."

* * *

The next day, Kate drops in to say goodbye before she leaves for Nantucket with Jessie and Exalta.

"Dad will be home in case of emergency," Kate tells Blair. She sets down an assortment of magazines—*Good Housekeeping, Ladies' Home Journal, Woman's Weekly*. Nothing with any real news. Blair knows her mother wants to keep her from being shocked or upset, but Blair doesn't want to read "Ten Cold Suppers for Summer" or "Weekend Embroidery Projects." She needs a far less wholesome magazine with articles like "What to Do When Your Husband Is Seeing a Prostitute." She needs *Cosmopolitan.*

"And I'll be back on the first of August, like we discussed, so I can be with you for the birth."

"I'm leaving Angus," Blair says.

Kate doesn't even blink. "I know he's been working hard, sweetheart. But the moon landing—"

"Damn the moon landing!" Blair says. Liftoff for Apollo 11 is scheduled for July 16, although any one of a thousand things could delay it, pushing it back a few weeks to Blair's due date. At this point, she hopes Angus *is* in Houston when the baby comes; she doesn't want him anywhere near her. "He's having an affair with some woman named Trixie." She can't bear to admit the prostitute part to Kate, but perhaps the name *Trixie* makes that obvious.

"Really?" Kate asks. She sounds skeptical. "Are you sure? It's common, you know, to *imagine* he's being unfaithful because you're feeling undesirable—"

"This *isn't* a figment of my imagination, Mother," Blair says. "She *called* here. I heard her voice."

"Well, I'm sure Angus will come to his senses once the baby is born," Kate says.

Blair closes her eyes and sees red, and all she can imagine is her blood pressure spiking to such an alarming level that the baby shoots right out of her. She needs to calm down. She opens her nightstand drawer, pulls out a pack of Kents, and lights one up. "So you suggest I just wait for this to end on its own? You suggest I *tolerate* this?"

"You're seven months pregnant, sweetheart," Kate says. "You can't leave and you can't get divorced and you can't confront Angus because the emotional turmoil is bad for the baby."

Blair should never have told her mother. She should have just swallowed her pride and confided in Kirby. Kirby would never advise Blair to stay with a cheating husband. "That's such an old-fashioned view, Mother," Blair declares. "What would Betty Friedan say?"

"Who?" Kate says.

Blair shakes her head and collects herself. "I thought maybe I could move into Nonny's house," she says. "Since she's away."

Kate laughs.

"The house is just sitting there, empty," Blair says. Her grandmother's town house in Beacon Hill is large, cool, and gracious, with clocks that chime and hand-knotted silk rugs that feel like heaven under bare feet. The bed in the guest room is a king, and the windows look out over the back courtyard, where there's a tall, wrought-iron fountain that makes a soothing gurgling sound. It wouldn't be as good as escaping to the islands but it would be better than staying here on Comm. Ave.

"And empty it will remain," Kate says. "I'm sorry, sweet pea. You're twenty-four years old, a grown woman, married, and pregnant, and you need to act like an adult and not a child who runs away from her problems. Angus has a remarkable career and provides very well for you. If he is having a dalliance with this... *Trixie,* it's probably because he's under so much pressure. Really, you might think to be grateful."

"Grateful?" Blair says. "*Grateful,* Mother? He's never home, he works all the time, and on the rare occasions he does make an appearance"—she pauses, unsure how much more she wants her mother to know. Kate looks at her expectantly—"he's...moody. Unpredictable. Sometimes he seems like a completely different person than the man I married."

"Oh, honey." Kate seems to soften a bit. She reaches over to brush a stray hair from Blair's forehead, and Blair briefly leans into the cooling comfort of her mother's palm, remembering how she used to pretend she felt feverish just so that her mother would rest that soft and steady hand against her face. The memory ends when Kate stands up briskly and leaves the bedroom. She returns a moment later with a glass of brown liquid over ice. At first, Blair thinks it's iced tea, but when she smells it, she's happy to find it's scotch.

"Isn't your doctor's appointment tomorrow?" Kate asks.

The appointment with Dr. Sayer, yes. The deplorable Dr. Sayer with the grotesque overgrown beard who feels Blair up with cold hands while his googly eyes swim behind his glasses.

"Yes," Blair says. She stubs out her cigarette in the ashtray by the bed and takes a sip of scotch. Immediately, she relaxes. "At ten."

"Is Angus going with you?"

"He's *supposed* to," Blair says. "But he may have forgotten and planned a rendezvous with Trixie."

Kate laughs and says, "It's best to keep a sense of humor about it. Let me know how it goes. We should be on Nantucket by four in the afternoon tomorrow. Love you, sweet pea. Be well." Kate leans over to kiss Blair on the forehead and give her shoulder a squeeze, and for one instant, Blair feels okay.

"Bye," Blair says. She can't believe her mother is being so non-chalant about the news. Blair should have disclosed the prostitute part; maybe then Kate would have been appropriately aghast. Her mother grew up in a time when young women were expected to just put up with unfaithful husbands. But now it's 1969 and Blair won't stand for it. If moving into Nonny's isn't an option, then Blair will just go to Nantucket for the summer. She'll have the baby on the island, at the cottage hospital.

But…Blair won't last two hours in the car and two hours on a ferry; merely driving up the cobblestones of Main Street might send her into premature labor.

She's trapped.

Angus remembers about Blair's doctor's appointment the next day, which is a relief to Blair because the notion of going anywhere alone in her condition is daunting.

Ruth, the office receptionist, takes one look at Blair and Angus and leads them right back to the office where Dr. Sayer is sitting at the desk, smoking. Blair can't tell if Ruth is alarmed by her size or if she's impressed that Dr. Whalen has chosen to accompany his wife to the appointment when he's such a busy man working on a matter that's so important to the nation's pride. Maybe it's a little of both.

There is no mistaking Dr. Sayer's reaction, however. When he sees Angus, he jumps to his feet and starts pumping Angus's hand. There follows a long conversation about the moon launch and the merits of various astronauts—Angus wholly defends Armstrong and Aldrin, but Dr. Sayer feels Jim Lovell should be included—and then Angus shifts into technical talk about thrust, elliptical or-bits, and Hohmann transfers, and Dr. Sayer nods along, though Blair is certain he's just as lost as she is.

When she can't stand being ignored another second, she clears her throat.

"Oh, yes," Angus says. "My wife is concerned about—"

"My size," Blair says. She finally has Dr. Sayer's undivided attention and she knows she'd better take advantage of the opportunity. "I'm huge. A hippo. I've outgrown every dress but this one."

Dr. Sayer gives her an appraising look, then comes around his desk and puts a hand on her belly. Blair feels the baby kick. "Let's send you to X-ray," he says.

Angus chooses to stay in the examining room while a nurse leads Blair down the hall and asks her to lie on a cold metal table. While the X-rays are taken, tears leak out of Blair's eyes. She's certain they're going to find she's carrying a giant, a monster, an octopus. She regrets ever marrying Angus and allowing herself to get pregnant. She imagines her life if she had taken an alternate path: Blair Foley, slender of body and nimble of mind, becomes a renowned scholar in the field of twentieth-century women's literature, starting with Edith Wharton and moving on to Shirley Jackson, Flannery O'Connor, Anne Sexton, Adrienne Rich. She would date different men, as Sallie does, an architect one weekend, a museum curator the next. She would not be here, lying on a metal table like a side of beef, awaiting news of what horrific creature is growing within her; she would be lounging on Cliffside Beach on Nantucket, and Marco, the lifeguard from Rio de Janeiro, would watch her trim, firm backside when she strolled from her umbrella to the water.

She would be having a mad, passionate affair with Marco, who would be devoted solely to her; she would not have to share Marco with a call girl named Trixie.

Blair closes her eyes to better focus on her rapture, and she must have dozed off because the next thing she knows, the nurse is shaking a blurry black-and-white film in front of her face and saying, "Would you like to see a picture of your twins?"

Twins.

Blair bursts out sobbing.

The next afternoon, there's a knock on the apartment door, and Blair suspects that, on receiving the news that there will be two grandchildren instead of one, her mother immediately left Nantucket and is now back in Boston. When Blair opens the door, she finds a tall, attractive man in a neatly pressed khaki suit. It takes Blair a moment to recognize Joey Whalen, Angus's brother.

"Joey!" Blair says. "Are you a sight for sore eyes. You look wonderful. What a surprise!"

"A surprise that I look wonderful?" Joey says, beaming. He kisses Blair on the cheek and hands her a bottle wrapped in brown paper and a bakery bag that smells of chocolate.

"Babka, right out of the oven," Joey says. "And our old friend, cold duck."

"You sure know how to cheer a girl up," Blair says, and she holds the door open for her brother-in-law.

Twins.

Every time she says the word in her mind, it seems more outrageous. Twins. Two babies. Two babies at once. The enormous life change that is *having a baby* has doubled in an instant. She presently has one of everything—one bassinet, one crib, one stroller—and now she needs a second of each. It's overwhelming.

Joey steps inside, loosens his tie, and sheds his jacket while Blair admires him. Right after Angus and Blair got married, Joey moved to New York City and landed a job with a prestigious advertising agency that specializes in food products. He worked on the Sara Lee campaign and has been chosen to promote the brand in New England and parts of eastern Canada. He's going to be in Boston for three to six months, he tells Blair; the agency rented him a suite at the Parker House hotel on Tremont, right down the street from the Marliave, Blair's favorite restaurant, and gave Joey a house account. He's wearing a beautiful suit, tailored for him at Alan David in New York, and gleaming Florsheim loafers. He's clean-cut and freshly shaved, and he smells good—in distinct opposition to Angus, who often forgets to brush his teeth and apply aftershave before he dashes headlong into his days.

Blair pours two glasses of the cold duck for old times' sake as Joey gets plates and a knife and slices into the warm, fragrant babka. They sit next to each other on the sofa and Blair feels happy for the first time in a long while, despite the fact that she won't be able to get up off the sofa without help.

"Babka," she says. "I don't think I've ever tried it before."

"New York has the greatest Polish bakeries," Joey says. "I eat so much Sara Lee that it's a nice change to have something made from scratch. But I'd never tell my bosses that." He takes a sip of his cold duck. "The other thing I love about New York is the Thai food. Have you ever had Thai food?"

"*Thai* food?" Blair says. She can't believe that Joey Whalen, who used to pedal the Swan Boats and whose idea of a gourmet meal was the oyster stew at Durgin-Park, has become so sophisticated. She remembers how he held Angus's notebook filled with calculations over the candle flames in a plea for attention and how, at that time, it had been crystal clear that she would be far better off with Angus.

Now she's not so sure. If she had married Joey instead, she might be living in New York City, visiting the Metropolitan

Museum of Art on Sunday afternoons and hanging out in Greenwich Village with the likes of Bob Dylan and Allen Ginsberg.

"How's your brother?" Joey asks, which Blair supposes is a natural segue—from Thai food to the battlegrounds of Vietnam.

"Still alive," Blair says. "He sends letters."

"It's an immoral war," Joey says. "Our guys are over there killing women and children."

The babies kick with the first bite of babka. Blair can't believe that Joey now has political opinions. She privately agrees the war is immoral. The last three administrations have valued the eradication of Communism over the lives of American soldiers. But Blair knows Tiger is over there fighting for their continued freedom and she's proud of him for that.

"So I have two pieces of news," Blair says. "The first is, I'm having twins."

Joey gives a whoop and then, crazily, he moves the coffee table out of the way and gets down on his hands and knees in front of Blair so he can rub her belly. "That's incredible. Not one human life contained inside you, but two. Two!" His touch feels good and Blair feels faintly aroused, *sexually* aroused, which is wrong on many levels. She laughs and swats at him. "Get up." She prefers Joey's enthusiasm to Angus's reaction yesterday, which fell somewhere between apathy and scientific interest. He had studied the X-ray, trying to see if the twins would likely be identical—one egg that split—or fraternal, two separate eggs, both fertilized. And then, all the way home from the hospital, he wondered aloud if at least one of the twins would be a boy.

Joey sits back down on the sofa, closer to Blair than he was before. "What's the second piece of news?"

Blair takes as deep a breath as she can manage. The babies have started to crowd her lungs. "Angus is having an affair with someone named Trixie," she says. Every time Blair says the name, she pictures a character from a Disney movie. "He meets her during the workday. She called here on the phone."

Joey's elation at the news of twins twists into something fierce and angry. "You have *got* to be kidding me."

"I wish I were," Blair says, and she starts to cry.

"Oh, hey," Joey says. "Hey, Blair, come on now." He puts an arm around Blair's shoulders and she falls into his arms and sobs all over his fine white shirt. "Angus is a dope. He's a heel. He's never known what he has—he's so damn smart, he just takes everything as his due."

"I thought he *loved* me!" Blair wails.

"I'm sure he does," Joey says. "I know he does. This is just… well, he must be panicking about the moon launch…or the babies."

"Panicking about the babies?" Blair says. "He sees the babies as my responsibility and mine alone. Babies are women's work, and rocket ships are men's work." Blair bursts into a fresh round of tears.

"Aw, Blair, don't cry," Joey says. "You're so pretty and smart and such a catch for someone like Angus…I'm sure this Trixie person doesn't hold a candle to you. I mean, how could she?"

Maybe it's that these words are *exactly* what Blair needs to hear or maybe it's that the hormones from not one but two babies are making Blair delirious, but whatever the reason, the next thing Blair knows, she's kissing Joey Whalen and he is kissing her back. Blair can't believe something so outrageous is happening and yet it feels so good that she is powerless to stop it. Angus never touches her anymore. Sex stopped last month because Blair read that it was unsafe in the final trimester of pregnancy, but along with the sex went handholding, back rubs, and kissing.

Joey tastes of the cold duck and warm chocolate; Blair can't get enough of his lips, his tongue, his touch. She is transported right back to that afternoon on the Swan Boat. She had felt this same passion then, back when she thought she would be marrying Joey. One of Joey's hands travels up Blair's thigh and one gently massages her nipple through the thin material of her threadbare dress.

She needs to put an end to this, Blair thinks, right now. But instead, things heat up. Joey starts unbuttoning the front of Blair's dress; honestly, Blair would like him to rip it off.

She is just reaching for Joey's belt buckle when Angus bursts into the apartment holding a huge bouquet of lilacs and peonies, Blair's favorite flowers.

Young Girl

Bright and early on Tuesday morning, Jessie and Exalta walk to the Field and Oar Club for the first day of Jessie's tennis lessons. It's so early that the shops aren't open yet, though there is the smell of bacon coming from the Charcoal Galley and there's a gentleman sweeping up pieces of a broken bottle on the walk outside of Bosun's Locker.

"Bar fight?" Exalta asks the gentleman.

"Good a guess as any," he says, and Exalta laughs in such a carefree way that Jessie isn't sure if she should be pleased or worried. She glances at her grandmother out of the corner of her eye and sees what appears to be a genuine smile. Maybe her grandmother is happy because she's back on Nantucket for the hundredth summer in a row, or maybe she's happy because she has finally gotten her way and Jessie has agreed to take tennis lessons. She resisted until now—her one small act of defiance—but this year, right after Tiger was deployed, Kate had *begged* Jessie to reconsider ("It would mean so much to Nonny"), and Jessie, unable to disappoint her mother, had acquiesced.

Jessie is uncoordinated, bordering on clumsy. She's certain tennis will only highlight her athletic shortcomings. She would rather spend every morning of the summer sitting in the dentist's chair having her teeth drilled.

Jessie decides to take advantage of Exalta's good mood. "Why is Mr. Crimmins living in Little Fair?" she asks.

"Oh!" Exalta sings out. The day isn't yet bright enough to require sunglasses, so Exalta's are perched in her blunt-cut silver hair. This allows Jessie to study her grandmother's expression. She looks like she's trying to decide whether to tell Jessie the entire truth or just part of it. "Well, he needed a place to live for the summer."

"Doesn't he live on Pine Street?" Jessie asks. "In the house with the church windows?"

"The old steamboat-terminal building," Exalta says. "Yes, he's rented the unit in the back for years and years, but that's an efficiency, big enough for only one person. And this summer, he has his grandson with him. Pickford. Bill says the boy was named after some tenth-rate musician. I had rather hoped he was named for Mary Pickford, the greatest actress of our time." Exalta seems to drift off in a reverie. "America's sweetheart...the girl with the curls. Pickford is a strong name, even if there aren't any family ties behind it. I have to say, I was pleasantly surprised to find Lorraine hadn't named her child something like Oleo or Bangladesh."

"Lorraine is Mr. Crimmins's daughter, right?" Jessie says.

"That's correct."

"You *know* her?"

"Knew her, years ago," Exalta says. "She used to clean for me. And cook. She was quite a baker, very precise with her measurements. It's a shame she ran off; she could have made something of herself."

"She cooked and cleaned for you?" Jessie says. "I never knew that."

"It was before you were born," Exalta says, and Jessie knows what that means. She often feels like everything important happened before she was born, back when Wilder Foley was alive and her siblings were young and her mother was happy. It's unsettling how much envy Jessie feels for a stretch of time. Those years, in the retelling, always sounded golden, like they could never be matched or recaptured.

"I just found out Mr. Crimmins had a daughter yesterday," Jessie says. "He's never talked about her."

"Her time here didn't end well," Exalta says. She seems to realize she's revealed too much. "Come along, we don't want to be late."

The Field and Oar Club occupies five acres of precious real estate on Nantucket Harbor. Jessie understands that it's a fancy club, meaning exclusive, but the actual clubhouse is a simple wooden building that even Nonny admits has seen better days, though it's given a fresh coat of white paint each spring. The club is populated by old people like Exalta who have children Kate's age and grandchildren Jessie's age, and all three generations are supposed to care about only two things once they cross the club's threshold: excellence in tennis and dominance in sailing. Jessie once asked Exalta about the name of the club and Exalta said, "It's charming, isn't it? But anachronistic. *Field* refers to the tennis courts, which used to be grass."

"Really?" Jessie said. The courts were orange clay now.

"And the *Oar* refers to boats, of course," Exalta said.

Of course, Jessie thought, except there wasn't a rowboat, canoe, or kayak in sight. Instead, there were motorboats, cabin cruisers, and sailboats of every size. Jessie grew up seeing groups of children yoked in bright yellow life preservers heading out for sailing lessons; she supposed she should be grateful to have escaped that fate.

Jessie's mother adores the club because the Field and Oar is all she has ever known. She and Exalta come here for lunch on the patio two to three times a week, and Kate enjoys the dinner dances. She claims the club is the last bastion of elegance on this island; the hippies and the freethinkers have infiltrated every other institution.

Jessie follows her grandmother to the reception desk, but then Exalta sees Mrs. Winter, whom Exalta has known since the previous century, and Jessie is left alone. The receptionist smiles at her. Her name tag says LIZZ. Lizz is pretty with blond hair and dazzling white teeth. Everyone who works at the Field and Oar is attractive enough to model in catalogs.

"I came for my tennis lesson," Jessie says. "The last name is Levin."

"Levin, you say?" Lizz scans her clipboard. "I don't see a Levin. What time was your lesson?"

"Um...eight?" Jessie holds her breath, wondering if a miracle has occurred and Exalta made a mistake. Maybe Jessie will be set free. She can go home, climb on her bike, and follow Pick to Surfside Beach. He leaves for the beach every morning at nine, he told her, then he comes home for lunch around two, although he sometimes gets a burger at the shack. He goes into work at the North Shore at four thirty, gets home between ten and eleven, and does it all over again the next day.

Suddenly, Exalta swoops in. "Jessie has a tennis lesson at eight. Jessica Nichols."

"Nichols," Lizz says. "Ah, okay. She told me Levin."

"Levin is my last name," Jessie says.

"Nichols," Exalta says. "Nichols is the member name."

"I'll go tell Garrison you're here," Lizz says. "You can head out to court eleven."

"The court closest to the water," Exalta says. "Aren't you lucky."

"I don't understand," Jessie says as they start walking. "Mom uses the name Levin when *she* comes here."

"She does that only to distress me," Exalta says.

"And Blair, Kirby, and Tiger use Foley," Jessie says. There's a challenge in her voice. "Right? They do. You and I both know they do."

"Foley is different," Exalta says.

"Because it's not Jewish," Jessie says. She stops in her tracks. She can't believe the fury that has taken hold of her. She grips the handle of her racket, which Exalta bought her brand-new for these lessons, a Jack Kramer–autographed Wilson. She would like to smash it against the brick walk.

"No," Exalta says. "Because Lieutenant Foley was on his way to becoming a member here before he died. *Your* father has no interest in becoming a member here."

Jessie wants to ask if he *could* become a member here if he wanted to. But the words get stuck; the sun is beating down on the part in her hair, and she can see a boy in whites standing patiently outside the court closest to the water—Garrison, her tennis instructor.

"I'm *not* taking my necklace off," Jessie whispers angrily.

"No one is asking you to," Exalta says.

Jessie fears that Exalta is going to stay and watch Jessie's tennis lesson, offering commentary and criticism, but the allure of drinking mimosas on the patio with Mrs. Winter proves too great. Exalta hands Jessie over to her instructor and says, "I'll see you in an hour. Listen to this gentleman, please." And then to Garrison, the instructor, Exalta says, "Under no circumstances are you to teach her a two-handed backhand."

"Yes, ma'am," Garrison says. His voice has a Southern twang. Jessie realizes she was wrong in thinking that everyone who worked at the club could be a catalog model because Garrison is funny-looking. He has a long torso and long, thin arms and legs, and the way he holds his racket vertically in front of his chest reminds Jessie of a praying mantis. He wears thick glasses that make his eyes look small and far away under the shade of his visor. Jessie had been hoping to get Topher for her instructor. Topher has thick brown hair and a strong jaw and is popular with ladies of all ages at the Field and Oar Club. Last year, Jessie overheard her mother say, "My *goodness,* that young man is handsome." Topher might have made the tennis lessons bearable.

Jessie waits until Exalta is out of earshot, then she offers a hand. "I'm Jessie *Levin,*" she says. "Levin, not Nichols."

"Garrison Howe," he says. He glances back at Exalta. "That your granny?"

Jessie sighs. "Yes."

"She's all business," Garrison says. "I like it."

Exalta called Garrison a gentleman, but the first five minutes of their acquaintance reveal that Garrison is only nineteen years old.

He's entering his sophomore year at Sewanee, a men's college in Tennessee. He applied for this job at the suggestion of his tennis coach at Sewanee, who went to summer camp with the pro here.

"And by jeezy if I didn't get the job," Garrison says. "Pro'ly because everyone else is off fighting the gooks."

Jessie bristles at the term. Her father has informed her it's a racial slur. "My brother is in Vietnam," Jessie says. She hopes this news will make Garrison more kindly disposed to the ungraceful and unskilled display he will no doubt witness while teaching Jessie tennis. "He's your age. Nineteen. If he'd stayed in college, he would be a rising sophomore, just like you."

Garrison stares at Jessie. She wonders if it was rude to point out that her brother is serving their country in the swampy jungles of Vietnam while Garrison is here doing this cushy job at the Field and Oar Club. Maybe he's going to say something rude in return. Maybe he's going to express a strong antiwar sentiment. And what will Jessie do then? Will she stomp off the court and demand a new instructor? She, too, is antiwar; her entire family is antiwar. These feelings coexist simultaneously with concern for and pride in Tiger.

Finally, Garrison speaks. "You have pretty eyes, Jessie."

Jessie is so taken aback by this non sequitur that she laughs.

"I like a woman with dark eyes," Garrison says. "I find them mysterious. And I love long dark hair like yours. I guess you could say I'm a brunette man." He holds the gate open and ushers Jessie onto the court. "Now, let's play some tennis."

Like many sports, tennis is deceptively simple. The objective is to hit the ball over a net with a racket, wait for one's opponent to hit it back, then hit it again. But also like many sports, there are nuances—speed, power, and an elusive element called *spin,* which depends on the angle at which you hold the racket and the way you hit the ball.

Garrison starts with the basics, forehand grip and forehand stroke. He places Jessie's hand in position, then stands just behind her and shows her how to move her arm.

"You might try loosening up," Garrison says. "You're very stiff, which will result in wooden play."

Jessie can't loosen up. The words *wooden play* give her a vision of a figure like one of her grandmother's whirligigs, a girl holding a racket that swings again and again. Jessie is disconcerted by Garrison's body positioned so close behind hers, his hands on her arm and back, and, most alarmingly, his declarations right before they began. She has pretty *eyes?* He likes her *dark hair?* No one but her parents has ever told Jessie she's pretty, and even those statements had been whittled down to a single aspect or instant. *You look lovely in red. You've been blessed with beautiful skin. That dress is becoming.* Jessie has never had a boy tell her she's pretty, and she might have been tempted to think Garrison was making fun of her, but she could tell he was speaking in earnest.

Garrison has a cart filled with bright yellow tennis balls and he drops each one with a precise bounce so that when Jessie swings the way he showed her, the ball clears the net with inches to spare, again and again.

She's doing it!

Garrison calls out words of encouragement—*Way to go! Good job! Keep it up!*—as Jessie hits the entire cart of balls with only two that smack the tape at the top of the net and fail to clear.

"And no bloopers," Garrison says. "That's impressive. I believe you just might be the next Billie Jean King."

Jessie knows he's exaggerating but hope unfurls in her chest nonetheless. She wonders if maybe she *will* prove to be good at tennis. It stands to reason, after all—Exalta is good at tennis, or she was, and both Kate and David play. Jessie's siblings all took the obligatory year of lessons, but none of them showed any real promise. Perhaps all of the tennis genes fell to Jessie. She grows warm thinking of how proud Exalta will be of her if that's the case. Jessie may even replace Kirby as the favorite.

"I think we should move on to backhand," Garrison says. Together, he and Jessie gather up all the balls. At one point, Jessie catches him looking at her and she feels…what does she feel? Something brand-new. She feels *desired.*

They move on to backhand. Jessie steels herself for the challenge.

Garrison says, "Your granny was clear that I am not to teach you a two-handed backhand but I don't think you're going to have the arm strength to clear the net with one hand."

Jessie is disappointed to hear this. "Can't I try it?" she asks. She's terrified of not following Exalta's exact instructions.

"We can," Garrison says. "Maybe you'll surprise me." He shows Jessie how to hold the racket, his hand lingering on her arm and back even longer than before. His touch makes Jessie self-conscious. Garrison drops the ball and Jessie swings and misses completely. Garrison drops a second ball and she misses again, and then yet again on her third try. Her eyes brim with tears of humiliation. She's hot, she's sweating, she's certain she smells. She should never have let herself believe she would be any good at this game.

"Let's try a two-handed grip," Garrison says. "It's easier. Here, I'll show you." He stands behind Jessie and wraps his arms around her so that his chest is pressing up against her back. She tenses. He speaks into her ear, his voice nearly a whisper. "Just relax, *relax.* Send your arms back like this and then…follow through." With the movement, Jessie feels a part of Garrison poking her. She prays she's imagining it but then she feels it again, hard and straight as the handle of a racket—his *erection*—the word plucked right out of the puberty talk they all received at the end of the school year. Garrison has gotten an erection from showing Jessie how to hit a backhand and now that erection is rubbing against her. Jessie tries to pull away but Garrison holds her arms in place.

"I don't feel well," she says, but Garrison doesn't respond. He stands behind her rocking back and forth with the ostensible mission of showing her how to swing her racket. At that instant, the horror becomes more than just Garrison and his erection. It's also Exalta disrespecting Jessie's last name and Tiger at war in the jungle. Jessie twists out of Garrison's arms with a strength she didn't know she possessed and she runs off the court and over to the patio, where Exalta is signing the chit. There are empty champagne glasses in front of Exalta and Mrs. Winter.

Exalta beams at Jessie. Her eyes have that glint that only alcohol produces in her. "How did it go?"

Jessie clears her throat. "I'd like a different instructor tomorrow."

"What?" Exalta says. "Whatever for?"

Jessie widens her eyes, hoping to convey her distress. Her grandmother was quite beautiful in her day. Surely she received her share of unwanted attention. But Jessie doesn't have the words to explain what happened, much less in front of Mrs. Winter. *Tumescence,* she thinks. The word from Blair's novel. She hears Blair say, *There's no reason to be grossed out by sex.* But she is.

"He taught me a two-handed backhand," Jessie says.

Exalta pushes herself up from the table. "Does the boy not have ears? That won't do at all," she says. "We'll find you someone else."

"A girl," Jessie says. "Please."

Mrs. Winter is stuck to Exalta like lint to a sweater, and when Mrs. Winter says, "Tell me, Exalta, how is Blair? She married an astronaut, didn't she? I've always been so fond of her, even though she broke my Larry's heart," Jessie excuses herself and goes to the locker room. She splashes water on her face; it's burning, whether from the sun or the humiliation she just endured, she isn't sure. The sensation of Garrison rubbing up against her won't go away. It's like he's branded her. She wants to cry, wants to scream, but she's at the club so she can do neither. When she gets home, she'll tell her mother what happened, and Garrison will be fired and sent back to Tennessee. But Jessie fears she will never, ever have the courage to tell her mother. Nor can she imagine telling her father. She could tell Blair or Kirby, but her older sisters aren't here. They've abandoned her.

When Jessie emerges from the locker room, Exalta is still out on the patio chatting with Mrs. Winter. Jessie wants to leave and just walk home by herself, but she knows there would be a price to pay for such rudeness, and so she lingers at the reception desk. Lizz has vanished; the desk is unmanned. On a shelf just behind the desk are polo shirts, visors, cocktail napkins, and stationery emblazoned with the kelly-green-and-white club burgee. Jessie's blood quickens. She glances around, sees no one. She leans over the counter and snatches the first thing within reach—a pair of terry-cloth wristbands, packaged in cellophane. The cellophane crackles; Jessie thinks that surely someone will appear and ask her for Exalta's member number so her account can be charged. But no one notices and Jessie stashes the wristbands in the roomy pocket of her tennis skirt. She goes to wait for Exalta on the front porch.

Everyday People

After twenty-one years of swimming against the tide—questioning authority, rebelling against the rules, and making poor decisions—Kirby Foley is surprised to find that quiet order and routine are the best parts of her front-desk job at the Shiretown Inn. The inn has twelve rooms, each with an en suite bath, and because of the location in downtown Edgartown, the clientele is upscale, as Mrs. Bennie promised. They have a few honeymooning couples, but most of the guests are Kirby's parents' age or older. During Kirby's first week of work, she finds everyone she comes in contact with polite and delightful.

Her shift quickly develops a rhythm. Between the hours of eleven p.m. and one a.m., the guests return from their evenings out—dinner at the Dunes, bonfires on the beach, a nightcap on the deck at the Navigator. Kirby has been trained by Mrs. Bennie to look for signs of trouble, but all of the guests seem happy and relaxed, maybe a bit tipsy, although not problematically so. Kirby's favorites are the Eltringhams from New Hope, Pennsylvania. (Kirby simply *adores* the name New Hope and applies it to her own situation now. After two arrests and the unspeakable situation with Scottie Turbo, for her, living and working on the Vineyard offers just that—new hope. Mr. Eltringham is a banker in Philadelphia, and Mrs. Eltringham owns a small antiques shop in the village of New Hope. It's the second marriage for both Mr. and Mrs. Eltringham; Mr. Eltringham has grown-up children by his first wife, and Mrs. Eltringham, in her life before him, was a nurse in the burn unit at St. Vincent's Hospital in New York City. Kirby is surprised at how much she learned about the Eltringhams with just a few thoughtful questions. On Kirby's third night of work, the Eltringhams bring her a piece of peach cobbler from the Art Cliff Diner. This gesture is so unexpected and so kind that for a second, Kirby is suspicious. But the cobbler is delicious. Kirby needs to start trusting people again.

The overnight shift isn't easy, by any means. Right around two a.m., Kirby starts to nod off. By then, she has reviewed the bills for guests checking out in the morning and has tidied the small lobby and made sure that all twelve room keys have been claimed. She nearly yearns for some drama—an unclaimed key, for example, or a noise complaint—because then there would be an impetus to stay awake.

Kirby sometimes steps out to the front porch to reinvigorate herself with the fresh night air, and she does that now; she takes in the silent, dark streets of Edgartown and tries not to think about everyone else on the island fast asleep.

Kirby wonders how things are going eleven miles away, on Nantucket. When Kirby called her mother from the house phone to tell her about the job, Kate responded, "Oh, good for you," and then informed Kirby that Blair was having twins. Kirby had been irritated to have her good news trumped. Of *course* Blair was having twins! Anybody with one good eye could see that Blair was big enough to require her own zip code.

"How's Jessie?" Kirby asked. Poor Jessie was pretty much raising herself, Kirby suspected, while Kate fretted about Blair and Tiger. Jessie was a sensitive kid, and smart; she liked to read and daydream. Kirby had tried to imbue her younger sister with some of her own passion and ferocity, but it hadn't taken root. Yet.

"Jessie?" Kate sounded like she didn't know who Kirby was talking about, and that said it all.

Kirby decides that when she gets her first paycheck—ninety dollars!—she'll buy Jessie a tie-dyed T-shirt that says MARTHA'S VINEYARD across the front, and she'll mail it to the house on Fair Street and suggest Jessie wear it to the Field and Oar. That will get Exalta's goat. Kirby should write a handbook called *How to Horrify Nonny and Get Away with It.* She laughs, then goes back in, settles down in the armchair in the back office, and turns on the small radio for company. The song playing is Procol Harum's "A Whiter Shade of Pale." Kirby loves the song, but it had been playing in Scottie Turbo's car on the way up to Lake Winnipesaukee. Kirby and Scottie had thrown their heads back and sung at the top of their lungs. *That her face, at first just ghostly, turned a whiter shade of pale.*

She turns the radio off.

She wakes up with a start when Mr. Ames, the night watchman, dings the bell on the front desk. Kirby hops to her feet, straightens her skirt, and hurries out to greet him. Mr. Ames is in his midsixties; he's a former policeman from South Boston who retired to the Vineyard with his wife, Susanna. They live in a cottage on East Chop, which is technically a part of Oak Bluffs, though not the Methodist Campground part. During Kirby's first night on the job, Mr. Ames showed Kirby a snapshot of Susanna, and Kirby was shocked to find that Susanna was black. Kirby had tried not to let any surprise show on her face or in her voice. "She's beautiful. How did you two meet?"

"In Boston," he said. "We both rode the Red Line of the T and

I would see her every now and again in her nurse's uniform. One day the train was crowded and I offered her my seat."

"That's so romantic!" Kirby said. "Do you have any children?"

"Susanna has a daughter from her first marriage," Mr. Ames said. "But Denise is grown and has kids of her own now."

Kirby had wanted to ask if it was difficult being part of an inter-racial couple or if it was no big deal. Her interest in this topic was pressing. Ever since Darren had picked Kirby up hitchhiking, her mind kept returning to him. She wanted to see him again.

Mr. Ames hands Kirby coffee in a Styrofoam cup. "Thought you might need this," he says. "I remembered that you take it sweet and light."

"Thank you," Kirby says. It's three o'clock now; she can't imag-ine staying awake another four hours. "Everything okay upstairs?" Mr. Ames does three walk-throughs, one at eleven thirty, one at two thirty, and one at five thirty.

"The gentleman in room eight snores like a black bear," Mr. Ames says. "Though I'm hardly one to talk." He points a finger at Kirby. "There's no shame in dozing off. If there's an emergency, I'll wake you."

"Thank you, Mr. Ames," Kirby says. She takes the coffee to the back office and thinks about how much she enjoys living without shame.

Shame.

There's a far bigger problem with Kirby dating Darren Frazier than just his being black. It's his mother. Dr. Frazier knows who Kirby is... maybe. Or maybe all young blond students look the same to her. Kirby should forget about Darren; the last thing she needs is a complicated relationship. Although what appeals to Kirby about Darren is that he seems so easy. He was nice enough to pick her up and drive her all the way to Edgartown; he's smart enough to go to Harvard; he takes pride in his summer job; he's confident and self-assured. And he has a gorgeous smile. How divine would it be to bask in that smile all summer long? How lovely to ride shotgun in Darren's Corvair and go pick up lobsters from Larsen's and eat them in the blue fairy-tale house?

Kirby sighs. Divine, lovely, but just a dream. He was nice to her because she's friends with Rajani. Possibly, he's interested in Rajani. This thought bothers Kirby more than it probably should.

She tries again with the radio and gets Peter, Paul, and Mary. *The answer, my friend, is blowin' in the wind.* She closes her eyes.

Kirby wakes with the sun at quarter after five and snaps into action. She goes through the bills one more time and hurries to the restroom to freshen up. She sets up the coffee percolator and arranges powdered doughnuts from a box on a plate for the guests. At precisely six o'clock, a guest named Bobby Hogue from room 3 appears in a pair of shorts and tennis shoes. Bobby Hogue is missing his left hand. It was blown off by a grenade during a search-and-destroy mission in Quang Nam during his second tour with the Marines. Once a Marine, always a Marine, Bobby Hogue says, so he still gets up early every day and goes for a five-mile run.

"Good morning, Mr. Hogue," Kirby says.

"Good morning, Kirby," Bobby Hogue says.

The newspapers land with a thud on the front porch, and Kirby rushes out from behind the desk to get them, but Bobby Hogue picks the bundle up with his right hand and sets them on the pedestal table in the middle of the lobby. Kirby feels a rush of admiration, then sneaks a glimpse at the rounded stump where his hand used to be.

"I'm not going to read the news today," Bobby Hogue says.

He gives her a kind smile; Kirby has told him that her brother is stationed in the Central Highlands. "And you shouldn't either."

"Deal," Kirby says. She's only too willing to play along, to pretend that the rest of the world is as serene as Edgartown, Massachusetts, at six o'clock on a summer morning.

Bobby Hogue waves to her with his stump, then runs down the porch stairs.

On her first day off, Kirby decides she'll try Inkwell Beach. She has considered it every day since Darren extended the invitation but she's exercised uncharacteristic restraint. She thinks about her first, heady days with Scottie Turbo, how eager she was to climb into his convertible and drive up to Lake Winnipesaukee. She had been a fool once, but she wouldn't be again.

Monday is picture-perfect—warm sun, low humidity, a silken blue sky, a delicious breeze off the water that Kirby enjoys through the open window of Mr. Ames's pickup truck. Kirby had spent six precious dollars of her disposable income on taxis to and from work before Mr. Ames saved the day by offering to drive her back to Oak Bluffs in the mornings, since they kept the same schedule. Normally, both Kirby and Mr. Ames are too tired for conversation, but on Monday morning, Kirby is excited about the day ahead.

"I'm going to Inkwell Beach," Kirby says to Mr. Ames. "Do you ever go there?"

"Used to when I was younger," Mr. Ames says. "With my wife's family." He pauses. "You and your friends might like Katama or the state beach better."

"I don't really have any friends yet," Kirby says. "I mean, I have one friend from college who's working as a nanny out in Chilmark, and I'm becoming friendly with a girl who lives in the house with me."

"So what's the interest in Inkwell Beach?" Mr. Ames says. "If you don't mind my asking."

"I met a boy who invited me," Kirby says. "Darren Frazier? He's a lifeguard at Inkwell."

"Yes, I know Darren," Mr. Ames says. "My wife's sister is married to Judge Frazier's cousin."

"Right on," Kirby says. Darren is the son of Dr. Frazier, who may or may not know about Kirby's unfortunate past, *and* of Judge Frazier, who may or may not have access to Kirby's arrest record. Darren Frazier is the last boy in Massachusetts that Kirby should be interested in.

"Darren invited you to Inkwell?" Mr. Ames says.

Kirby nods.

"Well, okay, then," Mr. Ames says. "Have fun."

Kirby is too nervous to join the other girls for breakfast and she is too agitated to sleep or even nap. She heads straight up to her room and puts a record on her Silvertone—*Stand!*, by Sly and the Family Stone, the album she brought for her hopeful moods. She turns the music up as loud as she dares. (One of the Irish Ms— Michaela—came storming upstairs a few evenings earlier when Kirby was playing Crosby, Stills, and Nash, her introspective-mood album, and said in her thick Irish accent, "Teern et doone!" To which Kirby responded, "Sorry, I didn't know you were fifty years old.")

Kirby puts on her red bikini and over it an extra-long tie-dyed T-shirt that has a hand-painted peace sign on the front. She wore this T-shirt with jeans and a pair of fringed suede boots to the protest where Scottie arrested her. He had cherry-picked her out of that teeming crowd because she looked "so good in that top," he'd said. Kirby ties a red bandanna over her hair—out of its bun for the first time in a week—and puts on her sunglasses. She's ready to go.

She needs a sidekick, an Ethel to her Lucy. Rajani nannies all day during the week, so she isn't an option. Kirby hurries down the stairs with her straw bag, which still contains sand from Madequecham Beach and a handful of shells that Jessie collected, and knocks on Patty's door.

Patty is still in her pajamas; she's eating a Payday bar.

"I got drunk last night," she says. "With my brother's friends. I let one of them, this rich kid from New York City named Luke, get to second base."

"Second base, huh?" Kirby says. "You liked him, then?" She leans against the door frame and watches Patty blush. She misses having girlfriends, she realizes. In a dorm at an all-girls school, there was no shortage of gossip like this.

"He's cute," Patty says. "I couldn't believe he was interested in me. But…he told me he likes full-figured girls with long hair he can pull."

This makes Kirby laugh. "He probably just meant he likes beautiful girls like you." She pokes Patty in the arm. "Come to the beach with me today, will you?"

"I need to go back to bed. I was up late and I work tonight," Patty says. "But maybe I'll meet you later. Where are you going?"

"Inkwell," Kirby says.

Patty makes a sharp noise, a bark or a yelp. "Didn't anyone tell you?"

"Tell me what?" Kirby says.

Patty lowers her voice. "That's the Negro beach," she says. "*Inkwell,* meaning 'black'—get it?"

Kirby feels her stomach lurch. "I know," she says. Suddenly, her cheeks are burning and she can't decide if she wants to retreat or fight. *Fight,* she thinks. "I met someone who's a lifeguard there. He invited me."

Patty stares at Kirby for a second and Kirby wonders if her favorite of all the girls in this house, the one she pegged right away as a potential friend, is going to turn out to be a racist. She is suddenly sixteen years old again, sitting in her civics class and overhearing Steve Willard and Roger Donnelly call Miss Carpenter, who was Kirby's favorite teacher, the N-word. Kirby had stood up and spat on Roger's desk, which had caused a giant brouhaha—and Kirby was the one who had been kept after class. When Miss Carpenter asked what on earth would cause Kirby to do something so beneath her, Kirby refused to say. She didn't have the heart to tell Miss Carpenter that she had been defending her. Miss Carpenter must have intuited this, however, because she said, "The best way to combat behavior or language that you find offensive is to *peacefully* protest. Do you understand me, Katharine?"

Kirby said she *did* understand. She'd apologized and scrubbed Roger's desk, and the next week, Miss Carpenter asked Kirby to march alongside her with Dr. King.

"I support the civil rights movement," Patty says, and Kirby exhales in relief. "My sister Sara was one of Robert Kennedy's Boiler Room Girls. But I still can't go with you."

"Why not?" Kirby says. She's impressed that Patty's sister worked for Bobby Kennedy, but if Patty believes Inkwell is an inferior beach because it's frequented by Negroes, then she's a racist.

"Because we don't belong there," Patty says. "They don't *want* white people there."

"Darren invited me," Kirby says. "He didn't seem to think it was a big deal and he knows what color I am. 'The times, they are a-changin'.'"

"Not that much," Patty says with a wistful smile. "You'll see."

* * *

Kirby marches off to Inkwell on her own, her head held high. She entertains some ungenerous thoughts about Patty—Patty must have loose morals if she let a boy she doesn't even *know* get to second base, and clearly, she has zero willpower. She says she wants to lose twenty-five pounds, but the second she wakes up, she reaches for a Payday bar. She must keep a stash of them in her nightstand. And what kind of boy says he likes long hair that he can *pull?* Some kind of *maniac?* Kirby doesn't want to think badly of Patty; right up until that conversation, she *liked* Patty. It's possible Patty doesn't know any nonwhite people personally. Kirby decides she'll introduce Patty to both Rajani and Darren. Her goal this summer is to turn Patty into a progressive.

Kirby walks onto Inkwell Beach as though it's the most natural thing in the world, and in some ways, it is. Summer for Kirby has always meant sun and sand. Her mother brought her to Steps Beach on Nantucket when she was a baby, and they returned to Steps each summer until their father died. After that, Kate replaced their babysitter Lorraine (who ran off) with a babysitter named Ivy (nicknamed "Poison Ivy" by Blair), who started taking them to Cisco Beach, where the big waves were. Blair had been afraid to swim, but not Kirby or Tiger, and to this day, Kirby feels the most alive when she's jumping waves and then drying off in the sun. When she was little, she was famous for not even bothering with a towel. She would just lie right down in the sand, and when she stood up, she was breaded like a fish stick.

Inkwell Beach is on the sound, so the water is calmer than Kirby likes, though it's hard to argue with the view; the water looks like a blue satin sheet. It's not so different from Steps Beach on Nantucket. There's a group of women who have arranged their chairs in a semicircle to facilitate conversation;

some of the women wear hats, and others raise their faces to the sun. At the shore, little kids dig for China, and girls with plastic buckets collect shells. Teenagers are up to their waists in the water, splashing one another; beyond them, an older gentleman swims a slow but steady freestyle. There are two guys around Kirby's age lying on towels; one is asleep on his stomach, one is reading *Slaughterhouse Five,* his face inscrutable behind his sunglasses.

Everyone is black. Everyone.

Well, right—what did Kirby expect? She expected everyone to be black but what she didn't anticipate was how this would make her feel. She doesn't feel threatened, certainly, or intimidated. She feels *conspicuous,* as though everyone notices her, and what people are thinking isn't that she's thin or fat or pretty or ugly—no, those things don't matter. What matters is that she's white.

She walks past the semicircle of women and their conversation drops off for a second, then starts up again in hushed tones. Kirby thinks she hears her name, but obviously that isn't possible. She moves closer to the water, past the little kids digging. They look up at her but appear unfazed, which heartens her somewhat. Children are color-blind.

The young man reading Vonnegut glances up and shakes his head at her, as if he's warning her to go away. He's as bad as Patty! Surely he understands that Kirby has as much of a right to be here as anyone else.

Patty's words echo: *We don't belong.*

Kirby hears a whistle and turns to see Darren, who's perched on the white latticed lifeguard stand. He's waving at…*her?* She checks the water behind her—there's no one—and then walks through the sand in her bare feet, her huarache sandals dangling from two fingers as though she doesn't have a care in the world.

"Hey," she says. She feels like Darren just threw her the life preserver that's hanging from the side of the stand.

"You came!" he says. "I can't believe it."

"Of course," Kirby says, shrugging. "Today is my first day off and it's an easy walk from the house."

"Great," Darren says, and she tries to read his face and his tone to see if he really does think it's great. "Welcome to Inkwell Beach. This is where I grew up."

"It's pretty," Kirby says truthfully.

Darren's gaze floats over Kirby's shoulder, and his smile tightens. Kirby turns to see one of the women from the semicircle standing up with her hands on her hips. It's a woman wearing a floppy hat.

"My mother," Darren says, and Kirby's spirits hit the sand. "She wants me to get back to work, I guess."

"I met your mother," Kirby says. She waves but Dr. Frazier just glares. "At your house."

"She told me," Darren says.

"Did she say anything about me?" Kirby asks.

Darren shakes his head. "Just that you showed up with Rajani." He stares at the ocean. "She doesn't like it when I get distracted from my job."

Is *that* what she doesn't like? Kirby wonders. Or does she not like *white girls* distracting Darren from his job? Or does she not like Kirby Foley, aka Clarissa Bouvier—the name Kirby made up back in Boston—distracting Darren from his job?

Does Darren's mother know that Kirby is Clarissa Bouvier?

"Thanks for coming to say hi," Darren says. He's leaning forward now in an active posture of lifeguarding, and Kirby can see he's eager for her to leave. "I'll swing by your house sometime this week and take you to the carousel. Would you like that?"

She should say no. She isn't interested in riding the carousel, and even if she were, she shouldn't encourage Darren. A relationship between them wouldn't work. But, as usual, Kirby doesn't listen to her own good advice. "I'd love it!" she says. "I'll see you later this week, then." She wanders off the sand at the next set of stairs, then stands on the hot sidewalk in a daze.

Was that a failure or not?

Not, Kirby decides. Darren asked her to come see him at Inkwell, and she did. The next move is his.

It's still early. Kirby decides she will hitchhike to the south shore and pass out on her towel. She's exhausted.

No sooner does she stick her thumb out than an olive-green Willys Jeep pulls over with a couple sitting up front but plenty of room on the back bench seat for Kirby.

The guy driving is cute; he's wearing a white polo shirt and sunglasses. The girl has her long dark hair braided down her back. Then Kirby realizes the girl is Patty.

"Hey, Kirby!" Patty says. "Meet Luke."

Kirby grins. "Hey, Luke," she says. "Glad to see somebody got this girl out of bed." She climbs into the Jeep and even feels a small surge of excitement when Patty lifts her hands in the air.

"Katama, here we come!"

More Today Than Yesterday

Sunday, June 22, 1969

Dear Tiger,

I was hoping Dad would bring a letter from you when he came yesterday, but he said none had arrived, which put me in a bad mood and Mom in an even worse mood. She got drunk last night at the Skipper, and not the kind of drunk where she came home singing, but the kind where she came home crying. Nonny slept right through it because she started with her Hendrick's and tonics at four o'clock instead of five, even though she was supposed to be minding me while Mom and Dad were out. She went up to bed at seven and put in earplugs. I made a peanut butter sandwich and watched My Three Sons *in the den.*

I hate my tennis lessons.

Jessie crosses this last line out. She will *not* complain about tennis lessons while her brother is loaded down with forty pounds of gear and slogging through hip-deep water in the rice paddies. Jessie does hate her tennis lessons but most of that hate is due to her experience with Garrison. Just walking into the Field and Oar makes Jessie queasy now. Exalta still refuses to let Jessie use the name Levin when she signs in or when she signs for something, like after her most recent lesson, when she went to the snack bar to get a chocolate frappe and a grilled cheese.

"N-three!" Exalta had called out as Jessie headed to the snack bar. "Nichols!"

Jessie had been so furious with her grandmother that while the grill boy's back was turned, she lifted a package of Twizzlers from the counter and slid it into her skirt pocket. Again, she'd waited for a hand to clamp on her shoulder announcing she'd been caught, but none came.

My tennis lessons started out badly but have gotten better since I asked for a new instructor. Her name is Suze, short for Susan; she was named for Susan B. Anthony, who, in case you weren't paying attention in history class, fought for women's right to vote. The cool thing is that Suze is a feminist just like Susan B. Anthony. She told me on the first day that she only accepts female tennis students because the world has enough male tennis stars as it is. She also told me she found out she was being paid less than the male tennis instructors at Field and Oar and she marched right up to Ollie Hayward, the head of tennis, and she threatened to quit if he didn't give her equal pay. Ollie said yes—probably not on principle, she says, but because Suze is the best player of all the instructors.

Jessie stops there, though she could talk about Suze all day. Suze has short hair like a boy—bright red, due to her Irish heritage—and pale, pale skin. She has to play tennis in a white long-sleeved shirt so her skin doesn't burn, and she paints her nose with zinc. When Jessie told Suze that Garrison Howe said she didn't have enough arm strength for a one-handed backhand, Suze said, "Let me tell you something about Garrison Howe."

Jessie held her breath. She waited for Suze to confide that Garrison had rubbed his tumescence against her as well.

"He's a half-witted sewer rat," Suze said.

"He is?" Jessie said.

"He is," Suze said. "But name-calling is for the weak. Actions are for the strong. Got it?"

"Got it," Jessie said.

I've had four lessons so far and I'm just starting to get the hang of it. I can hit a decent forehand and my backhand clears the net at least half the time. I also know how to score the game: love, fifteen, thirty, forty, game. Six games wins a set, but you have to win by two games. Two sets wins a match for women, three for men. (Suze feels it should be three sets for both sexes. Tennis is the most male-biased sport in the world, she says.) Next week, I'll learn to serve. Suze says she's had great luck teaching kids to serve; the junior champion here was once her student.

Other than that, nothing to report.

This isn't precisely true. Jessie wants to tell Tiger what happened with Pick, but Tiger is her brother and Jessie isn't sure how he would handle it. She has considered writing about it to Leslie or Doris, but it feels too new and too private to share.

When Kate and David came home from dinner at the Skipper, Kate started crying and woke Jessie up. She knew her mother missed Tiger, that she worried every second of every day that he would be shot and killed or, worse, captured and tortured. Her baby. Her only baby boy. Jessie lay in the dark listening to them talk in the kitchen, her eyes wide open as she, too, imagined the fates that might have befallen Tiger—without a letter, it was impossible to know if he was okay. David said all the right things, that Tiger was strong and fast, and, despite his disappointing grades, he was smart, he had a good understanding of the physical world, how to take things apart and put them back together. Most of all, he was mentally tough. David's words put Jessie at ease but Kate still cried and David took her to their bedroom. Once the door was closed, all Jessie could hear was her mother's muffled sobs.

Jessie realized she was starving—the peanut butter sandwich had been skimpy—and so she'd tiptoed downstairs for a snack.

She saw a flash of white moving outside the window and she froze for an instant, wondering if the house was haunted after all, if the ghost of Ebenezer Raymond or one of his children might be floating around, but when Jessie moved closer to the window, she saw Pick in his T-shirt and Levi's, returning home from his shift at the North Shore Restaurant.

Without thinking twice, Jessie stepped out of the kitchen door onto the brick patio and whispered his name. "Pick!"

He swung around, saw her, and waved her over. Jessie tiptoed across the patio and down the flagstone walk to where Pick was untying a parcel secured to the back of his bike. It was a cardboard takeout box.

"Let's go up to the deck," he whispered.

They stepped lightly into Little Fair, passed the closed door of Mr. Crimmins's room, and sneaked up the stairs. Jessie had forgotten that Little Fair had a deck that overlooked Plumb Lane; in the past, Kirby and Tiger had smoked their marijuana joints there so that Kate and Exalta wouldn't detect the smell. The deck was small, just big enough for two people. Pick appeared with two green bottles and the cardboard box. At first Jessie thought the bottles were beer and she quickly calculated just how rebellious she wanted to be, but then she saw they were ginger ale. Still technically forbidden, but not nearly as bad.

Pick sat on the deck next to Jessie and opened the box. "They give me leftovers every night," he said. "It's Saturday, so we really scored big."

Jessie warmed at his use of the pronoun *we,* and also, her stomach rumbled. "I'm starving," she admitted. "My grandmother passed out before she could make me any dinner."

"Bill told me your grandmother likes her gin," Pick said.

"She does," Jessie said, though she hardly thought it was a good idea for Mr. Crimmins to share this detail with Pick. But Jessie supposed that the family secrets would all be revealed, now that the Crimminses were living among them. Jessie eyed the cardboard box. "What did you get?"

Pick unfolded the flaps. "Meat loaf," he said. "And cod cakes. There's plenty, so help yourself."

Jessie loathed cod cakes and would eat meat loaf only under duress, but she was hungry and she was so happy to be sitting alone with Pick that the food tasted more delicious than any she could remember. They both ate with their fingers and a couple of times their hands met when they reached into the box. Then Pick offered Jessie the last bite of meat loaf, which she declined, but he said, "Come on," and popped it into Jessie's mouth, and his fingers touched her lips in a way that made her feel faint.

She drank some of her ginger ale—it was cold and spicy—and wondered if she should leave, but Pick cleared away the box, then turned around so that his back was to the railing and he was facing Jessie. He stretched out his dungareed legs, one of which was grazing Jessie's bare knee. He might not have noticed it, but Jessie was 100 percent nerve endings, all of them alert and yearning. It was funny the way being touched by Garrison had been offensive and gross but the slightest contact with Pick made her feel like she had eaten magic beans.

"So, Jessie," Pick said. "How are things?"

"My father got here last night," Jessie said. "He's a lawyer in Boston and only comes on weekends. I thought he would bring a letter from my brother, Tiger, but he didn't."

"Tiger is in Vietnam," Pick said, as if Jessie didn't know.

"I miss him," she said.

"He's your half brother, right?" Pick said. "And you have two half sisters?"

"Blair and Kirby," Jessie said. She bristled at the fact that Mr. Crimmins seemed to have shared even more family particulars. If *they* weren't allowed to use the qualifiers *half* and *step,* why should Pick be able to? She decided to turn the tables on him. "Do you miss your mother?" she asked.

Pick blew out a stream of air but said nothing, and Jessie felt like a complete heel for asking.

"There's stuff I didn't tell you," Pick said. He leaned forward. "She left for a reason. There was a man at the commune named Zeppelin, and he and my mother were together, but he used to hurt her, so she ran away."

Jessie thought of how badly she had wanted to get away from Garrison. "Did she tell you she was going?"

"No," Pick said. "But when I woke up and found out she had left, I knew that was why. It had nothing to do with me."

Jessie wondered if this story was true or if Pick had invented it to make himself feel better.

Pick said, "I was afraid Zep might come after me when my mom left, but he took up immediately with a woman named Bunny."

"Oh," Jessie said.

"Things were kind of like that at the commune," Pick said. "Sharing, partner swaps, no traditional relationship roles. My mom knew it was okay to leave me because there were plenty of other people to care for me." Pick stood up and peered over the railing like Plumb Lane was a pool that he was about to dive into. Jessie stood as well. She should get back to the main house. It wasn't impossible that Kate, in her melancholy state, would want to put her eyes on Jessie, the only child remaining at home. If she found Jessie's bed empty, who knew what she might do.

"I know where to find my mother," Pick said.

"You do?" Jessie said.

"There's going to be a big concert in August," Pick said. "In a town called Woodstock, New York. Jimi Hendrix is playing, and Creedence, Janis Joplin, Jefferson Airplane, the Who, Joe Cocker, Joan Baez, the Band, Crosby, Stills, Nash, and Young—"

"The Beatles?" Jessie asked hopefully. She had heard of most of the people Pick just mentioned but they weren't her favorites. "What about Joni Mitchell?" Jessie thought about what it would be like to hear Joni Mitchell singing "Both Sides Now" in person. Jessie had yet to even play her record on the Magnavox.

"The point is, *everyone* is going to be there," Pick said. "And my mother...well, she wouldn't miss it, I know that much."

"So you're *going?*" Jessie asked. "You're going to Woodstock, New York?"

"In August," Pick said. "I'm saving my paychecks. I figure I'll hop on the ferry a couple days before, take the bus to Boston, and hitchhike from there."

"And then how will you get back?" Jessie asked. She supposed what she was really asking was if he was coming back at all.

Pick shrugged. "My mom and I will figure it out. There are going to be thousands of people there; I'm sure someone can give us a ride. My mom is good at making friends." Pick turned to Jessie and a smile lit up his face. "Why don't you come with me?"

Jessie opened her mouth to laugh at the absurdity of the offer or maybe to lament that she was still too young to leave the island alone. But instead of doing either, she said, "Okay."

"Okay, you'll come?" Pick said.

Jessie nodded. She was in love, she realized then. Completely in love with this offbeat boy whose mother had abandoned him.

Pick stuck out his hand. "Shake on it," he said.

They shook hands and Pick held on for a few extra seconds. "This is great," he said. "Now I don't have to go alone."

He doesn't have to go alone; she will go with him, though she hasn't the foggiest idea how she will manage to do this. But it's still nearly two months off, so she has time to figure it out. Maybe Kirby will take her, or maybe the war in Vietnam will end and Tiger will make it home in time to go with Jessie and Pick. That, of course, would be almost too good to be true.

Jessie stares at the letter she's writing, then out the window at Fair Street, and she wonders what Tiger will be looking at when he reads it.

I hope you're well. I think of you every day, and just in case you're wondering, nothing is the same without you. Write soon please.

Love, Messie

Piece of My Heart

For the ride to the Cape in Joey Whalen's Lincoln Continental, Blair ties her Pucci scarf over her hair and puts on her round black sunglasses, a fashion statement she flat-out stole from former First Lady Jackie Kennedy Onassis. Joey wants to ride with the Lincoln's top down because it's a nice day, and Blair says fine; she's just happy the vehicle is spacious enough to accommodate her girth.

Joey is wearing a blue suit and a pair of Wayfarers. They cruise down Route 3 toward Cape Cod with the radio blaring; right now, it's Janis Joplin. Blair sneaks a glance at Joey through half-closed eyes. His expression is placid and carefree as he pretends to play the drums against the steering wheel.

The scene that ensued when Angus caught Blair and Joey in flagrante was so harrowing that, in retrospect, Blair can't believe she didn't go into labor right then and there. She's incredulous that Angus, who hadn't surprised Blair at home even once since they'd been married, showed up at the exact moment that Blair succumbed to her desire for Joey Whalen.

Angus had gaped at Blair and Joey, and then the bouquet of flowers—which h e m ust h ave b ought t o c elebrate n ews o f the twins—dropped to the floor.

"What the hell is going *on?*" he roared.

Joey and Blair had tried to pull apart, but a string from Blair's rapidly deteriorating maternity dress had caught on one of the buttons of Joey's bespoke shirt and so there was that awkwardness to contend with, which left time for Angus to storm over to the couch and loom above them.

"How long has this been going on?"

Blair let Joey speak. There was nothing going on, he said. Joey had stopped by and Blair was upset. Joey was only trying to comfort her and they'd gotten carried away.

"You expect me to *believe* that?" Angus said. He narrowed his eyes at Joey, and Blair was puzzled over how *furious* Angus seemed. She hadn't seen him show that much emotion since the summer of their wedding. When they'd returned to Boston that September and Angus went back to MIT, he had become more and more like a robot, programmed to move through life's daily routine. "You've had the hots for my wife from the beginning."

"Well," Joey said, straightening up to stand at his full height. He was taller than Angus, and broader. "She *was* my girlfriend first."

Blair opened her mouth to protest, but before she could get a word out, Angus landed a punch under Joey's eye and Joey delivered a blow to Angus's gut. Soon the brothers were engaged in a full-on brawl, circling each other, venting old grievances. Angus resented Joey for carrying a torch for Blair and for giving Blair such a suggestive wedding gift, the silver lighter engraved with the words *I loved you first. Eternally yours, Joey.* (Blair brought her hands to her mouth—Angus had actually noticed the lighter!) Joey said that he resented Angus for stealing Blair away without a word of apology. They grabbed each other and tumbled to the ground. Their boxing became a sort of wrestling and Blair wanted to yell at them to stop but she was interested in what the brothers had to say.

"You always get exactly what you want and then some," Joey said. "Because supposedly you're a genius."

"What about you?" Angus spit. "Coasting on your good looks, your charm, your athletic ability. People *liked* you better. I could never have gotten a girl like Blair if you hadn't brought her to me."

"That's right!" Joey said. "You married a woman who's too good for you and you're blowing it!" Joey had Angus's arms pinned over his head, and he pulled his arm back to punch him. Angus steeled himself and Blair let a cry escape. Joey seemed to reconsider, and then he let go of Angus and got to his feet. "She says you're having an affair."

Angus sat up. "If that's not the pot calling the kettle black, I don't know what is."

"You're lying to your pregnant wife," Joey said. He turned to Blair. "I would never do that. If you were still my girl, I would be true blue."

Angus pointed at the door. "Get out."

"Gladly," Joey said. He jammed his arms into his suit jacket and bent down to look at Blair. "If you need me, just call the Parker House."

Blair waited with her head bowed as Joey left. Angus dusted himself off and disappeared into the kitchen. Blair remained on the couch, summoning the energy to get to her feet. She felt oddly glad that Angus had come home and caught her and Joey. She *was* a catch! She *was* desirable—even when pregnant!

She hauled herself up and waddled to the kitchen. Angus's back was to her.

"Who is Trixie?" Blair asked. "And how long have you been seeing her?"

Angus stared at the wall behind the kitchen sink where Blair kept a needlepoint sampler that said AS YE SOW, SO SHALL YE REAP. She nearly laughed at the irony of it.

"You know what I think?" Blair said. "I think you've been seeing her since before we were married. I think you were talking to her on the phone *on our honeymoon*."

She watched Angus's shoulders tense. He looked like he was thrumming with the things he wanted to say—a confession, maybe.

"And that day I came to your office? Dobbins told me you had a *personal appointment*."

"We've been over this," Angus said.

Blair tried for a haughty laugh like the one her grandmother had perfected, but it came out as a whinny. "I think you were with her. And then the other day on the phone, I *heard* the two of you, Angus. She said her *name*. You said you wanted to *see her*."

Angus turned around. He was holding his glasses in his hands. They were in two pieces; Joey had broken them. Blair rarely got to look directly into her husband's eyes the way she did now. His irises were brown and flecked with green. As many times as Blair had cursed his name in the past year, she remained in his thrall.

"You're right," he said. "I was on the phone with Trixie while we were in Bermuda. And I went to see her the day you came to my office."

Blair felt like she'd been blindsided; even though this was what she'd suspected, it came as a fresh pain to hear him say it.

"Now, I've told you the truth and I'd like you to return the favor, please. Have you been carrying a torch for Joey all this time?" Angus laughed unhappily. "I mean, I *saw* the two of you in the act. *In our home*. So obviously the answer is yes."

Blair was at a loss for words; she didn't know where to start.

Angus's confession was straightforward: Yes, he'd been with Trixie. But Blair wasn't sure what had just happened with Joey. *Did* she have feelings for him? There was no denying there was a physical connection, but Blair thought that was because she had been so lonely—and so, so angry. Angus had stripped away Blair's personhood bit by bit. He'd made her quit her job, and now, with this pregnancy, she'd lost not only her body but also her autonomy. Angus expected her to stay home and keep house and prepare the meals. She had faithfully done that while also serving as an incubator for their children. But Angus had given Blair nothing in return—not his time, not his affection, not an apology, not a word of praise or thanks.

"You're never home," Blair said. The words sounded pale and limp, but that lay at the heart of the matter. She and Angus never *did* anything together anymore because Angus was always at work—or, apparently, with Trixie. Someone else was getting the best parts of him—either Trixie or his students or the U.S. government.

"I think you should go to Nantucket and wait out the rest of your pregnancy there," Angus said.

Blair was too proud to show him how this statement wounded her. *"Nantucket?"* she said. "How do you propose I get there? I certainly can't drive in my condition."

"I'm sure Joey will take you," Angus said. "Pack your things."

Joey has taken the entire day off from work and he even brought a picnic; it's in a basket on the back seat. Near the exit for Plymouth, they pass an older gentleman driving a cherry-red Mustang convertible. He honks at them and gives them the thumbs-up, and Joey waves. Looking at Blair from the shoulders up, no one can tell she is pregnant. To the gentleman in the

Mustang, Blair supposes, she and Joey look like any other young couple out for a ride.

Joey puts a hand on Blair's knee and she considers removing it. Is he being a sweet brother-in-law and a good guy by driving her to Hyannis, or is he claiming her? Has she been handed off like a baton from one brother to the other? Blair doesn't have to wonder what Betty Friedan would think about this; she already knows the answer.

At Blair's suggestion, they don't stop for lunch until they're up over the Sagamore Bridge and on Cape Cod. Joey drives to Craigville Beach, where there are picnic tables overlooking the water. He spreads out a red-checkered tablecloth and then a lunch that was prepared by the chef at the Parker House: cold roast beef, soft rolls, hard-boiled eggs, pickles, coleslaw, sliced strawberries, and pound cake. Blair would like to say that being thrown out of her own home by her unfaithful husband has diminished her appetite, but in fact, she's as hungry as ever. Joey watches with rapt attention as she devours a roast beef sandwich topped with sliced egg, coleslaw, and pickles—lots and lots of pickles!—and then cuts a thick slice of pound cake and smothers it with berries.

"My kingdom for some whipped cream," she says.

Joey holds up a finger and Blair thinks he's about to inform her she's a spoiled brat, but instead he races down the beach to the ice cream concession. Blair squints to see him pulling coins out of his pocket, and the next thing she knows, Joey is headed back toward her, holding a can of whipped cream. He sets it next to her plate.

"Ask and you shall receive," he says. "Go crazy."

This, Blair thinks, *is what it feels like to be adored.*

When they arrive at the ferry, Joey loads Blair's suitcase onto the luggage rack and holds her arm as he walks her to the pedestrian ramp.

"I should take the ferry over with you," he says.

"No, no," Blair says. She can't imagine her mother's and grandmother's expressions if they were to see Blair arriving on Nantucket with Joey Whalen instead of Angus. Her grandmother, especially, would be cross and confused, and there would be a lot of explaining to do. "You've done so much already. I'll be fine." She holds up a battered copy of *The House of Mirth,* which she brought for the ferry crossing. She has read it half a dozen times; it's her literary security blanket.

Joey takes the book from her and inspects it. "Edith Wharton," he says. "I should read this. That's how Angus won you over, isn't it?"

"Oh, Joey," Blair says. She stands on her tiptoes and gives him a chaste kiss on the lips.

He says, "I'll let you get settled over there and then I'll come see you."

"More than likely, I'll return to Boston next week," she says. What she means is that she will return when Angus comes to his senses and begs her to come home.

Joey grins. "That would be great!" He hugs Blair close and hard, so hard Blair fears for the babies, and then, after a final squeeze of her hand, he heads back to the car.

Blair turns around to see him one more time before she steps into the dim hold of the boat. Joey is behind the wheel of the Lincoln, waving like crazy. Blair waves back, though she feels an undeniable sense of relief when he finally drives away.

Everybody's Talkin'

June 24, 1969

Dear Tiger,

You aren't going to believe this.

I've been on Nantucket an entire week and have only been to the beach once, Sunday afternoon, just me and Mom and Dad, and Dad insisted on going all the way out to Great Point because he wanted to surf-cast. The trip out there took over an hour and we almost got stuck because Dad lets the tires down to only fifteen pounds when it's supposed to be eleven. Mom put a bottle of Chablis in the cooler and once we finally got to Great Point, she started drinking. She seems to have given up all her mom duties—like, she didn't offer to make sandwiches, so Dad made them, and he put mustard on my cheese sandwich and I had to throw it to the seagulls. There was nobody out there except for fishermen and one seal that was swimming off-shore. Dad said the seal meant there were fish but Mom said the seal meant there would be sharks so I couldn't swim. Mom didn't offer to put Coppertone on my back and I was afraid to ask her, so I got sunburned.

It was the worst beach day of my life.

(But that's not the part you won't believe. I'm coming to that part...just wait!)

Mom promised she would take me to Cisco Beach so I could hang around with kids my own age but after Dad left Sunday night, Mom was so sad she said she needed a day to recuperate. So we were supposed to go today (Tuesday) after my tennis lesson. My tennis lessons with Suze are going okay...

Here, Jessie pauses. Today, she had adamantly signed herself in as Jessica Levin, and Exalta had ripped the pen from Jessie's hand and crossed *Levin* out with a bold, angry stroke. She'd said, loud enough for everyone, including the Dunscombe twins and Mrs. Winter, to hear, "Jessica, this membership has been in the Nichols family since 1905 when this club was founded. *I* pay the bills, *not* your father. Therefore, you will use *my* name while you use this club or I will revoke your signing privileges altogether. *Do you understand me?*"

To keep herself from crying, Jessie imagined Exalta crossing North Beach Street without looking both ways, as she often did, and getting hit by a car.

Jessie excused herself and went to the locker room, where one of the Dunscombe twins—Helen or Heather, she couldn't tell which—disappeared into a bathroom stall. Whichever twin it was had left her Bermuda bag with a navy-blue linen monogrammed cover on the counter between the sinks. Jessie eyed the Bermuda bag. The monogram was HAD; she wasn't sure what either twin's middle name was, but it was possible, even likely, that Helen and Heather had the same initials. While Jessie was thinking that she would never steal from the Dunscombe twins—it seemed much worse, somehow, than stealing from the club—she lifted the wooden handle and grabbed the first things she could get her hands on, a five-dollar bill and a Bonne Bell lip gloss, root beer flavor. She jammed the items into the pocket of her tennis dress.

The toilet flushed. A second later, the twin emerged and smiled at Jessie.

"Hi, Jessie," she said.

Jessie's heart sank as she realized it was Heather, the nice twin. "Hi," she said.

But Jessie decides not to burden Tiger with this story. The last thing Tiger needs to know is that while he's off being a hero, Jessie is on Nantucket turning into a hardened criminal. She doesn't *intend* to steal. It just happens.

...but I have a long way to go when it comes to serving. I asked Suze whether anyone had ever double-faulted through an entire match and she told me I needed an "attitude adjustment."

Jessie realizes she's making Suze sound mean, which she isn't; Suze is just tough in the most admirable way. She doesn't want Jessie to even *consider* double-faulting through an entire match. Instead, she encourages Jessie to use positive visualization. She has a few pet phrases: *Follow through with your stroke! Charge the net!* But she has also given Jessie advice that has nothing to do with tennis, such as *Don't ever change your maiden name.* And *Make your own money.*

"You don't want to be financially dependent on a man, do you?" Suze had asked that very morning as they collected balls off the court.

"Um...no?" Jessie said.

Suze rolled a tennis ball up the side of her white sneaker, and in one swift motion with foot and racket, she flicked it up and caught it. "Tell me, Jessie, do you have any role models?"

"My brother is in Vietnam," Jessie said. "Serving our country."

"*Female* role models," Suze said.

Jessie thought about this. The obvious answer would be her mother, although Kate didn't have a career or make her own money, and neither did Exalta. Blair used to have a job but she quit when she married Angus. Kirby was working over on the Vineyard—she'd gotten a job at a hotel—but Kirby was a free spirit and smoked marijuana besides, and although Jessie loved and idolized her sister, the term *role model* didn't seem to apply.

"You?" Jessie said.

"Damn straight," Suze said, and she flicked up another ball.

Jessie returns to the letter. She tells herself to stay focused.

So here's the part you won't believe. When I got home from my tennis lesson, I ran upstairs to put on my bathing suit AND GUESS WHO WAS SITTING ON MY BED???

Blair, that's who.

The story she told Mom and Nonny is that she was lonely in Boston because Angus was always working and she was afraid she would go into labor while she was in the apartment by herself so she came to Nantucket.

She's big, Tiger. She looks like she swallowed a Volkswagen Bug.

The real story . . .

Here, Jessie stops. She promised Blair she wouldn't tell *anyone* the real story, but Tiger is far away and she hasn't heard from him in weeks, so who knew if he was even getting her letters. She might as well be sticking them in bottles and tossing them into the ocean.

. . . is that Angus is cheating on Blair with some woman named Trixie. Then, the day before yesterday, Joey Whalen came to

visit. Blair told him about Angus's affair and she started to cry. After that, Blair said, one thing led to another. You know how that can happen.

As though Jessie might indeed know.

    And Angus walked into the apartment and caught Blair and Joey kissing! Then Angus threw Blair out!
    I'm happy she's here except that Mom gave Blair my room, which means I have to go over to Little Fair and sleep in the second bedroom upstairs. I can't remember if I told you this but Mr. Crimmins's grandson is staying in the other upstairs bedroom and Mr. Crimmins himself is staying downstairs. It will be weird, all of us together in that tiny house, but my other option was to stay in the second twin bed in Nonny's room.
    No, thank you.
    On Thursday night, Mom is taking me to the Mad Hatter to celebrate my birthday. She picked Thursday night because, as you may recall, Nonny plays bridge on Thursday. Blair says she's too big to go out in public, so it will be just me and Mom.
    The only other person I would want to come is you. I wish you were here.
    Please write soon. You can write to Mom or Kirby or Blair or even Nonny but please just write so we know

Jessie nearly writes *you're alive.*

you're okay.

                         Love, Messie

Mother's Little Helper

Sunday night, Kate drives David down to Steamboat Wharf to catch the last ferry home, and when they get there, he leans over, kisses her cheek, and says, "You're drinking too much."

Kate opens her mouth to protest, but before she can say a word, David adds, "If you keep on like this, you'll turn into your mother. And neither of us wants that." He gets out of the car and joins the long line of people heading back to real life after a well-spent summer weekend. Kate waits to see if he'll wave, but the car behind her honks and she has to move along.

David has made his point.

He's right. She's drinking too much.

The drinking started on Sunday, May 25, the day after Tiger finished up his basic training and was deployed overseas to the Central Highlands of Vietnam. They went to brunch with Exalta, and Kate got so drunk that David had to carry her out of the Union Club. When she got home, she passed out in her darkened bedroom even though it was only three in the afternoon. She woke up at midnight, realized it was noon in Vietnam, and started to wail. Mothers all across America were standing strong, fortified by their love of country and their hatred of Communism, but Kate couldn't muster those emotions. Tiger possessed good instincts and had an abundance of street smarts; he was everything you could ask for in a soldier, and his father had been a career military man. Kate should have felt confidence and pride—but all she could think was that she might never see him again.

Alcohol is the only thing that helps, pathetic as that might sound.

At home in Brookline, after David left for work and Jessie for school, Kate opened a bottle of Chablis, which she finished by lunchtime. She drank vodka and sodas all afternoon—unlike gin, vodka had no smell—and then, when David got home, she poured a scotch for each of them, which they drank while watching Walter Cronkite. Then they opened a bottle of wine with dinner and Kate finished her day with a nightcap of either cream sherry or blackberry brandy.

It wasn't quite as bad as it sounded, Kate didn't think. It was only nine or ten drinks per day, less than one an hour, although some nights she drank martinis through dinner, as she had at the Skipper on Saturday night. They'd started that dinner with champagne to celebrate David's first weekend on the island, although, really, this was a farce. David *hated* Nantucket. He would argue that he loved Nantucket; what he hated was living under Exalta's roof. The house, even with the inclusion of Little Fair, was too small for all of them, and it was a trial to live by Exalta's rules. David also disliked the way their social lives revolved around the Field and Oar Club, a place he didn't feel included, or even welcome.

At dinner at the Skipper, David had said, "We had a banner year at the firm and I'm due a good bonus. Let's buy our own house here." He went on to describe a listing he'd seen for a house out in Madaket, a summer cottage that had uninterrupted views of the Atlantic. "Six bedrooms," he said. "Four and a half baths. And a yard big enough for a tennis court. Our *own* tennis court." Here, he'd reached for Kate's hand, but she lifted her champagne coupe and drained her glass. She understood David's desire for their own house, and it was tempting to dream of telling Exalta that they were moving out. But…Madaket? Madaket was six miles to the west. It was the wilderness. How would Kate ever adjust to not being in town? Not being able to walk to Charlie's Market or the club or the Skipper? And as for building their own tennis court, surely David was joking. That would be a gauche way for them to advertise the banner year David's firm had enjoyed, even worse than putting in a swimming pool.

The sad fact was that Kate was a captive of her own mother, of All's Fair, and of the life she'd known for the past forty-eight years on Nantucket. She didn't want to move. She didn't want to change.

"Mother won't live forever," Kate said.

David, because he was a gentle, kind man and wouldn't argue with her even when she had summarily dismissed his hope for a new life here, smiled. "Wanna bet?"

The night had deteriorated on the walk home. Kate hadn't yet told her husband that Bill Crimmins and his grandson were living in Little Fair; he knew nothing about the arrangement she'd made.

She said, "I think I forgot to mention that Mother offered Little Fair to Bill Crimmins for the summer."

David said, "Actually, Exalta told me *you* offered it to him. And his grandson."

Kate nodded. She was so drunk it felt like she was moving underwater. "It *was* me. Are you mad?"

"It's very thoughtful of you, Katie. Bill Crimmins has always done right by you, hasn't he?"

Kate bowed her head and watched the toes of her pink Pappagallo flats move forward, left, then right. She was so drunk it was like watching someone else's feet. Had Bill Crimmins always done right by her? Their relationship was far too complicated for that kind of blanket statement, but David, of course, knew nothing about Kate's past with the Crimmins family. She couldn't tell him about that, nor could she tell him about her agreement with Bill Crimmins this summer. David would think she was simply being kind when, really, she had traded Little Fair for Tiger's safety.

Kate started to cry. David hadn't brought any letters from Tiger. Letters were oxygen, and without oxygen, Kate could not survive.

She manages to make it all the way through Monday without a drink, which requires her to say no to Exalta for lunch at the club and no to Jessie for the beach because Kate can't endure either without wine. Instead, she shops at Charlie's for actual groceries and she visits the farm stand on Hummock Pond Road. It's too early for corn or tomatoes so Kate must be satisfied with radishes, lamb's lettuce, and a cantaloupe. She makes a final stop at Aime's Bakery for Portuguese bread, arriving just as they're pulling fresh loaves out of the oven. She wants to make a fine cold supper—the bread with salted butter, the lettuce and sliced radishes and some cold poached chicken with homemade Russian dressing, and she'll break out one or two of the cheeses they brought from Savenor's. This seems like a lot for just herself, Exalta, and Jessie, so Kate ponders inviting Bill Crimmins to join them. Will this seem pushy? Kate wants to know if he has heard back from his brother-in-law, the personal friend and confidant of General Creighton W. Abrams. She assumes that Bill will come to her as soon as he has news, and she decides that having Bill Crimmins sit at the table will make her speculation unbearable.

Kate watches Walter Cronkite, then she and Jessie and Exalta eat the cold supper in the kitchen. Exalta praises the dressing and eats four pieces of bread. She drains two Hendrick's and tonics packed with ice and garnished with a twist of lime—she prepares the twist herself, her only kitchen trick—and Kate volunteers to clean up in order to keep her hands occupied. At seven thirty, when the dishes are done and the leftovers wrapped up and put away, the sun is still shining. It's three days past the solstice, and sunlight hours are long, too long. The effort required to keep from drinking has exhausted Kate.

She goes up to bed.

Can she do it again on Tuesday? She hears Jessie and Exalta up early for Jessie's tennis lesson and she wants to go along but her mother will order a mimosa and it will be too much for Kate to resist. She lies back in bed, puts a pillow across her face to block the sun.

When she wakes up again, the house is quiet. Kate climbs out of bed and goes to the window just in time to see Pick disappear the wrong way down Fair Street on his bicycle. He's wearing only a pair of yellow swim trunks and a towel around his neck. He's barefoot. Off to the beach, Kate supposes, and she yearns for the summer days when she was a child. She has yet to be properly introduced to the boy; Bill Crimmins is probably avoiding it for the obvious reasons. But it will have to happen sooner or later.

Kate waits until Pick has disappeared from view, then she goes down to the kitchen to make herself a screwdriver, extra-strong.

She's halfway through her second drink when she hears someone coming in the back door. Kate has been sitting in the den, watching the summer breeze stir the moving parts of Exalta's whirligigs. The Indian chief in the canoe was always Tiger's favorite.

It's too early for Jessie and Exalta to be back, which means it must be Bill Crimmins.

Maybe he's been to the post office. Maybe he has her answer.

She abandons the screwdriver in the den. If Bill tells her what she wants to hear—what she *needs* to hear—she promises God that she'll quit drinking forever.

When Kate enters the kitchen, she cries out in surprise. It's not Bill Crimmins she finds—it's Blair! Kate blinks, thinking her mind is playing tricks on her thanks to vodka so early in the morning, and this notion is reinforced by the fact that Blair doesn't look like Blair. She looks like a cartoon rendering of herself—like Blair if someone pumped her with air to the point of almost popping.

"Sweet pea?" Kate says.

Blair bursts into tears.

Kate makes two fresh screwdrivers and leads Blair up to her own bedroom, where she turns the air-conditioning unit on high. Exalta doesn't like anyone to use the air-conditioning until July but it's already sweltering. Not only is poor Blair hysterical, she's shining with perspiration. She needs a cool room where they can talk privately; the noise of the air conditioner will mask their words should Exalta and Jessie come home.

Kate worries about Blair making it up the stairs. She is *so* big.

Blair flops on the bed and kicks her sandals off her swollen feet. Kate hands her a screwdriver.

"Take a sip," she says. "The vodka will calm you, and the juice is filled with vitamin C, good for the babies."

Blair accepts the glass and sucks the entire thing down. Kate takes a handkerchief from her lingerie drawer. If Blair is here, there must be very bad news indeed, but Kate welcomes the distraction from worrying about Tiger.

"What happened?" Kate asks.

Blair shakes her head. "It's over with Angus."

"Now, Blair," Kate says. "I told you—"

"It wasn't my decision," she says. "It was Angus's decision. He asked me to leave."

"What?" Kate says. She considers Angus a little strange, a bit socially awkward, possibly due to his unusually high IQ, but she never imagined him to be the kind of man who would put his pregnant wife out on the street. It's...barbaric, is what it is. And she's pregnant with *twins*. "Is this because of that woman?" Kate closes her eyes and bats away thoughts of Wilder and all the heartbreak she endured with him.

"He admitted he was seeing her," Blair says. "And then he asked me to leave."

"I'm...I'm *speechless,*" Kate says. "I can't fathom Angus being so cruel."

Blair casts her eyes down at her prodigious midsection. "It wasn't entirely Angus's fault. Joey Whalen came for a visit, and..."

Dear God, Kate thinks, *what is Blair going to say?*

"...and I kissed him, Mother. *Really* kissed him. And Angus walked in on us!" Blair starts weeping again. "Angus surprised me at home with *flowers* to celebrate the news about the twins and I was *necking with his brother!*"

Oh dear, Kate thinks. She has long suspected that Blair still carries a torch for Joey and vice versa.

"Surely Angus understands that you were upset about his relationship with the other woman? And surely you explained that you aren't yourself because of your condition?"

"He wouldn't hear any of that," Blair says. "Joey made it worse by proclaiming his love for me. They had a fistfight right in front of me and then Angus told me he thought I would be happier with Joey anyway."

"What?" Kate says. "Nonsense!"

"Joey drove me to the ferry," Blair says. "I think he still has feelings for me. In fact, I know he does."

"How Joey Whalen feels is not our concern," Kate says. "Our concern is how *you* feel, and you love Angus. Right?"

Blair hesitates, but her answer to this question doesn't matter. She married Angus for better or for worse. Angus is the father of these babies, not Joey. Fatherhood isn't something you can just pass off to another man. Although Kate did just that; David raised her three children like they were his own.

"Joey is thoughtful and dotes on me," Blair says. "I'm sure he would encourage me to work after the babies are born if I wanted to."

"Work after the *babies* are born?" Kate says. "You're having twins, sweet pea. They'll provide plenty of work."

"I wanted whipped cream on my cake and Joey ran and bought some from the ice cream man," Blair says.

Kate puts an arm around her daughter's shoulders. "You need to stop talking nonsense. You're married to Angus, you'll remain married to Angus, and you will stay home and raise those children just like I stayed home to raise you. Motherhood is a sacrifice. That's what makes it so rewarding."

"But—"

"Angus will come around in a few days," Kate says. "A week at the most. And then we'll ship you home."

While Blair sobs into the handkerchief, Kate considers the logistics of having Blair here for even a week. They'll need to call the cottage hospital that very afternoon to make certain there's a doctor who can deliver the babies in case of emergency. And where will Blair *sleep?* Kate can't put her in Little Fair with the Crimminses; she'll have to take Jessie's room, and Jessie can go over to Little Fair. That's not optimal, but it's only a week. Jessie will survive.

Poor Jessie. Kate promised her a beach day, and that's now out the window, plus she's being kicked out of her bedroom. Kate downs her screwdriver, and despite the chaos, a calm spreads through her. She'll take Jessie out to dinner Thursday night while Exalta is at bridge. And she'll start to give Jessie a little more freedom. That's what all kids want these days, Kate thinks. Freedom.

Magic Carpet Ride (Reprise)

Kirby spends her first days off being a third wheel with Patty and Luke, who have very quickly become a couple. Luke Winslow is a rising senior at Columbia University; he's majoring in business and when he graduates, he will head straight to Wall Street, he says, to work for his father's investment firm, Drexel Harriman Ripley. In fact, Luke's parents own the house on the Vineyard where Patty's brother Tommy and his roommate, Eugene, live. Kirby expects something halfway between a flophouse and a fraternity house, but when they pull into the driveway, after a beautiful, hilly, bucolic ride up-island to Chilmark, Kirby sees a compound that overlooks Nashaquitsa Pond. There are two ranch houses sided with cedar shingles like most of the homes on Nantucket. The slightly smaller one is where the boys live. Luke's parents live in the other, though they come to the Vineyard only on the weekends.

The house the boys live in blows Kirby's mind. Sliding screen doors open onto one long room with stark white walls and white beams. The furniture is modern and curvy. Against one wall is a lipstick-red sofa that looks like a woman lying on her side; it's flanked by two shell chairs, one turquoise, one electric lime green. There are enormous canvases on the walls, all female nudes, modern, reminiscent of Matisse and Chagall. At one end of the room is a minimalist kitchen—three swivel bar stools at a white marble countertop, on top of which is a wide wooden bowl filled with plums and bing cherries; open shelves stacked with rustic ceramic dishes.

At the other end of the house are two bedrooms, one with two double beds (for Tommy and Eugene), the other with one king bed (for Luke), all sheathed in crisp white linens. The bedrooms are connected by a white subway-tiled bathroom that has a floor paved with slate-blue river stones.

Okay, Kirby thinks. This is absolutely the grooviest house she has ever seen. There's a chandelier in the living room that looks like an origami fish. It's made of rice paper, Luke says.

"Who did all the paintings?" Kirby asks. The nude women are all voluptuous with long Botticelli-like hair.

"My mother," Luke says. "Elsa Winslow?" He says the name like Kirby might have heard of her. She has taken one art history course at Simmons, which is how she knows Matisse and Chagall. Kirby wonders if Elsa Winslow is famous. Maybe she has a cult following, like Andy Warhol.

"She's an *amazing* painter," Kirby says.

"Yeah," Luke says. "And she knows it."

Kirby looks at Luke with new eyes. She had originally thought him just a regular guy—privileged, obviously, given the painstakingly restored Willys Jeep, but not so different from guys in Brookline. Now that Kirby is standing in this super-hip beach bungalow, she's intrigued. Kirby imagines his parents—a midtown financial power broker and a Greenwich Village bohemian artist—with envy. They aren't hung up on budgets or rules like Kirby's parents are. They have given Luke his own house, essentially, to live in with his friends.

Kirby peers into the bedrooms. "Honestly, I thought with three guys living here, this place would be a mess. I can't believe how tidy it is."

"We have a housekeeper," Luke says. "Martine. She lives up at the other house." Luke grabs Patty and starts tickling her and Patty shrieks and the two of them fall over onto the red couch. When they start kissing, Kirby nearly asks them to quit it, but she doesn't want to be a wet blanket. She wanders over to the kitchen counter and considers the bowl of fruit. The plums and the cherries are nearly the same color, but not quite—deep purple and glorious purplish red—and Kirby realizes that even the fruit is meant to be art. She plucks a cherry out of the bowl. It's fat and juicy-looking, and Kirby can't resist popping it into her mouth. Her diet since arriving on this island has consisted of breakfast porridge, fried clams from Giordano's, and stale doughnuts at the inn. The cherry is sweeter than any she has ever tasted. She sucks on the pit until it's clean then discreetly spits it out in her hand. Behind her, on the sofa, she hears wet tongue noises and heavy breathing; she tries not to think about Scottie Turbo. No one would ever call Kirby a prude, but she doesn't want to stand here while Luke and Patty fool around. Kirby steps out the sliding door. In her peripheral vision, she catches sight of Luke leading Patty back to his bedroom. Kirby hears the door shut.

Fine.

She's not sure why she feels embarrassed. *They* should feel embarrassed. Patty might not know any better, but Luke has clearly been raised with some social graces. And yet, he's a boy...and boys want what they want when they want it. Kirby has learned this the hard way.

To distract herself, she takes in the view over the pond. It's nothing short of spectacular. Kirby halfway hopes that Patty marries Luke and inherits this compound from the banker father and artist mother so that Kirby can continue to visit this spot for the rest of her life.

She sits on the deck with her face to the sun, and a little while later, Patty and Luke appear. Patty looks flushed, Luke triumphant.

"Shall we go to the beach?" Luke asks.

Because Luke lives in Chilmark, he has access to Lucy Vincent Beach. "It's the most exclusive of all the Vineyard beaches," he explains. "You guys are lucky you met me." He grins, so Kirby can't hate him, though she's starting to, a little.

Once she steps onto Lucy Vincent, however, she agrees—they are lucky (*they* meaning Patty) they met Luke Winslow. The beach is wide and golden and backed by stark, dramatic cliffs. It's far, far more beautiful than Inkwell, not even in the same class, really, which makes Kirby indignant. She wonders if this is an example of institutional racism, but then she tells herself to relax—Inkwell is a town beach, and this is an up-island beach, windswept and wild.

Kirby quickly sees that, up ahead, there's a gentleman walking toward the water who is nude. As in, completely *nude*. She sees his penis hanging heavy between his legs. Kirby scans the beach and realizes that *everyone* on the beach is nude. They're reading in chairs; they're sleeping facedown, bippies to the sky; they're walking hand in hand, having conversations—all completely nude.

Kirby tries not to let her surprise show on her face. It's 1969; nudity is no big deal, she knows, but...my God. It's more disconcerting being a clothed person on a nude beach than it is being a white person on a Negro beach. Will Kirby be expected to strip down? She casts a sidelong glance at Patty. Her face is bright red, but whether with embarrassment or the sun, Kirby can't say. She's a good Catholic. This *must* come as a shock.

Luke finds a wide-open space and plops down their Styrofoam cooler, which is filled with Schlitz and chicken sandwiches prepared by Martine, the French maid. (Kirby caught a glimpse of her in her black uniform, complete with a white apron and frilled cap.) He sets up the chairs, and Kirby waits, wondering what will happen next. Patty pulls off her gauzy black cover-up to reveal a conservative black tank suit.

"We're at Lucy Vincent," Luke says. "Everything off."

Patty shakes her head.

"Patricia," Luke says.

"She doesn't want to," Kirby says. "And I don't want to either." Kirby pulls off her denim cutoffs and peasant blouse but decides her bikini is staying on.

Patty, however, peels away her black suit until she is standing before them in the splendid altogether. Her flesh is plentiful; she looks like a woman in a Rubens painting. She looks, Kirby thinks, like a woman in an Elsa Winslow painting, with her round breasts and ruddy nipples, her generous thighs and the curve of her belly that slopes down to her dark pubic hair. Kirby recognizes the romanticism before her: Luke has found his mother's art personified in Patty.

But then Kirby notices that Patty is trembling. Kirby sees a pronounced red mark on Patty's haunches—a handprint.

Luke shucks off his suit while facing away from Kirby so all she can see is his white behind. She busies herself by laying out her towel. She lies on her stomach and unties the string of her bikini top but that's as far as she'll go. She cranes her neck to see Luke leading Patty to the water, both of them naked as jaybirds.

Kirby sets her head down on her folded arms. What she told her parents is proving to be true: spending the summer on the Vineyard is quite educational.

A few days later, the temperature soars to the mid-eighties with 100 percent humidity. There's a breeze off the water early in the week, but by Friday, the sky is heavy, gray, and overcast; the air is hot and soupy. Naturally, the fan in Kirby's room picks this week to die a dramatic death. It stops spinning for no apparent reason, and when Kirby goes over to wiggle the plug, there is a sudden flash of electrical sparks followed by an acrid smell.

She can't live without a fan. Heat rises and she's in the attic, and although there's a window, without the fan the air is still. She corners Evan, Miss O'Rourke's nephew, who says he will go out and get her a new fan. It would be his pleasure.

That afternoon, there's a knock on Kirby's bedroom door. She's lying in bed listening to Aretha Franklin's *Lady Soul,* which is the album she brought for her rainy day/Sunday mood. If it's Michaela complaining about the volume, Kirby decides, she'll apologize profusely and then, once Michaela is back downstairs, put on her angry-mood album, Jimi Hendrix, *Electric Ladyland,* at top volume.

It might be Patty at the door. Luke picked Patty up earlier for a lobster-roll date in Menemsha, and Patty asked Kirby to go, but

Kirby declined. Patty, not Kirby, is Luke's girlfriend, and Kirby's beginning to find it strange that Patty wants her to join them every time they're together. Kirby wondered briefly if Patty was *afraid* of Luke. She had asked Patty about the red mark on her thigh.

"Did he *hit* you while you two were in the bedroom?" she asked. "Did he...I don't know...*spank* you?"

Patty laughed uncomfortably. "It's a game," she said. "Role-playing."

"*Role*-playing?" Kirby said.

"I'm an actress," Patty said.

When Kirby opens the door, she finds Barb standing before her. Kirby is surprised; she would have thought the hot, mouse-infested attic was the last place Barb would ever show her face.

"You have a visitor," Barb says.

"I do?" Kirby says. She assumes that Evan has arrived with the fan, and not a moment too soon. She throws on a polka-dot minidress and ties a bandanna around her hair. As she hurries down the stairs, she wonders what Evan might expect as a thank-you.

Barb waits at the top of the second-floor stairs along with Miranda and Maureen—Michaela is blessedly absent—and Kirby figures they must be really bored if they're that interested in seeing Evan in his brown polyester pants and Sunday-best shoes.

But when Kirby gets to the front door, she understands. It's not Evan. It's Darren Frazier. Kirby knows that for these girls, having a gentleman caller is a big deal. Having a Negro gentleman caller is, she suspects, brand-new territory for them.

Kirby's heart fills like a hot-air balloon. "Hey, you!" she says.

"Day off," he says. "I thought you might want to ride the carousel."

"I'd love it," Kirby says. She turns to wave at the girls who are loitering at the top of the stairs like they're watching *Guess Who's Coming to Dinner.* "See ya, ladies!"

As rotten, terrible luck would have it, they bump into Evan outside on the sidewalk; he's holding a huge rectangular box that Kirby can see is an air-conditioning unit.

"Is that for my room?" she asks hopefully.

"It's supposed to be." Evan grunts and drops the box onto the top step with a thud.

Air-conditioning is more than Kirby could have hoped for. "Evan, I can't thank you enough. You have no idea what it's like up there. I've been stewing in my own juices." She chastises herself for using that gross phrase in front of two gentlemen. Her mother would be appalled. "I'm very grateful."

Evan pulls a handkerchief out of his pants pocket and mops his brow. "I don't know how I'm going to get it all the way up to the attic."

"I've got it, man," Darren says, stepping up.

"Darren?" Evan says, blinking behind his square glasses. "Darren Frazier? Where did you come from?"

Darren has, of course, been standing there all along. How did Evan not notice him? Was Ralph Ellison right—were Negro men *invisible* to white people? It had seemed like hyperbole when Kirby read the book for her English class, but now that she's watching a real-life social interaction, she's not so sure.

Darren lifts the box with ease. "Fresh arms," he says, and Kirby thinks of how other guys might have flaunted their superior strength and stamina but Darren tries to downplay it. "We're going to the attic?"

"The attic," Kirby confirms.

Evan follows close on Darren's heels up the two flights of stairs and, realizing he's been shown up, offers to take the box back twice.

"I've got it," Darren says. He's not huffing or sweating and his biceps pop in a way that is undeniably attractive. Kirby brings up the rear, which means Evan can't look up her dress. Darren is proving to be a hero for so many reasons.

Kirby opens the door to the attic, and the hot, stale air nearly knocks her over. It's like having a damp mohair blanket thrown over her head. It's suffocating.

"Right on," Darren says. "I now understand the importance of this mission. You've been *living* up here?"

"I had a fan, but it broke," Kirby says. She scans the room for any embarrassing personal items; if she'd known she would be having guests, and if she'd known one of those guests would be *Darren,* she might have staged the room a little better—hidden the box of Kotex, for example, and maybe draped a bikini top over the back of her chair. Maybe set her paperback copy of *Invisible Man* on her nightstand. Earlier, she'd pulled a copy of Emily Post off the bookshelves at the hotel, thinking it would help her with her job, and she hopes Darren doesn't notice it splayed open on her bed; it seems hopelessly square.

Darren sets down the box, removes the air conditioner from the Styrofoam packing, then surveys the sole window. "Should fit?" he says. He looks to Evan, who shrugs, and Kirby's hopes sink because she's certain Evan didn't bother to measure the window, so her dream of air-conditioning may be short-lived. Darren sets the unit in the window; there are a couple of inches on each side.

Darren turns to Kirby. "Do you have a couple of books?"

This is Kirby's chance! She rummages through an old attaché case of her father's that she uses for her schoolwork. She brought six books for recreational reading but hasn't yet cracked one. She picks two that she thinks will make her seem erudite and well-read—*The Prime of Miss Jean Brodie,* by Muriel Spark, and *The Ginger Man,* by J. P. Donleavy.

Darren accepts them and holds up *The Ginger Man.* "Loved this one," he says. "I loved it so much it seems a shame to use it for this purpose, but this is just temporary. I have a couple of two-by-fours in my garage that I can cut down to fit in the gaps."

Kirby glances at Evan to see if he is hearing all this. Darren reads literature *and* he can cut down some two-by-fours to fit in the gaps of the window that Evan neglected to measure. Evan is standing back with his arms locked across his chest, glaring down at Darren. He isn't even pretending to help anymore. Kirby is annoyed, but a second later, the air conditioner is installed. Darren plugs it in and turns it on. Kirby stands before the blast of deliciously cold air and closes her eyes.

"It's heavenly," she says.

"You're welcome," Evan says. "Please don't make a big deal about it because I can't afford air-conditioning for anyone else. It's just that...it *does* get really hot up here."

"Thank you," Kirby says.

"Thank you," Kirby says to Darren once they're back down on the street.

"Evan bought *you* an air conditioner because he likes you," Darren says. "It's a twenty-six-pound love letter."

"Please stop," Kirby says. "I feel like I have to apologize for Evan. He just stood back and let you do all the work."

Darren shrugs. "I offered. I wanted to impress you."

Kirby grins. "You did?"

He reaches for her hand, and it feels like the most natural thing in the world.

* * *

Because the day is overcast and people aren't at the beach, the line at the Flying Horses Carousel is long. Darren buys their tickets and a box of popcorn for them to share while they watch people of all ages ride around on the antique horses, everyone grabbing silver ring after silver ring from the dispenser and stacking them on their animal's ears. The last ring, Darren explains, is brass, and grabbing the brass ring wins you an extra ride. It's a lot of hoopla for forty cents, he says, but it makes the ride more fun.

"Have you ever gotten the brass ring?" Kirby asks.

"Never once," Darren says. "My mother used to say it was because I was so lucky in the rest of my life."

Kirby says, "I don't think your mother likes me. She gave me a dirty look at the beach the other day."

Darren throws away the empty popcorn box and reclaims Kirby's hand. Her heart not only sings; it hits a soprano's high note. "My mother is protective," he says. "Trust me, it's not you."

Trust me, it is *me,* Kirby thinks. "Have you ever had a serious girlfriend?" she asks.

"One," Darren says. "My freshman year. Her name was Amanda."

Amanda. She sounds white, but Kirby is afraid to ask. She finds she's jealous of Amanda, which is ridiculous. "Did your mother like Amanda?" Kirby asks.

"Hated her," Darren says, and he laughs. "How about you? Have you had a serious boyfriend?"

Officer Scottie Turbo, she thinks. But there's no way she's going to tell that story. However, she finds she can't discount it either. "One," she says. "He was…older. A policeman."

"A policeman?" Darren says. He whistles. "Damn, that's tough to compete with. I'm jealous."

Kirby squeezes his hand. "You shouldn't be," she says. "It's over. And I mean *over*."

When it's finally their turn to ride the carousel, they pick horses next to each other, Darren on the inside and Kirby on the outside.

The carousel starts to spin and Kirby raises her hands over her head. She has never felt this happy.

Neither of them gets the brass ring—it goes to a little girl with custard-colored curls who looks like Buffy from *Family Affair*—but even so, Kirby gets off the carousel feeling like she's lucky in every part of her life.

Darren walks Kirby back to the house on Narragansett Avenue and says, "I'll be by tomorrow with those two-by-fours. And hey, why don't you come to my house for dinner on Sunday night? Sundays we always do steamers."

"Are you sure?" Kirby says. She loves steamer clams. On Nantucket, she and Tiger harvested their own clams using rakes that had belonged to their grandfather. No matter how thoroughly they rinsed them, they always ended up with sand in the bowl, and that was what made them authentic.

"Sure I'm sure," Darren says. "Come at five; that'll give us plenty of time to hang out before you have to go to work. You can get to know my mom a little better, and my dad is way easier than my mom."

His mom is the real *judge,* Kirby thinks. "Okay," she says. "I'll see you Sunday."

Darren leans over and kisses Kirby gently on the lips. Before she can register how good it feels, he's walking away with a wave.

Kirby floats into the house. Darren Frazier kissed her! He invited her for dinner! And the truly transcendent thing is, she doesn't even think of him as *black* anymore. She only thinks of him as Darren.

On a whim, Kirby knocks on Patty's door, and Patty calls out, "Enter at your own risk!"

Kirby finds Patty standing at her bureau wearing only a slip and staring into the mirror.

"Hey," Kirby says. She drops her voice to a whisper. "I have air-conditioning now. Want to come upstairs and luxuriate?"

"I have to go to work," Patty says. "Double feature, *The Italian Job* and *True Grit*." She tries for a light tone but Kirby senses something is wrong. And then she sees the purple bruise on Patty's upper arm.

"Hey," Kirby says, gently taking Patty's elbow so she can get a better look. "What's this?"

Patty yanks her arm away. "I told you," she says. "Role-playing."

"Patty," Kirby says. She locks eyes with Patty in the mirror, which seems easier than talking to her face to face. "Is he hurting you?"

"It's a *game,*" Patty says. "Now, please leave."

Help!

It feels like Blair is being held hostage in her own body. She's thirty-four weeks pregnant. There are still six weeks to go until her due date. She has heard that twins often come early, but she has also heard that first children are often late.

Early, she thinks, *come early. Today, tomorrow, right now.*

Of course, the babies will have no father.

Blair can't *believe* Angus asked her to leave. But then she tries to imagine how *she* would feel if she had walked in on Angus necking with her sister Kirby. It would be unspeakably horrible—much, much worse than finding out about the faceless Trixie.

She half expected there to be a bouquet of flowers waiting for her at All's Fair with a note of apology. When that didn't happen, she figured maybe Angus would show up in person. Blair would pretend to be indignant when she opened the front door. She would make him suffer for a few minutes before she relented and let him inside.

And then they would just pick up where they left off last summer. Angus could work at her grandfather's desk; they could walk into town for ice cream cones, go out for romantic dinners, share a cigarette on the bench at the top of Main Street. Anyone could see that Angus needed a vacation, and Angus and Blair needed a vacation together.

But Angus didn't even call to see if Blair had made it to the island safely, and Blair just hoped that he was bedridden with one of his episodes. It would serve him right.

On Blair's first full day on Nantucket, Exalta takes Jessie to her tennis lesson, and Kate has errands to run in town, so Blair is left alone in the house. She loves All's Fair, but she loves Little Fair even more. Little Fair was the backdrop to all of Blair's adolescent summers. She smoked her first cigarette there and poured her first gin and tonic into one of the jelly jars kept in the cabinet. She let Larry Winter kiss her on the deck overlooking Plumb Lane the summer she was fourteen, and for the rest of that summer, he would show up below that deck in the wee hours of the morning and call up to Blair as though they were Romeo and Juliet. In Little

Fair, she had played countless games of Monopoly and gin rummy with her brother and sister; she had made popcorn in a two-quart pot, burning it half the time; she had read the first novel she had ever truly fallen in love with, *Gone with the Wind;* she had taught Tiger and Jessie and the Dunscombe twins how to make sailors' valentines out of seashells and cardboard boxes.

Blair had been sitting at the small, round kitchen table in Little Fair when her mother told her she was getting married again, to her attorney, David Levin. Blair hadn't been sure how to react. On the one hand, she liked David Levin because David thought Blair was smart; he was always quizzing her on state capitals (Frankfort, Kentucky; Juneau, Alaska) and on the order of various American presidents (Zachary Taylor, Millard Fillmore, Franklin Pierce). On the other hand, she knew she owed some allegiance to her own father, who had died fairly recently. She considered pouting or even crying, but in the end, she had accepted the news cheerfully, and her mother had been visibly relieved. *You're the only child I worried about,* Kate said. *Kirby and Tiger are too young to understand.*

Blair had hoped to have Little Fair all to herself since Kirby and Tiger were gone, but Kate informed her that Mr. Crimmins was living in Little Fair with his grandson.

"Grandson?" Blair said. "You mean..."

"Lorraine's son," her mother said. "His name is Pickford. Pick."

"How old is he?" Blair asked.

"Fifteen," Kate said.

Well, yes, Blair thought. Lorraine had run off about that long ago. Blair had vivid memories of Lorraine; she had been Blair's babysitter once upon a time. Lorraine made delicious lemon sugar cookies. She used to let Blair crack the eggs. Blair still remembers how Lorraine taught her to knock the egg against the rim of the bowl, then place her thumbs on the sides of the fissure and gently pry it open to release the insides—the slimy white and the dense yellow globe of the yolk.

"So where's Lorraine?" Blair asked, and her mother said, "Nobody knows. She and Pick were living in a commune in California and one day this spring, Pick woke up and Lorraine was gone."

"She *left* him?" Blair had not yet embarked on her own journey of motherhood, but she understood how ghastly and unnatural this was. Then again, Lorraine had been a sad and damaged person, resistant to Mr. Crimmins's good-hearted parenting. Lorraine's most distinctive feature was her long dark hair. When she was baking, she kept it in a fat coiled bun, but she would let it down when she ventured out at night, and its length and beauty felt like a secret she was keeping. Lorraine also had a tattoo of a striped bass on the top of her foot. The tattoo fascinated Blair because when Lorraine walked, it looked like the fish was swimming. Blair had never known anyone but military men to have tattoos and she overheard her grandmother saying that the tattoo was a disgrace. *It's obvious the girl has no mother,* Exalta said. Lorraine was always meeting men at Bosun's Locker and staying out so late that she just slipped right into the Charcoal Galley for breakfast. Lorraine didn't like the beach but Exalta used to let Lorraine use the family's thirteen-foot Boston Whaler. Lorraine told Blair that she would take it out by herself, sail all the way up the harbor to Pocomo, and then lie across the bow of the boat in the nude. That detail was so shocking that to this day when Blair thinks of Lorraine Crimmins, she imagines her splayed over the bow of a boat, her mermaid's hair trailing in the water below.

Blair is ravenous. She's so big that she has given up on staying on any kind of diet; she'll worry about losing the weight once the babies are born. In the kitchen, Blair pours a cup of coffee and adds cream and sugar, then toasts some Portuguese bread, smothers it with peanut butter, and tops it with sliced banana. *Stop there,* she thinks. *That's a nice breakfast.* But she can't stop. When she finishes that, she attacks half a roast chicken, pulling the meat from the bones and licking the grease from her fingers. The impeccable manners drilled into her by Exalta and Kate have vanished; now she eats like an animal. In the freezer, she finds a carton of Brigham's butter brickle that is covered with ice crystals. It's clearly left over from the summer before, which makes sense because the only person in the family who likes butter brickle ice cream is Tiger. Blair eats it all, then helps herself to a heaping spoonful of grape jam. She sees a wedge of French brie from Savenor's and she polishes that off with half a box of stale melba toast, probably also left over from last summer.

She hears someone out in the yard. Thinking it's Exalta and Jessie, Blair hurries to clear her mess from the table—it looks like a family of raccoons has gotten into the kitchen—but then out the window, she sees it's a boy, a teenager with golden hair wearing yellow swim trunks and a shell necklace that glows white against his tan skin.

Blair hurries to open the back door. "Good morning!" she calls out. "Pick? How do you do! I'm Blair Whalen, Kate's oldest daughter."

Pick cocks his head. "Oh, hey there, howdy," he says. "You're Jessie's sister?"

Jessie's sister, Kate's daughter, Angus's wife, Exalta's granddaughter, the mother of two squirmy beings presently contained inside of her. In that instant, what Blair wants more than anything is not to be defined by other people.

"Yes," she says. "Pleasure to meet you."

"And you," Pick says. "I was just headed into town to use the pay phone. Wanna come?"

Blair hadn't planned on leaving the house. She's certain her mother and grandmother would frown on it, but for some reason, that suddenly makes it appealing. Blair has just eaten half the contents of the fridge; she could probably use a walk. And the idea of a pay phone has allure. Perhaps she'll try calling Angus. There's a phone in All's Fair, but it's a party line and the last thing Blair wants is someone listening in on her conversations.

"I'd love to," she says. "Let me get my purse."

Blair and Pick stroll down Fair Street to Main. Blair is mindful of the brick sidewalk and Pick holds her by the elbow when she has to step off the curb.

"You're having twins?" Pick says.

"Isn't it obvious?" Blair says.

"You're awfully big," Pick says. "Although I once watched a woman give birth to triplets."

"You...*what?*" Blair says.

"I assisted in a birth where a woman had triplets," Pick says. "My mother is friends with the midwife at the commune we live on in California."

Blair is rendered speechless. Lorraine allowed—or *encouraged*—Pick to assist in a *birth?* Blair also notes Pick's use of the present tense and she wonders if he's going back to California at the end of the summer. She's dying to ask about Lorraine but she holds her tongue all the way to the bank of pay phones alongside the Nantucket Electric Company. There's no one else using the pay phones, so Blair chooses the phone at the far end, and Pick, tactfully, chooses the phone closest to Main Street.

Blair opens her change purse. "Need a dime?"

"I'm planning to reverse the charges," Pick says, and he holds

Blair's gaze for a second. He has the long sun-bleached hair of a surfer and startling ice-blue eyes. He's a beautiful child, really. Blair can see Lorraine in his features and it's like bumping into someone she knew long, long ago. There's something so familiar about Pick that Blair immediately feels protective of him.

"Okay," she says. "Wait for me and we'll walk back together."

When she calls Angus at work, the newly hired receptionist, Ingrid, informs Blair that Dr. Whalen hasn't been in the office since Monday.

This is such startling news that Blair stammers when she asks, "H-h-has he gone to Houston?" That's the only explanation. Maybe the moon launch was moved up or possibly there's some problem that only Angus can fix.

"Houston?" Ingrid says. "No, not yet."

Blair waits, but she offers nothing else. "Thank you, Ingrid," Blair says, and she hangs up.

Blair dials the apartment next but the phone rings and rings.

Blair stares at her distorted reflection in the mirrored front of the phone. Angus must be having an episode. He's lying in bed in their darkened room, unable to move. Blair castigates herself for having wished this on him. She should have realized this would happen as soon as she left; they *both* should have realized this.

Blair calls the apartment again. *Pick up!* she thinks. But there's no answer.

She wishes she had befriended some of their neighbors. The other unit in their building is occupied by a couple from Japan; they're perfectly lovely but they don't speak much English. Blair supposes she could call her father or her friend Sallie to check on Angus, but then she imagines how mortified Angus would be to have either David or Sallie witness his infirmity. Nobody other than Joey knows about Angus's episodes. Should Blair ask *Joey* to check on him?

Blair's next thought is one she has been trying to push away. What if Angus *isn't* at home, immobilized by an episode? What if he's with Trixie? What if Angus and Trixie have gone away together? Angus has access to Blair's trust fund. What if he used it to take Trixie to Aruba or Tahiti?

Blair is hit by a strong wave of nausea and her stomach lurches. Is she going to vomit right here on Union Street? If so, that will be the humiliation that finally breaks her.

Breathe, she tells herself. *In through the nose, out through the mouth.* She presses her swollen feet into the sidewalk and imagines herself as a tree, strong and majestic. She inserts another dime to call Joey Whalen at work.

"Blair," he says when he hears her voice. "What's wrong? Is it time?"

She bites her lower lip. During the picnic on Craigville Beach, Joey described the first time he ever saw her. She had been walking down Newbury Street with Sallie. *You were wearing a sweater of robin's-egg blue,* he said. *Your hair was pulled away from your face with a tortoiseshell barrette. You were laughing and I thought, I want to be the one to make that girl laugh for the rest of her life.*

Remembering these words is a salve on the wound in Blair's heart. Had Angus ever noticed the color of one of Blair's sweaters or appreciated the sound of her laughter? She suspects not. The quality of Angus's love is different—more urgent, more desperate. Or at least it had been until his work consumed him and Blair got pregnant.

Blair is confused. Does she have feelings for Joey? Didn't she feel a secret, delicious rush every time she pulled out the silver lighter with the love note engraved on it? Hadn't she melted away in Joey's arms after only one sip of the cold duck and one bite of the chocolate babka? If Angus hadn't walked in, wasn't it possible that things might have progressed even further, not because her hormones were going haywire and not because she was upset about Trixie, but because she desired him?

"Not time yet," Blair tells Joey. "But I'm settled now and I want to see you. Will you come this weekend? Get a hotel? The Gordon Folger has nice rooms. Maybe not quite as nice as your hotel in Boston, but—"

"Aw, shucks, Blair," Joey says. "I just found out I have to go to Rhode Island this weekend. I have a client in Newport who invited me to sail on his friend's yacht, *Shamrock,* and then there's a cocktail party on the front lawn of one of the Vanderbilt mansions. I want to see you, but I'll have to take a rain check."

Sailing on a yacht. Cocktail party at a Vanderbilt mansion. This could have been Blair's life if she'd married Joey instead of Angus.

Rain check sounds vague and far away. Where is the man who hunted down whipped cream for her cake? She needs that man… now. Blair chastises herself—ten minutes earlier she yearned to be her own person, and yet here she is, pining away for a man, any man. But both of the Whalen brothers are proving unavailable.

"No problem," Blair says coolly. She can at least *sound* nonchalant. "Have fun in Newport." She hangs up and imagines Joey on a rolling green lawn with a Tom Collins in his hand, chatting up girls in patio dresses with hair piled high on top of their heads and long, dangly earrings. She knows there is no way he will give a second thought to his brother's hugely pregnant wife.

She bows her head. She has made *such* a mess of things. She should have listened to her mother and kept her mouth shut, let Angus's little affair run its course. She's so bewildered that she considers just giving the twins up for adoption. *She* will take a lover and disappear for days! She will go to parties with socialites and sail on yachts! She will pretend that none of this *ever happened!*

She turns around in time to see Pick slam down the receiver of his pay phone in obvious frustration.

"Everything okay?" she asks.

He clenches his fists and stares at the phone like he might sock it.

"Pick?" Blair says. It occurs to her then that the person he was trying to call was his mother. "Were you trying to reach Lorraine?"

"Lavender," Pick says. "She changed her name to Lavender."

"Oh," Blair says. "I see."

"I thought maybe she'd be back home by now," he says. "But she's still on the road, I guess." He shrugs. "It doesn't matter."

Who would have thought she and Pick would have so much in common? "My husband asked me to leave," Blair says. "And I thought by now he would have come to his senses, but he hasn't been to work in two days and he wasn't in our apartment. I'm pretty sure he's with his mistress."

"Really?" Pick says.

Blair knows she's being inappropriate but if Pick has seen a woman deliver triplets, then news of a mistress can't come as too much of a shock. "Really," she says.

"My grandfather told me your husband was incredibly smart," Pick says.

"Book smart," Blair says. "Not people smart."

"I'd rather be people smart," Pick says.

Despite her aching heart, Blair smiles at him.

Pick offers Blair his arm and they walk all the way back to the house in a bubble of respectful silence. When they reach All's Fair, Pick peels off. "I'm going to the beach before work," he explains.

"Where do you work?" Blair asks.

"The North Shore Restaurant," he says. "I want to be a chef when I grow up."

"You know what I want to be when I grow up?" Blair says.

He cocks his head, amused. To him, of course, she probably seems grown up already. Little does he know. "What?" he says.

"The mother of someone just like you," she says.

White Rabbit

Jessie expects her mother to forget about their dinner date, but on Thursday morning, before Exalta and Jessie leave for Jessie's tennis lesson, Kate pokes her head out of her bedroom and says, "Mad Hatter tonight, Jessie. Seven o'clock."

This announcement immediately brightens Jessie's mood. She and Exalta take their usual stroll down Main Street, past the Charcoal Galley and Bosun's Locker, but instead of crossing the street where they usually do, Exalta leads them down to Buttner's department store and stops in front of the window.

"How about we buy you a new sundress for tonight?" Exalta says. "We'll stop in after your lesson."

Jessie tries not to let her surprise show on her face. "Thank you, Nonny."

"I love nothing more than a new dress," Nonny says. "It cheers the soul. And everyone is so glum these days. Have you noticed?"

Yes, Jessie has noticed. Blair is a basket case, alternately stuffing her face, sleeping the days away, and weeping in front of the soap operas on television. (*Search for Tomorrow* is her favorite, followed by *The Edge of Night*. She has started talking about the characters as though they're friends of hers.) Kate isn't much better. She's in a fog for the first half of the day and busy getting drunk the second half. It has been nearly two weeks since they've received a letter from Tiger.

The only person who has been in good spirits—unusually good—is Exalta. She saunters down the street humming "I Get a Kick Out of You," her favorite Cole Porter song. *Humming!* Jessie can't understand it.

"Are you excited about bridge tonight, Nonny?" Jessie asks. She doesn't know the first thing about bridge, although she's fond of the snacks—peanuts, pretzels, cheesy crackers, and a rainbow of Jordan almonds—that Nonny puts out in heart-, diamond-, club-, and spade-shaped cut-glass dishes when she hosts bridge back home. Here on Nantucket, Exalta plays bridge at the Anglers' Club, which is a dim, dark-paneled bar overlooking Straight Wharf and the docks of the boat basin. The Nantucket Anglers' Club has mostly male members—Mr. Crimmins belongs to it, as Jessie's late grandfather did—but Nonny is a member as well. However, if it weren't for Thursday-night bridge, Nonny says, she would quit the club. She has never fished a day in her life.

"No one gets *excited* for bridge," Nonny says.

"No?" Jessie says. "But it's a game."

"It's mental calisthenics," Nonny says. "Keeps me sharp." She raises her sunglasses and looks Jessie in the eye. Nonny's eyes are light blue, and she has fine wrinkles in the skin around them. Nonny is so intimidating that Jessie usually avoids her direct gaze. "I realize that you don't like your tennis lessons, Jessica. But it's important that you learn the basic skills and vocabulary of the game. What if, ten years from now, you're invited to a house party on Hilton Head and your host suggests a game of mixed doubles and they need a fourth? You can volunteer confidently because you learned the game when you were young. When you find yourself in a situation such as that, you might think about your old Nonny and be grateful."

Jessie is taken aback by Exalta's words. She begins to wonder if Exalta's insistence on tennis lessons might come from a place of altruism, or even love.

Half an hour later, Jessie experiences the attitude adjustment that Suze has been hoping for. When Suze informs Jessie that she's ready to play her first real games against another junior student, Jessie rises to the challenge instead of protesting. When Jessie discovers that she'll be playing against the loathsome Helen Dunscombe, she clutches her racket like a caveman would his club. Jessie wants to beat Helen Dunscombe, not least because Helen Dunscombe's instructor is Garrison Howe, the molester.

Suze stands on Jessie's side of the court while Garrison stands on Helen's side. Garrison murmurs something to Helen that Jessie can't hear and Suze says, "Just keep a cool head and play your own game."

Jessie takes this advice to heart. She doesn't let herself get caught up in emotion. She allows herself to think of Garrison's inappropriate touching and Helen Dunscombe's asking Jessie when she's getting a nose job only at the instant when the racket meets the ball. She follows through with a ferocity that surprises even Suze, and all of her shots clear the net with an inch or two to spare. Jessie's backhand is weaker than her forehand, but it's clean and technically sound. Her serves land in the far corner of the service box, making them challenging to return. Jessie wins three games in a row handily. As she's bouncing the ball in advance of serving a fourth game, Helen Dunscombe throws her racket in frustration and Garrison shepherds her off the court.

"We need more practice," he calls out to Suze. And then, to Jessie, he says, "Nice backhand."

"I won!" Jessie announces to Exalta after the lesson is over and after Suze has patted her on the back and said, "Strong play, Jessica." Jessie can't help herself; she's beaming. "I beat Helen Dunscombe, three games to love."

Exalta is, as usual, sitting with Mrs. Winter, finishing her second or third or tenth mimosa.

"You'll have to excuse my granddaughter," Exalta says to Mrs. Winter. Exalta signals for the chit and wobbles a little as she stands.

"Excuse me for what?" Jessie asks once they're far enough away from Mrs. Winter. "I thought you would be proud of me. I won. I beat Helen Dunscombe." She swallows. "I'm learning the game, like you wanted."

"That's all fine and good," Exalta says. "But you bragged about it, which is very unbecoming in a girl. I'm not sure where you learned that was okay…or, rather, I fear I do know—from your father's side of the family. Your grandfather wears that horrid gold pinkie ring and Mrs. Levin drives a *Bentley* and they have their names plastered across the synagogue in Boca Raton, I hear. It's all very garish. The proper thing to do when you win at tennis or any other competition, Jessica, is to congratulate your opponent on a game well played and mention your victory to absolutely no one. Do you understand me?"

Jessie's face burns with mortification. She went into her lesson with such confidence and it had been satisfying to win against a person she disliked—*two* people she disliked. She's embarrassed because she knows Exalta is right—she was a braggart—but she hates that Exalta attributes any unflattering behavior in Jessie to her father or, in this case, her grandparents. Jessie didn't even realize Exalta *knew* her other grandparents, Bud and Freda Levin, whom Jessie calls Mimi and Grandpop. Grandpop used to be a jeweler and he'd owned a store on Boylston Street, and Mimi used to drive a Bentley, but now they live in Florida on a golf course and Grandpop doesn't work and Mimi has cataracts so she's forfeited her driver's license.

"Jessica," Exalta says. "Do you understand me?"

A nod won't suffice, Jessie can tell. "Yes," she whispers.

When they walk past Buttner's on the way home, Exalta doesn't mention stopping in to buy a new dress and Jessie doesn't remind her. The morning has been ruined.

By the time they reach home, Jessie's feelings about Exalta have reached a new low. She *hates* her grandmother. Her grandmother is a terrible person and most likely an anti-Semite. She's probably not as bad as a Nazi, but she might be the kind of person who would have turned in Anne Frank's family if she'd discovered them hiding in the attic.

Exalta's mood has remained buoyant. She steps into the kitchen, where Kate and Blair are drinking glasses of orange juice, and says, "Let's all go to the beach!"

"I can't, Nonny," Blair says. "I can't go anywhere."

"Nonsense," Exalta says. "It's a beautiful day. Let's drive out to Smith's Point in the Scout. That way you won't have to walk. We'll deliver you right to the water's edge. We'll pack a picnic." She looks at Kate. "Do we have groceries?"

"Yes, Mother," Kate says. "I have hard-boiled eggs and sliced ham and a fresh loaf of Portuguese from the bakery. And we still have half a melon."

"Wonderful," Exalta says. She studies Blair. "You haven't even dropped yet. We still have weeks before we see those babies."

Blair looks morose. "I can't swim. I have no bathing suit."

"You can get your feet wet," Exalta says. "It'll be good for you."

"I'm not going," Jessie says. "I have my summer reading to do. *Anne Frank: The Diary of a Young Girl.*" She stomps out of the kitchen to the backyard and slams the door behind her even though stomping and slamming are not allowed. She stands on the brick patio for a second, waiting for Kate to appear to either reprimand her or ask what's wrong. But enough time passes that Jessie figures she has gotten away with it. As she crosses the lawn to Little Fair, she sees Pick's bike is gone, but even so, she hopes to find him upstairs, maybe getting ready to make lunch.

Little Fair, however, is deserted. Jessie takes the tin of Jays potato chips off the shelf and absconds with it to her bedroom.

Her book is splayed open on her bed. She has reached the part where Anne is beginning to have feelings for Peter, which matches how Jessie feels about Pick. Like Pick, Peter is older. Jessie hasn't come out and asked Pick what religion he is but she can tell he isn't Jewish. She suspects he might not be Christian either. If he lived in a commune, they might have practiced their own religion.

Jessie tries to read but is too agitated. She is *so* angry at Exalta, and when she feels this way, there is only one cure. She can hear Exalta, Kate, and Blair going back and forth between the house and the street, where the Scout is parked. They're leaving for the beach without her. Jessie loves Smith's Point not only because they can drive right onto it but also because there are big, pounding waves on the ocean side and calmer water on the sound side and she can easily walk between the two. Tuckernuck is so close that, with binoculars, Jessie can see the people over there riding on the sand roads in their bare-bones Jeeps. Smith's Point also has shells and driftwood for collecting, and the sand is flat, good for walks. Despite this, Jessie is glad they're leaving her behind.

She waits until they all pile into the Scout with an umbrella, a stack of towels, the picnic basket, and a Styrofoam cooler. Blair seems to have a hard time climbing into the back seat and for a second, Jessie thinks Blair will have to stay home, but she manages to hoist herself up and Jessie silently cheers. Kate gets in the driver's side and the Scout takes off down Plumb Lane, then turns right onto Fair. Jessie waits five minutes, ten minutes, twelve minutes—just in case they've forgotten something and have to turn around. She predicts they'll be gone three hours at least.

Jessie slips out of Little Fair. The door to Mr. Crimmins's room is open but he's not home. During the day he works as a caretaker at other people's houses and is usually gone until dinnertime. Jessie pauses in the doorway, wondering if there is anything of value she could steal from Mr. Crimmins. She sees only a novel, *The Godfather,* a drinking glass by the bed, and the clothes in the closet. None of it is appealing, and it's not Mr. Crimmins she's after, anyway.

She goes back into All's Fair through the kitchen and sees that her mother has left her a ham and butter sandwich wrapped in wax paper and a spear of dill pickle, which is Jessie's favorite lunch. She takes a bite of the pickle but leaves the sandwich for later. She can't afford to get distracted.

In the den, she considers the whirligigs. Which one would Exalta miss the most? Probably the man on the tricycle—but what would Jessie do with it? Hide it somewhere in Little Fair? Bury it in the yard? Put it out with the trash? Exalta would immediately suspect that Jessie had taken it, and an inquisition would follow.

Then Jessie gets an idea.

She tiptoes up the stairs and down the hall to her grandmother's room. She turns the knob, steps inside, and closes the door behind her. The room is dim and cool; Exalta keeps her curtains drawn and her air conditioner running, even though she's not home. The rest of them are forbidden to do this—it's wasteful!—but the rules don't apply to Exalta because she owns the house. Kirby has long proclaimed that if she ever inherits the house, she's going to run the air conditioners full blast all day, every day.

Jessie takes a look around. She has been in this room only a few times before. There are two twin beds, side by side. They are so high off the ground that Exalta uses a step stool to reach hers. There's an armoire and a dressing table on top of which is a three-sided mirror, a silver hairbrush, and a matching hand mirror.

Jessie lifts the hand mirror. It's an antique, engraved on the back with Exalta's mother's initials, KFB, for Katharine Fox Baskett.

Over by the closet door is a triangular table on which Exalta keeps her jewelry. She brings only a few pieces with her because Nantucket is casual, and the rings she keeps in the porcelain boxes at home, for example, would be out of place here. But there on the table is the burgundy velvet box. When Jessie opens the box, she sees her gold-knot necklace with the diamond.

Jessie removes the necklace from the box but leaves the box itself, closed, on the triangular table. Then Jessie tiptoes out of the room and hurries back to Little Fair, where she wraps the necklace in a hankie and tucks the hankie into her drawstring purse. She will wear the necklace to dinner.

It isn't really stealing, Jessie tells herself, because the necklace is *hers*. But taking it without Exalta's knowledge or permission has done the trick. Jessie feels better.

Exalta leaves for her bridge game at five and Blair orders two pizzas from Vincent's to be delivered at six. Kate and Blair exchanged words about why Blair ordered *two* pizzas.

You're enormous, Kate said bluntly.

I'm hungry, Mother, Blair responded. *I'm eating for three.*

Jessie puts on her blue seersucker sundress from the year before but it's tight around the top, so Jessie has no choice but to go down to the kitchen and ask her mother and sister for help with the zipper.

"You've outgrown this," Kate says.

"You're getting *breasts,*" Blair says. She turns to Kate. "Have you bought her a bra?"

"She's only twelve years old," Kate says.

"Thirteen," Jessie says. Her cheeks are burning with both embarrassment and pleasure. She's getting breasts!

"You need to take her to Buttner's to get her a training bra, Mother," Blair says.

Kate sighs. "I'm not ready for this."

"Fine." Blair turns to Jessie. "I'll take you."

"Find something else to wear," Kate says.

Jessie goes back upstairs to put on her only other choice, a white eyelet A-line sundress, which is a bit more forgiving. She secures the chain around her neck, then studies herself in the mirror. She wishes Pick were here to see her but he has already left for work. Jessie should have suggested they go to the North Shore Restaurant.

When Jessie and her mother arrive at the Mad Hatter, the maître d' greets Kate with a bow. "Good evening, Mrs. Foley," he says.

"Mrs. *Levin,*" Kate says. "Come on, now, Shep, I've been Mrs. Levin for fourteen years." Her tone is light; she seems unbothered. It was a simple mistake, and Shep is an older gentleman who has known Jessie's mother since she was Katie Nichols. But Jessie can't help studying Shep. Does he seem like an anti-Semite?

"Of course. I'm sorry, Mrs. Levin. This must be young Jessica Levin, then. If I'm not mistaken, you're celebrating Jessica's birthday."

"Yes, correct, thank you, Shep," Kate says, and she ushers Jessie forward.

The Mad Hatter is Jessie's favorite restaurant because walking into it feels like entering another world. There are detailed murals on the walls depicting scenes from *Alice's Adventures in Wonderland* and *Through the Looking-Glass,* not only the Mad Hatter himself but also an imperious-looking Queen of Hearts, the White Rabbit, and a rendition of the Jabberwock that Jessie was afraid of when she was younger. The previous year, when they came here for dinner, Tiger and Kirby told Jessie that Lewis Carroll, the author, had written the books while smoking opium.

"That's why this world is so disturbed," Kirby said. "It's all about mind-altering drugs."

"It is?" Jessie said. She wasn't sure if they were telling her the truth; sometimes they told her things to see if she was gullible enough to believe them. Jessie had thought the Alice books were children's stories, like "Goldilocks and the Three Bears."

"Take the Cheshire cat, for example," Tiger said. "Do you know why he's smiling?"

At that point, Kate had told them to stop putting ideas in Jessie's head, which meant, Jessie assumed, that what they were saying was true.

Now their waitress arrives, wearing a blue dress with a white pinafore. She tells them her name is Alice, then she lowers her voice to a whisper and says, "It's *really* Alice."

Something is a little off with Alice, Jessie thinks. Her voice sounds spacey and her eyes are red, like Kirby's when she smokes marijuana. Jessie remembers one time after Kirby had been smoking that Exalta noticed her red eyes and asked if she had been swimming in a pool. Kirby and Tiger—and even Blair—had cracked up about that later, and "swimming in a pool" became their code for getting high.

Has their waitress Alice been swimming in a pool? Jessie wonders. She wishes her siblings were there so she could make them laugh by asking.

Kate orders a martini with two olives and Jessie orders a Shirley Temple with two cherries and Alice giggles. Kate scans the other tables and the chairs around the sunken Jabberwocky bar, but there is no one she knows, and she seems to relax. When her martini arrives, she loosens up even more. She actually *smiles*. Jessie realizes she hasn't seen her mother smile since the letter from the Selective Service arrived.

"Cheers to you, my darling," Kate says. "Happy birthday!"

It's ten days after Jessie's birthday, but this definitely qualifies as a case of better late than never. Jessie touches her mother's glass with her own, and together, they drink.

The relish tray arrives. Using the tiny, three-pronged fork, Jessie plucks out a piece of pickled cauliflower. She doesn't particularly care for the taste, but her siblings used to fight over the cauliflower, and because of this, it has become a prize.

Next, Alice brings the plate with the whipped cheese and an assortment of crackers. Kate nudges the plate closer to Jessie and says, "Go crazy, darling," because Jessie loves nothing more than the zesty cheese spread on an onion-salt cracker. She lifts the delicate piece of paper covering the cheese—it's stamped with a picture of the Mad Hatter—fixes herself two crackers, then offers one to her mother, who shakes her head. The basket of rolls is the next present to arrive—Nonny calls them "presents," because this is the food you get just for sitting down. Jessie has long wondered why anyone would order food you have to pay for when you could easily make a meal out of the relish tray, the cheese and crackers, and the rolls. Included in the Mad Hatter breadbasket are homemade cinnamon rolls, which were Tiger's particular favorite. Although Jessie wants one very badly, she leaves them both, as if Tiger might magically appear from the war and sit down to enjoy them. Instead, Jessie helps herself to one of the warm, pillowy Parker House rolls. She pulls it apart, then breaks it into smaller pieces and butters each piece as she goes, just as Nonny has taught her. She is showboating a little, willing Kate to notice her impeccable manners, but Kate is in a trance. She drains her first martini and orders a second, which Alice promptly delivers. Jessie's spirits sink because she senses her birthday dinner is going to end with her mother getting drunk and weepy and making a scene here at the Mad Hatter, and then they won't be able to return for the rest of the summer.

But the second martini might have contained a shot of adrenaline, because Kate perks up.

"Darling," she says. "I want you to tell me everything."

"Everything?" Jessie says.

"Yes, everything that's going on in that beautiful, brilliant mind of yours. Blair said you're getting breasts and now I can see that's true." Kate gazes at Jessie's chest and Jessie steels herself for questions about the necklace, but none come.

"I never told your grandmother anything," her mother says. "I kept secrets all through growing up, even silly things like Timothy Whitby down the street teaching me to drive in his Studebaker, and do you know what that did? It made me good at keeping secrets." Kate picks the olives out of her martini and pulls one off the toothpick with her teeth. Jessie is glad to see her mother eating something because she hasn't touched the relish tray, the crackers, or the bread. "And I'm still keeping secrets now, even though I'm a grown-up. Big secrets."

"You are?" Jessie says. She tries to imagine what kinds of secrets Kate could be keeping, but she comes up blank.

Kate nods, eats the second olive. "That's why I want you to know you can tell me anything, and I mean *anything,* and I won't be angry. I'm still going to love you just as much as I already do. Blair and Kirby are like me, you know, they keep secrets, but Tiger tells me everything and you will too, won't you?" She blinks rapidly. "Won't you please, Jessie, tell me everything?"

Jessie thinks about what it would be like to tell her mother *everything. Back home, in Brookline, Leslie made up a game where we all took something without paying for it.* The "game," Jessie knows, wasn't a game; it was stealing. *And even though I knew it was wrong, I liked it. So now, whenever I'm upset, I steal. For example, when my tennis instructor Garrison Howe wrapped his arms around me and rubbed . . .*

Jessie feels her face grow warm even thinking the words. There is *absolutely no way* she can tell her mother about Garrison.

Alice arrives with the blackboard menu and Jessie pretends to consider the options—veal Oscar, duck à l'orange, coquilles St. Jacques—as does Kate, but they both know what they're ordering because they always order the same thing: a Caesar salad to share, the shrimp scampi for Kate, and the filet mignon with béarnaise sauce and a baked potato with sour cream and chives for Jessie.

"One strawberry shortcake for dessert, please," Kate adds, because everyone knows the kitchen runs out of strawberry shortcake fast so you have to call dibs on it right away.

Alice writes down their order on her little pad, then reads it back. "'Caesar, two forks; one scampi, one filet medium rare with baked. And one shortcake, two forks.'" She gives them an inscrutable smile. "Remember what the Dormouse said."

"What?" Jessie asks.

Alice breaks into a fit of giggles; her tiny red eyes scrunch up and leak tears.

"I'll have another martini," Kate says.

Jessie finishes her roll and eats another cracker, even though she's getting full. She will never eat all of her steak, which is fine. She'll have it boxed up to go and maybe she can share it with Pick later.

I have a crush on Pick. Jessie thinks about telling her mother *this* but decides against it. If Jessie admits to having grown-up feelings, she suspects she will be whisked right out of Little Fair and forced to sleep next to Nonny.

Jessie realizes it's fine if she doesn't tell her mother everything, or even anything, because after Alice drops off the third martini, Kate smiles at Jessie in a dreamy way that lets Jessie know she's forgotten she even asked. For some reason, however, Jessie decides she doesn't want to be let off the hook.

"I do have something to tell you," Jessie says.

Kate snaps to attention and leans over the table. "Have you gotten your period, darling?"

"No." Jessie can't believe what she's about to say. But yes, she must say it. The words are collecting at the back of her throat like an angry crowd. Thirteen, she reminds herself, is an age of maturity and responsibility. "Nonny won't let me sign the name Levin at the club," Jessie says. "Because she's anti-Semitic."

Jessie isn't sure what she expected—shocked indignation, anger, incredulousness—but it isn't her mother laughing. Kate throws her head back to expose her neck and her pearls. "Ha-ha-ha-ha-ha!"

A lump rises in Jessie's throat. "Mom," she says in a wavering voice. "It's my *name*." *It's your name too,* she wants to say, but Kate, of course, has other names to choose from, so she might not feel as attached to Levin as Jessie does.

Kate notes Jessie's tone or perhaps the expression on her face and sobers. "Yes, darling, it's your name. You should be very proud of it and I will have a chat with your grandmother. I wouldn't go so far as to say your grandmother is an anti-Semite, although it's true she's not fond of your father."

Jessie is aghast to hear the words spoken so plainly. "But why not? Dad is—"

"The most wonderful man in the world," Kate says. "You and I agree on that. But your grandmother was partial to Wilder."

Jessie sinks into herself. Alice shows up with the wide wooden bowl and the ingredients for the Caesar salad. With a heavy heart, Jessie watches her surprisingly adept performance. Alice crushes the garlic and anchovies into a paste, streams the olive oil from a dramatic height, cranks a pepper grinder that's as long as Jessie's arm, adds an egg yolk and a teaspoon of French mustard, then tosses the crisp romaine lettuce until the leaves are evenly coated. For the finale, she shaves near-translucent pieces of Parmesan on top. The tableside preparation of the Caesar is one of the reasons Jessie loves the Mad Hatter more than any other restaurant, and yet tonight, she is too preoccupied to enjoy it.

Exalta was partial to Wilder Foley. So where does that leave Jessie? Nowhere good.

Once Alice goes, Kate regards the plate of salad before her. "Of course, Nonny had no idea what Wilder was really like. He was...well, he was a bastard is what he was."

Jessie tries not to be shocked at the swear word. She has never heard anyone in the family say one bad thing about Wilder Foley.

He was a career soldier—an infantryman in World War II, a lieutenant in Korea—and that automatically made him a hero. And he had died so tragically, a gun accident in his workshop, when Jessie's siblings were so young, when *he* was so young. Only thirty-three years old. Jessie has mixed feelings about the death of Wilder Foley. It's a sad and upsetting story and she feels broken-hearted for Blair, Kirby, and Tiger—but if Wilder hadn't died, Jessie wouldn't exist.

Blair kept a picture of Wilder Foley in her room growing up; in it, he wore a jacket covered with ribbons and medals. Jessie used to stare at the picture, trying to pick out the features that were replicated in her siblings. Wilder Foley was very, *very* handsome, much handsomer than David Levin, and so Jessie had always imagined that Kate had merely settled for the soulful, dark-eyed attorney after losing her gorgeous first husband. To hear her call Wilder a bastard is eye-opening, to say the very least.

"What did he do?" Jessie asks.

Kate sucks back the rest of her martini. "What didn't he do?" she asks, and then she nods at Jessie's plate. "Eat up."

They walk home with three to-go boxes: the scampi, the steak and potato, and the strawberry shortcake. Jessie decides she will wait up for Pick; Kate will forget all about the food, and Jessie can stash it in the fridge at Little Fair. Jessie isn't sure if her birthday dinner was a success or not; she's just glad they made it out of the restaurant without incident.

When they turn onto Fair Street, Kate says, "I know what you're thinking."

Jessie hopes this isn't true.

"You're thinking I didn't get you a birthday present," Kate says.

"I don't want anything," Jessie says. She touches her grandmother's necklace and thinks about her Tree of Life pendant and about the record album she has yet to listen to. The gifts themselves don't mean as much as the thoughts behind them. Jessie knows her mother loves her. Jessie also knows her mother is sad. All Jessie wants is for Tiger to come home, but if she says this, her mother will cry.

"I'm going to give you the gift of freedom," Kate says. They are now standing in front of St. Paul's Episcopal, their church, so the sidewalk is lit. She turns to face Jessie and takes both of her hands. "As long as you continue to go to tennis lessons with Nonny, I'll let you ride your bike to the beach by yourself in the afternoons."

"You will?" Jessie says.

"I will."

Jessie can't believe it. No more afternoons sitting home with Anne Frank. She can go meet Pick. That's all she's thinking. She can be with Pick.

When they get home, Kate goes up to bed and Jessie heads over to Little Fair with the bag of leftovers. She's dizzy with excitement. It's nine thirty already, so there's only an hour left until Pick gets home from work. Jessie is relieved to see the door to Mr. Crimmins's bedroom is closed; this means he's asleep or he's reading his novel and will soon be asleep. Jessie climbs the stairs quietly, *quietly,* and turns on only one light, the light over the sink, which is a forty-watt bulb that bathes the upstairs in twilight. She puts the shortcake in the fridge and leaves the entrées out; their boxes are still warm.

She hears footsteps on the stairs and scurries to her bedroom, where she lurks in the doorway. If it's Mr. Crimmins or her mother, she'll pretend she's asleep.

She sees a white T-shirt and dungarees. It's Pick. He must sense or smell the food because he goes right over to the boxes on the counter. Jessie steps out of the bedroom.

"Pick," she whispers.

He whips around, takes a look at her, then whistles. "Whoa, I almost didn't recognize you. You're all dressed up. You look really pretty, Jess."

Jessie feels like she might faint. He called her Jess, not Jessie, and she loves how grown-up the name sounds. "Thanks," she says. "I had dinner with my mother." She steps into the pool of lemony light so that Pick can better see her "all dressed up." He stares at her as she gets closer. He's going to kiss her; Jessie is certain of it. There's a yearning in his eyes. He likes her, she thinks. He likes her back!

She's unsure of how close to get and whether to stay silent or tell him to help himself to the leftovers. She brings her hand to her throat to touch the gold knot with the diamond, but something is wrong.

Wait, she thinks. *Wait!*

Jessie wraps both of her hands around her neck. Suddenly nothing else matters—not Pick, not the absence of letters from Tiger, not her mother's promise of freedom.

Nonny's necklace is gone.

Part Two

July 1969

Summertime Blues

The good news is that Kirby's air conditioner is doing its job. She has taken to calling the attic her igloo. As promised, Darren showed up the day after the carousel ride with the two-by-fours, and Evan must have let him in because when Kirby returned from the state beach that day, the unit was snug in the window and the novels had been returned to her bedside table with a note lying on top: *Enjoy! XO, D.*

The bad news is that this was nearly a week ago and Kirby hasn't heard from Darren since. She had thought the invitation over to his house for steamers was all set, but when Sunday evening rolled around, he hadn't called or stopped by to confirm the time. Even so, Kirby had gotten dressed and spent a torturous hour waiting on the front porch and listening for the phone to ring inside. She had considered strolling over to the Methodist Campground and simply knocking on the door of the blue house, but after consulting her Emily Post, she concluded that this would not do at all. Darren's plans must have changed. Maybe the Frazier family had decided on pizza instead or maybe someone had gotten sick...or maybe Darren had decided that he didn't like her after all. She had been thrilled with the *XO* preceding his initial in the note, but maybe she'd been imbuing those letters with too much meaning.

Or maybe, on hearing that Darren had invited Kirby for dinner, his mother had said, "Absolutely not."

If she had, it might have been because Kirby is white.

Or it might have been because Dr. Frazier knew that Kirby was Clarissa Bouvier.

Kirby tries to let thoughts of Darren go. He's not the reason she's on Martha's Vineyard, after all. If Kirby had learned anything from Officer Scottie Turbo, it was this: Never let a man be responsible for your happiness. Kirby will be responsible for her own happiness from now on.

There are good things to think about. Kirby loves her job. She enjoys the guests, and her friendship with Mr. Ames has earned her a ride to and from work and the opportunity to nap mid-shift in the back office without worry. In her first review by Mrs. Bennie, Kirby earned high marks. Mrs. Bennie let Kirby know that the inn would be getting even busier now that July was upon them, and the guests would be more renowned. There was a rumor that Frank Sinatra and Mia Farrow might be checking in, and Senator Kennedy was due to visit in two weeks.

"When we have VIP guests," Mrs. Bennie said, "we must exercise discretion. Their privacy is our number-one priority."

"Understood," Kirby said. She found it hard to believe that she might be the only person standing between Frank Sinatra or Senator Kennedy and a potential scandal—but one never knew. One couple who'd checked in under the names Mr. Light and Miss Shadow had informed Kirby that they would be experimenting with LSD during their stay. They'd asked to be left completely alone for thirty-six hours—no newspaper drop-off, no housekeeping. Kirby had assured them she would personally see to it that they were not disturbed. She worried that she was being too lenient, too liberal, too indulgent. What if one or the other of them had a bad trip and did a swan dive off the roof? Would it be

Kirby's fault? But all had apparently gone just fine, and when the couple checked out, Miss Shadow had slipped Kirby an envelope containing a fifty-dollar bill.

When Kirby isn't at work or asleep in her own private igloo, she hangs out with Patty and Luke. She worries about the role-playing or whatever it is they're doing when they're alone, but Kirby has learned that no one can judge a relationship except for the two people in it. And there's no denying that Luke Winslow makes life exciting. One Monday afternoon, Luke appeared in the Willys Jeep with a cooler full of beer and a fat joint and drove Patty and Kirby all the way out to the cliffs of Gay Head. Kirby had heard all about the cliffs and they did not disappoint. They were striated in earth tones—ocher, rust, brick red—and dropped straight down to the churning ocean. The three of them sat on a blanket, cracked some beers, passed the joint around, and experienced the majesty of the place—breathtaking, ancient, holy. When Luke and Patty started necking, Kirby closed her eyes and fell back on the blanket, enjoying the sun on her face. She was nearly asleep when she heard them sneak off, and she was envious, not only because they were having sex in the great outdoors with an unparalleled view of Mother Nature, but also because they had each other and she had no one.

Being responsible for her own happiness, she has realized, is a lonely proposition.

Patty must sense Kirby's loneliness because the following night she invites Kirby out for dinner and dancing with herself, Luke, and her brother Tommy. They go to the Dunes restaurant at the Katama Shores Motor Inn. It's an old army barracks that has been converted into a modern, low-slung motel overlooking the ocean. The Dunes has a curved wall of windows, delicious finger foods, and live music, all of which makes Kirby feel like she's walking into a sophisticated cocktail party.

Kirby *loves* the vibe. She thinks, *I'm fine! I'm happy!*

Luke gets them a table for four and Tommy sits next to Kirby and pulls his chair close to hers. Tommy is a male version of Patty. He's a little overweight with a mop of dark hair and freckles. He's not bad-looking or good-looking; he's just a regular guy whose night has clearly been *made* by meeting Kirby.

"You're a knockout," he says. His mouth is right at Kirby's ear, which Kirby thinks is a bit forward, although it's difficult to hear with the music. There's a four-person band playing songs by the Beatles, the Turtles, and the Cyrkle.

"Oh, thanks," Kirby says. For no good reason, the compliment sends her into a downward spiral of Darren-thought. After Scottie Turbo, Kirby was sure she would never like anyone again, but she likes Darren and she thought Darren liked her. Until his disappearing act. Kirby has gone over every word of their last conversation hundreds of times, wondering what she misconstrued, and she can't figure it out. Maybe she isn't meant for someone as quality as Darren. Maybe her life will be populated by ho-hum fellows like Tommy O'Callahan.

Across the table, Patty and Luke are enclosed in their usual love bubble. Luke summons the waitress in her high white patent leather boots and orders something; Kirby can't hear what it is, but she hopes it's potent. Her only hope is to get drunk.

The band plays "Red Rubber Ball."

"Wanna dance?" Tommy asks.

"Sure," Kirby says, though she doesn't at all. The song is neither fast nor slow, though Tommy, of course, chooses to dance slowly. He encircles Kirby with his beefy arms and pulls her close. She makes space between them the way her mother taught her to when she was eleven years old. She regrets agreeing to dance; she should have had a drink first.

"So," Kirby says. She isn't sure what to ask Tommy O'Callahan. She knows he's Patty's brother, two years older, seventh in line behind Joseph, Claire, Matthew, John, Kevin, and Sara and ahead of Rose and Patty. She knows he grew up in South Boston and attended UMass Boston before coming to the Vineyard to manage the Strand movie theater. She considers asking about his political views—what does he think about the war? How does he feel about Nixon?—because his answers will either rule him out as a boyfriend entirely or make her more kindly disposed toward him. But the setting is too convivial for such dreary questions and Kirby is in such a fragile state of mind that talking about the war might break her. "How did you meet Luke?"

"Dumb luck," Tommy says. "I was on my way over on the ferry and Luke approached me and said he was looking for roommates. So me and my buddy Eugene took a look at the place, and I mean, there was no question. Fifteen bucks a week for that house? *With* a maid? It's too good to be true. I pinch myself every day."

Luke makes only thirty dollars a week in rent, Kirby thinks. She wonders if he gives the money to his parents or pockets it. It's odd that Luke picked two strangers off the boat to be his roommates, isn't it? Doesn't he have *friends?* He's wealthy, good-looking, a man of leisure. Something doesn't add up.

"Is he a nice guy?" Kirby asks.

Tommy shrugs. "Sure."

The song ends and Kirby couldn't be happier. They head back to the table, where four enormous electric-blue cocktails are waiting. Kirby sits down and takes a healthy slug of hers. A platter of shrimp arrives and another of Swedish meatballs. Patty locks eyes with Kirby and cocks her head toward Tommy, unmistakably asking, *Do you like him?*

Kirby casts her eyes down at her cocktail. She would like to swim in it.

Three cocktails, four shrimp, and six meatballs later, Kirby is in a better frame of mind. The band plays "I Am the Walrus," and Kirby gets up to dance without checking to see if Tommy is following her, though of course he is, and he gamely tries to imitate her moves, which include floating her arms over her head one at a time as if they were tentacles. She also spins and dips, covering large swaths of the dance floor, leaving the other dancers bemused and Tommy visibly frustrated. He eventually gives up and skulks off, and Kirby finishes the dance by herself up front. When she returns to the table, Tommy is gone and Patty looks miffed.

"He went for a walk on the beach," Patty says. "He told me you were ignoring him."

A fresh round of drinks arrives and all Kirby wants to do is sit down and enjoy hers. She watches Luke feed Patty a meatball off a toothpick and decides she can't stay and watch that kind of grotesque display, so she goes outside to hunt down Tommy and apologize.

She finds him at the entrance to Katama Beach, lighting a cigarette.

"I'd love one, thanks," Kirby says, as flirtatiously as possible.

Tommy adds a second cigarette to his mouth and lights both without comment. Kirby instantly likes him better.

"Want to walk?" she asks as he gives her the cigarette.

He nods and kicks off his loafers. Kirby puts a hand on his shoulder as she pries the straps of her sandals off her heels. Then they trudge through the cool sand to the beach. Kirby loves the beach at night, always has. On Nantucket, she would go to bon-fires out in Madequecham, pulling on jeans and an Irish fisher-man's sweater over her bikini. She and her friends would drink beer, roast hot dogs on sticks, sing along as their friend Lincoln played corny old songs on his guitar *(Michael, row the boat ashore...).* They passed joints around, then bags of chips or paper sacks of snickerdoodles from Aime's Bakery. Always, someone would strip down and dash for the water, and Kirby was never far behind. You'd think the water would be colder at night, but in fact, it felt warmer. It was also scary. She couldn't see the size of the waves coming up, or her own legs, or what lurked beneath. There was a very real fear of sharks, who were rumored to feed at night. But this only heightened Kirby's sense of exhilaration. There was nothing quite like floating on her back, gazing up at the stars and moon.

She misses those nights, so much so that she considers asking Tommy to swim. They'd have to go in their underwear, she sup-poses, or go nude. She dismisses the idea.

Instead, they walk—to the right, which is west. Tommy doesn't speak or reach for Kirby's hand and Kirby figures he's probably sore, but she isn't going to apologize for dancing. This isn't a date, not really. They are only adjuncts to Patty and Luke's growing pas-sion. Kirby thinks briefly about sharing her concerns about Luke with Tommy but he's Patty's brother and the last thing he likely wants to discuss is his sister's sex life.

Kirby meanders toward the water and gets her feet wet. The wa-ter glows where she kicks it up.

"Look," she says. "Phosphorescence."

Tommy ventures in and the two of them spend a few minutes splashing, laughing when the water lights up. Then, on the beach, Kirby spies the bone-white shape of a quahog shell.

"Excellent," she says, picking it up. "I've been looking for one of these."

"Ashtray?" Tommy asks.

"Soap dish, actually," Kirby says. She rinses it at the water's edge; it's perfectly intact, with a swirl of blue and white, like the ocean itself, inside the shell. "I'm on a tight budget."

Tommy laughs at this and Kirby knows she's forgiven. He takes her hand and pulls her to him and she knows what's coming. Sure enough, when she lifts her face, he kisses her. His timing isn't bad—it's dark, they're on the beach with their ankles awash in sparkling water. Things couldn't really get any more romantic. It's his execution that's the problem. His mouth is open too wide; his tongue is thick and meaty and he seems intent on choking Kirby with it. She tolerates a second or two of this, wondering if things will magically improve, ruminating on the mystery of human chemistry. Will Tommy someday meet a woman who thinks his kissing is amazing and who can't get enough of it?

Kirby presses her hand to his chest and, to his credit, he stops.

"We should get back," Kirby says.

"I guess you're right," Tommy says miserably.

A few days later, Kirby hears from Rajani.

"The Aldworths have taken their boat *and* their bratty kids to Cuttyhunk," she says. "They're paying me to stay at their house with their cat."

"You're kidding," Kirby says. She has had so little contact with Rajani that she knows almost nothing about the family she nannies for; she didn't know they owned a boat, that their kids were bratty, or that they had a cat. All she knew was that they lived in Chilmark.

"Why don't you come over?" Rajani says. "We can swim at their private beach and then go to Menemsha for lunch. They left me the keys to their Porsche."

Kirby doesn't have to be asked twice. She borrows Patty's bike and rides all the way out to the address Rajani gave her on Tea Lane. It's farther away than she thought, but it's pretty along State Road; she passes rolling farmland and stone walls, ponds and big trees. The landscape is different from Nantucket, where the brush is low and windswept and most of the trees are scrub pines.

Finally, Kirby turns onto Tea Lane and pedals all the way out to the water. At the end of a shell driveway, the house number she's looking for is carved into a stone. A little farther down, the house itself comes into view. It's palatial—three stories, with a turret at one end. Around the side is a swimming pool and tennis court. As Kirby is kickstanding her bike, Rajani appears in the entrance, her arms spread wide.

"Welcome to my home," she says. "Away from home."

The house is grand. There's a white piano and leopard-skin rugs and what Kirby thinks is an Andy Warhol hanging in the kitchen next to the fridge, in the same place that another family might hang their children's crayon drawings. The kitchen is modern. All of the appliances are avocado green, a color that pops against the white tile floor and the pink-and-orange mosaic backsplash.

Kirby follows Rajani outside to the deck. The pool is off to the left. Down three steps and over one small dune is the ocean.

"Are you kidding me?" Kirby says. "You work here every day? Why didn't you tell me?"

"Too busy running after Eric and Randy," she says. "The demon twins."

Kirby is stunned. She was wowed by Luke Winslow's place on Nashaquitsa Pond, and in some ways, she prefers it to this. Who needs a grand piano and leopard-skin rugs and a Warhol in a *summer home?* Kirby always felt privileged growing up because of their house on Fair Street, right in town, and the mural in the living room, and their long legacy at the Field and Oar Club. But now that she has seen this house and Luke's house, she understands that Fair Street is nothing special.

"Wanna swim?" Rajani asks.

Kirby strips down to her bikini and races for the water.

At lunchtime, Rajani plucks the car keys out of a ruby-colored glass bowl ("I think the Aldworths have key parties," she whispers) and they climb into Mrs. Aldworth's Porsche 911 and zip across Chilmark to Menemsha.

Menemsha has been built up in Kirby's mind because she's been told it's a can't-miss destination, but when they arrive, she finds it's a teeny-tiny fishing village, a *working* fishing village. There's a small harbor crammed with fishing vessels. All of the boats now, at midday, are unloading their catches; the avalanches of slippery silver fish look like quarters running out of a slot machine. There are enormous wooden traps bursting with lobsters.

Kirby blinks behind her cat's-eye sunglasses. "Who is going to eat all those lobsters?"

"We are," Rajani says. "Come on." She pulls Kirby into a non-descript building with a sign that says HOMEPORT. Guests at the inn *rave* about the Homeport, and Kirby loves how understated it is. If people aren't coming for the decor, they must be coming for the food. Rajani marches up to the counter and orders two lobster lunches. Kirby marvels at how confident her friend sounds and how beautiful she looks with her bronzed skin and dark hair and hazel eyes. She's so much more relaxed now that it's summertime and she's away from the pressure cooker of the college.

The lobster lunch turns out to be a pound-and-a-half boiled

lobster, an ear of corn, a cup of chowder, a dish of coleslaw, a mini-loaf of dense white bread, and lots of butter, both in packets and drawn. Over Kirby's protests, Rajani springs for both of their lunches. "What the Aldworths pay me is obscene," she says.

They sit at the only unoccupied table and Rajani crushes a claw between the silver arms of the cracker. "So, what's new with you?"

Kirby blows across a spoonful of creamy chowder flecked with fresh parsley. What to say? She has already filled Rajani in on her job—the serenity she finds in the wee hours, the kind guests and wonderful Mr. Ames, the pending visits from singers, movie stars, and senators. Should she tell Rajani about Patty and Luke? Should she tell Rajani about Darren? Rajani has known Darren for years, but if Darren told Rajani that he and Kirby met and that they went on a date to the carousel, wouldn't Rajani have said something?

The good news is that before Kirby has to decide what to say, their lunch is interrupted.

The bad news is that the lunch is interrupted by…Darren himself. Kirby blinks. Darren Frazier is standing next to their table flashing that drop-dead gorgeous smile as if he can't believe his fantastic luck. He's with an older gentleman whose completely bald head gleams like a polished bed knob. His father, the judge.

"Fancy seeing you two Oak Bluffs girls all the way out here," Darren says.

"Darren!" Rajani jumps up to give him a hug, then turns to his father. "Your Honor."

"Rajani," the judge says. He takes her hand in both of his, then kisses her cheek. "We haven't seen you once all summer. How is this possible?"

While Rajani explains her nannying job, Darren turns to Kirby.

"I'm glad we bumped into you," he says in a voice meant only for her. "I've been meaning to stop by to apologize for Sunday night. Something came up."

Something came up. Kirby wants to know what, exactly, but she can't very well get into a deep discussion with him right now, and so she shrugs and says, "Don't worry about it."

Darren reaches for her hand and gives it a surreptitious squeeze. Kirby feels a thrill zip up her spine.

"Meet my dad," Darren says. He clears his throat. "Dad, this is Rajani's friend Kirby Foley."

The judge shakes Kirby's hand. "Pleased to meet you, Kirby."

"We go to Simmons together," Rajani says. "And I converted Kirby to the Vineyard way of life, even though her family has a home on Nantucket."

The judge's eyebrows lift. "Ah! You're the one who lives on Nantucket. Yes, my wife mentioned you."

Kirby feels her smile drop a fraction of an inch. "The Vineyard is a lovely change," she says. "I'm working the front desk at the Shiretown Inn."

"Well, please give Mrs. Bennie our best," the judge says. "Darren, should we get this lunch home before it's cold?" He smiles at Rajani. "Enjoy your lunch."

Kirby runs through the entire interaction over and over again as she bikes home from Tea Lane. The judge was perfectly amiable, she thinks, until he figured out who Kirby was. Then he cut things short. Or maybe Kirby is being paranoid.

A paper bag holding the remains of her lunch swings from her handlebars. The bad news is that, after Darren and his father left the Homeport, Kirby was unable to eat a bite of food.

The good news is that Rajani was so caught up in describing

what happens at the Aldworths' key parties that she didn't even notice.

The next morning, when there is only a scant half hour left in Kirby's shift, Mr. Ames comes into the back office holding a red rose surrounded by greens and baby's breath and wrapped in cellophane.

"For me?" Kirby asks. She knows the flower can't be from Mr. Ames himself—he's married and has never shown anything more than an avuncular interest in Kirby—but she worries it might be from Mr. Rochester in room 3. Mr. Rochester is a rotund, bespectacled, bald man of at least thirty who has been sent by AAA to rate the hotel. Mr. Rochester had leered at Kirby upon his return from what must have been a Chianti-and-sambuca-soaked evening at Giordano's and invited Kirby up to his room for a nightcap, which Kirby had, naturally, refused, even though she realized that it might sabotage their chances for a respectable rating.

"Not Mr. Rochester?" Kirby asks.

"I've been sworn to secrecy," Mr. Ames says.

Kirby puts the rose in a bud vase and sets it on the desk. She supposes the flower could be from Bobby Hogue, who is back at the inn this week. He's such a nice man, though even older than Scottie Turbo, and Kirby wonders whether she could be in a relationship with a man with a missing hand. Yes, she decides. If Darren were missing a hand, she would still like him.

When it's time to leave work and head home, Mr. Ames tells Kirby to go on out front; he has to check in with Mrs. Bennie for a moment. Kirby thinks this is strange—they don't usually overlap with Mrs. Bennie, who arrives at nine—but she steps outside anyway.

There, idling at the front curb, is Darren in his red Corvair.

When he sees Kirby, he hops out of the car and races around to open the passenger door.

"Ride home?" he says.

She can't believe this is happening. Darren is here at the inn at seven o'clock in the morning to take her home. He's not wearing his white T-shirt and shorts, which means he isn't on his way to work. He came only to see her. And Mr. Ames is in on it. *Darren* is the one who brought Kirby the rose!

Kirby keeps her cool. "I'd love it," she says as she folds her legs gracefully into the front seat. "Thank you."

I Heard It Through the Grapevine

Kate never would have guessed it, but Bitsy Dunscombe drinks even more than she does. It's a Friday night in July and they have managed to score a decent table at the Opera House. This alone is reason to celebrate. Bitsy calls their waiter over and orders champagne, the best, a vintage Krug.

Bitsy Dunscombe, née Entwistle, of Park Avenue, New York City, and Main Street, Nantucket, was born an aristocrat. She married Ward Dunscombe, whose family owns platinum mines, and now Bitsy has more money than everyone else on Nantucket combined—or close to it, anyway. Kate finds Bitsy's blatant displays of wealth obnoxious, except in situations like this one.

As the piano tinkles away and the regulars sitting at table 1 hoot with laughter, Kate and Bitsy make quick work of the Krug, and

Kate eats one of the tiny gougères brought out by their waiter before they order their martinis.

Bitsy isn't Kate's first choice of dinner companion on a Friday night but the two of them do make a tradition of getting together once a summer, and neither David nor Ward is coming to the island this weekend, so when Bitsy called, Kate thought, *Why not,* and accepted the invitation.

David called the night before to say he was bogged down in a case and couldn't get away, but Kate knows he's keeping his distance on purpose. He'll show up when she cuts back on her drinking, when she can make it through a short phone conversation without hiccupping or slurring her words, which hasn't happened since she arrived.

As for Ward…well, everyone knows that Ward Dunscombe has a mistress on Long Island; her name is Kimberly Titus and she's the daughter of Reggie Titus, flour king. Even Bitsy knows and she seems to accept it as a matter of course. When Kate informed Bitsy that David wasn't coming this weekend, Bitsy said, "Does David have a Kimberly in Boston?"

"No," Kate said. "He has a job." As soon as the words were out of her mouth, she knew Bitsy must find her naive and way too trusting, but Kate had been married to a philanderer once and she wasn't crazy enough to do it a second time. David is principled; if anything, he's *too* principled. Kate is the one with the dark secret and questionable morals.

One martini, two martinis. Kate orders the escargots to start and Bitsy the hot appetizer—a crepe of seafood tossed in béchamel—which she barely touches.

"Shall we order wine?" Bitsy asks. This seems excessive. Kate is already seeing double, and the garlic from the escargot is repeating on her, so she eats a piece of bread slathered with the sublime

French butter. But the question was, of course, rhetorical. Bitsy calls over their waiter and keeps him at the table far longer than is necessary, hanging on to his arm, asking obnoxious questions about Sancerre versus Chablis when she has already announced that she's ordering *le boeuf* for her main course.

When poor Fernando or Arnoldo—Kate can't remember the man's name for love or money—finally escapes, Bitsy looks at Kate across the table and says, "I'm sleeping with him."

Kate nearly chokes on her bread. "With whom?"

"Arturo," Bitsy says. "He comes to the house after service and throws pebbles at my window."

Kate brings her menu up to her face to shield the aghast expression she can't wish away. Bitsy Dunscombe is sleeping with an Opera House waiter. Kate realizes there's a sexual revolution going on in the rest of the country, but she never thought it would infiltrate the upper echelons of society here on Nantucket.

"Don't *judge* me, Katie Nichols," Bitsy says. Kate dislikes her childhood nickname, although Bitsy is one of the few people who has known Kate long enough to use it. They'd taken sailing lessons together when they were only eleven years old. "I know you've always thought you were better than me with your four perfect children, but I have news for you..."

So this is Bitsy Dunscombe fueled by one too many, Kate thinks. She gets ugly—not only her language, but her face as well. Her expression contorts into a hideous mask with narrowed, accusing eyes and twisted lips. If she says anything about Tiger, Kate will slap her or throw a drink in her face. The piano player will stop right in the middle of "Try to Remember," and the revelers at table 1 will gape first and gossip later, and who could blame them? Kate Levin and Bitsy Dunscombe are two middle-aged matrons, both impeccably bred and raised, who should be able to get through dinner at the Opera House without making a scene.

No, Kate thinks. She pulls her comportment out as though it were something tucked away in her pocketbook. "I never thought I was better than you, Bitsy. You have beautiful twin girls. You were much smarter than I—you didn't make the mistake of marrying too young."

"Don't patronize me," Bitsy whispers fiercely. "I won't have it."

At that moment, Arturo arrives with the wine, a cabernet that will complement both Bitsy's *boeuf* and Kate's *canard*. As Bitsy goes through the theatrics of tasting the wine, Kate gazes around the room. The Opera House is tiny, a jewel box, really, dark and magical, with the iconic velvet-lined phone booth in the corner where Kate once caught Wilder kissing the Broussards' Swedish au pair. Wilder had been drunk, too drunk to know what he was doing, so Kate had forgiven him, despite the public humiliation.

Kate thinks of poor Blair, probably at that very moment lolling on the couch in front of the television like a walrus on an ice floe, stuffing her face with grilled-cheese sandwiches and pudding cups. Kate encouraged Blair to stick it out with Angus even though Angus is engaging in an affair with the woman named Trixie (who can only be a prostitute) because that was what Kate herself had done—she stuck it out. But why should poor Blair have to suffer as Kate did? For propriety's sake? Propriety means next to nothing these days, as Bitsy Dunscombe is so plainly demonstrating. Why shouldn't Blair be with Angus's brother, Joey, if that's who she really loves? Blair deserves to be adored. All women deserve to be adored.

"I'm sorry, Bitsy, your words came as a shock," Kate says. She lowers her voice. "I assure you, I would never judge—"

"You should be positively ashamed of your daughter," Bitsy

says. She takes a long drink of her wine; it stains her lips purple. Kate wonders if Bitsy has heard about Blair; her presence on the island can hardly be kept hush-hush. The news must have circulated that Blair and Angus are having marital problems and perhaps someone got hold of the sordid story about Angus kicking Blair out of the apartment because he caught her with *his own brother*. But who would have leaked such a story? Exalta? Exalta meets Mrs. Winter for mimosas every morning. She might have said something accidentally, and everyone knows how Mrs. Winter holds a grudge against Blair for dumping her grandson, Larry.

Or maybe Bitsy is referring to Kirby? Maybe news of Kirby's arrests made it from Boston to New York? Or maybe Kirby was involved with something even more nefarious? That spring, Kirby came home from college unannounced for three days midweek. She had offered no explanation and stayed holed up in her room, refusing all meals. Kate was traumatized by Tiger's recent departure, but even so, she expressed concern and asked Kirby a few probing questions, which were batted back in her face like shuttlecocks. Over the years Kate had learned that with Kirby, emotions ran hot and hard for a time—much like the outdoor shower at All's Fair—and then returned to normal. Sure enough, when the weekend rolled around, Kirby returned to Simmons, resigned if not cheery. Kate was secretly relieved that Kirby had decided to spend the summer on the Vineyard because it gave her one less person to worry about on a daily basis. Four children had seemed so perfect, so *square,* but Kate has to admit, much of the time it feels like too many.

"To which daughter are you referring?" Kate asks. She tastes the wine—it's exquisite, but that only serves to annoy her—and regards Bitsy with open curiosity.

"Jessica," Bitsy hisses. "She stole five dollars from Heather's pocketbook while Heather was using the ladies' room at the club. Five dollars *and* a lip gloss. Heather didn't want to say anything but Helen was in the next stall and she spied on Jessie through the crack in the door. She said that Jessie reached right into Heather's Bermuda bag, took the money and lip gloss, and walked out."

Kate rolls her eyes. "Spare me, please. Jessie would never do such a thing. I would bet my life on it."

"Helen *saw* her, Katie," Bitsy says. "And Heather admitted the money was missing. She earned that money by—"

"Reading to the blind?" Kate interjects. She's sick of hearing what a tireless do-gooder Heather is. She's a Girl Scout, she feeds stray dogs, she takes the elderly for walks in their wheelchairs. Admittedly, Heather is far better than that little minx Helen. Helen has been trouble from day one. Of *course* she's trying to pin this robbery on Jessie. Helen probably took the money herself! "Helen probably took the money herself," Kate says. "And she's trying to blame Jessie. How have you not considered that?"

"Helen said Jessie did it. That's enough proof for me. Helen doesn't lie."

"Jessie doesn't steal."

"Maybe she was doing it to get attention," Bitsy says. She leans back in her chair and lights a cigarette. "I'm sure that's it, poor girl. One sister is pregnant with twins, one sister is raising hell on Martha's Vineyard, and she has a brother at war. I feel sorry for Jessie, which is what I told my girls. Let her keep the money and the lip gloss if it makes her feel better."

Arturo arrives with their dinners and Kate stands up. "You two enjoy," she says. "I'm going home." She tosses her napkin on her chair and weaves her way through the dining room, past the godforsaken phone booth, and out to the patio, where she waves goodbye to Gwen, the owner, who is deep in conversation with the artist Roy Bailey.

"It was a wonderful evening, as always," Kate calls out. "Thank you."

She rages as she walks back to the house. Bitsy Dunscombe is a...a...well, frankly the right word eludes Kate, but Bitsy certainly knows how to put an end to a lifelong friendship. Kate will never speak to her again. How *dare* she accuse Jessie of *stealing* and then insinuate it's because Kate doesn't pay enough *attention* to her!

Kate passes Bosun's Locker and considers stopping in for a drink. All the regulars would likely fall off their bar stools or laugh her right out of the place. Wilder used to go to Bosun's and Kate would either call and ask for him to be sent home or march down and yank him out of there herself. Those nights were preferable to the nights when she stormed into the bar expecting to find him and he wasn't there.

She will not go to Bosun's Locker.

But maybe the Charcoal Galley? The six escargots and piece of bread didn't do much in the way of filling her up. She could go for a greasy cheeseburger with griddled onions and a side of gravy fries, but she figures she's likely to bump into the same characters from Bosun's at the Charcoal Galley this time of night, either filling up after a day of drinking or fueling up before a night of drinking.

She turns left onto Fair Street. She's loaded for bear, as the saying goes. She has let Bill Crimmins have enough time. She will knock on his door—who cares if he's asleep?—and demand answers. Has he heard from his brother-in-law about Tiger's discharge?

She knows that he hasn't. If he had, he certainly would have let her know. But Kate will ask anyway. She expects results—and soon!

Kate is two houses away when she sees a taxi pull up in front of All's Fair. For an instant, her heart soars. It's Tiger, come to surprise her. Or it's Kirby—yes, Kate *does* miss her wild second daughter terribly. She would be delighted if it's Kirby; her night would be salvaged. Or...maybe it's David. Kate wishes she hadn't drunk half a bottle of champagne, two martinis, and a glass of cabernet. David has come after all, but he will see that nothing has changed. Kate is a lush. Worse—a drunk.

Even in the dark, she distinguishes the figure of a man. So, David. Kate rushes forward, thinking her only hope at this point is to throw herself on his tender mercies. But as she gets closer, she sees the man isn't David. It's Angus, Dr. Angus Whalen, who sees fit to cheat on his wife while she's pregnant with twins.

"Stop right there," Kate says, and Angus does indeed freeze in his tracks on the sidewalk in front of the house. Angus is smart but not particularly strong or intimidating. With his glasses and his pointy nose, he resembles nothing so much as an intelligent mouse. Kate feels affronted on her eldest daughter's behalf, plus she's furious with Bitsy. This does not bode well for Angus.

"*What* are you doing here?" Kate asks.

"I came to see my wife," he says. His eyes follow the taxi as it drives off down Fair Street.

"First of all, she's asleep," Kate says. "Second of all, you have some nerve showing up here unannounced after throwing your pregnant wife out." Kate squints. The street is dark and she's having a hard time seeing Angus clearly. She's happy that the anger in her voice masks her advanced state of drunkenness. "How dare you."

"I caught her with my brother," Angus says. "Did she tell you *that?*"

"She did, in fact, Angus. She said you misconstrued their embrace. She was merely seeking comfort from Joey because she'd discovered your infidelity."

"About that..." Angus says.

But Kate doesn't want to hear any excuses or explanations from Angus; she was married to a serial philanderer for *ten years!* She has heard enough excuses and accepted enough apologies to last the rest of her life! Kate notes how satisfying it is to reject this disgusting behavior instead of accepting it as Bitsy Dunscombe is doing and as Kate once did. Blair may end up divorced, but at least she'll retain her pride.

"I'm asking you nicely to leave this island and never return," Kate says. "Blair deserves better. Maybe your brother will know how to treat her, and if he doesn't, she will easily find someone else. You and I both know that, Angus. Go now, please."

"I need to talk to her," Angus says. "I need to see her." He pulls at his hair—*Like a mental patient,* Kate thinks. "She's carrying my babies."

"You should have considered that before you strayed," Kate says. "And before you asked her to leave. Good night, Angus, and goodbye."

"Kate, *please,*" Angus says.

Kate tries to recall if Angus has ever used her Christian name before. He's ten years older than Blair so he might feel like a contemporary of Kate's, though he most certainly isn't one, and they aren't fond enough of each other for him to call her Mother. He should be addressing her as Mrs. Levin, but to correct him now would only keep him here longer.

"My next step is calling the police," Kate says. Anyone who

knows Katie Nichols Foley Levin would realize there's absolutely no chance of her bringing lights and sirens into a family matter. But Angus Whalen *doesn't* know Kate, and so he backs up to the street, holding his palms up.

"All right, all right, I'm going," Angus says. "Just please tell Blair I came to see her."

Kate nods, a gesture that could mean almost anything. She waits outside until Angus heads down Fair, turns onto Main, and disappears.

Summertime Blues (Reprise)

Her grandmother's necklace is gone. Every time Jessie says these words in her mind, she feels a wave of nausea. Twice, she has actually vomited, though she hasn't eaten much in the days since the necklace went missing. Her mother asks each morning if she's feeling okay. She looks peaked, Kate says. And then to Blair she says, sotto voce, "It's probably puberty. Before long, Jessie will be a woman!"

To which Blair responds, "Poor Jessie."

Neither of them has any idea about the predicament Jessie is in. The gold-knot necklace with the diamond is *gone*. Jessie *lost* it.

The only person who knows about it is Pick. The instant Jessie made the gut-wrenching discovery, she started to shake and cry, and her hopes for her first romantic interlude changed into something else entirely.

"What's wrong?" Pick asked. "Jessie, what is it?"

She was back to being Jessie, not Jess. She was a child who had been entrusted with something valuable—indeed, something *priceless*—and she had lost it. She tried to explain to Pick between sobs, but she had to be quiet because the last thing she wanted to do was alert Mr. Crimmins. Mr. Crimmins, most certainly, would go straight to Exalta.

"My grandmother's necklace…I wore it to dinner and now it's gone," Jessie says.

"Oh jeez," Pick had said, but it was clear from his tone that he didn't understand the situation. He was a boy. Boys didn't care about jewelry or about sentimentality, even though Jessie went on to explain that her maternal grandfather, Penn Nichols, long dead, had given that necklace to Exalta for their first wedding anniversary, in 1919. The necklace was valuable too, gold with a diamond. This, Pick had an easier time grasping, and so they got down on their hands and knees and searched every inch of the floor of Little Fair.

Then they sneaked outside and checked the flagstone walk and the strip of grass between the houses. Pick had pulled a flashlight out of the utility drawer in the kitchen but the batteries were nearly dead; the light was watery and barely any help at all. They checked the deck, and then, once inside All's Fair, they ran their hands across the linoleum of the kitchen floor; they came away with toast crumbs, dried tomato seeds, and cereal flakes, but no necklace. They moved out into the hallway and that was when they heard footsteps on the stairs. Pick grabbed Jessie by the hand and pulled her through the half-size door to the buttery, the cramped closet where Kirby had been punished so many years earlier. The buttery was dark and smelled like damp brick and mold but it was a decent hiding place; no one would think to look for a person in there. They crouched down side by side, by necessity their bodies pressing together. Pick squeezed Jessie's hand, but she was too nervous to enjoy any thrill. She could tell by the weight and the pace of the footsteps that the person awake was Exalta. A moment later, they heard low voices in the kitchen, one of them a man's, so it must have been Mr. Crimmins. Jessie was trembling. Pick slid an arm around her back and maybe tried to kiss her but he ended up burying his nose under her jaw.

"Turn your face," he said. So it was true, he *was* trying to kiss her—but at that moment, the footsteps came back their way and Jessie froze and couldn't help thinking of Anne Frank hiding in the attic of the skinny house in Amsterdam and how frightened she must have been with the constant threat of the Nazis.

Exalta went back up the stairs. Pick and Jessie stayed quiet and still for a few minutes after all noises in the house had subsided, and then Jessie pushed the door to the buttery open and stepped out, and Pick followed.

Wordlessly, they went back to Little Fair, and when they'd climbed the stairs, Jessie said, "There are leftovers. Help yourself."

"You're going to bed?" Pick asked. "Don't you want to go out on the deck and eat?"

She shook her head. There was a lump in her throat that would make it impossible to swallow. She wanted to curl up in a ball and die quietly of anxiety. It could have been, should have been, the best night of her young life, the night of her first kiss, but it was ruined. She didn't deserve happiness.

Even so, she managed a weak smile. "I'll look for the necklace again in the morning. I'll retrace my steps all the way back to the Mad Hatter if I have to."

"Good idea," Pick said, but his mouth was full. He was already into the scampi.

* * *

Jessie slept fitfully, waking up for good when the sun rose at five thirty. She had fallen asleep in her dress, which she took off and kicked to the back of her closet. She would never, ever wear it again. She put on shorts and a T-shirt and her Keds and hurried down the stairs and out the door and through the side gate to the alley.

Nantucket was pretty at seven thirty, when she and Exalta would walk to the club for tennis, but at five thirty it was even more beautiful. The air was dewy, the light pearlescent. Fair Street was still; Jessie might have been the only person awake. She wished she could enjoy it, but she was too agitated. If she had lost the necklace on the street and someone had found it, then it was gone forever. It could have been picked up by a bird and woven into a nest. It could have been run over by a car, the chain broken, the knot flattened, the diamond dislodged. It could have fallen into a sewer grate and become mired in the muck and gray water that ran beneath the island.

Jessie cast her eyes down as she traveled the exact path back to the Mad Hatter that she and Kate had taken home. Glints in the sidewalk turned out to be mica, which felt like a cruel trick; ditto the tabs from beer and soda cans that littered the brick outside of Bosun's Locker. As Jessie crossed Main Street, she looked in the crevices between the cobblestones. Meanwhile, she tried to imagine telling Exalta that she had lost the necklace. Jessie wasn't even supposed to *have* the necklace; she had, essentially, stolen it from Exalta's bedroom. This made it so much worse—two things to admit to instead of one.

Jessie got all the way across town without encountering another soul, which was fortunate because she had no explanation for what she was doing out and about this early. When she arrived at the Mad Hatter, she climbed the steps and knocked on the glass pane of the door, but no one answered. She could hardly be surprised; it was barely six in the morning. As she wondered what time the cleaners came in, wondered if maybe they had found the necklace last night—under her chair, say—she gasped. The necklace wasn't at the Mad Hatter because Jessie had touched it at her throat on the way home. On Main Street!

Jessie hurried back across town to the spot in front of the Pacific National Bank where she remembered fingering the necklace. She started there and searched every square inch of pavement diligently until she was back at All's Fair.

It had to be somewhere, she reasoned.

But it wasn't. It was gone.

Now, a week later, worry about the necklace has grown into a full-blown crisis. Every day when Jessie wakes up, she fills with dread, expecting that this will be the day Exalta realizes the necklace is gone.

Thursday evening, when Exalta goes to bridge at the Anglers' Club, Jessie sneaks back into her bedroom. The air is chilled, the high single bed is made with crisp white linens, and the burgundy velvet box is on the triangular table. The sight of the velvet box is as gruesome to Jessie as a severed hand.

She experiences a glimmer of hope as she pries the box open; for one second, she imagines that she can change the past, that a week ago, she did not abscond with the necklace out of anger but left it right where it was.

The box is empty. Jessie's stomach lurches.

She thinks about taking the box. Will Nonny notice its absence? Will taking the box lessen the chances of Exalta suggesting, on some future special occasion, that Jessie wear the necklace?

Maybe Jessie should take *all* the jewelry from the triangular table. She can leave the boxes open and askew, make it look as if they've been robbed.

Yes! Jessie thinks. This would solve everything. And it's not too far-fetched. They leave the doors unlocked night and day; anyone could just come in and walk off with the jewels.

But there is rarely, if ever, a time when the house is completely unoccupied, especially now that Blair is here. And somehow Jessie knows that if she stages a burglary, the person who will be blamed is Pick.

Blair, Jessie thinks. She will confide in Blair and ask her advice. Blair seems pretty miserable; she could probably use a distraction. Maybe, just maybe, Blair will give Jessie the money to replace the necklace. She can go down to S. J. Patten on Main Street, describe the necklace, and commission a new one.

Jessie leaves the burgundy box where it is and heads down the hall to her room, which is now Blair's room. The door is closed, so Blair is inside and not downstairs in front of the television, thank goodness. It's impossible to tear her away from *The Flying Nun*.

When Jessie knocks, Blair utters a froggy "Come in."

The air conditioner is humming and Blair has the drapes closed against the sun, which is still fairly bright even at seven in the evening. Blair is wearing the yellow dress that is starting to come apart at the seams. When she sees Jessie, she offers a smile and heaves herself up to sitting. Her hair is messy; she wears no makeup, not even lipstick; and her girth is so shocking, she looks as if she's harboring an entire family under her dress.

"Hey," Blair says.

"Hey," Jessie says. She closes the door and sits on the bed next to Blair. "I have a problem."

"Boy troubles?" Blair asks.

Jessie shakes her head as she thinks of being crammed into the buttery with Pick and how he basically *asked* to kiss her and what a missed opportunity that was. Yet this concern is pale and distant compared to the red-hot urgency of the missing necklace.

"Is it...did you get your..."

"No," Jessie says. She thinks back to her last evening in Brookline—Leslie announcing that she had officially entered puberty, Doris clutching her belly against imaginary cramps—and she marvels that she had ever been so innocent. She takes a deep breath. "Nonny gave me a necklace for my birthday. It was a gold knot with a tiny diamond in the center on a gold chain. I guess Gramps gave it to her for their first wedding anniversary."

"Wow," Blair says. "And she gave it to you...to *have?* Like, *permanently?*"

Jessie's eyes fill with tears. "She did. It was supposed to be a special-occasion necklace."

"I should think so," Blair says.

"But she was keeping it for me in her room. And last Thursday night when Mom and I went to the Mad Hatter, I put it on... without asking Nonny, I mean. She was at bridge, so I couldn't ask her..."

"Yeah?" Blair says warily.

"And I lost it!" Jessie says. "It must have fallen off my neck. I've looked everywhere in this house, I retraced my steps through town, I checked to make sure it wasn't caught inside my dress. It's *gone,* Blair."

Blair falls back against her pillows with her fingers laced across her belly. "Jessie," she says.

"I know!" Jessie cries. "You don't have to make me feel bad about it because I already feel rotten and you don't have to tell me I'm irresponsible with nice things because that much is obvious."

"Oh, Jessie," Blair says. "I'm so sorry."

"It's priceless," Jessie says, wiping a hand under her nose. "Gramps gave it to her in 1919. It lasted fifty years and then I had it for one night and now it's gone."

"I take it you haven't told Nonny," Blair says.

"I can't tell Nonny," Jessie says. "I just can't."

"She's going to find out sooner or later, though. You know that, right?"

"I was hoping you could give me money so I could go to the jeweler and ask them to make another one," Jessie says. "It doesn't have to be exact. Nonny's eyesight isn't that great. If she doesn't look closely, she won't notice. And I'll pay you back every penny, I swear."

Blair laughs. "Oh, honey."

Jessie assumes that means no. She bows her head. Her only hope now is that Exalta won't notice the necklace is missing for the next six weeks, at which point Jessie will go with Pick to Woodstock and never return.

"Wait right here," Blair says. She lumbers across the room to the bookshelves and scans the titles. These books are mostly old. Some belonged to their mother growing up; some belonged to Nonny. Blair extracts a slim volume and presses it on Jessie.

"Read this," she says. "Then you'll know what to do."

The book is *The Necklace and Other Stories,* by Guy de Maupassant.

Jessie takes the book back to Little Fair and lies across her bed to read it; she is out of options. The first story, "The Necklace," is about a woman who wants to impress people at a fancy party and borrows an expensive necklace from an acquaintance—and then loses it. She finds a similar necklace in a jewelry store, and she and her husband sell everything they own and take out multiple loans to buy it. She gives this necklace to the acquaintance without mentioning that it's a replacement, and the couple spends years in poverty, the wife doing scullery work in order to repay the loans. A decade later, she runs into the acquaintance and finds out that the necklace she lost was not valuable at all; the jewels were made of paste.

When Jessie finishes the story, she slams the book shut. This doesn't help her because the necklace she lost wasn't a fake. It was real, the real necklace that Nonny received from Gramps. Right? It had the heft of gold, and the diamond looked genuine. Maybe Blair thinks Nonny gave her a decoy to see if she was ready to care for a fine piece of jewelry.

That would be such a relief! But Jessie doubts it's true.

She understands why Blair suggested the book. There's only one correct course of action: tell Nonny the truth.

When is the right time? On their way to tennis lessons? On their way home from tennis lessons? In the evening, after Nonny has had a couple of gin and tonics? Jessie starts scrutinizing her grandmother's moods. Every time she imagines telling Exalta the truth, she feels sick. She can't do it.

Then, after the Fourth of July, Exalta spends a long stretch of time in the den watching Wimbledon on TV. Her favorite player, Rod Laver, wins his quarter-final match, then his semifinal match. And then he wins the final match against John Newcombe. He is the Wimbledon champion once again and Exalta claps her hands with glee. When Jessie sits down next to her on the sofa, Exalta turns to her and says, "Isn't that *marvelous?*"

Jessie wants to blurt out the words *Nonny, I lost the necklace.* But she can't bring herself to ruin Exalta's good mood.

* * *

That evening after dinner, Jessie returns to Little Fair to find an envelope on the kitchen table. She creeps toward it as though it's a dove that might fly away. What are the chances that someone found the necklace and left it in this envelope for Jessie? She squeezes her eyes closed then bravely opens them, thinking that whatever the envelope is, it will be fine.

It's a letter, addressed to her here at All's Fair.

The return address is *Private Richard Foley, U.S. Army.*

It's from Tiger.

Jessie falls into a seat at the table and fingers the envelope; she wants to rip it open. She holds the letter in both hands and considers doing that—but somehow she knows she has to wait.

Wait until after she has told Nonny the truth.

The next morning, Jessie wakes up to pouring rain. She puts on her whites and pulls her hair into a ponytail, though clearly there'll be no tennis today; just a run through the backyard to All's Fair leaves her drenched. Nonny is sitting in the kitchen in the green kimono with the embroidered hibiscus that she got in Japan before World War II. She's drinking a cup of coffee and reading the newspaper, which is unusual, but then Jessie sees she's reading the sports page. There's a large picture of Rod Laver.

"Tennis lessons canceled," Exalta says. She gives Jessie a kind smile. "You can go on back to bed."

If Jessie was looking for a sign, she has found it. Going back to Little Fair and burrowing under the covers as she listens to the patter of rain against the roof is a tempting choice—but it's also a cowardly one.

Jessie takes a seat across from Exalta. "Nonny, there's something I have to tell you."

Her grandmother gazes at her with interest. Exalta isn't wearing any makeup, so her wrinkles are revealed, and there are pouches under her blue eyes. Her lips are the same color as her skin. Her hair, which looks silvery blond when combed, now looks gray, the color of steel. Jessie tries to imagine her grandmother as a thirteen-year-old. Of course, that would have been in 1907, before most people had automobiles or flew on airplanes, before Russia was an enemy.

"I lost your necklace," Jessie says. "The one Gramps gave you for your anniversary."

Exalta blinks, and this split second while Exalta is processing what Jessie just said is the worst moment of Jessie's life.

The silence that follows is equally awful. Jessie sees no choice but to fill it. "I took the necklace from your room. I wore it to dinner with Mom last Thursday."

Exalta executes a nod so slight Jessie wonders if she has imagined it, but it's followed by a change in Exalta's expression. The corners of her mouth fall a fraction of an inch. She isn't frantic at the news, or appalled. She is simply disappointed. Jessie has revealed herself to be as untrustworthy as Exalta feared. Not worthy of the necklace. Not worthy of the family.

"You took it without asking," Exalta says. "Do you know what that's called, Jessica?"

"Stealing," Jessie says. A bolder, braver version of herself—Jessica Levin at eighteen, or even sixteen—might have pointed out that since Nonny had given her the necklace, it was hers, and by definition, she couldn't steal something that already belonged to her. Nonny might then have pointed out that she had decreed that the necklace was for special occasions only—but dinner at the Mad Hatter qualified, right? Nonny hadn't meant that Jessie had to wait for her high-school graduation or her wedding, had she?

"Stealing," Exalta repeated. She made the word sound vile. Only criminals stole—Bonnie and Clyde, John Dillinger. "And this isn't the first time you've stolen something, is it, Jessica?"

"I..." Jessie falters. What does Nonny know? Jessie inhales and prepares to...what? Lie? Cowards lie. She sits quietly for a second and regroups. Telling the truth when you've done something wrong is the most terrifying thing in the world. Never mind that Jessie was angry—her tennis instructor touched her inappropriately, her grandmother refused to let her use her own last name, her brother had been called up by Selective Service—her actions weren't justified.

"No," she says. "It wasn't the first time."

"Mrs. Winter told me that Bitsy Dunscombe told her that you took five dollars and a lipstick out of Heather Dunscombe's bag. And I told her that I would bet all of my worldly belongings that this was not the case. Do you know why I said that, Jessica?"

Tears rise at the vision of her grandmother defending her against Mrs. Winter and Bitsy Dunscombe. "Why?" Jessie says.

"Because I thought you were different from the other three children," Exalta says. "I thought you were sensitive and thoughtful. Trustworthy."

At this, tears fall.

"Now I see I was mistaken."

Jessie cries. She sobs. It's too awful—not that Exalta is disappointed; this, she could have predicted. What's awful is that Exalta had believed in Jessie, that she attributed wonderful qualities like sensitivity and thoughtfulness to her, and Jessie hadn't realized it. She knew she was different from the other three children, yes, but she had always felt lesser, somehow—small, dark, strange.

"I'm going to sit here while you retrieve the five dollars and the lipstick," Exalta says. "I will return them."

Exalta will return them? Isn't the correct punishment to make Jessie give the money and the lip gloss back to Heather along with a full, mortifying confession and apology? But then Jessie understands that Exalta needs to save face.

Jessie runs through the rain back to her bedroom at Little Fair. She opens her top drawer and pulls out the five-dollar bill and the Bonne Bell lip gloss—and the wristbands and the Twizzlers. When she gets back to the kitchen and drops the items on the table, Exalta looks unsurprised.

"Is that everything?"

"Except the necklace," Jessie says. The matter of the precious heirloom, lost forever, seems to have been forgotten.

"Mr. Crimmins found the necklace caught between the floorboards in the hall," Exalta says. "Lucky for you. And I have tucked it away for safekeeping."

Jessie's relief can't be described. She feels so light she could float. Mr. Crimmins *found* the necklace! She is happy not because she's been let off the hook but because she genuinely cares about the necklace.

"Don't worry, I'm not taking it away from you," Exalta says. "But I will retain custody of it until you're older. Sixteen, perhaps."

"I don't deserve it ever," Jessie says. This is how she feels. The necklace would be safer with Blair or Kirby or even, eventually, one of Blair's children.

"Don't be ridiculous," Exalta says. "You're perfectly worthy of the necklace, Jessica. You simply need to grow up a bit." The corners of Exalta's mouth turn up ever so slightly. "I wouldn't choose to be thirteen again for all the tea in China."

Jessie can see why. So far, thirteen is turning out to be a terrible age.

"You'll be punished for the stealing," Exalta says. "Grounded for a week. Extra chores. You'll keep on with your tennis lessons but you won't be allowed to eat at the snack bar afterward. You can come home and eat. It's against my nature to keep a child inside on a summer day but you leave me no choice. You'll stay home in the afternoons and, of course, the evenings. Do you understand me?"

"Yes," Jessie says. She swallows. "Does my mother know?"

"Your mother doesn't need anything else to worry about," Exalta says. "Now go. Get out of my sight."

Back into the rain, back up the stairs of Little Fair, back to her room, where she closes and locks the door, sheds her damp tennis clothes, and puts her pajamas on again. She is disgraced for certain, but curiously, she feels better, not worse. She feels clean. She feels cured.

She picks up her copy of *Anne Frank* and takes out Tiger's letter. Her hands are steady.

June 20, 1969

Dear Jessie,

I need you to promise you won't show anyone else this letter.

Our company was ambushed last week near the village of Dak Lak. We lost over half our men.

Jessie, both Puppy and Frog were killed. Frog was hit by sniper fire—one clean shot to the head. Puppy ran out to grab Frog's body and he stepped on a grenade. His right leg was blasted off. So I went to grab Frog and I brought him back to where Puppy was. I ripped Frog's shirt off and used it as a tourniquet on Puppy's leg, and I thought maybe I'd save him.

He was still talking, first praying to the good Lord Jesus Christ, then calling to his mama, and I was praying too, saying, "God, please don't take both my brothers in the same day, but if You must, take me too."

Puppy died in my arms while we were waiting for the chopper.

So many men were lost that they've reassigned those of us who survived to other companies. I'm heading out on a top secret mission so I'll be out of touch for a while. I'll write as soon as I can.

I miss home, Messie. I'm not sure you even know the real reason I call you that; probably you thought all these years that I was teasing you, the way a big brother is supposed to. But really, I call you that because when you were a baby, Mom used to let me feed you your baby food. I would hold the spoon with your squash or pureed plums and half the time you would open your piehole like a baby bird and take what was on the spoon. The other half, you would reach a little hand out, grab the food from the spoon, and smear it all over your face. Then you would laugh so hard that I would laugh too.

That's why I nicknamed you Messie.

Since Frog and Puppy died, I've been wondering what the point to all this is—not just the war, but life in general. I've had some real dark thoughts. I try to picture your baby face covered with plums and I hear that laugh like heaven's bells and that keeps me tethered. My kid sister. Who knew?

Please don't tell Mom or Nonny or anyone else about this letter or about me going on a secret mission. I already wrote to Magee to tell her. Since I'm sharing secrets in this letter I might as well tell you that I've asked Magee to marry me. I sent her

Gramps's Harvard class ring to stand in for a diamond. We will have a big wedding, if I make it out of here alive.
  I hope I do, Messie. I hope I do.

                                        Love, your brother, Tiger

Nineteenth Nervous Breakdown

No one has said so out loud, but on July 7, when Blair is less than four weeks from her due date, it becomes clear that she won't be returning to Boston for the delivery. She will give birth to the twins here, on Nantucket. Buried deep beneath the many layers of emotion that Blair feels on any given day is a fluttery pride, and even joy, about this. Her children will be native Nantucketers. They will have the same claim to the island as the Coffins and the Starbucks and (this is what *really* thrills Blair) an even greater connection to it than the summer residents who have been coming to the island for decades—people like Exalta.

Blair announces over breakfast toast with her mother (for when Kate is around, Blair is offered only dry toast in an attempt to keep her from gaining any more weight) that they should probably go see Dr. Van de Berg, who delivers all of the island's babies.

"I suppose you're right," Kate says with a heavy sigh. "I'll set something up for today."

The appointment is scheduled for twelve thirty, and despite the heat, Blair is grateful to get out of the house. She has watched day after glorious day slide by while she lies about in bed or watches soap operas in the den.

"Could we possibly go to lunch after?" Blair asks.

Kate shocks Blair by saying, "Where should we go?"

"The Galley," Blair says. She wants a lobster roll with French fries and a tall glass of iced tea with lots of lemon and sugar. Even a few days ago, lunch at the Galley would have been too upsetting to contemplate because that was the spot Blair favored for lunch the summer before, back when she was married but not pregnant, back when she was thin, back when she was herself. But with her due date in sight, she realizes that pregnancy isn't a life sentence. It will end. She will give birth to the babies and her present misery will become a distant memory.

Kate nods in approval. "Wonderful," she says. "They make the best gimlets."

The Nantucket Cottage Hospital is country medicine but what it lacks in big-city sophistication, it makes up for in personal attention. Dr. Van de Berg is a wonderful, welcome change from the smug condescension of Dr. Sayer at the Boston Hospital for Women. Dr. Van de Berg is a short man who has the countenance of a cheerful elf. He's tanned and healthy; he looks as if delivering babies is something he does between sailing in regattas and playing rounds of golf. He's wearing a white lab coat over a baby-blue polo and a pair of snappy madras pants. Blair loves everything about Dr. Van de Berg; he is the apotheosis of a summer doctor. She doesn't even mind when he asks her to lie back on the metal table so he can check her.

Being "checked" in this instance means Dr. Van de Berg reaching up inside of Blair, which makes Blair think of Julia Child's instructions about removing the gizzards from a raw chicken. That leads her to remember her three failed attempts to make *poulet au porto* the previous autumn. She wonders if Trixie is an accomplished French cook whose pan sauces never break. Blair is so consumed with envy over Trixie's imagined skills in the kitchen that she isn't listening when Dr. Van de Berg says something from his post between her legs.

"I'm sorry, what?"

"You're a hundred percent effaced and two centimeters dilated. The babies should be here in a week, maybe two. Maybe sooner."

Blair sits up on her elbows. "What?"

When Blair returns to the waiting room and Kate asks how everything went, Blair says, "Just fine. Let's go to lunch, I'm starving."

As they drive to the Galley, Blair practices her breathing. She needs to calm down. On the one hand, the news is exhilarating— a week, maybe two, maybe sooner. On the other hand, Blair is forced to consider her circumstances. If she gives birth tomorrow or next week or in two weeks, she will be doing it alone. There has been no word from Angus and no word from Joey. The situation is enough to send Blair back to the solace of her bed, but she doesn't want to miss what might be her last chance to get out of the house.

The Galley offers simple lunch fare, and it's right on Cliffside Beach, a mere forty yards from the lapping waves of Nantucket Sound. Kate and Blair are seated at a coveted two-top on the outer edge of the restaurant, along the rope railing. Blair positions her arm so it's resting in the sun. The maître d' is the same man as the year before, though he doesn't recognize Blair. When he saw her approaching, he cleared the way for her as though she were a Mack Truck about to barrel through the restaurant. Blair is so happy to be here that she doesn't even feel self-conscious about her yellow dress. The Galley isn't a formal place; nearly all the diners are in bathing suits and cover-ups.

If Blair's motivation for being here is to get out of the house and dig into a lobster roll and French fries, Kate's is to start drinking.

"I'd like a gimlet," Kate tells the waitress, a girl of about seventeen who has her hair in pigtails. "And another one in ten minutes."

Behind her sunglasses, Blair raises her eyebrows but doesn't comment. She orders an iced tea and studies her mother—Katharine Nichols Foley Levin, the summertime version. Kate seems to have aged ten years since Tiger was deployed. Kate's skin is lightly tanned and her hair is loose, held off her face by a grosgrain headband, but there are tense lines around her mouth and etched into her forehead, and Blair knows that if Kate removes her sunglasses, her eyes will be bleary. She wears her pearls with a crisp white short-sleeved blouse, so she's still recognizable as herself, but she drains the first gimlet in under a minute. Three long sips. Blair counts as she drinks her iced tea.

"Mother," Blair says.

Kate gazes at the sea until her second gimlet arrives and once that, too, is gone, she turns to Blair and says, "I have some things to tell you that might be difficult for you to hear."

Blair presumes her mother is going to list the reasons why Blair must forsake Joey Whalen and reunite with Angus. "Mother—"

"Just listen," Kate says. She flags down the waitress and says, "Two lobster rolls, please, with French fries. And another gimlet."

"Yes, ma'am." The pigtailed waitress departs. What must she think about a woman who is on track to drink half a dozen gimlets before lunch is over?

Kate leans forward and says, "Your father, Wilder Foley, was a philanderer. He slept with...scores of women while we were married."

Blair stirs up the sugar from the bottom of her iced tea with her straw. She isn't exactly surprised to hear that her father stepped out—she'd always had a feeling—but *scores*? Surely Kate is exaggerating.

"I'm not exaggerating," Kate says. "There were upwards of forty." She taps her finger against the weathered wood of the table. "And those were the ones I knew about here at home. While he was at war..." She laughs unhappily. "Well, the sky's the limit."

"Why did you stay?" Blair asks.

"Three little children," Kate says. "Plus, it was what was done back then. Women turned a blind eye. And I was afraid of what your grandmother would say if I left. She *adored* Wilder."

Yes, this is common family knowledge; Nonny had favored Wilder, just as she now favors Kirby. And Angus too, Blair realizes with a heavy heart. Nonny is particularly fond of Angus.

"Were you...*sad* when he died?" Blair asks. She had often imagined the moment when Kate went searching the house for Wilder and found him shot dead in his workshop. Kate would have let out an ear-piercing scream. Or maybe not. After all, she had children sleeping.

"There aren't words to describe how I felt. There just...aren't words. A person is alive one minute, dead the next. The human mind really can't process it. *Sadness* comes long after all of the other, more difficult and destructive emotions have passed. But, yes, at some point, I was sad. Profoundly sad," Kate says. She lights a cigarette and offers one to Blair, who declines. She's having enough trouble breathing as it is. Blair does pull her silver lighter from her purse to light her mother's cigarette and this gesture threatens to deliver Blair back to her despair over Angus and Joey, but after the first drag of her cigarette, Kate adds, "We'd had quite a blowout. Right before he died."

"Blowout?" This isn't a word Blair has ever heard her mother use. "About what?"

At that moment, their lobster rolls arrive, with a third gimlet for Kate. The delicate moment pops like a soap bubble; Blair can tell from Kate's expression that she has no intention of disclosing anything further.

Blair regards her beautiful lunch—the toasted, buttered roll overflowing with snowy chunks of lobster meat tossed with mayonnaise and a pale dice of celery to add crunch, and crisp golden fries. The lunch nearly has sexual appeal. Blair vows to go slowly and enjoy every bite.

"Mother?" Blair asks. She is angry that Kate has broached a subject then left it to die in the sun. "Tell me about the blowout."

Kate dips a fry in ketchup. She always looks elegant no matter what she's doing, Blair thinks. It isn't fair.

"The point," Kate says, "is that I don't want you to be afraid of me the way I was afraid of Nonny. Angus is conducting an affair, he's admitted to it, and you don't have to tolerate it." She lifts her lobster roll and takes a bite, then dabs the corners of her mouth with her napkin. "That's why I sent him away."

"Sent who away?" Blair asks. She, too, starts with a French fry but she doesn't have the restraint to nibble just one. She pinches a few and does her best not to cram them into her mouth.

"Angus," Kate says. "He showed up at the house a few days ago. Friday. I saw him on the way home from my travesty of a dinner with Bitsy Dunscombe."

Blair fights to swallow. "Angus showed up at which house? Not All's Fair? He wasn't here on Nantucket, was he, Mother?"

"Yes, darling," Kate says. "But please don't worry. I sent him away and told him never to come back."

Blair could dress Kate down for meddling in her marriage, then rise from the table, storm out of the restaurant, and hail a taxi back to Fair Street. But what she actually does is pick up her lobster roll and take a huge, satisfying bite. Also on the plate is a side of peppery coleslaw and a kosher dill spear.

Angus had come to Nantucket and Kate sent him away. *Yes,* Blair thinks, *serves him right.* She is secretly delighted—and very, very relieved—that Angus has not completely forsaken her. Although she supposes it's possible that Angus came to ask for a divorce.

She'll call him later. She needs to tell him about the babies anyway.

That evening, Kate and Exalta go to the Straight Wharf Theater to see a production of *Damn Yankees*. They've had their tickets for weeks, since long before Blair arrived, and they purchased one for Jessie, but Jessie is grounded for losing the necklace. They ask Blair to go, but Blair can't possibly sit for two hours wedged into one of those narrow seats, so she invites Mr. Crimmins. Once they're all out the door, Blair picks up the phone. The line is being used, so she hangs up and tries again after five minutes, then ten, all the while cursing Exalta for not spending the extra dollar a month for a private line.

When Blair picks up the phone the third time, the line is free. It's half past six, the hour that normal people sit down to eat, but Blair knows Angus will still be at work. She dials the office but Ingrid must have gone home because the line rings and rings. Eventually Blair is put through to the university's answering service but she declines to leave a message.

She takes a breath and chastises herself for not calling earlier in the day, but this house affords no privacy.

She calls the apartment on a lark. No answer. She hangs up and calls Joey Whalen at his hotel. He picks up on the fourth ring. In the background there's music playing and Blair hears a woman laughing.

"Blair?" he says. "Is everything okay? Is it time?"

"No," she says. "Not yet. I was just hoping to talk. Ask how Newport was. But if you're in the middle of something—"

"I'm entertaining right now," Joey says. "How 'bout I give you a call tomorrow—hey, hey, pass that over here—from the office?"

Blair can practically smell the marijuana smoke and taste the martinis and see the svelte body of a sexy brunette in a clingy red dress with a plunging neckline. A girl Joey met in Newport, no doubt, who works at the cosmetic counter at Filene's. That's who Joey *should* be dating. He was never really interested in Blair. Well, maybe at first, when she was single and free, but all of his recent attention, she realizes suddenly, is just old, unfinished business between him and Angus.

Blair hangs up without saying goodbye. She plucks the silver lighter from her purse, carries it out back, and throws it as far as she can—which, admittedly, isn't far. It does clear the gate, however, and skitters across Plumb Lane. Some car will flatten it, or possibly a passerby will spy it, pick it up, read the engraved message, and wonder about this fellow Joey and the woman who was lucky enough to receive his eternal love.

Blair plans to call Angus first thing the next morning but she doesn't wake until nearly ten. Jessie and Exalta are at the club for Jessie's tennis lessons and Kate is shopping in town. (Or drinking, Blair thinks. And she hasn't forgotten about the *blowout.*) The phone line is in use so Blair waits ten minutes, then fifteen, then she picks up the phone and asks, as nicely as possible, for the woman who is talking to wrap up her call because Blair has a rather urgent matter to deal with. The woman makes no promises to be brief, and, in fact, she stays on the line until ten forty-five, at which time Blair finally calls Angus at the office.

Ingrid says, "I'm sorry, Mrs. Whalen. I'm afraid he's gone."

"Gone?" Blair says. "What do you mean, gone?" For one ghastly second, she thinks Angus is dead, possibly by his own hand due to being banished from Nantucket by his mother-in-law.

"He flew to Houston early this morning," Ingrid says. "He'll be there until the mission is over. He isn't scheduled to return to Boston until the twenty-fifth."

Blair hangs up. The twenty-fifth is two weeks away. Blair spreads her hands across her belly.

"Stay put for two weeks," she says. "Just stay put."

A Whiter Shade of Pale

It's Kirby's belief that each summer is characterized not only by its special occasions but also by its routines. For example, the summer of 1957, when Kirby was nine and Blair was twelve, the girls owned and operated a lemonade stand they called Foley's Finest on the corner of Main and Fair Streets and made at least a dollar fifty a day and often more. Blair saved her half of the money to buy an electric curling iron, but Kirby often walked with her mother or Nonny down to Robinson's to buy bubble gum or a yo-yo or an *Archie* comic book. Then there was the summer Kirby was fourteen and Blair was seventeen. Blair was dating Larry

Winter, whom Kirby had a painful crush on. Exacerbating the situation was that Kirby's job in that summer of 1962 was to babysit Larry's little sisters, Eve and Carolyn, ages four and two, which was done at the Winters' house out in Quaise Pasture because the girls took a long afternoon nap. Often, Larry would be dispatched to drive Kirby home when he finished his shift at Aime's Bakery, and these minutes alone with Larry in the car cemented Kirby's ardor. Larry Winter was tall and good-looking and played varsity squash at Phillips Exeter. He was a shoo-in for the Ivies, though Kirby learned during these drives that he had his heart set on Georgetown; he wanted to study government and someday become president of the United States. Kirby had been dazzled at the time, though now she can see how unoriginal Larry Winter's dreams were. It was 1962, and the papers were filled with images of the sun-kissed, carefree Kennedys summering over in Hyannis Port. *Everyone* had wanted to be president.

Larry used to bring treats home from the bakery, boxes of doughnuts or oatmeal cookies studded with dried cranberries. He always offered a little something to Kirby, but these were gifts of kindness rather than hints that he returned her feelings. Always, when Kirby got out of the car in front of All's Fair, Blair would be waiting to get in, and sometimes she and Larry would neck right there in the car until either Kate or Exalta appeared in the doorway of the house to put an end to it.

This summer, the summer of 1969, the routine is different, obviously—Kirby is on a different island!—but she suspects that when she looks back on this year from a distance, she will remember the house on Narragansett—Patty, Barb, the three Ms, Evan; the porridge and brown bread for breakfast; the relief, after walking up two flights of stairs, of her air-conditioned lair. (The other girls, Patty has confided, are fiendishly jealous, and Kirby doesn't blame them. She has gotten so lucky with her accommodations that she worries she'll pay for it somehow and something bad will happen before summer's end.) She will remember her tasks at the front desk of the Shiretown Inn—checking the bills, making the coffee, arranging the newspapers and doughnuts—and she will remember the kindness of Mr. Ames and Bobby Hogue and the hours she spent in half sleep as the transistor radio played "Up on Cripple Creek" and "Crystal Blue Persuasion."

As the first half of July unspools, it seems like Kirby will also remember starting a romance with Darren Frazier. Since the morning he picked her up outside the Shiretown Inn and drove her home, they have seen each other every day. Darren lifeguards from nine to five and he spends nearly every evening with his parents and the extended Frazier family, who keep a nonstop social schedule—lobster dinners, bonfires, house parties, boat parties, pig roasts, bingo, ice cream socials, dances, and steamers on Sundays. Darren doesn't offer to bring Kirby to any of these events, which she understands at first—they're still getting to know each other—but she assumes it's only a matter of time. Darren leaves these social engagements early so that he can pick Kirby up at ten o'clock and drive her to work, and the next morning he's always stationed out front at seven on the dot to drive her back to Narragansett Avenue before he has to report to the beach.

At night, they neck in the front seat of the car—they park on little-used Thayer Street—but in the mornings, they keep themselves to just a hand squeeze in case any of Kirby's housemates are looking out the window. Kirby longs to be more intimate with Darren—sexually, certainly, but also emotionally. They talk in the car and they kiss in the car; the mere sight of the red Corvair turning the corner makes Kirby's heart breach like a whale. But she wants another *date*. She wants to go to the movies or to dinner at the Boston House or even to shoot a game of pool at Lou's Worry. She'd like to double with Patty and Luke, although ever since that night with Tommy O'Callahan, Patty and Luke have kept to themselves, and Kirby understands. All she wants is to be alone with Darren.

"Can we do the carousel again?" Kirby asks him. "Maybe tonight before work?"

"It's my auntie's birthday," he says. "The judge is making oyster stew."

"I love oyster stew," Kirby says, though this is an outright lie. She likes clams, shrimp, and mussels and she's a fool for lobster, but the pleasure of the oyster still eludes her. She's just angling for an invite.

None comes.

"We'll go back to the carousel," Darren says. "Just not tonight."

But then... serendipity! They have the same day off, Tuesday, and Darren proposes a beach outing.

"I'll plan everything," he says. "All you need is your bikini and a book."

Kirby loves that he said she needed a book—what is the beach without a good book?—but she hopes they are too busy swimming and kissing and splashing and tussling in the sand to read. Even so, she packs *Myra Breckinridge,* which she hasn't even cracked open, and she decides she's finally tan enough to wear her white crocheted bikini.

Darren asks Kirby to meet him at Tony's Market; he wants to pick up beer and ice, and they can leave from there. Kirby agrees... but as she's walking from Narragansett Avenue to Tony's, she passes right by Darren's house and his car is still out front.

Should she go knock on the door or keep going and meet him at Tony's like he asked her to?

Her head advises her to keep going. Her heart tells her differently.

She marches up the walk and knocks on the door.

"Come in!" a voice booms from inside.

Kirby pulls open the screen door and enters. She peers into the sunny front room with its bright furnishings; on the white kidney-shaped table there's a glass pitcher holding periwinkle hydrangeas that make the room even more summery and inviting. In addition to being beautiful and accomplished, Dr. Frazier has impeccable taste. Kirby is nearly frantic to win her over. She continues down the hall, passing a small powder room with green bamboo-printed wallpaper, to the last door on the right, which opens to an eat-in kitchen that is decorated to resemble a Parisian brasserie. There is a black-and-white-tile floor and marble countertops and frosted-glass globe pendant lights and a wooden sign that says CAFÉ, CHOCOLAT, PÂTE, ET SIROPS over the copper sink. There's jaunty clarinet music playing.

The judge is leaning against the counter, bifocals on, with the newspaper spread out in front of him. He's wearing green golf pants and a yellow polo shirt. There's a couple sitting at the round bistro table drinking coffee and helping themselves to a rainbow pinwheel of fruit and a platter of muffins.

"Hi," Kirby says. The man and woman at the table are older, the judge's age, and Kirby tells herself to act natural, as though she were meeting friends of her own parents. "Sorry to interrupt. I'm looking for Darren."

The three adults stare at her for a second as though she's an alien arrived from Mars. Kirby is, frankly, relieved that Dr. Frazier isn't present. This is her chance to charm the judge, maybe. She gives him her best smile. "Your Honor, I'm Kirby Foley. I met you at the Homeport with Rajani?"

"Yes," the judge says. "I remember. Good morning."

The woman stands up. "I'm Cassandra Frazier," she says, offering her hand. Her hair is in a towering bun that's wound with a colorful scarf. She's wearing wooden bangles that clatter as she shakes Kirby's hand. "And this is my husband, Hank," she says as she sits down.

Hank has a mouthful of muffin but he rises to shake Kirby's hand, and then, once he's swallowed, he says, "Hank Frazier, first cousin of the honorable judge."

Kirby looks at Cassandra. "Are you by any chance the sister of Mr. Ames's wife, Susanna?"

Cassandra cocks her head and offers a half smile. "I am, yes. How do you know Susanna?"

"Oh, I've never met her. But I work the night shift with Mr. Ames at the Shiretown Inn and when I mentioned that I was friends with Darren, he said his wife's sister was married to the judge's cousin." Kirby feels a small sense of triumph, as though she has just plugged the last piece into a jigsaw puzzle.

"Yes!" Cassandra exclaims. "You're the young lady from Nantucket, then? Cal raves about you."

"That's very nice to hear," Kirby says. She checks to make sure that Judge Frazier has taken note of this, that his cousin's wife's sister's husband raves about Kirby. *See?* she wants to say. *Someone you know, even ever so tangentially, thinks I'm worth raving about.*

The judge says, "And you're here to see Darren?"

"I am," Kirby says. "We're going to the beach."

"The beach?" the judge says, as though he's never heard of the place. He turns to face the doorway. "Darren! You have a visitor!"

Kirby wants to compliment the room—it's so *cool,* with all the art deco flourishes, so unexpectedly fun and fresh. She wants to take a mental picture of the fruit plate so that at some point in her own adult life, when she has money for that kind of exquisite produce, she might re-create it—pale green slices of honeydew melon, brighter green kiwi, fresh pineapple, pale disks of banana, strawberries cut into fans, a pile of blueberries and blackberries in the center. She wants to ask Cassandra where she got her scarf and her bracelets. Is the scarf from Paris? The bracelets look vaguely African; were they purchased at a market in Nairobi? Kirby also wants to ask about the music. She usually listens to rock 'n' roll but the clarinet has a cheerful cadence that makes it perfect for a summer morning. Is it Benny Goodman? Basically, Kirby would like to be invited to be a part of this world, but she's afraid of sounding pushy, and so she says nothing, and the four of them stew in awkward silence until Darren comes down to the kitchen. When he sees Kirby, his expression is one of unadulterated alarm.

"What are you doing here?" he says.

Kirby tries to smile. "We're going to the beach…right?"

"I didn't know your friend works with Cal at the Shiretown Inn," Cassandra says. "You should have told me."

Darren gives his aunt a distracted nod. To Kirby he says, "I thought I said Tony's."

"You did, but I was in the neighborhood."

"You're off to the beach?" the judge asks.

"The nudie beach?" Hank crows.

"Lobsterville," Darren says. "We're meeting people there."

They are? This is news to Kirby.

The judge takes his time folding the newspaper and everyone watches as he does so. Kirby can tell he's deliberating over something. What will his verdict be?

"Go on, then," he says. "Get out of here before your mother gets home."

They head out to the car in silence. Kirby feels she owes Darren an apology; it was rude of her to show up unannounced. She wanted to prove something, but what? That she wasn't afraid? That she could hang out with Darren's family and fit in? In the end, she has proved nothing and now Darren's angry. He parks the Corvair in front of Tony's Market and runs in without a word. Kirby nearly calls out to offer him money, but in the end, she just folds her hands in her lap and bows her head. *Get out of here before your mother gets home.* It doesn't take a Rhodes Scholar to figure out what the judge meant by that.

When Darren emerges from the store, he's grinning. He's himself again. He puts the ice and beer on the floor in the back seat, starts the engine, turns up the radio. It's Dylan singing "Lay, Lady, Lay."

"Let's get out of this town," he says. "I want to relax."

It's Kirby's fourth time up-island and she's beginning to recognize landmarks—the Ag Hall and Alley's General Store in West Tisbury and then the long stretch of Middle Road. They pass the turnoff for Tea Lane, where Rajani nannies the demon twins in the beachfront castle with the Warhol, and then, once Middle Road turns into State, Kirby recognizes the driveway to Luke's compound on Nashaquitsa Pond. They pass through Menemsha, turn right, and end up at Lobsterville Beach.

"I've heard about this beach from guests at the inn," she says. "One man got such a bad sunburn, he renamed it Turned-into-a-Lobster-Ville Beach."

Darren laughs and it sounds genuine. The day started out a little topsy-turvy, but Kirby feels it righting itself.

Lobsterville Beach is nearly empty; they are very clearly not meeting anyone else. Darren carries the chairs and the cooler to a secluded cove where they can see the cliffs of Gay Head jutting out into the ocean. It must be the most picturesque spot on the island, Kirby thinks, and he sought it out for her. He sets up the chairs and towels and then he strips off his T-shirt. His skin is such a beautiful color that Kirby wants to compliment it, but she isn't sure what words to use.

He notices her staring at him. "You ready to swim?"

"Hell, yeah," she says and she races him to the water.

Darren bought Schlitz beer, her favorite, and it's icy cold. They crack a couple open, and then, because there's no one else in sight, Kirby produces a joint that she tucked into her change purse before she left the house.

"Smoke?" she says.

"I don't usually," he says. "But today I'll make an exception."

Kirby lights the joint, takes a toke, and passes it over to Darren, who inhales with deep appreciation. They smoke the joint down to an itty-bitty roach and then Kirby falls back on her towel, suffused in a cloud of sweet smoke and a sense of great well-being. Drugs are a public scourge and yet they make absolutely everything better, at least temporarily. Before she knows what's happening, Darren pulls her up by the hand and leads her behind a giant boulder at the edge of the cove. He starts kissing her. It's novel for them to be standing, with their hips pushed together, and then, as if that isn't seductive enough, Darren lifts her up. Her back scrapes against the rock but she doesn't care. She wraps her legs around him and squeezes and gets lost in the kissing and in the pressure and in the heat between their bodies. When she opens her eyes, she sees the green, raging sea beyond and she knows she will never forget this moment.

She breaks away. "I want to wait."

"You do?" Darren says. He eases her feet back down to the sand. "I mean, yeah, that's cool. We can wait."

"I'd like a bed," Kirby says. "I'm sure that sounds old-fashioned."

Darren kisses her. "Not old-fashioned at all. I'd like a bed too. You deserve a man who lavishes you with attention, who takes his time with you."

For no reason, tears burn Kirby's eyes. Or *not* for no reason. She is suddenly assaulted by memories of sex with Officer Scottie Turbo. It was fast, it was rough, it was about his pleasure, not hers; it was about his needs, his schedule, his agenda.

He used her, then threw her away.

"Hey," Darren says, running a thumb under her eye. "What's wrong?"

"Your parents don't know we're seeing each other, do they?" She uses the phrase *seeing each other* because that's all it is. It isn't dating. They never *go* anywhere together. They are never seen in public. She's a secret for him, just like she was with Scottie Turbo.

Darren sighs. "No," he says. "They don't."

"It's your mother who objects."

"Yes, and she persuaded my father that you're…I don't know. Inappropriate? I'm not sure why."

"I know why," Kirby says. She squints down the beach; it's deserted. "Want to walk?"

"Sure," Darren says.

The story is easier to tell while they're in motion. Kirby can stare straight ahead instead of at Darren, which gives her some emotional distance.

"Remember when I told you about the policeman I dated?" she says.

"Yes," Darren says. "He's haunted me since you mentioned him."

"I went to an antiwar protest this past winter," Kirby says. "In Cambridge."

Darren shrugs. "I didn't go to any. I mean, I'm against the war, but I had so much work . . ."

"Protesting takes time," Kirby says. "You don't have to explain to me." She had spent countless hours making signs and convincing other women at Simmons to go. This was in February, after the second year of surprise Tet attacks but before Tiger was drafted, so at that time, Kirby's opposition to the war had been pure and uncomplicated. She had marched, she had chanted, she had disobeyed police orders to the crowds to stand down, to clear the streets and go home. She had called one policeman a pig and was preparing to spit on his shield just as she had spit on Roger Donnelly's school desk years before when he grabbed her, pinned her hands behind her back, cuffed her, and said, "You're coming with me, dollface."

It gives Kirby chills thinking of it even now.

She quieted down once she was cuffed; her situation had become very real very quickly and all she could think was how angry her parents would be, and Exalta would be worse than angry. Kirby was being *arrested*. The officer remained silent as he did his best to skirt the mob and lead Kirby back to his squad car. He pulled her along by the upper arm, though his grip loosened, and indeed, he was nearly gentle with her, protective. Kirby was relieved for a moment. This man was going to deliver her from the mayhem. What was she *doing* here, anyway? She *did* want an end to the war and she wanted her voice to be heard by the people in charge—Nixon, John Mitchell, Spiro Agnew, Henry Kissinger. But now there would be very real consequences for her idealism—expense and public shame.

"I'm sorry I called you a pig," Kirby said. "I don't think the police are pigs. I'm not sure why I said that."

The officer shrugged. "Nobody's right if everybody's wrong."

Kirby suppressed a smile. He was quoting Buffalo Springfield! Had she managed to get arrested by the one member of the Boston Police Department who had a rebellious streak?

When they got to the squad car, the officer read Kirby her Miranda rights, but his heart didn't seem to be in it. Kirby focused on his name tag, TURBO, and thought that it was a name better suited to a fighter pilot. Then she noticed that his eyes were green, her favorite color, and there was a sly cast to his expression that had long been her downfall with men.

"How old are you, dollface?" he asked.

"Twenty-one," she said. "I'm a junior at Simmons."

"Oh yeah?" he said. "I thought maybe you were one of those uppity Wellesley girls."

"They rejected me," Kirby said. Blair had gone to Wellesley, but Kirby's grades hadn't been as good and she didn't make the cut, much to Exalta's dismay.

"Rejected *you,* dollface?" he said. "You're kidding me."

"Stop calling me that," she said. *Dollface.* It was such a demeaning term. She wasn't a doll. She was a woman, a person.

Before she knew what was happening, Officer Turbo lifted her chin and kissed her. She thought of resisting, pushing him away, even kicking him in the nuts. He was abusing his authority! But she instantly felt attracted to him. She was helpless anyway, with her hands shackled behind her back, but the thing was, this *turned her on.* It was so wrong, so counter to the principles of being a strong female, that she felt betrayed by her body.

He was the one who pulled away. He looked as startled as she felt. "I'm against the war too," he said. Before she could respond, he said, "I'm not going to haul you in. But I am writing you a ticket for disturbing the peace."

She had thought, *Ha! That's ironic.* It was Richard Nixon who was disturbing the peace—and Johnson before him, and McNamara. Kirby stood quietly while Officer Turbo wrote out a ticket then uncuffed her and handed her the citation as though nothing had happened, as though he hadn't just given her the best kiss of her young life.

"My name's Scottie," he said. "Stay out of trouble."

Kirby had turned her misadventure into an empowering anecdote. Yes, she had been arrested, put in handcuffs and everything, but in her greatly modified rendition of the story, she talked sense into the arresting officer and he let her go with just a fine. Seventy-five dollars. It was too much money for Kirby to come up with on her student budget and so she had to tell her parents. They should be grateful, she'd told them. He'd let her off easy.

Kate and David were not grateful; they were appalled. But Kirby pointed out that all she had done was protest the government's foreign policy, a right guaranteed her by the U.S. Constitution. It was the policeman who should be judged, not Kirby.

"What was the officer's name?" David asked.

"I forget," Kirby lied. David was an influential lawyer and could probably find a way to have Officer Scottie Turbo disciplined or even suspended, which wasn't what Kirby wanted. What Kirby wanted was to see Scottie Turbo again—but how? All she knew about him was that he was an officer with the BPD who had been assigned to the protests in Cambridge that day. She had no way to determine what his regular beat was. Did he write parking tickets around Fenway or investigate break-ins in Back Bay or set speed traps on Route 93? Kirby realized her best hope of seeing Scottie Turbo again was to do what she had been doing the first time, and so a few weeks later, when another protest was scheduled at Harvard, Kirby attended.

She tried to remember where she had been when he grabbed her; she thought it was on Russell Street, across from the Coop. And sure enough, there he was, standing in exactly the same spot.

"Pig!" she shouted. She considered pretending to spit but she couldn't bring herself to do it. Instead, she winked at him, and he immediately grabbed her by the arm—harder this time—pinned her wrists behind her, and threw on the cuffs.

"Hey, dollface," he said in her ear.

He led Kirby to his squad car, read her her Miranda rights, then opened the back door.

"Get in," he said.

Fear rumbled through Kirby's gut. Was he taking her in for real this time? She ducked her head and folded into the back seat of the car, which was separated from the front by a metal grate. She felt like an animal. He drove south through Boston, past UMass, past Quincy, and into Braintree, where he pulled over behind an abandoned warehouse. It started to rain, which only made the circumstances bleaker. What were they *doing* here? Officer Turbo parked and got out to survey the area. Kirby couldn't help craning her neck too. There was no one else around. He could shoot her and dump her and he would never be caught.

He opened the back door. "Move over," he said. He slid in beside her and unlocked her cuffs.

They started seeing each other every few days. They went to first base, second base, third base—and then Scottie would stop. It was excruciating. Kirby wanted to sneak him into her dorm, but she had a roommate who was always around.

"What about your place? Can't we go there?" she asked.

"No," he said. "I live with my mother. She's older but still sharp. And she has a German shepherd who is very territorial."

"Motel?" she said. It seemed sleazy and low-class, but what choice did they have?

"I've got a better idea," he said. "I own a little fishing shack up on Lake Winnipesaukee. First nice day, we'll go."

The first nice stretch of days came the second week of April, right after Easter. Officer Scottie Turbo pulled up to the Simmons campus in a royal-blue Dodge convertible, picked Kirby up, and drove north on I-95 to a town called Wolfeboro, New Hampshire, on the lake.

"I went to school in this town," he said.

"You *did?*" Kirby said. She realized then that she knew almost nothing about Scottie's background except that he lived with his mother and her German shepherd, that he graduated in the middle of the pack from the police academy, and that he'd made a name for himself in crowd control. His regular beats included Fenway Park and Alumni Stadium.

"Brewster Academy," he said. "My parents sent me there after I got expelled from Weymouth High School for fighting." He pointed out the campus—a cluster of white clapboard buildings on a green with a darling chapel—and Kirby tried to picture a teenage Scottie Turbo walking to class. It was nearly impossible; he was so sturdy, serious, surly. It seemed like he had been born a full-grown man.

The fishing shack was exactly that—a wooden structure that featured four walls, a floor, and a roof. It was furnished for survival; there was a metal sink, a small icebox, a cot with a bare mattress. Scottie threw open two doors, and voilà—the gloom became illuminated with the day's sunlight. Outside was a small deck with a table and two chairs, and beyond the deck lay a steep muddy bank that descended to the expanse of Lake Winnipesaukee.

The lake was beautiful in an austere way. The trees were only starting to bud but the unseasonably warm day hinted at how appealing this place must be in summer and early fall. Unsure of what to do, Kirby lingered at the railing of the deck, gazing out. Scottie came up behind her, moved her hair, and kissed the back of her neck.

They made love three or four times that day, then slept intertwined on the cot; they even went skinny-dipping in the lake. The water was so cold it burned, but when Kirby emerged she felt clean and strong, as though she had been dipped in steel. When the sun started to descend, they got back in the Dodge and drove to a little tavern downtown for hot roast beef sandwiches and cold beer.

When Scottie dropped Kirby back at Simmons, she knew she was in love.

Kirby doesn't tell Darren all of this, naturally, just the gist of it, and she doesn't check to see how he's processing everything. They reach the point on the beach where they can't go any farther, and that seems like a natural place to turn around and head back.

Now comes the hard part, Kirby thinks.

Once Kirby and Scottie had slept together, the genie could not be put back into the bottle. There followed a string of days when all Kirby could think about was how they could be together. Another trip to Winnipesaukee was impractical, so they resorted to fast, furtive interludes in the dark corners and crevices of Boston. Behind the warehouse in Braintree was a favorite spot, as was a certain hidden nook in the park along the Charles River; one time, it was the bathroom of an Irish bar next to Fenway during one of the first Red Sox games of the season.

And then Kirby felt a change. She was dizzy; her breasts were tender; she was tired.

No, she thought. Blair was pregnant but she was married to Angus, which made it a proper and joyful event. Kirby being in the same boat was a disgrace. There was also the undeniable fact that Kirby didn't want children, ever.

When she started to feel nauseated, she made an appointment at the free clinic in Roxbury under the name of Clarissa Bouvier— the name Clarissa had been plucked right from the book she was reading in her contemporary literature class, *Mrs. Dalloway,* and Bouvier was a tribute to the former First Lady, Jackie Kennedy. After the nurse confirmed that yes, Kirby was probably about six weeks along, she said, "The doctor will be in to examine you."

The woman who walked in was named Dr. Frazier. Kirby had started to cry.

Dr. Frazier had cocked an eyebrow. "So…I take it this wasn't planned?"

No, not planned, not wanted. "I can't have this baby," Kirby said. "I *cannot.* I can't even go away, have the baby, and come back. I'm in college. My brother just went to war. My family can't handle any more shocks. Plus they'll disown me."

"I highly doubt that," Dr. Frazier said. "Where do you live?"

"Brookline," Kirby said.

"So you have resources, then," Dr. Frazier said.

If by *resources,* she meant money, then yes. The Foley-Levins had financial resources. But they were growing short on emotional resources. "I can't have this baby. It's not an option."

"Legally, that's your only option," Dr. Frazier said. Kirby can remember hating Dr. Frazier at that moment. The doctor was in her mid-forties and very attractive, very put-together, too put-together to be working at this crappy clinic. Kirby guessed that she volunteered here a day or two a week.

"Surely there must be *someplace,*" Kirby said. There were rumors at Simmons about ways to handle an unwanted pregnancy, like a storefront in Chinatown. If you knew the secret password, they'd give you a magic potion, and when you woke up, it was done. "In Chinatown?"

The doctor sighed. "I could get in trouble for telling you this, but here's an address. Don't wait on this"—Dr. Frazier checked the file for her patient's name—"Clarissa. It's safe but it's not cheap."

This was the worst event of Kirby's life, but for the doctor, Kirby supposed, it was just another day in the office. The address was on Washington Street, somewhere in the desolate South End. Kirby clutched the piece of paper like the life preserver it was.

Don't wait on this, Dr. Frazier had said, but Kirby had to take care of something first. She arranged to meet Scottie that evening behind the warehouse in Braintree. She didn't let on that anything was wrong but when she saw him, she tells Darren, she stuttered until she got the words out: *Scottie, I'm p-pregnant!*

"And what did he say?" Darren wants to know. "Did he do the honorable thing and ask you to marry him?"

Would she be standing here if he had? She had been so blindly infatuated with Scottie Turbo that if he had said he wanted to marry her and keep the baby, she would have said yes. But Scottie Turbo had said no such thing. He had pulled all the cash out of his wallet—a hundred and forty-two dollars—and said he hoped that was enough. Kirby didn't say, *Enough for what?* She knew what it was for. And even though an abortion was what she wanted, it hurt her that it was what *he* wanted too.

She took his money and said, "You don't live with your mother, do you? You're married, aren't you?"

He said, "What are you, a detective?" And then he'd kissed her forehead and hurried back to his squad car.

She never heard from him again.

Later that night, she had awoken with painful cramping, and in the morning, she started to bleed.

"Things took care of themselves," Kirby says to Darren now. "But I couldn't believe it when Rajani took me to your house and…there was Dr. Frazier. At first, I didn't think she remembered me. But now I know that she does."

Darren squeezes Kirby's hand. "I'm sorry you had to go through all that. This doesn't change my feelings for you one bit. People have histories, Kirby. I don't care what my mother thinks."

"But you *do* care," Kirby says. "You're here with me, sure—at an unpopulated beach. But you should have seen your face when you walked into your kitchen today."

"You took me by surprise—"

"You didn't want me there. And your father told us to shoo before your mother got home."

"I don't think my mother would *judge* you," Darren says. "She's not like that. She sees girls in that predicament all the time."

"I think your mother is a lovely person," Kirby says. "And she helped me when I desperately needed it. But she doesn't want you to date me. You're her only child, a son who goes to Harvard. She wants you to be with someone virtuous and principled and unsullied. It doesn't matter that I didn't end up having an abortion. It matters that I was careless and exercised poor judgment and let myself get into trouble." They arrive back at their towels. Kirby's heart is dense and cold, like a hunk of ice in her chest. She gathers up her things. "I want you to take me home."

"Kirby."

"Darren."

They stare at each other and it feels like a standoff. "Fight for me, then," she says. "Invite me to the beach picnic at Lambert's Cove on Friday or for steamers on Sunday. Tell your parents and your aunts, uncles, and cousins that we're dating and too bad if they don't like it."

"I'm afraid they'll make you uncomfortable," Darren says.

"You're afraid they'll make *you* uncomfortable," Kirby says.

"I think if we just take it slow—"

"Meaning keep it a secret."

"You're being unfair."

"It's doomed!" Kirby says. Being with Scottie Turbo had taught her how to recognize a doomed relationship. "There are things we can change and things we can't. I *can* change how your family sees me, I promise you that, but only if you give me the chance to spend some time with them."

"Kirby..."

He knows she's right, she can see it on his face, but she can also see he's too afraid to do anything about it.

"Take me home, Darren," she says. "Please."

Darren dutifully collapses the chairs, folds the towels, packs up the cooler, and heads back to the car, Kirby trailing him. As she climbs in the passenger side of the Corvair, in her mind, she travels back four weeks, to the first time she laid eyes on Darren, when he stopped to pick her up hitchhiking. She had no idea that saying yes to that ride would lead to this crushing disappointment, but she has to admit that if she had the moment to do over, she would still say yes.

Whatever Lola Wants

The evenings that Kate has spent at the Straight Wharf Theater over the years have been some of the happiest of her life, and although she's miserable to her core this summer, she still brightens when Exalta reminds her they have three tickets, front row, for that evening's performance of *Damn Yankees.* Kate has never seen the show but she loves Adler and Ross and she loves seeing shows on Nantucket in an intimate theater with familiar faces in the cast.

They were planning to take Jessie but she's been grounded because news of the stealing incident at the club reached Exalta's ears and Jessie confirmed it was true. When Exalta relayed this to Kate, Kate said, "I'll have a talk with her," and Exalta said, "I've handled the matter, darling. Believe me, she has learned her lesson."

Kate knows she should address the issue with Jessie nonetheless, but she doesn't have the energy. Jessie is grounded for the rest of the week—no beach, no town, and no theater tonight. Fine.

Blair says she's far too big to sit comfortably for two hours, so Exalta offers the third ticket to Bill Crimmins, which makes sense, since he is the only other grown-up in the house, but it makes Kate uncomfortable.

"Really, Mother?" Kate says. "We're taking Bill?"

"He loves the theater," Exalta says. "And please wipe that look off your face, darling. He's hardly our *servant.*"

"Not our servant, obviously," Kate says, though he is their employee and also, this summer, their tenant. But Kate holds her tongue because she knows that her real issue with Bill Crimmins isn't his social status; he has worked for them for so long he can be considered family. Kate's issue is that Bill Crimmins owes her an answer about her son and he seems unaware of the agony that Kate is enduring while she waits. Normal interaction with the man is impossible.

For this trip to the theater, then, she will have to call upon her own inner actress. Kate, Exalta, and Bill leave the house with plenty of time to spare for a seven-thirty curtain. Bill looks more than respectable in pressed slacks and a navy blazer. He is solicitous and polite, careful to act as escort to both Exalta and Kate. He knows absolutely everyone on the island and is greeted what feels like a hundred times as they walk to the theater and then a hundred times more once they enter the theater.

"You're quite the social butterfly," Exalta says. She sounds put-out, nearly jealous, and Kate itches to remind Exalta that they don't know anyone because in the decades that they've lived here, they have socialized only at one place and that's the Field and Oar Club. The club often *feels* like the center of the island but as Kate looks around, she sees there is an entire community of people—summer and year-round—whom she doesn't know. She can't be bothered about her limited circle this summer; that's a luxury for a woman whose son is not at war. For now, it will be all Kate can do to pay attention to the performance. It doesn't have a military theme, which is good; she couldn't have handled *South Pacific,* for example, or even *Bye Bye Birdie*. This musical is about baseball.

But as the house lights dim and the show begins, Kate grows uneasy. The plot seems innocent enough—a longtime Washington Senators fan desperately wants his team to beat the Yankees and win the pennant. But it quickly turns into a tale of selling one's soul to the devil. The character of Mr. Applegate is going to turn old Joe Boyd into Shoeless Joe Hardy, who will have the talent to lead the Senators to the pennant...in exchange for his soul.

Kate struggles not to draw parallels. She and Bill have an agreement, an understanding. He and his grandson can stay indefinitely...if he finds a way to get Tiger home.

But if that doesn't happen?

The show is entertaining. Kate loses herself in the story for long stretches. Bill Crimmins is sitting between Kate and Exalta, but Kate notices Exalta pitched forward in her seat, in thrall to the actors and the music.

The woman who plays Lola is a knockout. Kate recognizes her as one of the people who were sitting at table 1 at the Opera House the other night. When she sings "Whatever Lola Wants," Exalta sings along softly.

Well, yes, Kate thinks, her mother *would* like that song.

Kate decides she will talk to Bill Crimmins tonight. She can't wait another day. Nixon has promised to start sending boys home but there are still half a million troops in Vietnam, and the ones who will leave first are the ones who have been over there the longest, meaning not Tiger. Kate wants to believe that the peace talks taking place in Paris will work, but the negotiators can't even decide on a round table versus a rectangular table, so how can they possibly iron out their ideological differences?

The play has a happy ending—Shoeless Joe wins the pennant *and* escapes eternal damnation *and* is reunited with his one true love, his wife. *I don't need everything tied up with a bow,* Kate thinks. She just needs Tiger to come home.

At the curtain call, Exalta jumps to her feet, clapping wildly, and then Bill Crimmins stands, presumably in deference to Exalta.

(*Whatever Exalta wants,* Kate thinks, *Exalta gets.*) And soon the rest of the audience members get to their feet. There are whistles and hollers of approval. The cast bows, then bows again.

The lights come up, and, as much as Kate enjoyed the show, she's glad it's over.

Walking down Fair Street, Exalta gushes, "That was just marvelous, wasn't it?"

"It was indeed," Bill Crimmins agrees heartily.

"Let's go to dinner," Exalta says.

"Mother," Kate says.

"At the Woodbox," Exalta says. "I haven't been once all summer and it's right across the street!"

"I could go for some popovers," Bill Crimmins says. "And Madame T. is quite fond of me, you know."

"Everyone on this island is fond of you, Bill," Exalta observes.

"I'm going to pass," Kate says. She likes to eat at the Woodbox when they come up for the occasional autumn weekend, but in the summer, it's beastly hot, and beyond that, Kate doesn't have the patience to sit and make small talk about the show when she has such pressing business to discuss with Bill Crimmins. She's positive that once she demurs, Exalta will as well, because what is Exalta going to do? Go to dinner with Bill Crimmins by herself?

Yes, apparently. Bill Crimmins links his arm through Exalta's and they saunter across the street, leaving Kate to stand out in front of All's Fair.

Kate tells herself she doesn't care. She goes inside to pour herself a vodka.

Kate is three drinks in when she hears her mother and Bill Crimmins come home. There are brief good-nights exchanged and then

273

Kate hears Exalta's footsteps on the stairs, and Bill Crimmins strides into the kitchen whistling "Shoeless Joe from Hannibal, Mo.," his blazer dangling off one hooked finger. When he sees Kate sitting in the near dark with a vodka over ice in front of her, he startles and his expression becomes fearful, as though he has encountered the devil herself.

"Bill," she says.

"Katie."

Again, the loathsome nickname. Kate stands up, steadying herself against the table. "I need to know about Tiger."

Bill's face falls and Kate grips the table's edge.

"I overestimated my brother-in-law's influence," he says. "He isn't able to pull the strings to get Tiger home."

"Bill," Kate says. She isn't sure which emotion to indulge first, anger or agony. She *knew* things would turn out this way—the U.S. military isn't inclined to grant personal favors, even when the request comes from the very top—and yet she still feels swindled. Bill's suggestion had been prompted by desperation. He needed a place for himself and the boy to live; he might have flat-out *lied* to bargain his way into Little Fair. Did Bill's brother-in-law even *know* the general? Had Bill's brother-in-law really served in World War II? Did Bill even *have* a brother-in-law?

"I do have information, however," Bill says. "I was able to get that."

"Information?" Kate says. "What does that mean?"

Bill pulls a chair out as though to sit down, but Kate shakes her head. "Tell me right now."

"Tiger has been sent off on a special mission." Bill bunches his blazer up in his hands and stares down at it. "It was unexpected. Tiger's company ran into a bad firefight"—Kate squeezes her eyes closed—"and so many men in his company were killed that the survivors were reassigned to other companies and Tiger was sent..."

"Where?" Kate asks.

"To Cambodia," Bill says. "He was sent on a special mission to Cambodia."

Cambodia, Kate thinks as she falls into bed. Tiger has supposedly been sent on a mission to disrupt the flow of supplies along the Ho Chi Minh Trail. Kate is skeptical. Is this information reliable? Bill Crimmins has proved untrustworthy; who's to say that he's not making this up? Although it would explain why there have been no letters.

When Kate asked Bill Crimmins how long he had known about Cambodia, he said, "I found out only a few days ago. I've been waiting for the right time to tell you."

This answer made Kate livid. Granted, she hadn't seen much of Bill Crimmins the past few days, but he'd just sat through an entire musical with her without giving a hint or a clue that he had news of any kind. When he entered the kitchen, he had been *whistling!* The news obviously didn't weigh on him at all. If Kate hadn't asked him directly, would he have kept the information a secret so that he and Pick could continue to live in Little Fair?

Yes, undoubtedly.

Kate was so furious—and so, so upset about Tiger in Cambodia, which was a place she couldn't picture and that she wasn't sure she could point to on a map—that she ordered Bill Crimmins to move out. He could stay until the end of the weekend, she told him. But that was it.

Even in the dark kitchen, she had seen Bill's face turn ashen. "But it's July, Katie," he said. "Where are we going to live? All the summer rentals are booked and I couldn't possibly afford one of those anyway."

"I agreed to let you stay because you told me you could help Tiger. You promised." Kate wasn't sure that Bill *had* promised, exactly, but the message in his letter had been clear: He would use his connections to keep Tiger safe. But he hadn't, and now he had to face the consequences. A good-faith effort on his part wasn't enough, not when Tiger's life was on the line.

"Pick has a job here," Bill said. "He's working his tail off every single day. And I have a business to run. I have clients who depend on me."

"Well, then, maybe one of your other clients will offer you a place to live," she said.

"Katie," he said. "Come on. You're not like this."

True; Kate *wasn't* like this. Exalta was the tough, uncompromising one. Kate had always been distinguished by her loveliness, her graciousness, her empathy, her charity—qualities her mother counted as weaknesses. It was only with Tiger's deployment that Kate had developed a carapace around her heart. "Have you ever thought what it feels like for me?" she asked. "Having him here?"

"He's almost never around..."

"Even so," Kate said. She moved toward the hallway. "Good night, Bill."

"You don't want to do this, Kate," he said. His voice from the dark void of the kitchen was menacing. "I know I promised never to tell anyone about what happened...but you've put me in a spot where it might be impossible to keep quiet."

He was threatening her, then—and under other circumstances, this might be effective. Bill Crimmins was the only person on the planet who knew Kate's secret. But oddly, it didn't scare her. If he told anyone what she'd admitted to him so many years ago, it would be his word against hers. No one would believe Bill Crimmins.

Except for Exalta. If Exalta heard what Bill Crimmins had to say, she would know it was true.

But Kate didn't care anymore. Nothing mattered to Kate but getting Tiger home.

Sunshine of Your Love

During her truly miserable week in captivity, Jessie finishes *Anne Frank: The Diary of a Young Girl*. The diary ends abruptly, and sure enough, the afterword states that Anne and her sister, Margot, were discovered in their hiding place and taken first to Auschwitz, then to Bergen-Belsen, where they died of typhus. Jessie blinks back hot tears, thinking she must have misread something. She assumed that Anne survived, because why would anyone assign this book to a seventh-grader if Anne had *died?* But reading it again does nothing to change the outcome. Anne died; only Otto Frank, her father, survived. Miep Gies found Anne's diary; she gave it to Otto Frank, who allowed it to be published.

The line that finally makes Jessie burst into sobs is *In spite of everything I still believe that people are really good at heart.*

Jessie cries and cries. What about Helen Dunscombe? she wonders. Is *she* good at heart? What about Garrison Howe? What about Exalta? Jessie is so angry at Exalta that she suspects the answer is no, Exalta is *not* good at heart. She's judgmental and prejudiced. But how did she get that way? She has everything a person could want.

Jessie tries to get a grip, but the tears keep coming. Tiger is on a secret mission. Jessie has no details but it sounds dangerous, even more dangerous than the regular Vietnam War.

Are the *Vietcong* good at heart?

Some of them, probably. The Vietcong support Communism, which is a system in which everyone shares. This is bad because in exchange for this sharing, individuals give up their freedom, and to Americans, freedom is the most important thing.

Jessie has had her freedom taken away this week, so she understands its value.

There's a knock on her door and Jessie reaches for a tissue to mop her face. "Hello?" she says.

The door opens a bit and Pick pokes his head in. "You okay?" he says. "I heard you crying."

Jessie can't possibly admit that she's weeping over her summer reading. "My brother was sent out on a secret mission," she says.

Pick comes in, closes the door behind him, and sits on Jessie's bed, facing her. He's half an arm's distance away. Jessie's mother would explode like a grenade if she knew that Pick and Jessie were in Jessie's bedroom with the door closed. Jessie would be grounded for another week, at least, but she isn't about to ask Pick to leave.

"That's so *cool*. Maybe he's an assassin or something. Maybe he's going to be a hero."

Jessie wants to inform Pick that Tiger is already a hero; every American soldier fighting in Vietnam is a hero. "Maybe," she says. "What are you doing home?" It's eleven thirty in the morning, a time Pick usually goes to the beach.

"It's kind of a blah day out," he says. "Plus I wanted to sleep in. I'm going to a party after work tonight. Some of the waitstaff are having a bonfire on the beach."

"Sounds fun," Jessie says.

"I wish I could invite you along but it's my first time being included and I'm not sure it would be cool if I brought a date."

Date. Despite Jessie's abject misery, her heart sprouts wings.

"I can't go anywhere anyway," Jessie says. "I'm grounded."

Pick reaches out and wipes away Jessie's tears and she stays stock-still, feeling warmth where he touched her. "Grounded?" he says. "What'd you do?"

"Nonny found out I lost the necklace," Jessie says. "I took it without asking."

"Sticky fingers," Pick says. "I like it." Without warning, Pick leans over and kisses Jessie on the lips.

Jessie is dumbstruck. The kiss was light, fleeting, sweet. *Do it again!* Jessie thinks. *Do it again!*

He must read her mind, because he kisses her again and his mouth stays on her mouth and then his lips part and she feels his tongue. It's foreign—someone else's tongue in her mouth—but it's also electrifying. She feels like someone just plugged her in. Their tongues touch and in another instant, they are necking, just like people in the movies, and Pick shifts closer and puts a hand behind her head and pulls her in.

How long does it last? A couple of minutes, the most sublime, intoxicating minutes of Jessie's life. Kissing is...well, Jessie now understands it's the secret to happiness. She never wants to stop. She tries not to think, just surrenders to their tongues and Pick's soft lips and the way he smells and tastes.

Finally, he pulls away. She's dizzy.

He grins. "I've been wanting to do that for a while now."

"You have?"

"Yeah," he says. "Haven't you?"

She has no answer to this.

Pick stands up. "I'm going to grab lunch at Susie's Snack Bar," he says. "Do you want me to bring you something?"

Jessie is still in a daze. "Chicken?" she says.

"The fried chicken?" he says. "Okay, I'll be back."

From her window, Jessie watches Pick ride off. He's so self-assured, the way he swings his hips from side to side on his bike and then stands straight up on the pedals, head held high. There isn't a boy on earth as magnetic and irresistible as Pick Crimmins. Jessie is in love with him and she will be in love with him until she dies, and maybe even after that.

Jessie and Pick eat their lunch on the tiny deck and when they finish, Pick clears their trash away. What will happen now? Jessie wonders. What happens is that Pick pulls Jessie inside, away from anyone who might pass by on Plumb Lane, and there is some more necking. This time is even better than the first; Jessie is more relaxed, she knows what she's doing—or at least she does until Pick lifts the bottom of her shirt.

Jessie swats his hand away. She doesn't even mean to do this; it's involuntary, a reflex.

Pick pulls back. "Sorry," he says. He holds both hands up in surrender. "I'm getting carried away. We'd better stop. I should get ready for work."

Jessie doesn't want to stop and she knows that Pick still has hours before he has to leave for the North Shore. But she also isn't ready for anything more than kissing. She is thrilled that Pick is getting carried away, but it's scary too. Terrifying.

* * *

That afternoon, Jessie writes identical letters to both Leslie and Doris.

How's your summer going? My summer is fine. I have to take tennis lessons every morning at the Field and Oar Club. My backhand and my serve are coming along, so if I get invited to a weekend party on Hilton Head, I'll be prepared.

Jessie considers crumpling this up and starting over. Leslie might understand what a weekend party on Hilton Head meant, but it'll most certainly go right over Doris's head.

The only "news" I have is that I'm dating someone. His name is Pickford Crimmins but he goes by Pick. He's fifteen years old, from California, and very cute—blond hair, light blue eyes, and tanner than even George Hamilton! His family is actually living with my family this summer, which is how we met. I would not say we are going steady yet, although we probably will be soon.

Jessie leans back to consider just how blown away Leslie and Doris will be by this news. Of the three of them, it's Jessie Levin who has gotten a boyfriend first. The fact that Pick isn't technically her boyfriend doesn't matter because Leslie and Doris will never meet him.

Also, we are going to Woodstock together in August.

Jessie crosses this out. She can imagine Leslie reporting this startling fact to her mother and then Leslie's mother calling David Levin to ask what on earth he's thinking, allowing his thirteen-year-old daughter to go to Woodstock.

Blair is pregnant with twins! Due August first. She's here on Nantucket now and she'll have the babies at the hospital. My brother

Jessie pauses. She doesn't want to say too much about Tiger's secret mission, although Jessie can't imagine that two adolescent girls in Brookline, Massachusetts, knowing about it would matter.

sends letters full of things I can't tell anyone. Kirby

Jessie wants to mention Kirby because all of Jessie's friends, especially Leslie, are obsessed with Kirby. But Jessie hasn't seen or talked to her all summer. Kirby sent a package that contained a tie-dyed Martha's Vineyard T-shirt with a card that said *Miss you!* Other than that, it's like Kirby has fallen off the face of the earth.

is spending the summer on Martha's Vineyard. I'm hoping to be allowed to go visit but my mom probably won't let me because she's upset about Tiger and doesn't want to say goodbye to any more of her children, even for a couple of days.

These are the truest words in the whole letter, Jessie realizes.

That's all for now! Write back!

> *Your best friend,*
> *Jessie*

P.S. Thank you again for the record album. I listen to it all the time!

White lie, Jessie thinks. She hasn't listened to it even once, and now that she and Exalta are at odds, she can't ask to use the Magnavox. Plus it's in the den with the television that Blair watches all day, every day. But again, Leslie and Doris will never know.

Jessie seals the letters in envelopes and puts a stamp on each but she's not allowed to leave the house, so going to the mailbox will have to wait.

She leans back in bed and thinks about kissing Pick.

I'm getting carried away.

Carried away isn't a phrase Jessie has given much thought to before but now she sees how accurately it describes her mood. She feels like there is wind beneath her, like she is being lifted up into the air; she feels like she's soaring.

Her life was one thing when she woke up that morning, and now it is something else entirely.

As Jessie and Exalta are walking home from tennis lessons the next morning, Exalta says, "Well, Jessica, today is the last day of your grounding. Tomorrow you'll be free to do as you please."

Free to do as she pleases. Jessie thinks back to the dinner at the Mad Hatter with her mother. Kate *said* that Jessie's birthday present would be permission to ride her bike to the beach in the afternoons. Has Kate learned what happened with the necklace? Jessie assumes so, though Kate hasn't said a word about it. It's possible—no, probable—that even Jessie stealing hasn't managed to catch Kate's attention, which is a bad thing but also, for Jessie, a good thing.

Tomorrow, she will go to the beach with Pick.

That night, Jessie is awakened by someone yelling. It's Mr. Crimmins, she realizes. She creeps out of bed and cracks her door so she can hear better. Not every word is distinct but Jessie gets the gist of things. Mr. Crimmins is reprimanding Pick for breaking curfew.

Curfew? Jessie didn't realize Pick *had* a curfew, or rules of any kind. He seems not to need them; he sticks to a routine—beach, work, sleep. But when Jessie checks her clock, she sees that it's three o'clock in the morning.

Three o'clock in the morning? Is Pick just getting home? Then Jessie remembers the bonfire—but that was the night before. Maybe the staff at the North Shore have a bonfire every night, the way Kirby and her friends used to. Maybe Pick has been accepted by his peers and now has a standing invitation, and maybe in another week or two, he'll be able to bring Jessie with him. (There's no way she'll be allowed to go, so she will have to sneak out and will likely get caught, and the only punishment she can imagine that would be severe enough for two major infractions in one summer is being sent to boarding school.)

Jessie worries that Pick will get grounded just as Jessie's own sentence has been lifted.

"Do you want to get us kicked out of here?" Mr. Crimmins asks.

"No, sir."

"We're on thin enough ice as it is."

"Yes, sir."

Jessie hears Pick's feet on the stairs so she shuts her door and climbs back into bed. There was no mention of grounding. Jessie closes her eyes. Tomorrow she will wear her yellow bikini.

The next morning before tennis, Jessie checks Pick's door, but it's closed tight; he's still asleep. When Jessie gets back from tennis, his bike is gone and his bedroom door is open.

He went to the beach, as usual.

Jessie changes into her suit and considers packing a lunch, but she doesn't want to waste any time. She races downstairs to the den, where Blair is lounging across the sofa with a pillow crammed between her legs. The big news with Blair is that she's wearing a new dress that Kate ordered for her from a catalog. It's orange corduroy and has a ruffled neckline and long sleeves, and although it's unseasonal—Blair's sweating just lying there—it's an improvement over the disintegrating yellow dress.

"Can I borrow a dollar?" Jessie asks. "I'm biking to Surfside and I want to get a burger at the shack."

She worries for a second that Blair will check to see if Jessie is allowed to bike to Surfside or that she will tell Jessie that spending fifty cents on a burger, a quarter on fries, and a quarter on a Coke is a waste of money when there is perfectly good food in the kitchen.

But Blair doesn't even look up. "My purse is in my bedroom," she says. "Take as much as you want."

"Okay, thank you," Jessie says. She eyes Blair for a second. Should she be worried about her sister? She looks like an enormous, sad orange zombie, entranced by the soap operas on television. "Can I get you anything?"

"Me?" Blair says. "No. Thank you, though."

Jessie decides she is never getting pregnant.

It's amazing how freedom changes everything. The sun is brighter, the sky bluer, the window boxes of the houses on Fair Street are all first-prize winners. Her breath comes easier, and her legs feel sure and strong as she pedals along.

She's going to meet Pick at the beach!

Once at Surfside, she hunts for Pick's bike in the rack. When she doesn't see it, she panics. What if he went somewhere else?

Cisco, Madaket, Steps? Jessie imagines herself on a wild-goose chase around the island. But then she sees his bike on the very end, the telltale greenish-black color, the white tape on the handlebars. It's not locked up, which is careless of him but not surprising. Probably Pick is used to life on the commune, where everyone shared and there was no need for locks. Jessie chains her bike to his and then chains her bike to the rack.

There's the enticing smell of burgers and grilled onions wafting over from the shack. Jessie thinks of stopping but she wants to find Pick first. She took two dollars from Blair's wallet so that she could offer to pay for Pick's lunch.

Surfside Beach is packed. The wide swath of sand is dotted with colorful umbrellas and blankets and competing music from transistor radios. First Jessie hears "Proud Mary," by Creedence, and then, a few seconds later, "Touch Me," by the Doors. The crowd is mostly families, but here and there are groups of teenagers—boys tossing a football, girls rubbing baby oil on their arms and legs. Jessie scans the beach for Pick. She imagines he swims a lot, then naps; maybe he's invited to join these football games. She hopes he is. This is a busy, happy beach, and for that reason, sitting alone seems like a maudlin prospect.

"Jessie!"

Jessie lifts her gaze, and yes—down toward the water she sees Pick in his mustard-colored trunks waving at her. She can't hide her smile as she shuffles through the hot sand in her flip-flops.

Pick grins. "I thought that was you," he says. "But imagine my surprise. You've not only been sprung from jail, you ventured all the way out here on your own." He checks behind her. "You're alone, right? Or did your mom come?"

"I'm here alone," Jessie says. Her cheeks burn; he certainly didn't think she'd come to the beach with her mother? Then Jessie notices that behind Pick, lying on a beach towel that Jessie recognizes from All's Fair, is a girl in a black bikini. When Pick sees Jessie notice her, he says, "Oh, hey, come meet Sabrina."

Jessie's legs suddenly feel weak and watery. She tells herself to breathe. This is nothing to worry about.

Sabrina jumps to her feet. Sabrina is Pick's age, fifteen or sixteen, and Sabrina is beautiful. She has a blond ponytail, a toothy smile, actual breasts, and toenails painted the color of strawberries.

"Hey," Sabrina says. She offers her hand, like an adult. "I'm Sabrina. You must be Jessie. Pick talks about you all the time."

"Hi," Jessie squeaks. She's slightly bolstered by this statement— Pick talks about her all the time—but she's afraid it doesn't mean what she wants it to mean. And sure enough, Pick wraps an arm around Sabrina's shoulders and kisses her cheek.

"Sabrina is a waitress at the North Shore," Pick says. "And last night, she agreed to be my girlfriend." He beams at Jessie. It feels as though he has just crushed her heart under his bike tire or picked her heart up like a shell at the shoreline and chucked it out to sea. *Agreed to be my girlfriend.*

Sabrina elbows Pick in the ribs. "You know I only said yes because I'm dying to go to Woodstock."

"Woodstock or bust!" Pick says. "Four weeks from now I should have a pile of money saved."

Sabrina smiles at Jessie. "Set your things down," she says. "Then we can go for a swim."

"Oh," Jessie says. "I'm not staying. I just came to say hi." She squints out at the ocean through her gathering tears. The water sparkles and Jessie is hot from biking, so hot, but there's no way she can stay here at the beach, no way she can swim with Sabrina and Pick. Sabrina is Pick's *girlfriend.* They are going steady, and

Sabrina, not Jessie, is going with Pick to Woodstock. But what about the other day? The necking in Little Fair? It wasn't just a peck on the cheek; they had really been kissing. What changed? Pick had gone to a bonfire, maybe two bonfires, and it's true that Jessie hadn't really seen him since then, but she had relived the kissing in her mind a thousand times and she assumed he had too. But the necking with Jessie must not have lived up to his expectations because now look—she has been relegated to little-sister status.

She should have let him go further. She should have let him put his hand under her shirt. But it had been so new then, and she hadn't been ready. It seems wildly unfair that now Pick is kissing Sabrina and putting his hand beneath Sabrina's shirt. Now Pick and Sabrina are getting carried away and Jessie is left behind.

She turns and wanders through the maze of blankets and towels; she's careful, even in her agitated state, not to kick sand on anyone.

One of the transistor radios is playing "Suite: Judy Blue Eyes." *It's getting to the point where I'm no fun anymore.*

"Jessie!" Pick calls out. She hears him but she doesn't look back. She knows not to do that, at least.

In the parking lot, she unlocks her bike from Pick's and from the rack, and in one small, juvenile gesture, she kicks Pick's bike to the ground.

When Jessie arrives back at All's Fair—*All's fair in love and war,* she thinks, and she shudders at how cruel her own house's name now seems—she hears her mother's raised voice in the kitchen. Jessie couldn't care less. She will write to her father and tell him about Garrison rubbing against her, or about Exalta's anti-Semitism, or that Kate is drinking so much Jessie doesn't feel safe, and she will be allowed to return home. She needs to get off this island. If she stays, she will die, or at least the inside of her will die.

Even now, her stomach hurts. She's certain she will never eat again, never sleep again, never be happy or carefree again. She has learned the hard way that love ruins everything.

As Jessie is heading up the stairs to Little Fair, she hears her mother say Mr. Crimmins's name, and then Pick's name, and curiosity gets the better of her and she heads for the kitchen.

Kate and Exalta are facing each other with their arms crossed. Jessie has walked in on a showdown.

"What's going on?" she asks.

"The Crimminses are leaving," Kate says.

"Leaving?" Jessie says.

"Moving out," Kate says.

Jessie can't believe her good luck. She feels a little lighter.

"Nonsense," Exalta says. "Bill Crimmins is well into his seventies and the boy is fifteen. We can't just put them out on the street."

"We most certainly can," Kate says. "Bill Crimmins is a fraud."

"I'm sure he tried his best," Exalta says. "And I hate to remind you of this, darling, but this is *my* house and the only person with a say about who stays or goes is me."

"Mother, please," Kate says. "Try to see it from my point of view. Think how difficult it is for me—"

"Jessie and Pick are friendly," Exalta says. "It's good for her to have another young person around." She looks up and sees Jessie. "Aren't you fond of young Pickford, Jessica?"

Jessie is finally starting to think like a tennis player. It feels like Exalta has just lobbed a ball to her forehand. *Charge the net!* she thinks. "Actually, Nonny, I don't like Pick. I don't like him at all. I think he's..." She tries to be strategic with her choice of words. "Common." She looks at her mother. "And dangerous. A bad influence. He asked me to go with him to Woodstock."

"Woodstock!" Kate cries.

Exalta looks nonplussed. "Think of how the boy has been raised. Or not raised, as the case may be. We can hardly evict him. And I won't do that to Bill, not after the years, the *decades,* he has faithfully served this household."

"He's caused us more trouble than he's saved us," Kate says.

"That's nonsense and you know it, Katharine," Exalta says. "I will hear nothing else about it. They are staying put."

"Mother," Kate says.

"Nonny..." Jessie says.

"Enough," Exalta says.

Jessie trudges up to her bedroom. She feels doubly cheated now. Triply cheated—no beach, no Pick, no chance to be rid of Pick.

She can't even bring herself to hate Sabrina. Sabrina was nice. Pick is right to make Sabrina his girlfriend. She's pretty, kind, friendly, and older. The problem isn't Sabrina; it's Jessie herself.

Jessie's stomach hurts something awful. Even though it's a bright, sunny day, Jessie decides she's going to put on her pajamas and climb into bed. She has a book to read for pleasure: *From the Mixed-Up Files of Mrs. Basil E. Frankweiler,* about some kids who run away from home and end up living in the Metropolitan Museum of Art.

Jessie wants to run away. That was what Woodstock was all about, but Pick must not even remember that he asked Jessie to go. He must not remember that he tried to kiss Jessie in the buttery and then he *did* kiss her, passionately, two separate times.

It happened. It wasn't something she dreamed—although now, it's destined to feel that way.

Jessie gasps when she slips off her bikini bottoms. They're stained with blood. Her period, she thinks. It came. This is something she had been wishing for, praying for, even, but now it doesn't matter. Now, she couldn't care less.

Can't Find My Way Home

Tiger is in Cambodia. Exalta has overridden Kate's decision to evict Bill Crimmins for his ineffectiveness. David won't come to the island. Kate called him at the office with the intent of telling him about her deal with Bill, but when his secretary put him through, he said, "I'm very busy right now. Can we talk later?"

Kate nearly pushed and said, *Later* when? *How about tonight at eight o'clock?,* but she couldn't bear to hear him say that eight o'clock wouldn't work, that no time would work, because the issue *wasn't* that he was busy; he was always busy. It was that he didn't want to talk to Kate at all.

Her problems, she realizes, are all interconnected. Since she's not allowed to throw Bill Crimmins out, she might persuade him to believe that he's staying due to her good graces as long as he continues to pressure his brother-in-law for information about Tiger. Part of Kate clings to the idea that this mission in Cambodia—blocking the flow of supplies to the Vietcong—is less dangerous than combat in Vietnam, but who is she kidding? It's all dangerous. Once she has a reliable source confirming that Tiger is, at least, safe, Kate can stop numbing herself with alcohol and she will be restored to David's favor.

Kate catches Bill bright and early on his way out to his pickup truck, which he parks on Plumb Lane, and says, "I'm sorry about my temper the other day, Bill. I was distraught about Tiger..."

Bill softens immediately; she can see forgiveness in his face. He is a good man, and Exalta is right, he *has* placed himself in service to this house and their family for over three decades. That Kate now harbors some anger and resentment toward Bill Crimmins and, worse, that she feels *disillusioned* by him is breaking her heart along with everything else in her life.

Bill puts a hand on her shoulder. "I understand, Katie. I've lost a child myself."

Kate nearly says, *You have?* She wonders if maybe Bill's wife, who died so long ago that Kate never knew her, lost a baby. But then she realizes he means Lorraine and she nearly growls at him.

Lorraine isn't lost the way Tiger is lost. Comparing them is nothing short of offensive, but Kate will let it go. She supposes that, regardless of the circumstances, Bill must miss his daughter.

"I'm happy to let you and...Pick stay," Kate says. The child's name sticks like a fishbone in her throat. "Stay for as long as you need, of course. It was cruel of me to pull the rug out from under you. But if you would please continue to pursue your brother-in-law for any news he has about Tiger..."

"Of course," Bill says. His eyes shine. "I miss him too, Katie. I think of him like one of my own."

There's a lot of emotional distance between having a child of one's own and thinking of a child as one's own, although Bill has known Tiger since he was born and they were always close. They both love the Red Sox and tinkering with cars. Would Tiger trust Bill Crimmins with his life? Probably, Kate has to admit.

"Thank you," she whispers.

There is one other action she can take to fix the mess she finds herself in. Something previously unthinkable. Once Jessie and Exalta leave for the club, Kate secures a scarf over her hair, puts on her sunglasses, and climbs into the Scout.

Up the cobblestones of Main Street she goes; it feels like being inside a cocktail shaker. Kate rumbles around the Civil War monument and along Upper Main. She passes her two favorite houses. They both back onto the grassy fields that border Quarter Mile Hill. One is rustic and barn-like with crisscross ironwork over the wavy leaded-glass windows; the other is a luscious white confection that features a front portico with Ionic columns and two glassed-in porches. These homes are the best mix of town and country and Kate fantasizes about telling Exalta that she has bought a house on Upper Main, the only address that would qualify in everyone's mind as superior to Fair. But alas, Kate doesn't have that kind of money and those houses stay in families for five or six or ten generations.

At the flagpole at Caton Circle, Kate checks her watch—four minutes. Four minutes isn't so bad. But she's still quite a distance from her destination.

She drives out Madaket Road. The Chase Barn is on the left, but after that, homes are few and far between. Still, it's a lovely ride, isn't it? On the right, Maxcy Pond glitters like a mirror, and then Kate sails up to the top of the hill to overlook the rolling green acres of Sanford Farm. There are twenty-seven curves on Madaket Road; Kate wonders what it would be like to drive them in the dark after a few cocktails.

All the way out at the end of the road is the hamlet of Madaket. Madaket Millie lives in one of the cottages out here on Hither Creek; she's the closest thing Nantucket has to a folk hero. She served as a coastal-defense specialist in World War II and spent long hours watching for ships in distress and German U-boats. It's well known that she's curmudgeonly and will befriend only children, animals, and her Madaket neighbors. Kate considers introducing herself to Madaket Millie and inviting her to lunch at the Field and Oar Club. This feels like a radical idea, but is it? Bitsy Dunscombe will likely never speak to Kate again; Kate could use a new friend to replace her, so why not Madaket Millie?

The island is much bigger than she realized.

Kate turns left at the first unmarked dirt road after the harbor, Massasoit Bridge Road. She cruises over the eponymous bridge and checks her watch—sixteen minutes from town. When Massasoit Bridge Road dead-ends, Kate turns left and immediately spies the structure that originally gave Red Barn Road its name. The barn is faded to a dusty pink and part of the roof is caving in. It's no longer in use but it retains a certain charm; Andrew Wyeth might have painted this barn, with the flat, windswept acres behind it and the ocean in front.

There's only one other structure on this road: the six-bedroom home David found listed for sale in the newspaper. Kate spies it up ahead. She pulls into the spacious drive. The house has gray shingles and white trim that are weathered and peeling, respectively, in a way that suggests gravitas and character rather than neglect. The house is tall and wide; both All's Fair and Little Fair would fit inside. From the front porch, there are uninterrupted views of the ocean. Kate is enraptured; here, there's no mistaking you're on an island.

Kate tries the front door. It's unlocked, so she walks right in.

The house is immediately welcoming. There's a living room on the left, a dining room with a grand pedestal table surrounded by ten ladder-back chairs on the right, and a flight of stairs up the middle. The back of the house features an eat-in kitchen with big windows that look back on what used to be farmland. There is, in fact, plenty of room for both a tennis court and a swimming pool, and although Kate scorned David for suggesting it (she cringes remembering her own sharp tongue. Why does he remain married to her?), she now thinks how wonderful it would be to create a proper summer estate out here. She had previously thought it garish and gauche, but neither is true if there are no neighbors to witness it.

Upstairs, Kate finds a medley of bedrooms and bathrooms and closets. The entire upstairs is painted white and every time Kate turns a corner, there's another bedroom, another bath. Some of the bedrooms have twin beds, some a double bed; two connect through a Jack-and-Jill bathroom with a double vanity. There's a spacious linen closet and a nursery that still contains a crib. There is one room where the walls are lined with books, the swollen paperbacks of summer, and Kate imagines a future time when her mind will be quiet enough that she can read again.

Expecting another closet, she opens a door to find a set of stairs, which she climbs up to an attic. It's a finished space—though brutally hot; it needs a powerful standing fan—that's furnished with six built-in bunk beds. The quality of the bunk beds is high; the wood is solid and true, and the mattresses look new. Kate imagines that the man of the house built these for his grandchildren, maybe at their behest, maybe as a surprise, and the brothers and sisters and cousins treasured their time up here away from the adults, telling secrets, making up ghost stories.

Kate wonders if she will ever have enough grandchildren to fill this room.

She returns to the second floor to find the room that will be Tiger's. One of the front rooms, she decides, with a big bed and a half bath. When Tiger comes home, he can marry Magee and the two of them can sleep in this room and wake up to the sun's first rays hitting the water.

The other front bedroom will be for her and David; it's the master, and it has an en suite bath with a claw-foot tub. There are rooms for Blair, Kirby, and Jessie, and one guest room that will be home to boyfriends or college roommates or in-laws.

Kate stands at the top of the stairs looking down. She hadn't expected to like the house this much; she had not expected to like it at all. She came to see it with dual purposes, neither of them noble—to escape Exalta and to appease David. But what she has found is a place that the entire family can call home. It's not fancy—there's no crown molding, no priceless murals, nowhere to hang proper drapes. There are no brick floors, and there's no kitchen fireplace or quaint buttery. It has no pedigree, really—if Kate had to guess, she would say the house was built with stock-market money in the prosperous twenties as a summer resort by people who loved nature and their privacy.

The house feels like home. It feels like the place where she and David might happily spend the 1970s, the 1980s, and, if they're lucky, the 1990s. Maybe they'll even watch the sun rise on the new millennium here.

The year 2000; it's only thirty-one years away, and yet it feels like science fiction.

The thought sustains her. She will usher in the next thousand years here, on Red Barn Road.

* * *

Kate can't risk calling Laundry Real Estate from the house, nor can she go to the office in person, as someone she knows might see her and report back to Exalta. She decides to call from the bank of pay phones at the Nantucket Electric Company building. It's midday and another scorcher. Town is deserted, which is a good thing. There's always a chance someone might notice her using the pay phone and wonder if Kate is having an affair. Bitsy Dunscombe would most definitely suspect that.

Kate needs to be quick.

There's only one other person at the bank of phones, a blond teenager with his back to Kate. He's yelling into the receiver, "Where *is* she? Have you heard from her? No? Not *anything?*" When he slams down the phone, Kate gasps.

"Pick?" Kate says. It's the first time she has used his name. Bill Crimmins tactfully skipped a proper introduction, though naturally Kate and Pick have seen each other in passing. He's always on his bike, either heading to the beach or to work or returning from the beach or from work. If he looks over and sees her, he waves and she waves back.

Pick seems upset by the call and embarrassed to be recognized. He draws his forearm across his eyes. Was the boy *crying?* Kate replays his words and suddenly she understands: he must have been looking for his mother.

"Hey, Mrs. Levin," he says. He gestures toward the phone with a theatrical flourish. "All yours." He turns to go; she sees his bike resting against the telephone pole. She would normally be grateful for an easy exit—she has sensitive business to discuss that she doesn't want him to overhear, plus she feels very uncomfortable around him. She can't bring herself to look at him too closely. But he's in such obvious distress, she can't let it go unremarked.

"Pick, are you okay? Is everything all right? Are you trying to find Lorraine?"

He nods while looking at the pavement, then he meets Kate's eyes. "You knew her, right? My mom?"

"Oh," Kate says. It serves her right for opening her mouth. "I knew her a long time ago. But yes, she worked for our family for years." Kate swallows. "She used to keep an eye on the children, my older children, when they were very young."

"I don't know where she is," Pick says. "I don't know where she went or when she's coming back. There's stuff I want to tell her. This whole summer...I mean, I got a job and got promoted to the hot line—"

Kate smiles. "Congratulations."

"And I have a new girlfriend. Her name is Sabrina. She's the prettiest waitress at the restaurant and she's funny, too, and smart. There are these two old ladies who come to eat at the restaurant all the time and Sabrina calls them Arsenic and Old Lace." Pick's eyes, she notices, are Lorraine's eyes, the frosted blue of sea glass. "I'm sorry."

Kate places a hand on his arm. He's as brown as a berry, as the saying goes. "Don't apologize. If anyone understands missing someone, it's me. My son is overseas."

"Jessie told me," Pick says. "You must be proud."

"I am," Kate says. "But it's difficult, of course." They stand together another few seconds without anything to say, then Kate turns to the phone. "Well, I'd better make my call."

Pick climbs on his bike. "See you at home."

Home, she thinks. He's lived there four weeks with people he barely knows, and he considers it home. That's either wonderful or the saddest thing Kate has ever heard; she can't decide which.

She drops a dime in the slot and dials the number.

"Laundry Real Estate," the receptionist says.

"Yes," Kate says. "I'd like to make an offer on a house."

Fly Me to the Moon (Reprise)

Almost by magic, Blair wakes up one morning and feels fine. She feels better than fine; she feels energized. She climbs out of bed and puts on her dress. The orange corduroy dress Kate bought her is just too hot to wear in mid-July but having it has given Blair the chance to wash, iron, and mend her trusty yellow dress, which she has nicknamed "Old Yeller." She gets downstairs to breakfast before Exalta and Jessie leave for Jessie's tennis lesson. Jessie stares morosely into her bowl of cereal. Two days earlier, Jessie had tapped on Blair's door to tell her she had gotten her period.

"What do I do?" Jessie asked.

Blair had nearly said, *Go find Mom,* but these days talking to Kate was as effective as talking to someone on television; Kate couldn't be relied on or confided in these days. That was okay; Blair would use this opportunity to hone her maternal skills. She hauled herself up off the sofa.

"I'll go to Congdon's Pharmacy," Blair said. "Run up and fetch my purse."

Later, after she showed Jessie how to best manage her monthly, she said, "We should go out and get you a bra."

Jessie had reddened.

"Facts of life," Blair said.

This morning, after Exalta excuses herself to get dressed before they leave for the club, Blair touches Jessie's shoulder. "You and me, this afternoon," she says. "Buttner's."

For breakfast, Blair eats a banana with peanut butter, then she cleans up everyone's dishes and sets a glass of orange juice and a bowl of lightly sugared strawberries at her mother's place. She heads back upstairs and changes the sheets on her bed for the first time since she's arrived. She loves the feeling of fresh, clean sheets; the ones she has chosen are white with sprigs of lavender printed on them. When the bed is made and the pillows plumped, Blair takes the dirty sheets down to the washing machine, then sets up the clothesline in the yard. It's a glorious day and she wants nothing more than to sit on the steps and raise her face to the sun, but there's no time to waste. She has a lot to accomplish.

She goes upstairs to pack her bag for the hospital: a nightgown she abandoned four months ago that she hopes will fit once the twins are born, slippers, hairbrush, perfume, curlers, toothbrush, compact, and a copy of Dr. Spock that she has yet to even crack open.

She straightens her room, dusts the top of the dresser, then pulls the vacuum out of the hall closet. She runs the sweeper over the wood floors and the braided rug.

She goes downstairs, pulls the linens out of the washing machine, and hangs them on the line. She hears Exalta and Jessie arrive home. *Perfect timing!* she thinks. She'll take Jessie to Buttner's and then to the Charcoal Galley to celebrate her entry into womanhood.

Blair intercepts Jessie as she's striding across the backyard to

Little Fair. "Hey, get changed, we're going to Buttner's then out to lunch."

"Okay," Jessie says. She looks a little happier than she did that morning, but then Blair hears voices and Jessie's expression collapses like a soufflé. Blair peeks out from behind the hanging bedsheets to see Pick approaching on his bike with a pretty blond perched on the handlebars. They come to a screeching halt on Plumb Lane and the girl laughs as she tumbles off the bike and onto the street, just barely managing to stay on her feet.

"Hey, Jessie!" Pick calls out.

"Hey, Jessie," the girl with him says.

Jessie storms into Little Fair without a word.

Uh-oh, Blair thinks. She strides over to the gate to let the happy couple through. "Hey, Pick," she says. She offers her hand to the girl. "Hello there, I'm Blair."

"Sabrina," the girl says. She gives Blair a winning smile. She is all white teeth, blue eyes, small, perky breasts. She reminds Blair of a sugar cookie. "I'm Pick's girlfriend."

Pick's *girlfriend!* This is the first Blair has heard of a girlfriend, though she realizes she has hardly paid attention to anyone but herself this summer.

"Nice to meet you," Blair says. She supposes Jessie's rebuff of these two can mean only one thing. "Where are you guys headed?"

"I'm going to make Sabrina some lunch," Pick says. He nods at Little Fair. "Upstairs."

"Your grandfather isn't home," Blair says. "So I'm going to have to put a damper on those plans, I'm afraid. I can't let the two of you go up unchaperoned."

Pick makes a face so familiar that Blair gets chills. She must be having flashbacks of Lorraine. "Jessie just went upstairs," he says. "She can be our chaperone."

"I'm taking Jessie out," Blair says. "Sorry, Pick, I know it's a drag, but those are the house rules. They've been in existence since I was your age. You guys are welcome to go to the big house. I believe both my mother and grandmother are around."

Pick sighs. "No, thanks. I guess we'll just go get a burger at the Charcoal Galley."

Foiled! Blair thinks. But that's quite all right. She can take Jessie to Cy's Green Coffee Pot.

"Toodle-oo," she says.

On the way down Main Street to Buttner's, Blair tells Jessie, "So...I met Pick's girlfriend."

No response from her sister.

"She seemed nice."

Jessie shrugs.

"She's very pretty."

"I guess," Jessie says.

"Not as pretty as you, of course," Blair says.

Jessie stops in her tracks. "Blair?"

"Yes?"

"Please stop."

Blair feels a pain in her midsection, as though the words pierced her. "Okay, sorry, sorry."

"Let's just get this *over with,*" Jessie says, and she flings open the door to Buttner's.

Buttner's smells the same, Blair thinks. Like the new leather of school shoes and the boiled wool of peacoats and the saleswomen's perfume and floor polish. Blair has been coming to this store her entire life; she prefers it to any place in Boston, even Filene's.

She leads Jessie back to the lingerie department and finds Miss

Timsy, the same woman who fitted Blair for her bra twelve years earlier. Francesca Timsy is a spinster, a Nantucket native who lives with her sister, Donatella Timsy, in a tiny cottage on Farmer Street. Both Timsy sisters sing in the choir at St. Paul's. They're as old as the hills and yet, curiously, Miss Timsy looks exactly the same as she did twelve years ago—blue hair (set once a week at Claire Elaine's Beauty Shop next door), steel-rimmed glasses, pencil skirt, and tape measure draped around her neck.

"Katie Nichols?" Miss Timsy says. "Is that you? You're having *another* baby?"

Blair puts a hand on Miss Timsy's stick-thin forearm. "It's Blair Foley, Miss Timsy, Kate's daughter. I'm pregnant with twins." Blair is tickled to be mistaken for her glamorous mother, although she's certain it's because Miss Timsy is almost completely senile.

Miss Timsy seems to snap right back to the summer of 1969 because she says, "Oh, Blair, dear, of course. My eyes were playing tricks on me, not surprising with the heat we've been having. I heard you were pregnant with twins. Donatella ran into your mother at the market."

"Well, we're here today to get my sister Jessie a bra!" Blair says. Jessie curls into herself and Blair realizes her voice is louder than normal because she's trying to accommodate Miss Timsy's ancient ears. "Her first bra!"

Miss Timsy regards Jessie. "Sister?" she says. "This isn't Kirby. Kirby's blond."

"This isn't Kirby," Blair says. She notices Jessie trying to make herself even smaller and she hopes she doesn't have to run through the family calculus with Miss Timsy. "This is Jessica, the youngest."

Thankfully, Miss Timsy has moved on to business. She eyes Jessie's chest.

"Well, I can tell you're going to have a magnificent bosom in a few short years. Come, let's get you fitted."

Jessie throws Blair a pleading look but Blair pretends not to see. Miss Timsy is a professional, and being fitted by her is a rite of passage. Blair survived; Kirby survived; Jessie will survive.

"I'll be over in the layette section!" Blair calls out.

She meanders through the women's department, admiring the fall fashions—out already, even though it's only mid-July—and feels another sharp pain. She wonders if she'll even fit into regular clothes by fall.

She moves on to the children's section and is haunted by memories of back-to-school shopping with Kate and Exalta. She even remembers one year when Tiger was in a baby carriage, so Blair's father must have still been alive. She remembers another year when she chose a paisley blouse that had a matching orange skirt but somehow the skirt hadn't made it home to Brookline and Blair cried because she had wanted to wear the outfit on the first day of school. Kate had called Buttner's and they mailed the skirt, but had it made it in time? Blair can't remember. So much of what seems painfully important in the moment fades away. Jessie is embarrassed about being fitted for a bra now, but ten years from now when she has the magnificent bosom that Miss Timsy predicted, she'll be buying black lace bras and push-up bras to impress her boyfriends, and maybe one afternoon, as she's having brunch with girlfriends at the Marliave, she'll tell them the story of getting her first bra at Buttner's.

Finally, Blair arrives at the baby section—toddler, infants, newborn layette. She has nothing for the twins, and no one has sent anything. Blair decides to choose four outfits for each gender, just to cover her bases. The clothes are precious, tiny and delicate like fine doll clothes. Blair gets four basic white onesies, two with pink piping, two with blue, and four sailor suits, two male, two female. The sailor suits are impractical, she knows, but she can't resist. She hands the outfits over to the salesgirl, who takes them to the register.

"You'll need to wait to ring these up," Blair says. "My sister is being fitted for a bra."

Blair heads back to lingerie to see how Jessie is faring. She can hear Miss Timsy's incessant patter: "You see, my dear, how this one provides lift? Shoulders back now, chin up..."

Suddenly, Blair feels a staggering pain; it's like giant hands are squeezing her midsection. There's a sound like the muted pop of a balloon, and water comes gushing out from between Blair's legs.

She screams.

Miss Timsy pokes her head out from behind the dressing-room curtain, and the salesgirl rushes over to take Blair's arm. "Are you okay, miss?" Then the salesgirl notices the puddle forming at Blair's feet. Liquid is running down Blair's bare legs, and Blair is mortified and confused, thinking she somehow lost control of her bladder and *wet* herself, but a split second later she realizes her water has broken *right in the middle of Buttner's* next to a carousel of boys' dungarees. A pain comes that is so rude and insistent that Blair knows this is it. Contractions. Labor.

"Jessie!" she says. "We need to go *now!*"

Jessie pops out of the dressing room in just her shorts and a white bra.

"Put your shirt on!" Blair says. "We have to go. I'm in labor. It's time."

Miss Timsy says, "Let us call an ambulance."

"No, no," Blair says. She isn't about to make a scene; it's bad enough she's leaving them to clean up after her. "We have to go. My bag, my things—my mother will take me, it's fine."

Blinding pain. Blair grits her teeth, counts to ten. It passes.

She and Jessie walk up Main Street, Blair holding on to Jessie's arm for dear life. Right outside of Mitchell's Book Corner, Blair feels another contraction coming on; it's like a truck is about to hit her.

"We have to stop for a minute," Blair says. There's a bench outside the store and Blair hears Jessie asking her if she wants to sit but Jessie's voice is faint and far away. There is only room in Blair's head for her own thoughts and this searing white-hot pain. She doesn't think sitting will help; it may make things worse—if anything *could* be worse than being in labor on Main Street in the broiling-hot sun.

The contraction barrels down. Blair's knees buckle but Jessie holds her steady.

"Should I run for Mom?" Jessie asks.

Blair can't talk until the contraction is past. "And *leave* me here? No, let's go."

They make it to the corner of Main and Fair, but another contraction is coming. Blair says, "You go. I'll be right here."

Jessie races up the street. Blair braces herself against a tree. The Quaker Meeting House is across the street—quiet, calm, serene. Blair wills herself to think about the Quaker Meeting House, but the pain is overwhelming. It consumes her. She's crying and sweating and cursing the day she ever met Angus. Angus, who is a thousand miles away in Houston. Blair tries to recall today's date. She thinks it's the fifteenth, so the moon launch is tomorrow. Right? It doesn't matter. Angus is so unavailable, he might as well be *on* the moon.

A car pulls up and Blair casts her eyes down, willing it to move on. Her legs are sticky with fluid, the back of her dress is soaked, and she wants to disappear; what she fears most right now is a Good Samaritan.

"Blair!"

It's her mother and Jessie in the Scout. Jessie hops out and walks Blair over to the passenger side, but how will she ever get up and in? She faces the car while Jessie pushes from under her buttocks and somehow boosts Blair up. Another contraction is coming.

"We can't go down the cobblestones," Blair says.

"What?" Kate says. "But darling, there's no other way."

"We! Cannot! Go! Down! The! Cobblestones!" Blair says in a voice that sounds nothing like her own. "Back up."

"Back up?" Kate says. "Fair Street is one-way, darling."

"Back up, Mom," Jessie says. "No one is behind us. I'll keep watch."

Another contraction is coming. Blair howls.

Kate backs up.

"Keep going! Keep going!" Jessie says. "It's clear all the way to Lucretia Mott."

Thank you, God, Blair thinks. Lucretia Mott Lane to Pine Street, Pine Street to Lyons, Lyons to South Mill, which meets Prospect Street right across from the hospital. Kate screeches to a stop in the emergency room parking lot, and two orderlies appear with a stretcher.

"You're not leaving me, are you?" Blair asks her mother.

"We'll be right behind you, darling," Kate says. "You won't be alone."

Blair closes her eyes. She won't be alone. Kate and Jessie will be here. Someone is missing, Blair thinks. "Someone is missing," Blair mumbles to the orderly.

"Oh yeah?" he says. "Your husband?"

Angus? she thinks. *No.*

The person missing is Kirby.

Blair is in labor for eighteen hours, which sounds grueling, although, truthfully, it's only the beginning and the end of labor that are challenging. The contractions come fast and hard until Dr. Van de Berg arrives and instructs the nurse, Myrtle, to give Blair something to make her "comfortable."

"Here comes your glass of wine," Myrtle says as she shoots something into Blair's IV.

She's in twilight sleep much of the night. She wakes up at dawn when the nurse tells her it's time to push.

Kate is there at the bedside and Jessie is sitting on a stool in the corner of the room. This would never be allowed in a big-city hospital, Blair knows, but she's glad they bend the rules here a little. Jessie is wearing a surgical mask, which looks so funny on her that Blair actually laughs.

Dr. Van de Berg reappears in blue scrubs. "Who wants to have a baby or two?" he asks. He checks Blair and says, "The first baby is crowning, Blair. Bear down."

This is happening. Blair is overcome with emotion. She is going to have a baby, two babies. She is about to create a family, right here, right now, on July 16, 1969, the same day that man will head to the moon. Angus must be consumed by the imminent launch, checking and rechecking calculations, in constant contact with Cape Kennedy. He will have no idea that on an island thirty miles from the Massachusetts shore, his children are about to enter the world.

"Push, Blair, push," Dr. Van de Berg says.

Blair pushes.

"Again," Dr. Van de Berg says.

"Push, darling," Kate says. Blair looks at her mother. Kate's hair is in its usual chignon; there are pearls at her neck; she's wearing a peach dress. She has an iron grip on Blair's hand, and Blair can feel Kate passing her her strength, gifting her her fortitude. Blair knows her mother endured this, and Nonny before her, and Nonny's mother before her, and so on and so on. Blair hopes Jessie is watching so she learns that all women are strong and miraculous.

Strong, Blair thinks. *Miraculous.*

"It's a girl!" Dr. Van de Berg says. "She's perfect."

A girl! Blair thinks, and her heart soars. Jessie is on her feet, her eyes wide, her fists clenched with nerves or joy. Kate sniffs, wipes a tear.

"My granddaughter," she says.

Dr. Van de Berg hands the baby to Myrtle as though it's a loaf of bread he pulled from the oven. "We aren't finished," he says. "You can take a couple of deep breaths until we're ready to go again."

Blair turns to her mother. "I bought outfits."

"Miss Timsy brought them up to the house," Kate says. "Along with three bras for Jessie. Thank you for handling that. I meant to do it—"

"Here we go," Dr. Van de Berg says. "The head is crowning."

"I'm wagering on another girl," Myrtle says. "Probably identical."

"Push," Dr. Van de Berg says.

Blair bears down.

Kate squeezes her hand. "You are such a champion, darling."

Blair lets a great moan go as she pushes with all her might.

"Again, please," Dr. Van de Berg says.

"I can't," Blair whimpers.

"You can, darling," Kate says. "Come on, now."

Blair pushes again and she feels a loosening, a lightening.

"It's a boy," Dr. Van de Berg says, his voice jubilant. "A beautiful baby boy. You have a girl and a boy, Mama. A son and a daughter."

Blair bursts into tears.

TELEGRAM TO DR. ANGUS WHALEN, MISSION CONTROL, HOUSTON, TEXAS

  GENEVIEVE FOLEY WHALEN 6 LB 2 OZ BORN 6:38 A.M.
  GEORGE NICHOLS WHALEN 5 LB 14 OZ BORN 6:44 A.M.
  MOTHER AND BABIES DOING FINE.

Two hours later, after the babies have been cleaned and swaddled and after Blair has delivered the placentas and been stitched up and successfully latched each baby to her breasts for the first meal of their lives, Blair asks to see a TV. It's almost nine a.m. The launch is supposed to take place in half an hour.

Myrtle frowns. "Don't you want to sleep?"

"My husband is an astrophysicist," Blair says. "He has been working on this mission for years. That's why he's not here. He's in Houston, at Mission Control."

"Hold on," Myrtle says. She disappears down the hall and returns a few minutes later holding a small boxy black-and-white TV, which she sets on the table at the foot of Blair's bed.

"This is the TV we keep in the nurses' station," Myrtle says. She plugs it in and fiddles with the antennas until the picture becomes clear—Cape Kennedy in Florida and the thousands of people who are attending the launch. There are photos of the three

astronauts—Neil Armstrong, Buzz Aldrin, and Michael Collins—
on the screen and Blair gets chills. She wants to announce that although those gentlemen are going out into space, there are lots
of other people who made it possible—among them Dr. Angus
Whalen. The happy drugs are definitely working because, after a
quick self-inventory, Blair doesn't find a hint of anger or resentment toward Angus for missing the birth. He was busy doing his
job while Blair did hers. This isn't a feminist position, she knows,
but she can't be moved to care. She has twins! A matched set!
A daughter and a son. When Dr. Van de Berg said, "Good job,
Mama," he was referring to her, Blair. *She's* the mama!

The candy striper in the maternity ward, Tracy, follows Myrtle.
She's carrying two bottles of Asti Spumante in a bedpan full of ice.

"We broke out the champagne because twin births are so rare
here," Myrtle says.

Blair claps her hands. "Let's all have some when the rocket
takes off!"

"We're on the clock," Myrtle says. "But a sip or two won't hurt.
After all, this is a monumental event. Twins and the moon launch
on the *same day*."

Tracy the candy striper goes to fetch paper cups while Myrtle
pops the cork.

The engines thrust, a fiery cloud bursts from below the rocket,
and the newscaster, excitement barely disguised in his voice,
counts down: "Five…four…three…two…one…*blast off!*"
Blair raises her paper cup of Asti Spumante to the others in the
room and lets out a whoop.

"Cheers!" she cries. "Here's to the next frontier!" *This toast,*
she thinks, *works on so many levels.*

Dr. Van de Berg appears in the doorway and watches as the
rocket breaks through the atmosphere. He turns to the room with

an expression of genuine wonder. "Your children are entering a remarkable world," he says.

TELEGRAM TO BLAIR FOLEY WHALEN, NANTUCKET COT-
TAGE HOSPITAL, MATERNITY WARD
  RECEIVED THE HAPPY NEWS OF THE TWINS. SENDING
MY BEST WISHES AND CONGRATULATIONS. WILL RETURN
TO BOSTON JULY 25. ANGUS.

Ring of Fire

July 17, 1969

Dear Tiger,

Jessie now thinks of Tiger as her own version of Anne Frank's Kitty because she isn't at all convinced that Tiger will ever read this letter. This doubt gives her freedom. If it's a letter that will never be read, then she can write the entire, unfiltered truth.

It has been a busy week.

Jessie nearly starts by telling Tiger that she got her period, but then she hesitates, because what if he *does* end up reading this? He'll be so grossed out—and rightly so—that he might crumple up the letter and throw it away without getting to the good stuff.

On Tuesday afternoon, Blair took me to Buttner's to get some new clothes.

She considers mentioning that they were, in fact, *bra* shopping, but again, she censors herself, though she's certain Tiger would laugh at Miss Timsy's declaration that Jessie would one day have a magnificent bosom.

While I was in the changing room half dressed

Jessie had been standing in a bra and shorts while Miss Timsy stood behind her, fiddling with the length of the straps.

I heard a shriek. I poked my head out to find that Blair's water had broken all over the floor of Buttner's. She was in labor.

The salesladies at Buttner's offered to call an ambulance but Blair insisted we walk home, even though she was in a lot of pain. We had to stop a bunch of times, once right in front of Bosun's Locker, and I was afraid the babies were going to come then and there and that one of the Bosun's regulars would have to deliver them, but finally, Blair let me run ahead to get Mom. Blair refused to drive over the cobblestones so Mom drove in reverse the wrong way down Fair Street in order to get to the hospital. Thank goodness Nonny didn't see!

So now comes the important news: You're officially an uncle! You have a niece named Genevieve Foley Whalen and a nephew named George Nichols Whalen.

Jessie wonders if Angus will object to both babies being named after Blair's family, then she wonders if Angus picked the names Genevieve and George, though she kind of doubts it. No one at the hospital asked about Angus, which Jessie found surprising until she reasoned that, historically, there were a lot of fishermen—whalers and the like—on Nantucket, as well as a lot of summer wives like Kate, women whose husbands worked in the city during the week, so maybe a birth with no father present was more common than Jessie imagined.

Angus wasn't here because yesterday was the day the Apollo 11 mission took off for the moon.

Would Tiger know about the moon launch? Jessie wonders. Do they get newspapers? Tiger and Jessie had watched Apollo 8 in its moon orbit on Christmas Eve and listened to the astronauts read from the book of Genesis, and they'd agreed it was a good way to end a terrible year.

He's in Houston, working at Mission Control, and when Blair told the nurses this, they brought a television into the room so we could watch. They also brought two bottles of champagne and they even gave me a cup!

Jessie considers how much she wants to share with Tiger. Because the fact is, Jessie had more than one cup of champagne. Everyone had been engrossed by the moon launch, so when Jessie finished her own champagne, she drank Blair's and Myrtle the nurse's. Jessie had never tasted alcohol before and after an initial aversion to the taste—it was fizzy like soda but sour and bitter—she felt a sparkly, bubbly rush, and the world suddenly seemed like a wonderful place, able to contain both the intimate miracle of childbirth and the widely anticipated miracle of space travel.

From outer space, the astronauts would be able to see the entire Earth—Nantucket Island and Vietnam both—and something about this comforted Jessie.

If she had stopped after the champagne, things might not have spiraled out of control. But when Kate and Jessie came home from the hospital later that morning, Jessie felt a dull headache threatening and she had learned enough from her mother and grandmother to know that this state was called a hangover and the only way to stave it off effectively was to continue drinking.

When Jessie climbed the stairs to Little Fair, she expected to find Pick—his bike was leaning against the fence—but his bedroom door was closed. Frankly, Jessie was relieved. She opened the refrigerator. The bottom shelf in the door held a regiment of stout brown bottles of Budweiser. Jessie counted; there were nine. The bottles had been there all summer long. Would Mr. Crimmins notice if one was missing? Jessie doubted it, but just to be safe, she spread the bottles out to erase the gap.

She retreated to her room with the beer bottle and an opener from the utensil drawer. As she flipped the top off, she was reminded of the lesson about simple machines in her science class. A bottle opener was a lever.

She drank the beer. It tasted even worse than the champagne had initially, but after a few concentrated sips, Jessie felt the warm fuzzy feeling return. She was able to ignore the taste and just gulp it down. She belched.

Another beer? she wondered. Her head was starting to swim.

That was when she heard voices—Pick's and a girl's. Sabrina. Here, upstairs, in the house. Had they been in Pick's *bedroom?*

Jessie slammed open the door to her room and stormed out.

"Hey, Jessie!" Pick said. "I heard the babies were born. A boy and a girl. That's so cool."

Jessie glared at Sabrina. "You know you two aren't allowed up here without an adult present."

Sabrina, who up until that point had been nothing but nice to Jessie, transformed into the witchy person Jessie had been hoping she was. "What are you going to do, tell on us?"

"I could," Jessie said. "My family is already considering tossing Pick and his grandfather out. If my mother finds out Pick has you up here, I bet she'll be pretty angry."

"Jessie," Pick said. He was afraid; Jessie could see it on his face. Jessie realized she had power.

Sabrina shrugged. "Whatever. I have to get home to shower." She turned to Pick. "See you at work." She kissed him and the kiss turned into something long and sloppy. Jessie's stomach lurched and she nearly vomited right there, but Pick pushed Sabrina away. He, at least, had some sense of propriety.

Sabrina vanished down the stairs, leaving Jessie and Pick to stare at each other.

"Jessie," he said.

"A few days ago," Jessie said, "the person you were kissing like that was *me*."

"I know, Jessie, but..."

"But what?"

"That was before I knew Sabrina liked me back," he said.

This answer was a slap in the face, but Jessie was proud of herself—she didn't even flinch. She simply stared at him with all the hate she could muster.

"I like you, Jessie, but you're only thirteen. Sabrina is fifteen. We work together. I've liked her since the second I saw her.

She's so pretty. I mean, you're pretty too, and you're really nice, but—"

"But you like Sabrina. You asked her to go steady and you asked *her* to go to Woodstock with you. You do remember that you asked *me* to go to Woodstock, right?"

"Right," Pick said. "But I was only kidding." He swallowed. "Not kidding ha-ha, but, I mean, we both know you were never going to be allowed to go to Woodstock."

"*You* aren't allowed to go to Woodstock!" Jessie said, her voice growing belligerent. "There's no way Mr. Crimmins is going to let you go so you'll have to sneak away with Sabrina, and I'm sure you'll get caught." Jessie wanted to believe this was true but she also had confidence in Pick's street smarts. He and Sabrina would go to Woodstock, hear the bands, dance together, and fall asleep curled up in the back of someone's truck. Pick would find his mother and introduce her to Sabrina, his girlfriend. Jessie could see it all clearly: Pick and Sabrina—and not Jessie. Jessie would be here on Nantucket, dutifully going to tennis lessons and changing diapers and waiting to hear if her brother was dead or alive.

"Jessie," Pick said. "I'm sorry. I didn't mean to…I think you're terrific. I mean, we're friends still, right?"

Tears dripped down Jessie's face. It was him being nice that undid her because all she wanted to do was hate him.

"Friends?" Jessie said. She tilted her head. "I'm not sure about that, Pick. I'm not sure at all." She felt energized by this answer and she had watched enough soap operas with Blair to know what to do next. She spun on her heel, retreated to her room, and closed the door quietly but firmly behind her.

Jessie decides that Tiger does not need to hear about her grand humiliation, her broken heart, or her subsequent hangover—a headache so bad, it felt like her skull might crack. She now understands the appeal of drinking, but also the consequences.

Not worth it.

So that's the story of the birth of our niece and nephew. Blair isn't coming home until Sunday—because she had twins, she gets to stay in the hospital a really long time—and when the babies get here, I'm going to show them your photo and tell them about their brave uncle Tiger.

I miss you. Write soon!

Love, Messie

The next day, life returns to normal, though the very last thing Jessie wants to do is go to her tennis lesson. She tries to get out of it by asking to accompany Kate to the hospital to see the babies, but Kate informs her that George is being circumcised that morning and therefore the afternoon would be better for a visit. Jessie isn't sure exactly what circumcision is but when she asks, Kate shakes her head as if to say it isn't a subject for polite conversation.

And so Jessie and Exalta set out for the club, first swinging by the post office so Jessie can drop her letter to Tiger in the mailbox. Exalta looks on with an expression of indulgence and pity, as though Jessie were mailing a letter off to Santa Claus.

Jessie's anger at Pick is still lingering. She glares at Exalta. "Do you ever write to Tiger?"

Exalta says, "Come along or we'll be late."

But Jessie persists. She's tired of being ignored, disregarded, redirected. "Nonny, do you write to Tiger? Have you written to him even once since he's been overseas?"

"No," Exalta says. The syllable hangs in the air, naked and

cruel, and Exalta must realize this because she says, "Perhaps I should."

Jessie wants to scream, *Perhaps you should? Perhaps?* But she has learned recently that silence is more powerful than a furious outburst.

When they arrive at the club, Jessie feels the need to steal again, steal something right from under Exalta's nose, but that would backfire. Instead, she peels off for the locker room so she can calm herself before her lesson.

"Don't dilly-dally," Exalta says. "I'm off to find Mrs. Winter."

Jessie slams into the locker room. She's so angry she wants to smash the mirrors with her racket—but she stops short. Sitting on the love seat in the lounge is one of the Dunscombe twins, sobbing into her hands.

"Hello?" Jessie says gently. She isn't sure if it's Helen or Heather. If she knew it was Helen, Jessie would just ignore her, but she likes Heather and feels bad about stealing her money.

The twin looks up. Helen.

Now Jessie is stuck. "Everything okay?" she asks in a way that she hopes sounds rhetorical.

Helen struggles for a breath. "I *hate* my tennis instructor," she says.

Jessie nearly rolls her eyes. It figures that Helen Dunscombe is crying over something stupid like tennis.

"I want to...I want to *kill* him!"

What snags Jessie's attention aren't the words—everyone wants to kill *someone*—it's the guttural tone of Helen's voice and the way she's clenching her fists. Jessie starts to ask who Helen's instructor is, but then she remembers it's Garrison Howe. And *then* Jessie gets it. Although she does not like Helen *at all,* she sits down on the edge of the coffee table in front of her.

"Garrison," she says. "Did he..." She doesn't even have words at her disposal. She clears her throat. "He touched you, right?"

Helen stops crying for a second and looks at Jessie in astonishment before she whispers, "How did you know?"

"He rubbed against me during our first lesson," Jessie says. "I ran."

"I told my mother the first time it happened," Helen says. "She told me I was being dramatic and to stop exaggerating. Then he did it again—he ran the back of his hand over my breast while he was correcting my serve—and when I told my mother that time, she said all men are like that and I should just get used to it."

Jessie blinks. She wasn't brave enough to tell Kate—or anyone else—for exactly that reason. "We could both go and tell Ollie Hayward," she says. "With both of us, he would have to believe it."

Helen shakes her head. "He might believe it, but he won't *do* anything. Even Heather thinks I'm just looking for a way to switch to Topher."

If Jessie didn't know about Garrison, she might have thought this as well. "So you don't want to tell *anybody?*" Jessie asks. She does the previously unthinkable—she reaches a hand out to Helen.

Helen takes it and gives Jessie a weak smile. "Well," she says, "I just told you."

Jessie spends her entire tennis lesson smacking the ball like never before. Her forehand is a fireball, her backhand solid and true, and her serve is blistering—or at least that's how it seems to Jessie because she is just *so angry.* Garrison has been taking gross liberties with Helen Dunscombe and probably with all his other female tennis students, possibly some who are even younger than Helen and Jessie.

It's this thought that makes Jessie pocket the ball and approach the net. Suze is on the other side, bent over, both hands on the handle of her racket, in the ready position.

"Oh, come on," she says. "Don't stop now. You're on a roll. This is the strongest play I've seen all summer."

"Suze," Jessie says. "I have to tell you something."

Jessie remembers her father's advice to always think before she speaks. "Before I had you as an instructor, I had Garrison." She stops to breathe. "During our first lesson, he was showing me a two-handed backhand and he rubbed his body against mine."

"Rubbed it…suggestively?" Suze says. She puts her hands on her hips. "Are you kidding me?"

"I ran away," Jessie says. "And I asked my grandmother for another instructor, a girl, and they gave me you."

"Did you *tell* your grandmother what Garrison did?" Suze says. "Did you tell *anyone?*"

"No," Jessie says.

"Oh, Jessie," Suze says. Her voice is suddenly tender. "You could have told me. You know you could have come to me at any time."

"I'm coming to you now," Jessie says. The sun is blasting the orange clay court. Jessie is so hot, it feels like she's standing on the surface of the sun. She needs water and shade. But then she imagines the other girl or girls, some maybe only eleven years old or even as young as ten, maybe a girl who will be twelve or thirteen next summer if Garrison comes back, and so she keeps talking. "He touched Helen Dunscombe too. She was crying in the locker room about it. He touched her breast while he was showing her how to serve. Helen told her mother and her mother said that's just the way men are."

"What?" Suze shouts. She stands up to her full height and starts bouncing her palm off the face of her racket. "Well, I mean, she's not wrong. Men *are* like that. But we don't have to put up with it. Jessie, do you hear me? We do *not* have to put up with it."

"What are we going to do?" Jessie says. She suddenly regrets her decision to confide in Suze and she realizes she should never have mentioned Helen Dunscombe by name. "Are you going to tell Ollie Hayward?" Jessie envisions being marched into Ollie's office or maybe even the office of Mr. Bosley, the general manager of the Field and Oar, or—horror of all horrors—to the board of governors, old men like Mrs. Winter's husband. Jessie will have to speak the embarrassing truth and her name will be sullied and Helen Dunscombe's name will be sullied—and possibly Helen will turn around and deny it ever happened and then Jessie will be left exposed and alone. Any which way, it will be worse for Jessie than it will be for Garrison Howe. "Please. My grandmother, my family…they can't know about this."

Suze's face is shaded by her visor; all Jessie can see clearly in the blinding sun is the white stripe of zinc on Suze's nose. But Jessie can tell Suze is deep in thought.

"I'm not going to tell Ollie," Suze says. "He won't care and even if he does care, he won't punish Garrison properly. But *I* will punish Garrison properly. I will see to it that Garrison resigns."

Jessie lets her breath go. Suze understands. Suze is her role model. "How are you going to do that?" Jessie asks.

"I'm going to enlist the help of Jeffrey Pryor, who has pledged his undying devotion to yours truly." Suze smirks. "He'll do whatever I ask him to."

Jessie is fascinated but not at all surprised. Suze is a person who inspires devotion. "Are you going to ask him to beat Garrison up?"

"Better," Suze says. "Jeffrey works two jobs here. He's the grill boy at the snack bar"—meaning, Jessie thinks guiltily, that he's the one she stole the Twizzlers from—"*and* he's in charge of the men's locker room!" Suze raises her hands above her head in victory.

Jessie is confused. "I don't get it."

"Well, let me enlighten you," Suze says. "I'll ask Jeffrey to put BenGay in Garrison's jockstrap, itching powder in his socks, and *laxatives* in his Cokes!" Suze grins. "Trust me, Garrison will be gone within a week."

Jessie imagines Garrison hurrying off the court toward the bathroom mid-lesson, fearing he might have a very embarrassing accident in front of everyone. She wants to hug Suze. She can't wait to tell Helen Dunscombe!

"All right, get back to the baseline," Suze says. "You owe me one more volley."

All Along the Watchtower

As soon as Kirby gets to work on Friday, Mrs. Bennie informs her that Senator Kennedy and his cousin Joe Gargan have checked into their rooms but are out for the evening.

Kirby already knows that the senator is hosting a party out on Chappaquiddick for the Boiler Room Girls—the elite group of women who worked on Bobby Kennedy's 1968 presidential campaign. Patty's sister Sara was one of the Boiler Room Girls and she has come to the Vineyard to attend the party. That afternoon, when she swung by the Narragansett Avenue house to say hello, she extended an invitation to both Patty *and* Kirby. Sara O'Callahan was nothing like bland Tommy; clearly the females in the family received the superior genes. Sara had dark hair and milky skin like Patty, though Sara's hair was cut in a pixie just like Mia Farrow's, which made her blue eyes seem impossibly big and round. She was slender and fashionable in a red A-line dress and hammered-gold earrings. Sara brought along her friend Mary Jo, another one of the Boiler Room Girls who had worked as Bobby Kennedy's secretary. Mary Jo wore a navy-blue linen sheath and pearls. Kirby looked on both Sara and Mary Jo with awe. They were only five or six years older than her but they seemed worldly and sophisticated; Kirby wanted to be just like them.

She would *become* just like them, she decided. Since ending her relationship with Darren the week before, Kirby had been flailing. Who was she? What did she want from life? She needed to shrug off her heartbreak and disillusionment and start to forge a real identity. She would return to the person she was on the morning of the first protest march, when she pulled on her tie-dyed peace sign T-shirt and zipped up her fringed suede boots. That woman was passionate and self-possessed, carefree and confident. Kirby had been feeling like her love affair with Scottie and then her relationship with Darren diminished her, but now she understood she had that backward. Those two relationships, even in their failure, had given Kirby something—strength, she supposed, and resolve.

When she returned to Simmons in September, she would finally declare a major: political science. She would focus on her studies and apply for an internship, maybe at Tip O'Neill's office. Or maybe, just maybe, Kirby would encounter Senator Kennedy at the inn and he would take a shine to her and offer her his card. There were rumors that he would make a run for president against Nixon.

Kirby could not, however, attend the party on Chappaquiddick. She had to work at eleven.

"Just come for a little while," Patty urged. "It's a barbecue, starting at seven. You could leave right after dinner. I'm sure someone will give you a ride to the ferry, then you can just walk to the inn." She grabbed Kirby's hand and Kirby saw dark bruises the size of dimes on Patty's wrist.

"I wish I could," Kirby said. For one second, she considered calling in sick and going to the party—she hadn't missed a night all summer—but this was irresponsible and she knew there was no way she could endure the party without a drink or a toke. She didn't belong there, anyway. If she went, she would be the ultimate hanger-on—Sara's sister's friend. Her instincts told her the better course of action was to introduce herself to Senator Kennedy later, at the hotel.

Still, she'd felt insanely jealous as she helped Patty pick out an outfit. "Does Luke know you're going to this party?" Kirby asked. If *she* felt jealous, she couldn't imagine how Luke must feel.

"It's none of his business," Patty said, and when she caught Kirby's expression in the mirror, she said, "What? He doesn't *own* me."

Mrs. Bennie is rarely at the inn this late; Kirby supposes she's here to make sure that everything goes smoothly during the senator's stay. But her lipstick is faded and strands of hair are escaping from her bun. She looks frazzled and Kirby nearly tells her to go home, that she can handle things from here. But Mrs. Bennie feels compelled to issue one final reminder.

"Remember, Katharine, to exercise *discretion*. The senator's privacy and personal comfort are our first priority."

"Yes, ma'am," Kirby says.

Kirby proceeds as though everything is normal. Everything *is* normal except for Kirby's heightened state of awareness. At any moment, the senator might come strolling through the front door. It will be enough just to see him, Kirby decides, just to say, *Have a good night.* Teddy Kennedy is young and handsome, although not quite as handsome as Bobby and nowhere near as handsome as President Kennedy. What would it be like to be a member of such a family? Kirby wonders. She supposes Teddy Kennedy thinks of his brothers the same way that she thinks of Blair and Jessie.

Two by two, guests enter the lobby, then head up to bed. A few of the women stop to compliment Kirby's dress, a yellow shift embroidered with daisies that's the brightest, most cheerful dress she owns. She reviews the bills at the front desk rather than in the back office so she doesn't miss anything or anybody.

When she's finished, she allows herself fifteen minutes to indulge in thoughts of Darren. He had driven her home from Lobsterville Beach in silence and she thought he'd resigned himself to her way of thinking: he was too close to his parents for their relationship to proceed any further. But before she climbed out of the car, he took her hand and pressed it to his lips.

"I don't want you to go," he said. "I like you, Kirby."

"Yes," she said. "I like you too."

"Maybe when we're both back in the city, at school, we can—"

She opened the door and got out without letting him finish. She knew what he was proposing—that they revisit things in the fall, after they were back in school, after he was out of his parents' house. Kirby could see how that idea would be appealing; they would have nine months to let their love blossom and grow without static from that pesky little thing called family.

But it wouldn't be real.

Kirby was content to cast Darren as the weak one—but would she have the courage to bring Darren home to Kate and David? Yes, of course. Her parents were fair-minded. What about Exalta? Here, Kirby came as close to understanding Darren's predicament as she could. She would *not* relish the idea of introducing Darren to her grandmother.

It wasn't meant to be, Kirby thought.

She'd hitched her bag over her shoulder, marched into the house, ascended to the igloo, and thrown herself onto the bed.

The next day there was a knock on her door. Michaela. Kirby supposed she was there to tell Kirby to stop playing her Simon and Garfunkel album over and over again.

"Go away," Kirby said.

"Darren's on the phone," Michaela said.

"Tell him I'm out," Kirby said.

Michaela put a hand on her hip. "You're asking me to *lie?*"

"Yes," Kirby said. "If you object on moral grounds, then just hang up and take the phone off the hook. Please."

Michaela shrugged. "Maybe I'll see if he wants to go out with me," she said. "He's cute."

Kirby tries to put that conversation out of her mind. She shuffles the bills until they're in an even pile, then returns them to the file folder with a sigh.

At half past one, a man comes striding into the lobby and makes a beeline for the desk.

It takes Kirby a second to recognize Luke. He doesn't look like himself; his hair is wild and his face is bright red. He's sweating and his eyes are bulging like a bullfrog's. He's wearing a green

T-shirt with a rip in the neck and a pair of loose-fitting drawstring pants. He's in his *pajamas,* Kirby realizes, and immediately she knows something's wrong.

"Luke," she says. "Did something happen to Patty?"

Luke smacks both hands down on the desk and bellows, "You tell *me!* Where *is* she? She's not at home, she's not at the movie theater, and her brother, that idiot, said he hasn't seen her, so that leaves you. I thought you two were out whoring around since she said you broke up with your darkie boyfriend, but look, here you are." He leans across the desk and grabs Kirby by the wrist.

"Let go of me," she says softly. She doesn't want to wake any guests.

"Where *is* she?" Luke asks. He twists Kirby's wrist and it hurts so bad, she's sure it will snap.

"I have no idea," Kirby says, but her words aren't convincing even to her own ears.

"Tell me!" he roars.

The pain in Kirby's wrist is building; the more she struggles to free herself, the sharper the pain becomes.

She went to a party, Kirby nearly says, *on Chappy*—but before she can get the words out, she hears a deep voice.

"Hey!"

They both turn and Luke releases Kirby's wrist. It's Mr. Ames, sweet, kind, understanding Mr. Ames, who looks anything but that at this moment. He grabs Luke by the front of the T-shirt and nearly lifts him off the ground. "You bothering the lady?"

"No," Luke says.

"This is Luke Winslow, my housemate's boyfriend," Kirby says. "He came here looking for Patty, but I don't know where she is."

Mr. Ames lets Luke go. "You have no business showing up at this hotel to harass people. I saw you hurting Miss Foley here.

How 'bout I call the Edgartown Police?" He pulls his walkie-talkie off his hip.

Luke hangs his head and starts to blubber.

Kirby rolls her eyes. "He must be drunk," she says. "How did you get here, Luke? Did you drive?"

He raises his head. "Where is she?" he asks plaintively. "I just want to know the truth. Is she out with someone else?"

"For crying out loud," Mr. Ames says. "I'm calling the police."

"Wait," Kirby says. She comes out from behind the desk and speaks into Mr. Ames's ear. "The senator will probably be back any minute. I don't think we should call the police."

Mr. Ames checks his watch. "You're right."

"Could I maybe…borrow your car and drive him home?" Kirby asks.

"Where does he live?" Mr. Ames asks.

"Chilmark," Kirby says. "Off the State Road."

"That's too far," Mr. Ames says. "You'll be gone forty minutes at least. Call the kid a cab."

"Okay," Kirby says. She phones for a taxi while Luke collapses onto the sofa in the lobby and Mr. Ames stands guard over him. Kirby thinks back on all the quiet shifts she worked when she longed for action, and now she has action…on the worst of all possible nights. Senator Kennedy could appear at any moment, and instead of walking into a warm, welcoming lobby, he'll see Luke, who is alternately crying into his hands and angrily muttering that he's going to make Patty pay for what she's doing.

Maybe they *should* call the police, Kirby thinks. Yes, they should. Luke is dangerous. But then Kirby thinks about Mrs. Bennie's warnings and reminders. If Mrs. Bennie finds out that the police showed up at the inn on the senator's first night because of a friend of Kirby's…

They need to get him out of there.

"We need to get him out of here," Kirby says, mostly to herself. Outside, the cab pulls up.

"Let's go, Luke," Kirby says with false cheer.

"Go sleep it off, buddy," Mr. Ames says.

Reluctantly, Luke gets to his feet.

"You got it from here?" Mr. Ames asks. "I'm going back to my post."

"All set," Kirby says. She pulls Luke toward the front door. "Come on."

Luke stumbles down the stairs to the taxi. He's *so* drunk—and he's also, very clearly, a *psychopath*. This role-playing that he and Patty have been doing is just a euphemism or else a flat-out cover-up for him *abusing* her.

He doesn't own me, Patty said. But he *does* in a way, Kirby sees now. He hurts her to keep control, and she *lets* him.

The cabdriver gets out to open the door for Luke. He's young and slight of frame, a pip-squeak. Honestly, he looks to be about Jessie's age. Kirby wishes they had sent someone else.

"Where you headed?" the driver asks.

"He's going to Chilmark," Kirby says. "State Road."

"I'm going to Oak Bluffs," Luke says. "Narragansett Avenue."

"No!" Kirby says. She has, wisely, brought five dollars from the petty-cash drawer to pay for the taxi. "He's going to Chilmark. The address is...Luke, what's your address?"

Luke crawls into the back seat. "Narragansett Avenue, Oak Bluffs."

Kirby presses the five-dollar bill into the pip-squeak cabbie's hand. "Take him to Chilmark, *only* to Chilmark. He lives off the State Road."

"But *where* off the State Road?" the cabbie asks. "There aren't many streetlights up-island and there are a lot of houses tucked back in the woods. I don't want to be driving around all night looking for the right place."

"Oak Bluffs," Luke growls.

Kirby glances back at the inn. She can't leave—but she can't risk Luke going to Oak Bluffs either. He'll find Patty and make her pay. Kirby imagines a black eye or worse.

Mr. Ames told Kirby it was *not* okay for her to go to Chilmark because it would take too long, and it's obviously against the rules for Kirby to leave the property while she's on the clock; it wouldn't matter if this took only five minutes. But in the moment, it feels like Mr. Ames doesn't care about Patty's safety, which means he's technically siding with Luke, which makes sense because they're both men and the entire country is one big oppressive patriarchy!

Kirby slides into the front seat; there's no way she's sitting in the back with Luke.

"I'll tell you where to go," she says to the cabbie. "And then you can bring me back here. Just drive. Drive as fast as you can."

When Kirby gets back to the inn—she's gone the better part of an hour because they missed the turn and had to double back—the lobby is quiet and the senator's room key has been claimed. Kirby's spirits are in a free fall. Are things okay or not? She walks down the hall to find Mr. Ames dozing in his chair by the side entrance. Gently Kirby touches his arm, and he startles awake.

"Kirby," he says. He gets to his feet, shaking his head. "I told you not to leave. Who did you think was going to handle the desk when the senator got back?"

Kirby clings to what's left of her self-righteous rage. "I had to go," she says. "Luke wanted the cabbie to take him to my house in Oak Bluffs. He would have found Patty. He *hurts* her, Mr. Ames."

"I understand you wanted to help your friend, but you have a job, Kirby, and with that job comes responsibility. Any idea how concerned I was when you just ran off without telling me?"

"I'm so sorry," she says.

Mr. Ames says, "Well, you're lucky. The senator came in the side door and I was right here so I went and fetched his key. He didn't look much better than that other punk, to be honest."

"Really?" Kirby says. "Was he drunk?"

"He was something," Mr. Ames says. "Looked like he went swimming in all his clothes. He was disoriented, I guess, which was why he came knocking on the side door. He kept asking the time. I told him it was two thirty and he asked if I was sure it wasn't earlier, so I had to lead him over to the clock and show him. Funny thing is, he was wearing a watch." Mr. Ames shrugs. "Maybe it stopped."

Mrs. Bennie makes a surprise appearance at seven in the morning. She looks crisp and fresh in a shamrock-green shirtwaist dress and pearls. It's the first time Kirby has ever seen her boss with her hair down; she looks ten years younger, softer, prettier. Kirby supposes she wants to make a good impression on the senator. Compared to this new, glamorous version of Mrs. Bennie, Kirby feels wan and exhausted. Despite her keen desire to meet the senator, Kirby is relieved when Mrs. Bennie tells her she can go home. "I'm asking Mr. Ames to stay until nine," Mrs. Bennie says. "So you'll have to find another ride back to Oak Bluffs, I'm afraid."

It's not a problem. Kirby is too disconcerted by the events of the night to impose on Mr. Ames for a ride anyway. She calls a taxi, and they send a burly driver covered in tattoos who looks like a long-haul fisherman. Why couldn't they have sent this guy last night? Kirby wonders. That would have solved everything.

Kirby promptly falls asleep in the back seat, awakening only as they turn onto Circuit Avenue, at which point she sits up and gathers her things. She can't believe she missed the senator. She *hates* Luke Winslow! And then, as though she has somehow conjured him with this one thought, Kirby sees Luke pacing on the sidewalk in front of the house.

No! she thinks. No, this can't be happening, but yes, that's him, fists clenched, muttering to himself. He has showered and changed, at least. His hair is combed, and he's wearing a white polo shirt and blue seersucker Bermudas. This is almost worse, she decides; he looks respectable.

"I've gotten the address wrong," Kirby tells the taxi driver. "Keep going."

"Keep going *where?*" the taxi driver asks. Kirby leans over the seat and notices a tattoo of a snarling Elvis on his forearm.

"Methodist Campground?" Kirby says. She doesn't know Darren's exact address. "The big blue house? Judge Frazier's house? Do you know it?"

"I do, actually," the driver says. He winds around Ocean Park and a few moments later pulls up in front of Darren's house. "Buck twenty-five."

Kirby gives him a dollar fifty, then gets out of the taxi. She stands at the white gate for a second, wondering if she would be better off waking up Evan in the basement or finding a pay phone—there's one over by the fudge shop—and calling the police directly.

But...she's here. She strides up the walk and knocks on the front door. A second later, she's face to face with the good doctor. Dr. Frazier is wearing athletic shorts and a white tank top; her hair is held off her face by a striped sweatband.

"Hello," she says.

"Dr. Frazier…"

"Darren's asleep," she says. "He doesn't have to be at work until noon."

"I have an urgent situation," Kirby says. "I need his help."

"What kind of urgent situation?" Dr. Frazier asks. Her voice is arch. Kirby holds the woman in high esteem and she wishes the feeling were mutual but it just isn't, and now she can't even lean on Mr. Ames's good opinion of her.

"It's my roommate," Kirby says. "She's dating someone who hurts her, and he's waiting for her now outside the house on Narragansett."

Kirby watches Dr. Frazier struggle between doctor-mode and mother-mode. Mother-mode wins. "What does this have to do with Darren?"

"Nothing, but—"

"I think it's better that he not get involved," Dr. Frazier says. "He's a good boy. He stays out of trouble. I take it your roommate's boyfriend is white?"

Kirby nods. She doesn't understand what that has to do with anything.

"If Darren gets into an altercation with a white boy…" Dr. Frazier says. She narrows her eyes. "You should find someone else to help you."

"I thought maybe Darren could reason with him."

"Men who hurt women can't be reasoned with," Dr. Frazier says. "If it's serious, call the police."

"It's serious," Kirby says.

"Okay, then. Would you like to use the phone?"

Would she like to use the phone? Dr. Frazier is watching her closely, possibly to determine her motives. Do the police need to be called or is she really here only so she can see Darren?

"You're welcome to come in," Dr. Frazier says. "I have nothing against you personally, Kirby."

But you do, Kirby thinks. Though she doesn't have time to defend herself right now.

"I'll go get my landlord," Kirby says. "Thank you, Dr. Frazier. Sorry to bother you so early." Kirby turns and hurries back down the walk and out the gate while, she's sure, Dr. Frazier watches her from the doorway.

Kirby runs toward Narragansett Avenue. She won't wake Evan. She can handle Luke herself.

She's a block and a half away when things start to unfold. A black sedan pulls up in front of the house and Patty gets out of the passenger side. Kirby can't see who's driving but the car is unfamiliar. The car drives off.

"Patty!" Kirby yells.

Patty turns toward Kirby's voice but then Luke approaches her and...Patty hugs him. They start kissing right there on the sidewalk and Kirby thinks, *Okay?* Maybe Luke has had a chance to calm down. But still, Kirby is concerned. And sure enough, Luke pushes Patty away, hard, so that she stumbles, and then he grabs her by the hair and starts pulling her up the stairs to the house.

Kirby runs. "Let go of her!"

Luke doesn't let go. He's swearing under his breath, calling Patty a whore, asking Patty where she spent the night, who she was with, how many guys she slept with. Patty is crying softly, saying, "I was with my sister Sara. We were at a party on Chappy. Let go of me, Luke, you're *hurting* me."

"I thought you liked it when I hurt you," Luke says.

Kirby takes the front steps two at a time and starts pummeling Luke's back. "Let go of her. Luke, stop!"

Luke swings around and backhands Kirby right across the face.

She's stunned. No one has ever hit her before. She brings her fingers to her lip. She's bleeding.

"Are you kidding me?" a voice says.

Kirby backs up a few steps as Darren comes charging up the stairs. He regards Luke for one second, then punches him. The hit is solid; the sound, gruesome. Luke drops to the ground.

"Go inside," Darren says to Kirby. "Call the police."

Luke doesn't even bother getting up. He just lies splayed across the yard, whimpering.

Patty kneels down next to him. "He's hurt!" she says. She glares at Darren. "You hurt him!"

"He hit Kirby," Darren says. "Any man who would raise his hand to a woman does not deserve your sympathy."

"It was self-defense," Patty says. "Kirby was attacking him."

"*Attacking* him?" Kirby says. Her face stings; she's going to have a fat lip. "He was dragging you by the hair like a caveman."

"How many times do I have to tell you?" Patty says. "This is *none* of your business!"

"You don't deserve to be treated that way," Kirby says. "I've seen the bruises, Patty, and the marks from where he slaps you."

Patty casts a sidelong glance at Darren and speaks through gritted teeth. "It's none of your business. You don't know what I like or don't like—"

"It's 1969," Kirby says. "You don't have to tolerate him *abusing* you."

Patty gets to her feet and charges toward Kirby, and Kirby wonders if she's about to get hit for the second time in her life. "Butt out! I don't judge your…*preferences,* so please don't judge mine." She pulls Luke up.

"Well, the fact is, he hit *me,*" Kirby says. "I could press charges."

"Press away!" Patty says. Her eyes are wild with defiance, but beneath this Kirby spies fear or insecurity—or maybe it's just exhaustion. Kirby is guessing Patty didn't get much sleep on Chappy. "Come on, Luke." Patty yanks Luke into the house, blatantly violating the no-visitors-of-the-opposite-sex rule. The front door slams behind them.

Kirby and Darren stare at each other in dumbfounded silence.

"What should I do?" Kirby asks.

Just then, a police car rolls up and Kirby feels a wave of relief. Maybe someone else reported the disturbance; Patty's screaming could have woken the dead.

"Edgartown?" Darren says.

Kirby doesn't understand at first, but then she notices it's the *Edgartown* police, not the Oak Bluffs police, which is very unusual indeed.

An officer gets out of the car and strides up the walk. He nods at Kirby and Darren.

"I'm looking for Patricia O'Callahan," he says.

Kirby can't decide if she should linger and try to eavesdrop or if she should just head up to the igloo and go to sleep.

"I should probably get some ice," she says to Darren.

Gently, he touches her swollen lip. "I'm gonna wait until he comes out and then give him a proper licking."

"The police are handling it," Kirby says. She wonders if maybe it was Mr. Ames who called the Edgartown police.

"You're right," Darren says. He smiles at her and Kirby allows herself to be sucked into the warmth of his brown eyes. He's handsome, genuine, kind, and flat-out superior to every other boyfriend she has ever had—but he will never be hers. Kirby wants to blame this on history or society, but the fact is, her own bad decisions are the obstacle.

"Thank you for coming to the rescue," Kirby says. "My hero."

"Anytime," Darren says.

Kirby is lying facedown on her bed—too tired to remove her yellow daisy dress but not too tired to play Simon and Garfunkel—when she hears the scream. She lifts her head an inch.

It's Patty.

Although Kirby's first instinct is to leap into action, she stays put. Patty made it perfectly clear that she doesn't want Kirby's help.

There's a second scream and then footsteps on the stairs and pounding on Kirby's door. She rises to find Michaela and Barb.

"You need to come downstairs," Michaela says. "She's asking for you."

"Something's happened," Barb says.

Kirby isn't sure what she's going to find but she certainly doesn't expect to see both Luke and the police officer standing idly by while Patty wails. When Kirby descends the stairs, Patty looks up. Her face is crumpled and beet red.

"Mary Jo," Patty says.

Kirby blinks.

"Mary Jo Kopechne, Sara's friend?" Patty says. "Someone drove off the Dike Bridge with her in the car and she was trapped. She drowned, Kirby. She's dead."

A Whiter Shade of Pale (Reprise)

Kate called David with the happy news about the twins and he said, "That's wonderful, Kate. You must be overjoyed."

The "you" worried her. She didn't like the way he was distancing himself from her and the family. It was very unlike him. David adored Blair and, as he did with all of Kate's children, treated her like his own.

"Won't you come this weekend and meet them?" Kate asked. "Please?"

David issued a mighty sigh. This, Kate thought, was when he'd tell her he wanted a divorce.

"What if I got us a room at the Gordon Folger?" Kate asked. This was what they used to do when they were dating, back when Exalta made no secret of the fact that she disapproved of Kate getting involved with someone so soon after Wilder's death, and her own lawyer, to boot! Exalta insisted that there were rules about that sort of thing, but what she really meant was her own rule that Kate stick to Boston Brahmins.

"A room at the Gordon Folger won't be necessary," David said. "I'd like to spend some time with my daughter."

"Our daughter," Kate said.

"Our daughter, yes, Kate," David said. "But I'm not up to fighting traffic Friday night. I'll take a ferry midday Saturday and leave Sunday afternoon before the crush."

He would be on Nantucket a scant twenty-four hours, Kate thought, and from the sound of it, that was mostly so he could see Jessie. Apparently, Kate was no longer his first priority, nor was she worth sitting in traffic for. But she had behaved abominably this summer; she had no delusions about that.

"Thank you," she said. "It would mean the world to me. To us all."

David gave a dry laugh. "Please warn Exalta of my impending arrival."

"Actually, Mother was just asking why we haven't seen more of you this summer," Kate said. This was a lie, but at least Exalta hadn't said anything overtly negative about David, as she was wont to do.

"Kate, please," David said. "Don't make it worse." He hung up.

On Saturday morning, there's knocking on the front door of All's Fair that quickly turns sharp and insistent. Kate is exhausted; she stayed at the hospital until nearly eleven the night before, holding one baby while Blair nursed the other. She waits to see if either Exalta or Jessie will answer the door but then she remembers that it's a weekend—no tennis lessons, so they won't be up. Kate rouses herself. It must be David here early, she thinks, and she smooths her hair before she ties the belt of her robe. The knocking continues. Why make such a ruckus? she wonders. Why not just let himself in? He knows they never lock the door. He's probably trying to make a point: This isn't his house so he'll act like a guest.

Halfway down the stairs, she freezes. It's *not* David because the first ferry in doesn't arrive until ten. Who else would be knocking on the front door so early on a Saturday morning? Someone on a mission. Someone from the U.S. Army.

Kate feels light-headed. She sits on the step, fourth from the bottom. She won't answer the door. She can't. She'll sit here for the rest of her life if she has to, she will turn to stone, but she will *not* answer the door to the news that Tiger is dead.

The knocking persists. A female voice says, "Open up! I know you're in there!"

A woman? Kate thinks. She pushes herself to her feet.

Standing on the front step is a woman with long dark hair. She's wearing a black-and-white tie-dyed T-shirt, a denim skirt, and an anklet made of tiny bells. Her feet are bare.

"Can I *help* you?" Kate asks. This woman is a flower child, a hippie, and likely a beggar or here asking for money for some imaginary charity. But because Kate is awash with sweet relief, she'll give the woman a quarter and tell her to please be on her way. Maybe she'll send her down the street to Bitsy Dunscombe's house. Kate brightens at the very idea of this prank.

The woman is wearing a pair of tiny, round mirrored sunglasses. When she raises them, Kate sees ice-blue eyes.

Dear God, Kate thinks, and it takes everything in her power not to slam the door shut in the woman's face.

"Katie?" the woman says.

It's Lorraine. Lorraine Crimmins.

Kate falls back on her manners. "Lorraine," she says. "I'm sorry...you've given me a shock. I...we...weren't expecting you, were we? Bill...your father...didn't say anything..."

"He doesn't know I'm coming," Lorraine says. "He'll be more surprised than you."

"Ah," Kate says. She's at a *complete* loss. "I'm sure he'll be happy to see you."

"Doubt that," Lorraine says. "But I didn't come to see the old man. I came to get my boy."

"Well," Kate says. The polite thing to do is invite Lorraine in but Kate can't bring herself to do it. Now that she's recovering from her shock, she feels the old hatred surfacing inside her, like pollution in a river. "You'll have to check with your father about that. My understanding is you up and left Pick by himself. I'm not sure what reason a mother would ever have for doing such a thing, but if you ask me, you don't deserve the boy back. He's quite happy here with us. He has a job and a girlfriend. In the fall, he can go to high school here."

"Ha!" Lorraine laughs like Kate has told a joke. "Come off it, Katie."

"I heard him on the phone the other day, Lorraine, trying to call the…place you live, or used to live, looking for you, and no one could tell him where you were. He was upset."

"Well, then, he'll be happy to see me."

Kate shuts the door and leans against it. Lorraine starts pounding. Kate wants Exalta to wake up, but she sleeps with earplugs in so there is little to no hope of her hearing all this. Ever so stealthily, Kate slides the dead bolt; there's a telltale click. Lorraine stops knocking.

Good, Kate thinks. Lorraine gets the picture—she isn't welcome. Kate considers calling the police but she can't bear to make a scene so early on a Saturday—or at all.

Kate hurries down the hall, through the kitchen, and across the yard. She needs to wake up Bill Crimmins. But when she lets herself into Little Fair, she sees his bedroom is empty. A quick check out the window confirms his truck is gone. It's early, but not *that* early. Bill has already left for work.

Kate leaves Little Fair just in time to see Lorraine opening the back door and entering the kitchen at All's Fair.

"What are you *doing?*" Kate calls out in a furious whisper. "I did not invite you in!" She flies into the kitchen to find Lorraine already seated at the table. Lorraine chooses a peach out of the fruit bowl and takes a sloppy bite, her eyes defiant. Juice drips down her chin.

"Get. Out." Kate looms over Lorraine. She is so angry, she wants to strike her.

"Go ahead," Lorraine says. "Slap me. I know you want to. You've wanted to for sixteen years." She stands up and presents a cheek to Kate. "It will give me great satisfaction to watch Katie Nichols lose control."

"You're despicable," Kate says. "You were despicable then and you're even more despicable now. Where is your self-respect? You show up here barefoot like a common hobo. You stink to high heaven. And I'm sure you don't have any money."

"True," Lorraine says with a smirk. "I don't. But my father will give me some."

Kate silently concedes that point. "You are *not* staying here, Lorraine."

"It's actually Lavender now," Lorraine says. "If you don't mind."

"What I mind, *Lavender,* is you barging into our family home uninvited."

"You know, I've actually missed this house," Lorraine says. "It has so many unique features. The mural, the buttery…"

"Watch it, Lorraine," Kate says. She can't *believe* how brazen the woman is being. She must be on something.

"And so many fine antiques. Exalta's whatchamacallits—and that spinning wheel. Hey, do you remember when Kirby got in trouble for breaking the spinning wheel and she wouldn't apologize? That's because I was the one who broke it. I had taken a bunch of your diet pills and I was buzzing and wanted to see how fast it could go."

Kate stares at Lorraine. Of course she remembers the broken

spinning wheel. Was Lorraine confessing now, so many years later, that she had stolen Kate's diet pills (she had struggled to lose weight after giving birth to Tiger) and while speeding on those pills, she had broken the house's most valuable antique and then pinned the blame on a five-year-old?

"All the family secrets are coming out!" Lorraine says with a lunatic's smile. One of her side teeth is missing. "I would have spoken up if Kirby got into any real trouble, but of course she didn't. She was Exalta's lapdog. By the way, how is Blair? Did she ever stop sucking her thumb? And what about my favorite, little Tiger? How is our little Tiger?"

"You're a whore," Kate says. "A common whore."

"Lucky for your husband," Lorraine says.

That's it; Kate snaps. She grabs Lorraine by the arm and pulls her toward the back door, but Lorraine digs into the linoleum with her dirty heels. Kate prays for her mother to appear; Lorraine has always looked up to Exalta. But the person who materializes on the back porch is Jessie. Kate wonders how long she's been standing there and what, exactly, she's heard. Behind Jessie is Pick dressed in his mustard-yellow board shorts with a towel draped around his neck, climbing onto his bike.

Lorraine must see Pick also because all of a sudden, she bursts forward, eager to go exactly where Kate wants her to go—outside.

It's a messy reunion, and loud. Lorraine is sobbing; she begs for forgiveness and professes her love, but Pick seems to rebuff his mother. Finally, however, he lets her hug him and then they're embracing and rocking back and forth. Kate and Jessie watch from the back porch. Kate is...incredulous. She can't believe Lorraine

Crimmins has returned to Nantucket and that she had the gall to knock on the front door of All's Fair after the disgraceful way she left so many years ago.

And yet, the reunion between mother and son is strangely touching.

Tiger, Kate thinks.

But Tiger is off fighting a war for the U.S. Army. He's fighting so that rootless, toothless floozies like Lorraine Crimmins can wander the country in bare feet.

"Is she taking him back to California?" Jessie asks.

"Who knows," Kate says.

"What did she mean when—"

"I'll explain later," Kate says. "Right now, I have to find Bill Crimmins."

Kate starts by calling down to the Charcoal Galley to see if Bill was in for breakfast and if he said where he was headed later.

The waitress, Joelle, says, "He's been doing handyman work at the Congregational church all week."

Wonderful. Kate calls the Congregational church and asks the secretary in the office to please send Bill Crimmins home to Fair Street.

"His daughter has paid us a surprise visit from California," Kate says.

Bill pulls up a few minutes later. Kate and Jessie are at the kitchen table; Kate is drinking her morning coffee, and through the window, she sees him slam his truck door shut and then slam into Little Fair. Kate has no idea what will transpire. Jessie, drinking juice and nibbling a piece of toast, watches him as well.

"Do you think—" Jessie asks.

"I don't know and I don't care," Kate says. "You shouldn't care either. They're not our family." Kate throws back what's left of her coffee. "Not really."

Not really.

Lucky for your husband.

Kate fills her coffee cup again and resists the temptation to add whiskey because David is coming today and she cannot, *will not,* be drunk when he arrives. However, without alcohol, it's difficult to banish the ghosts.

Wilder.

Kate knew he was unfaithful early in the marriage—he had flirted with Kate's own cousin at their wedding reception in a way that was completely inappropriate—but it had taken her a while to realize just how crucial to his self-worth the philandering was. It didn't matter what Kate said or did. She would threaten to leave; he would earnestly promise to stop. A few weeks or months later, he would be back at the bars, coming home late, not coming home at all.

It was, frankly, a relief when he left for Korea.

When Wilder came home, he seemed like a new man—devoted, chastened, passionate about Kate and Kate only. On Nantucket that summer, Exalta fawned all over him—telling all the ladies at the Field and Oar that Wilder was a war hero—and Kate's father, Penn, indulged him with scotch and good cigars. But after only a few weeks, the highs of Wilder's personality dropped into deep troughs. Kate was aware that Wilder had started taking Benzedrine overseas in order to stay sharp and she suspected the habit had continued here at home. She could tell when he was high—his eyes had a certain glint and he talked a mile a minute. The only thing that could bring him down softly was alcohol. That summer, there were late nights at Bosun's Locker and then a string of nights when he didn't come home at all. One morning, he showed up with mud-caked shoes; he said he'd fallen asleep on a grave in the Quaker cemetery, weeping over the men he'd lost in Korea. Another night he brought half a pound of sand to bed with him. He told Kate he'd walked all the way to Surfside Beach, then from Surfside to Cisco, then from Cisco home.

She had chosen to believe him.

On what turned out to be the last of those nights, when Kate woke up and Wilder wasn't in bed, she went to the kitchen to make some warm milk. She heard a noise coming from the hallway and when she'd gone to investigate, she'd found Wilder hiding in the buttery. At first she thought he was in there alone, which wasn't too surprising—he was definitely drunk and he might have mistaken her for Exalta or Penn and tried to hide. But then Kate caught a glimpse of a ghost-white foot sticking out of the back of the buttery.

It was Lorraine. Lorraine Crimmins, who cooked and baked for Exalta and who, that summer, was also minding the children.

Their summer had ended abruptly right there. Kate packed up herself and the children that very night and they had left on the early ferry, before her parents were even awake.

"You can explain to them why I left," Kate told Wilder. "Stay here with her if that's what you want."

Kate had stood on the upper deck of the ferry with her car keys clenched like a weapon between her fingers as she watched Nantucket retreat into the distance. Lorraine Crimmins; it was *such* a betrayal. Lorraine had started working at the Nichols household when she was sixteen years old and Kate twenty, a sophomore at Smith College. That was during the war. Kate had invited Lorraine to listen to the radio with her in the evenings; together they had knit socks for the men overseas. Kate had been kind to Lorraine because she *pitied* her. Lorraine was a sad case—ruined by her mother's death when she was a baby, doomed to disappoint and underachieve every step of the way after that. Lorraine was very pretty, but her style tended toward tawdry. She wore too much makeup when she went out at night, and her clothes were tight and cheap. At Bosun's Locker she met men—scallopers, house painters, traveling salesmen—one after the other, no one special, no one serious.

Wilder and Lorraine, crammed into the buttery. Given away by Kate glimpsing that one pale foot. It wasn't a vision Kate could ever hope to forget.

Kate had told Wilder to stay with Lorraine but as the ferry crossed the sound, she feared that was exactly what he would do. Kate loved Wilder and she hated herself for that. It seemed the cruelest circumstance life had to offer—that someone she loved so profoundly could hurt her so badly and still that love did not die. If anything, it intensified. Kate wanted Wilder to love *her*, to desire *her*, not Lorraine Crimmins.

Why her? Why Lorraine, of all people?

Exalta had called the next day to check on Tiger's fever.

"Tiger's *fever?*" Kate said.

Yes, Exalta said, Wilder had explained that Tiger was running a high fever, which was why Kate had taken the children to Boston in such a great hurry.

The big war hero was a coward, Kate thought.

Just as Kate was summoning the courage to tell Exalta the truth—as humiliating as it was, Kate would also gain great satisfaction in stripping Exalta of her illusions about the man— Wilder had walked through the door. He dropped to his knees in front of Kate, and she felt the mightiest relief she had ever known.

* * *

A few minutes after Bill goes into Little Fair, Kate and Jessie watch all three of the Crimminses emerge from the house—Mr. Crimmins first, holding a duffel bag, then Lorraine, then Pick. Pick turns and sees Kate and Jessie and offers a halfhearted wave. Jessie gets up and takes a step forward but Kate says, "Let them go." The last thing she wants is a grandiose, overblown goodbye, and she can't get close to Lorraine again or she will do something she is sure to regret.

"But…" Jessie says. She gazes at her mother with her liquid brown eyes. "I'm in love with him."

Kate processes this information. "Come with me," she says. "I want to talk to you."

Midnight Confessions

Jessie follows her mother up the stairs of Little Fair. It's almost unbearable to be here now that Pick is gone, really *gone*. Jessie would even prefer him being here with Sabrina. She thinks back to the day she arrived, when she found Pick playing that dumb ball-and-paddle game. She feels like she walked into a trap. Pick was so cute with his sun-bleached hair and his rope bracelet and his easy charm, asking Jessie questions, taking an interest in her, making her a simple, delicious lunch when she was so hungry. It was impossible *not* to fall immediately in love with him.

Kate indicates that Jessie should sit at the table and Jessie does so, though her heart breaks because he didn't leave a note for her or anything, no sign that they'd been friends or that he'd miss her. Probably, he'd been worried about Sabrina—or maybe not. Maybe he was just happy that his mother came to reclaim him. Jessie hadn't been able to tell from the look on his face.

"You know what the happiest summer of my life was?" Kate asks.

"When you turned thirteen?" Jessie guesses.

"I was thirteen during the Great Depression," Kate says. "So, no."

Jessie doesn't venture another guess. Frankly, she doesn't care.

"It was the summer you were born," Kate says. "Your dad and I brought you here when you were only four weeks old, just a little peanut. And we lived up here in Little Fair all by ourselves, and the other three kids stayed in the big house with Nonny and Gramps."

"Oh," Jessie says. She's only old enough to remember when her siblings lived in Little Fair by themselves.

"I was happy...well, probably because I had a little bit of space from Nonny. It was just you, me, and Daddy. It felt like a fresh start...and I desperately needed a fresh start."

Jessie runs her Tree of Life pendant along its chain as her mind wanders back to the exchange she overheard between her mother and Lorraine Crimmins. Kate had called Lorraine Crimmins a whore, and Lorraine, instead of getting angry like Jessie assumed she would, said, *Lucky for your husband.* Jessie had gotten a funny feeling then, like a door was opening, a secret door, and she was finally getting a glimpse of what lurked behind it. She knows a whore is a prostitute, a woman who gets paid to have sex with men, and she knows that when Lorraine said, *Lucky for your husband,* she meant Wilder Foley, not David Levin.

Wilder Foley and Lorraine Crimmins?

Jessie thinks back to the puberty talk at the end of the school year and she feels herself flush because she suddenly knows what her mother wants to talk to her about.

Jessie hasn't been paying attention to her mother, who's been talking about how Kate and David brought Jessie everywhere that summer in her carriage and her baby basket. They had even taken her on a cabin cruiser all the way over to Tuckernuck.

"Mom," Jessie says, interrupting her. "Is Pick..." She doesn't know how to ask what she wants to ask but it hardly matters because she knows the answer is yes.

"Pick is Wilder Foley's son," Kate says matter-of-factly. "Wilder got Lorraine Crimmins pregnant. She ran off to California and had Pick, and I haven't seen her since then. Until today."

For a second, Jessie is suspended in sheer panic, thinking she has fallen in love with *her own brother*—but then she recalculates. Pick *isn't* her brother. His parents are Lorraine Crimmins and Wilder Foley. Her parents are Kate and David. Pick is, however, the half brother of Blair, Kirby, and Tiger, just as Jessie is their half sister. Pick is *her,* but on the flip side.

Jessie is dizzy. "Does Nonny know?" she asks.

Kate shrugs. "I'm sure she suspects. Although, actually, I have no idea. Your grandmother and I haven't talked about it because we don't talk about anything. I've had a very lonely life."

"You *have?*" Jessie says. In her mind, Kate is the center of everything. She's Exalta's daughter; she was Wilder's wife and now she's David's wife; she's Blair's, Kirby's, Tiger's, and Jessie's mother. How can she be lonely?

Kate's eyes fill with tears and Jessie gazes at her with wonder. Her mother is so beautiful, even in her bathrobe and pink silk pajamas, even without pearls or lipstick. Jessie knows her mother is sick with worry about Tiger but now it appears she's sad about all sorts of other things, older things.

"The night Wilder died…" Kate says.

"You don't have to talk about it," Jessie says.

"I have to tell *someone,* don't you see?" Kate says. She squeezes Jessie's hand, and for the first time ever in her life, Jessie understands that her mother is real.

It's a revelation. Her mother is a human being who feels pain—sadness, loneliness, confusion. Jessie thought all grown-ups lived in a different atmosphere, one that was like a cool, clear gel. Adults had problems, Jessie knew—money and their children—but one of the benefits of reaching adulthood, she thought, was that you outgrew the raw, hot, chaotic emotions of adolescence.

"The night Wilder died was a couple of days after I received a letter from Lorraine telling me that she was pregnant with his baby."

Jessie's stomach drops.

"I wanted to confront him while the children were asleep," Kate says. "I found him in his workshop, cleaning his gun."

Jessie bows her head and closes her eyes. She knows she should be honored that her mother has chosen *her* as a confidante…but she doesn't want to hear another word. Already the story is different from the one Jessie believed to be true her whole life. She thought that Kate had walked into the workshop and found Wilder dead.

"I let him read the letter from Lorraine," Kate goes on, "and I said, 'It looks like you're to have a bastard child. I'm taking the children and leaving you. I'm moving back to Beacon Hill with my parents. I'm through, Wilder, and there's nothing you can do about it. I've contacted a lawyer and I'm filing for divorce.'"

Jessie holds her breath. She had been told long ago—by whom, she can't remember—that Wilder shot himself accidentally and that Kate had hired David Levin to prove it wasn't a suicide and he had done that.

"I closed the door and walked away," Kate says. "But do you know what I regret?"

Jessie senses that she's not expected to answer, and she can't find her voice anyway.

"I regret not slamming the door," Kate says. "If I'd shown anger, Wilder might have snapped to his senses and come after me to argue or plead his case. He had...dramatic mood swings, problems with pills and whiskey...but I didn't realize how low his low points were. Honestly, Jessica, I wasn't thinking about him in that moment. I was thinking about myself. I was thinking that he had betrayed me. He had been unfaithful with someone I knew, someone I liked. And he'd been careless enough to get her pregnant, which meant that the whole wide world would know that Wilder preferred Lorraine Crimmins to me, and I would be humiliated on top of my heartbreak."

"What happened?" Jessie asks.

"A split second after I'd closed the door quietly but firmly, with a click, and walked away, I heard a shot."

"He killed himself," Jessie says.

"Yes," Kate says. "I wasn't a hundred percent certain at first because Wilder was prone to drama. I thought it was possible he'd fired a shot into the wall to make me *think* he'd killed himself. And he was so unstable that I also thought it was possible that I'd open that door and he would be pointing the gun at me."

"What did you do?" Jessie asks.

"I waited a few minutes and when I heard nothing but silence, I opened the door and I saw what he'd done." Kate's eyes are dry, her face is calm. She might be telling Jessie that she opened the door to find Wilder had fixed the vacuum. "My first emotion was

353

completely irrational: anger. I was furious that Wilder had taken the easy way out. I wanted him to face what he'd done. I wanted him to feel shame in front of my father, in front of my mother."

This is so unexpected, Jessie doesn't know how to arrange her expression.

"And then I felt guilt, like an ocean wave crashing over me, a really powerful wave, the kind that knocks you down and fills your nose and mouth with burning salt water. Because..." Kate laughs sadly. "I can't believe I'm telling you all this. I should stop."

Yes, Jessie thinks. *Stop. Stop!* But somehow she knows Kate isn't able to stop.

"I felt guilty because I had lied to Wilder. I hadn't contacted a lawyer and I didn't plan on divorcing him. I would have moved to Nonny's temporarily, then we would have worked it out. I only said what I did in order to upset him." Kate pauses, thinks for a minute, then says, "The only person in the whole world who knows the truth is Bill Crimmins."

"Mr. Crimmins?" Jessie says.

"I called him on Nantucket and told him what happened. He got on the ferry and made it to our house by midnight. He fixed it."

"Fixed it *how?*" Jessie asks. Her hands are numb, her lips are tingling. She will never, ever be the same. Nothing matters anymore—not Pick, not the Tree of Life, not Anne Frank discovered by the Nazis and dying in a concentration camp. Her mother lied about Wilder Foley's death. He killed himself because of something Kate said. And Mr. Crimmins knows.

"He just fixed it," Kate says. "He made it look like an accident."

"Dad?" Jessie asks.

"David was the main person we were trying to fool," Kate says. "And the insurance company, of course, because they wouldn't have paid a settlement for a suicide. And I wanted to hide the truth from my friends and neighbors. When they heard Wilder killed himself accidentally while cleaning his gun, they felt sorry for us. *That* is a tragedy. Suicide, however, carries a stigma. I couldn't bear to pass that legacy on to the children. So, only Bill knows. And now you. I'm trusting you with this secret, but I will not *burden* you with it. If you want to call the authorities right now, call the authorities." Her eyes are shining with tears. "It might be a relief. You have no idea what kind of *hell* it has been living with this for so many years. I waited each day to be punished. Because no one gets off scot-free, Jessie. And when they called up your brother, although the rest of the world might see that as random bad luck, I knew that Tiger was being drafted because of me. And he's likely going to die."

"Mom," Jessie whispers. "Please don't say that."

"It's my fault," Kate says forlornly. She lays her head on the table, and finally, the tears fall. "It's my fault. I drove Wilder to his death."

Jessie remembers seeing the destruction that the Bonneville caused after it crashed through the front window of Buttner's. The damage had seemed irreparable. And yet, Buttner's window had eventually been restored to brand-new, better than brand-new. So, too, with Kate's earth-shattering confession. Kate cries for a while; Jessie hands her some tissues, Kate wipes her tears, then heads back over to All's Fair. When Jessie checks on her a while later, Kate seems *happier*. She suggests that they go to the beach, just the two of them.

"It's the nineteenth of July," Kate says in a completely normal voice. "And we've barely been."

"What about Dad?" Jessie asks. She tries to keep her voice

steady but right now her world is hanging on her father's arrival. Her mother must know Jessie would never call the authorities to turn her in, but Jessie *is* going to tell her father. She *hates* that Kate and Mr. Crimmins set out to fool him. He needs to know the truth.

"He's arriving on the three-fifteen," Kate says. "If we leave here by eleven, we can still get half a day."

Jessie is afraid if she declines, her mother will think it's because she's horrified by the secret. Jessie *is* horrified by the secret. For sixteen years, her mother has been lying to everyone. And now Kate is being punished—no, they are *all* being punished, because Tiger was sent to Vietnam and might come back in a body bag.

The incomprehensible thing is that Jessie still loves her mother as much as ever, maybe more. Jessie remembers only too well how she agonized that week when she thought Nonny's necklace was gone forever and how that guilt was like a load of gravel in her gut, grinding away, weighing her down. What must it have been like for her mother, keeping the secret from Nonny and David and her own children all these years? No wonder she felt lonely.

Jessie will tell David, and David will confront Kate, and although things will then be messy, the truth will be out and Kate will feel better and maybe Tiger will be saved.

"Okay," Jessie says. "I'll put my suit on."

"I'll make sandwiches," Kate says.

"Mom," Jessie says. Kate stops. They look at each other and this is the make-or-break moment, Jessie can feel it.

"No mustard," Jessie says.

The day turns out much better than Jessie would have thought such a day could. Kate and Jessie go to Ram Pasture. Exalta tried to wrangle an invitation but Kate said, "I'd like some time alone with Jessie, thanks, Mother." The beach is practically deserted.

The sun is warm but not overbearing and because Exalta isn't there, Jessie gets to sit in her chair, a Sleepy Hollow, which did not get its name by accident. Jessie falls asleep in the sun but her mother remembered the Coppertone so Jessie doesn't burn. When she wakes up, she and Kate take a swim. The water is cool and refreshing and cleansing. When they climb out, they eat their sandwiches on their towels. Jessie has ham and cheese on lightly toasted Portuguese bread with butter and some nice lettuce and pickles, and it's the best sandwich she has eaten all summer if she doesn't count the BLT Pick made for her on the first day.

After lunch, Jessie lies on her stomach and reads *Mrs. Basil E. Frankweiler*. She stops every few pages to daydream about her older self graduating from college and moving to New York City or Paris or Amsterdam, which is where Anne Frank lived.

At quarter to three, they pack up their things and climb into the Scout, and they reach the ferry at the exact moment that David Levin is coming down the gangplank.

Kate says, "Go ahead, it's okay."

Jessie gets out of the car and runs into her father's arms and he holds her tight and says, "Oh, honey, you are a sight for sore eyes." Jessie squeezes him tightly and thinks that *he's* the sight for sore eyes; she didn't realize how much she missed him until just this second.

He pulls away and says, "I can't believe how grown-up and beautiful you're getting."

Her face grows warm, or maybe that's from the sun.

"Don't forget, we have an ice cream date," David says. "But right now, I want to kiss your mother."

They drive back to the house and Kate and David disappear upstairs and Jessie takes a long outdoor shower and then goes upstairs in Little Fair and sees an envelope on the table. Her heart seizes. Tiger? But as she gets closer, she sees it's just a letter from Doris. Jessie takes it into her room and stretches out across the bed. Her skin is tight from the sun, and despite the shower, there are still grains of sand hiding in the part of her hair and the whorls of her ears, but this is how it's supposed to be in summer.

Dear Jessie,

I can't believe you have a boyfriend. I hope he gets to visit Brookline so we can meet him in person.

Jessie realizes that this line means exactly what it says: Doris *doesn't* believe Jessie has a boyfriend. And Doris is correct, but she never needs to know that.

There's big news here and that is that Leslie got caught stealing a pair of pearl earrings from Filene's. She went shopping with Pammy Pope and told Pammy how easy it was to just take whatever she wanted without paying for it. Pammy said she wanted a pair of pearl earrings. Piece of cake, Leslie said. She took out her own gold studs and stuck them in her pocket. Then at the jewelry counter, she asked to see the pearl earrings. She stuck them in her ears and pretended to admire them in the mirror and when the saleslady got distracted, Leslie slipped into the next department, then the next, then she eased out the door to the street. Pammy was in awe. She thought Leslie had gotten away with it.
Leslie was stopped by the police two blocks away.
The police took her to the station, called her parents, said

they had witnessed the burglary on a hidden camera and they could charge Leslie and she would go to court and maybe even a juvenile delinquent center. Leslie's father managed to talk the police out of it and he took Leslie home.

But now... Leslie's parents have decided to send her to boarding school in Switzerland (which is where her grandmother lives) because they don't want Leslie going down a "wayward path."

So I guess that just leaves you and me, facing seventh grade together!

See you in a few weeks.

From your best friend, Doris

The drama of the day and the sun at the beach have worn Jessie down. She has every intention of using the dollar her father gave her to walk down to Vincent's for pizza, but the second her parents leave for dinner at the Skipper, she goes up to her room and falls asleep.

She wakes up in the middle of the night, absolutely ravenous. She knows the offerings in the fridge at Little Fair are meager—half a jar of pickles, grape jam, a package of hot dogs that would require boiling, which seems like too much work. Jessie tiptoes down the stairs but finds the door to Mr. Crimmins's room open. The room is empty and dark, and Jessie wonders if Mr. Crimmins will move back to Pine Street now that Pick is gone. She supposes the answer is yes.

Jessie crosses the yard and enters the kitchen at All's Fair, hoping that Kate brought home a doggie bag from the Skipper; her mother hasn't eaten a full meal since Tiger left. Sure enough, there's a paper bag on the counter and inside is a box containing cold fried chicken. Jessie is so hungry she bites into the drumstick right away. She hears voices. Maybe she's not the only person awake, or maybe someone left the television on.

Jessie tiptoes down the hall. No one has turned on the TV since Blair left for the hospital. But Jessie can see the watery light flickering into the hall.

She pauses at the doorway, drumstick still in hand, and peers in. She sees the silhouette of her parents sitting on the sofa, but what catches Jessie's attention is the television screen. There's a man in an astronaut suit emerging from a rocket.

A voice says, "We see you coming down the ladder."

It's the moon landing! Jessie knew it was happening soon but with everything else going on, she forgot it was tonight. She is *so* happy she woke up.

There's another voice, far away and distorted, like a man talking into a tin can. The voice says, "That's one small step for man, one giant leap for mankind."

Her parents stand up—but then Jessie realizes it's *not* her parents. It's…Nonny and Mr. Crimmins. Nonny turns to Mr. Crimmins, offering both her hands.

"Bill," she says. "Did you ever think we'd live long enough to see this?"

Mr. Crimmins pulls Exalta to him and kisses her—*really* kisses her, like a character in one of Blair's soap operas.

Jessie's mouth falls open. Behind Exalta and Bill Crimmins, Neil Armstrong walks on the surface of the moon.

Man is walking on the moon!

Exalta isn't pushing Mr. Crimmins away. She is kissing him back. They are *kissing* and Jessie realizes that Exalta, too, is real. She's a real person who has feelings for Mr. Crimmins.

Exalta breaks away. "Come upstairs with me," she says.

Jessie quietly, oh, so quietly, scurries back down the hall to the kitchen.

Sunlight floods Jessie's room the next morning and she awakens, blinking at the ceiling. Then, she starts to laugh. It's funny, isn't it? Funny peculiar but also, for some reason, funny ha-ha. Exalta is *old!* Mr. Crimmins is *older!* And yet, there they were. Jessie wonders how long their romance has been going on. Was it just a spontaneous moment inspired by the wonder of space travel? Or has it been happening all summer? Or...is Jessie going to discover that Exalta and Mr. Crimmins have been conducting a love affair for years and years, ever since Penn Nichols died, or even before that?

Jessie hops out of bed, pads past Mr. Crimmins's closed bedroom door, walks across the yard, and goes into the kitchen, where she finds her father reading the newspaper. Splashed across the front is the headline "Man Walks on Moon," and there's a grainy black-and-white photo of Armstrong and Aldrin planting the flag.

"We missed the moon landing," David says. "Too much wine at dinner. I'm sorry, Jessie. I wanted to wake you up so we could watch it."

"That's okay," Jessie says. She can't look her father in the eye or she'll give him a crazy-person grin. She pokes her head into the fridge looking for juice.

"Your mother went to the hospital to bring Blair and the babies home, so what do you say you and I get out of the house for a while to give them some space? We can go play tennis. You can show me what you've learned."

Tennis on a Sunday; it's worse than church. But Jessie needs to talk to her father alone, and this might give her the opportunity. "Okay," she says.

* * *

After breakfast, Jessie and her father put on their whites, grab their rackets, and walk to the club. Jessie has butterflies in her stomach that increase in number the closer they get to the club. She's obviously nervous about disclosing her mother's secret, but more immediately, she's nervous about her father signing in at the club desk. What if they don't let him in because he's Jewish? She nearly suggests they walk a quarter mile to play on the public courts at the Jetties but she doesn't want to alert her father to a possible problem or make him think he's not good enough for the Field and Oar Club.

When they approach the desk, Jessie's heart is hammering in her chest. It's not even Lizz at the desk; it's some fill-in person who won't recognize Jessie and know she's a member.

David smiles. "Good morning," he says to the fill-in girl, who has messy hair and dark circles under her eyes and looks like she was roused from bed five minutes earlier. "I'm David Levin, son-in-law of Exalta Nichols. My daughter and I are going to go hit."

The girl-who-just-woke-up—BRENDA, her name tag says—doesn't even blink. "Sign in," she says groggily.

Jessie watches her father sign: *Nichols N-3.*

He turns to Jessie. "Ready to play?"

"How come you didn't sign Levin?" she asks as they walk toward the courts.

"Because it's your grandmother's membership."

"Yeah, but Levin is your name," she says. *And my name!* "Did you not sign it because you don't want anyone to know you're Jewish?"

David throws his head back and laughs. He wraps an arm around Jessie and pulls her in close. "Trust me, everyone here already knows I'm Jewish. But you know what else they know?"

"What?" Jessie says.

They are right in front of court 11, which is closest to the water. It's the only court Jessie has played on all summer but she has been so racked with anxiety about her lessons that she has never once noticed how pretty her surroundings are. Today the sky is brilliant blue, and an American flag ripples in the breeze. The harbor is dotted with boats. The view from here is breathtaking but also exclusive because it's not for everybody.

David says, "They know I'm smart and that I have an important job and they know I'm a really, really good tennis player. They also know how much I love your mother and your sisters and your brother and you. And to most people here, Jessie, the good people, that's all that matters. Okay?"

Tears are standing in Jessie's eyes but she hopes they're hidden by the bill of her visor. She nods and leads her father onto the court.

They hit the ball around, Jessie accepting her father's compliments—"Your backhand is so strong and accurate! Your serving form is darn near perfect!"—but after an hour, the sun is high and hot, and both Jessie and David have had enough.

"How about we go to the Sweet Shoppe?" David says. "Get that ice cream I promised you."

Even though it's July 20, this is Jessie's first trip all summer to the Sweet Shoppe. It smells the way all good ice cream parlors should, like toasted marshmallows, melted chocolate, and the malt-and-vanilla scent of just-baked waffle cones. Jessie orders a double scoop of malachite chip in a silver bowl and David gets black raspberry in a cone and they sit at one of the tiny circular marble tables in uncomfortable wrought-iron chairs.

"It's time for you to pour your heart out," David says. "I'm not here to judge. I'm just here to listen."

Not here to judge. This is an unusual statement, Jessie thinks, which must be a sign that she can hand over her mother's awful secret.

She can't say it.

She wonders if maybe she can ease into the news about her mother. There are many other places to start: Garrison's unwanted liberties, Jessie's spate of thefts, her losing Nonny's necklace and the subsequent grounding, falling in love with Pick, her first kiss, her first heartbreak upon meeting Sabrina, the bra shopping that was interrupted by Blair's water breaking on the floor at Buttner's, her mother's drinking problem, Jessie's first period, her angst that Anne Frank did not survive the war, the scene with Lorraine Crimmins followed by Pick's departure that is maybe forever, Tiger's letter telling Jessie two of his friends, Frog and Puppy, had been killed and that he was being shipped off on a secret mission, the discovery that Exalta and Mr. Crimmins were…girlfriend and boyfriend?

Jessie opens her mouth to speak but her tongue is frozen, both literally and figuratively. She feels like a stunted, thwarted failure. She is unable to share any of the things that happened to her this summer. She just can't do it.

Instead, she digs into her malachite chip—it's just a fancy name for mint chocolate chip—which has reached that seductively melted stage.

She feels the cool weight of her Tree of Life pendant against her breastbone. When her father noticed her wearing it, his eyes lit up. *Maturity and responsibility,* she thinks. And then, a radical idea seizes her.

When she was a child, she told her parents everything: *I'm hungry, I'm tired, I need to use the bathroom, I skinned my knee, I like, I hate, I want, I need.* What if growing up means keeping some things to herself? The experiences of this summer will become as much a part of her as her bones and muscle, her brain and heart. Ten or twenty years from now, when she looks back on the summer of 1969, she will think: *That was the summer I became real. My own real person.*

She draws her spoon along the delicious melty edge of her ice cream and says, "I haven't been able to play my new record album even once."

"The Joni Mitchell?" David says.

Jessie loves her father for remembering. And then another radical thought strikes: to her father, she is already a real person.

"Well, let's remedy that as soon as we get home," David says. He tilts his head and catches her eye. "So it's fair to say this summer has turned out better than you thought?"

"Oh yes," Jessie tells her father. "Much better."

For What It's Worth

Senator Kennedy is in trouble.

Not long after Patty tells Kirby the ghastly news about Mary Jo Kopechne, Mrs. Bennie calls Kirby into work. Although Kirby's psyche is now frayed thanks to too much drama and not enough sleep, she has no choice but to go. She arrives back at the inn, still in her yellow daisy dress, and is immediately shuttled into the office with Mrs. Bennie and an Edgartown police officer named Sergeant Braga.

"Where's Mr. Ames?" Kirby asks.

"He has already given the sergeant his statement," Mrs. Bennie says. Kirby notes that her hair has been pinned back up in its usual bun, and any sense of fun or frivolity has been replaced with mournful gravitas. Kirby wishes she knew what Mr. Ames told the sergeant.

"We're trying to corroborate the senator's story," Sergeant Braga says. "He allegedly left the party at the Lawrence cottage around eleven fifteen and offered to give Miss Kopechne a ride to the ferry so she could return to her lodgings in Edgartown. However, the senator got turned around in the dark and accidentally drove off the Dike Bridge, where the car flipped over and submerged. The senator says he repeatedly tried to dive down to free Miss Kopechne, who was in the passenger seat, but he was unsuccessful. After a brief rest, the senator walked back to the Lawrence cottage to alert his cousin Mr. Gargan and a friend about what had happened. They too dove down in an attempt to free Miss Kopechne but were unsuccessful."

Kirby steadies her breathing. She can't believe that Mary Jo Kopechne, Sara O'Callahan's friend in the navy sheath and pearls, a person Kirby had met *only the day before,* was dead.

Dead.

The senator left the party with Mary Jo. This seems incriminating, doesn't it? Or maybe it was innocent. Maybe he was, as he said, driving Mary Jo back to the ferry. If Kirby had attended the party, it could easily have been *Kirby* he was driving to the ferry. It could have been Kirby trapped in the car underwater.

"The senator says he entered the hotel at around a quarter past one. Does that sound right to you?"

One fifteen? That does *not* sound right. Luke came into the lobby at one thirty, Kirby recalls. The cab arrived around two, and Kirby returned to the hotel at ten minutes to three. Mr. Ames said the senator had shown up at two thirty. Right? Surely Mr. Ames has told the police this, but if it differs from the senator's account, then Kirby's recollection would be very important—except she hadn't been there.

"I didn't see the senator at all," Kirby says.

"But he went up to his room," Mrs. Bennie says. "You must have given him his key."

"Mr. Ames gave him his key," Kirby says. She stares at her hands in her lap. "I was off the property when the senator returned."

"What?" Mrs. Bennie says.

"I was dealing with an intruder."

"An intruder?"

"My roommate's boyfriend came into the lobby. He was acting inappropriately, raising his voice. He was drunk and angry. We put him in a taxi."

"I should hope so!" Mrs. Bennie exclaims.

"I went along with him," Kirby says. She appeals to Sergeant Braga because she's too ashamed to look at Mrs. Bennie. "I knew I wasn't supposed to leave the inn but I needed to make sure Luke went straight home. I was afraid he would hunt down my roommate and hurt her."

Instead of being impressed by Kirby's brave display of devotion and friendship, Sergeant Braga looks disappointed. "So you didn't see the senator at all? You had no contact with him?"

"None," Kirby says.

The sergeant stands up. "All right, I'm finished here. Thank you for your cooperation, Mrs. Bennie. I'll let you know if I need anything else."

Mrs. Bennie rises while resting a firm hand on Kirby's shoulder to let her know to stay put. "Please do, Sergeant," she says.

The instant the door to the office closes, Mrs. Bennie says, "The senator did *not* kill that girl. It was an *accident*. We all take our lives into our own hands when we get into a car."

Kirby can sympathize with Mrs. Bennie's distress; in fact, she shares it. There's nothing quite so disheartening as discovering your hero is just an ordinary man. However, unlike Mrs. Bennie, Kirby thinks the senator might very well be responsible for Mary Jo Kopechne's death. It sounds like he was the one who drove the car off the bridge, and it also sounds like he left the scene without pulling Mary Jo from the car. The senator had asked Mr. Ames if he was sure it wasn't earlier than two thirty. He must have been looking for an alibi that would put him at the hotel and not on Chappaquiddick!

Kirby's theorizing is interrupted by Mrs. Bennie sighing. "Unfortunately, I'm going to have to let you go," she says.

"What?" Kirby says.

"You left the property without permission," Mrs. Bennie says. "We don't pay you to gallivant about, no matter how noble the crusade."

"But...but..." Kirby's protest sputters out.

Mrs. Bennie removes her reading glasses and lets them rest on her bosom. "I know it's difficult, Katharine," she says. "We've been very pleased with your performance here. I wish none of this had ever happened. The poor, poor senator—"

"And poor Mary Jo!" Kirby says. "Mary Jo is *dead*." Kirby nearly mentions that she met Mary Jo briefly. She *met* the young woman who drowned in an accident that was probably caused by Senator Kennedy. Maybe history wouldn't hold on to the name Mary Jo Kopechne, but Kirby certainly would.

"I'll write you a wonderful reference," Mrs. Bennie says. "And you'll be paid for the entire week."

Kirby sees that no amount of begging will get her her job back and she knows that Mrs. Bennie is being more than fair about the reference and the salary—probably because she wants Kirby to go quietly instead of adding more angst to this whole sordid situation.

As Kirby stands on the front porch of the inn waiting for her taxi back to Oak Bluffs, she puzzles over how things can be just fine one minute and so completely not fine the next.

She's going to miss Edgartown—the white clapboard houses with black shutters and overflowing window boxes, the blue stripe of the harbor visible through the side yards. It feels familiar, nearly like home, which means only that she has nothing left to prove.

She will head back to the house on Narragansett Avenue to pack her things. In the morning, she'll leave for Nantucket.

It's only eleven miles from Martha's Vineyard to Nantucket as the crow flies, but for Kirby to actually get there, she has to take the ferry to Woods Hole and then take a different ferry to Nantucket.

Darren offers to drive her to the wharf but Kirby insists she can walk.

"With all your luggage?" Darren says. "Just let me. Please, Kirby?"

Kirby agrees but she tells him her plan is to slip out early, before the other girls go to breakfast. She hates goodbyes, and especially in this case, because she's leaving halfway through the summer under ignominious circumstances. The only person Kirby will truly miss is Patty—even though Patty and Luke are now more together than they've ever been. In fact, when the summer was over, Patty told Kirby in a righteous tone, she would be moving to New York City with him. She's going to pursue her dream of becoming an actress the old-fashioned way—by reading *Backstage* and showing up at cattle calls.

"I'll be waiting out front at seven," Darren says. "No fanfare."

He's there, as promised, leaning against his car. When Kirby emerges, he rushes to help her with her bags. She climbs into the car and gives the house one long last look. She left a note for the girls, and she supposes that they will now quarrel over who gets to live in her igloo.

Darren parks at the terminal, despite Kirby's protests, because he wants to put her luggage on the cart. *Okay, okay, thank you,* she thinks, *now leave.* Her dislike of goodbyes is especially strong when it comes to saying goodbye to Darren.

After he deals with the luggage and Kirby gets her ticket, he gathers her up in his arms. Kirby is shocked.

"There are *people* around," she says.

"I don't care."

He *does* care—that's why they are where they are. What Darren means is that he doesn't care because he doesn't know the people here. They're tourists, and most of them—although not all—are white. There are families trying to comfort crying children who have been awakened too early; there are honeymooners snapping Polaroids; there is an elderly black couple, the woman's husband leaning on her as they shuffle toward the ramp.

"Darren…"

"I'll see you in the fall," he says.

"I'm not sure that's a good idea."

"Just one date," he says. "Let me take you to Mr. Bartley's Burgers. Okay? It's legendary. Or if you'd rather, we can go to the Rathskeller…"

"Burgers are fine," Kirby says. She would never admit it to him but she feels happy that he wants to see her back in the city. And one date can't hurt.

Darren kisses her goodbye and the kiss is longer and more intense than she anticipates. Soon, they are necking; it feels so good she can't tear herself away. She senses disapproving stares from the older black couple, or maybe she's imagining it. Maybe it's the summer of 1969 and things are different now and a black boy and a white girl can kiss in public and nobody cares.

"Right on!" a voice says. Kirby breaks away to see a very tall, very skinny guy about their age with a huge Afro of orange hair. He's wearing rainbow-striped velour pants with a matching vest and a black top hat. He's in his bare feet. He gives Kirby and Darren the thumbs-up and says, "Love is all you need."

Kirby feels pretty good as she boards the ferry. The foghorn sounds, which always plucks a sad string in Kirby's heart because it usually means she's leaving Nantucket. Today, however, she's *going* to Nantucket. She will rest her head tonight in her bed on *her* island; she still has six weeks of summer left. She will get to meet her new niece and nephew; she will make herself useful driving Jessie around; she will do her best to plant some revolutionary ideas—like racial equality—in Exalta's fusty old brain. She'll make Exalta listen to some Bob Dylan. And maybe, just maybe, this summer will end up being one that people write songs about.

As Kirby stands on the bow of the ferry, something catches her eye. A man. A woman with the man.

She's surprised, because she thought she was past the point where she stared hungrily at every man who remotely resembled Scottie Turbo. But apparently not, because what draws Kirby's eye is the crew cut and the impossibly strong, square stance, like a man built from bricks. At first, Kirby isn't 100 percent sure. She edges closer. There are plenty of people on the deck, so she can easily spy while still blending in.

He turns, and his profile is a punch to her gut. Unmistakable. Kirby grabs the railing for support. Scottie Turbo is on this ferry.

Which means he was on Martha's Vineyard. She's surprised by this. When she told Scottie her family had a house on Nantucket, he made a face and flicked his nose.

"Snobs," he said. "Those islands are infested with them."

She'd had a difficult time imagining bringing Scottie Turbo to All's Fair and introducing him to her grandmother. She'd tried to picture him complimenting the mural in the living room or appreciating Exalta's collection of whirligigs; tried to envision Scottie at a table at the Field and Oar Club, ordering a gin and tonic. She'd come up empty.

The more socially and economically democratic atmosphere of the Vineyard must have been okay. Kirby wonders where he stayed, then conjures up a nightmare scenario in which Scottie and this woman walk into the Shiretown Inn while Kirby is working.

Eeeeeeeeeeeeeeee!

After a moment, Kirby's shock subsides enough for her to properly evaluate the woman. Wife, she thinks. Not girlfriend. She can tell by how almost uninterested in each other they seem. They rest their forearms on the railing side by side, not touching. The wife has pale hair, though she's not quite as blond as Kirby and her hair is chopped blunt at the shoulders, much like Exalta's. Kirby edges a little closer to get a better look at Wifey; to do this, she positions herself behind Scottie's back. Wifey has sallow skin with ruddy spots on her cheeks. She wears no makeup and her eyes get lost in her face. She's plain. She looks a little bit like Scottie himself. They have the same coloring, the same grim set to their mouths, as if they're perpetually expecting bad news. What does she do for a living? Kirby wonders. She doesn't seem working-class, but neither does she telegraph the kindness and empathy of a nurse or a teacher. Probably she's a secretary. Yes, Kirby thinks. She seems organized and efficient, and she is no doubt indispensable to her important boss—an executive at a manufacturing company or maybe a real estate mogul. She can probably type a hundred and ten words a minute and take shorthand; she brings him his coffee and orders his lunch and picks up his dry cleaning. Maybe Scottie is even a little jealous of her boss because she is so devoted.

Kirby is simply projecting here; she has no idea what Wifey does.

Is there anyone in the world more fascinating than the woman you lost out to? Kirby wonders. She can't figure out what Scottie sees in this woman.

Then Wifey turns and Kirby gets it. She's pregnant, *roundly* pregnant—maybe five or six months along. Kirby does some quick backward counting. Wifey was already pregnant when Kirby told Scottie *she* was pregnant.

Ahhh.

Wifey notices Kirby staring at her and returns Kirby's gaze with an unapologetically frank challenge in her eyes.

"Can I help you with something?" she asks.

Kirby freezes. Her mind spins like a wheel on a game show. What should she say? She could pretend to be enraptured by Wifey's pregnancy. Blair told Kirby that a woman becomes public property once she's pregnant, and every Tammy, Dina, and Harriet on the street feels compelled to comment on her belly and sometimes even touch her without asking.

Scottie spins around to find who Wifey is calling out. He sees Kirby and his face turns to stone. It's not hate; she can see that plain enough. It's fear.

Kirby steps forward, positively beaming. "Forgive me for staring," she says. "It's just that you look familiar to me. I'm Kirby Foley. What's your name?"

"Ann," she says. "Ann Turbo. Maiden name Herlihy. I went

to Mt. Alvernia. Do I know you from there? You're way younger than me."

Younger by five years or so, Kirby guesses. She knew a girl who went to Mt. Alvernia—Deirdre Metcalfe—but Kirby can't fake having gone there.

"I went to Brookline," she says, shrugging. "Public-school kid."

Scottie speaks up. "You're probably mistaken, miss. You don't know us."

It's either the "miss" or the "us" that irks her. He's waving a verbal billy club, urging her to move along. Of *course* that's what he wants. He's petrified. His internal organs must be twisted up like Monday's washing.

"Maybe I'm just drawn to you because you're pregnant," Kirby says. "I was pregnant not so long ago."

"You were?" Ann looks behind Kirby for any sign of a child.

"I lost the baby," Kirby says.

Ann flinches like Kirby slapped her. "No!" she cries.

"It was probably a good thing," Kirby says. She flashes Ann her bare left hand. "I got in trouble. And the father"—she takes a step closer to Scottie. She's so close, she could slap him…or kiss him—"was a married man. Of course, I didn't know that at the time."

Ann gasps, apparently too overcome for words. Scottie opens his mouth to speak but Kirby raises a traffic-cop hand. "The man had absolutely no integrity and a dishrag for character," Kirby says. "But I'm sure he'll pay a price for this *somewhere down the road.*"

"I should hope *so!*" Ann says. She's now Kirby's champion and Scottie pulls out a handkerchief to wipe sweat off his brow.

"Lucky for you, you seem to have a good man right here," Kirby says, nodding at Scottie. "An honest, upright man."

"He's a policeman!" Ann announces proudly.

"Is he?" Kirby says. She allows herself a direct gaze into Scottie's green eyes; she might as well be leaping off the bow into the sound. *"What a field day for the heat,"* she sings. *"A thousand people in the street."*

She expects to meet a barrier, a boulder, a concrete wall—but instead she finds something softer. A field of grass.

I'm sorry, his eyes say. *I had a wife and a baby on the way. But please know that I did fall in love with you. I'm in love with you still and always will be.*

Or at least that's what Kirby *imagines* his eyes are saying. It's good enough.

She grins. "Have a nice day!" she says, and she saunters to the back of the boat.

Because all the ferries to Nantucket are sold out—"It's July, sweetheart," the world-weary ticket agent says—Kirby rides to Nantucket on the evening freight boat with her two suitcases perched on the starboard side atop some packing crates filled with dry goods. Kirby is tired—physically and emotionally—but she perks up when the twinkling lights of Nantucket town become visible on the horizon. She picks out the spire of the Congregational church and the clock tower of the Unitarian church, marking north and south, but what she loves the best is the way the lights of the boats scattered across the dark harbor mimic the stars in the night sky.

There are no taxis waiting to meet this boat when it docks, so Kirby makes her slow way with her suitcases—both so heavy they might contain gold bullion—and her beloved Silvertone record player down Easy Street and up Main Street. When she turns left onto Fair, she wants to break into a run.

Home; she's finally home.

She leaves her luggage on the front step—she will get it in the morning—and tiptoes inside and up the stairs. She isn't foolish enough to enter her grandmother's room or her parents' room but she has no problem waking up Jessie.

Surprise! The third bedroom is crowded—a rounded figure in the bed barricaded by two bassinets. Kirby doesn't want to disturb Blair, but she takes a moment to gaze at the tiny faces of her new niece and nephew. She can't tell which is which but it doesn't matter. She'll make their acquaintance in the morning.

Down the stairs, down the hall, through the kitchen that still smells of the cooking fireplace even though it hasn't been used in a hundred years, out the door, and across the lawn to Little Fair.

The downstairs bedroom is dark and empty. Tiger's room, Kirby thinks with an ache. Then up the stairs she goes. It's pitch-black but she doesn't need a light; this path is ingrained in her muscles and bones. She could navigate Little Fair with her eyes closed.

Bedroom one, Blair's room, is empty and Kirby could easily lie down and sleep for the next two days straight, but instead she eases open the door to the second bedroom.

Jessie is asleep, splayed across the bed like she fell out of an airplane. Her hair is spread out over her pillow. Kirby has always been jealous of that; Jessie's hair is as thick and lavish as mink. She doesn't have a single blemish, either on her face or on her soul. Oh, how Kirby wishes she could go back to this age and start over.

She lifts the dead weight of Jessie's arm and slides into bed next to her. Jessie stirs, and one eye flutters open.

"Who is it?"

"It's me. Kirby."

Jessie hugs Kirby with a ferocity that is childlike in its enthusiasm and adult in its strength. "Welcome home," Jessie says. "I missed you."

Kirby sighs as she closes her eyes. It has been a long day.

Get Back

The twins are eight days old when Neil Armstrong, Buzz Aldrin, and Michael Collins reenter the Earth's atmosphere. The only communication Blair has received from Angus is the telegram, now also eight days old. He hasn't called Blair at the hospital or at home, which means...what?

Blair received a dozen pink roses from Joey Whalen and a card that said *Congrats, Sis!* This, she notes, is a far cry from *I loved you first. Eternally yours, Joey.*

Blair feels untethered, like an astronaut whose lifeline to the mother ship has been cut. She's alone, aimless, abandoned.

Kirby shows up fresh off the ferry from the Vineyard and Blair brightens. She has her confidante back. But when Blair tells Kirby how bereft she feels because she has managed to lose both Angus and Joey, Kirby puts her hands on her hips and delivers a lecture. "What would Betty Friedan say? You don't need a man. You can raise these twins by yourself. I'll help. We'll all help."

Blair is skeptical about this. And to add insult to injury, she still looks pregnant! She isn't as big as she was just before she delivered the babies; she's back to where she was in month four or five. Her breasts are gigantic and as heavy as sandbags, her nipples two points of fire.

Despite this, Blair loves nursing the twins. When their tiny mouths tug, the milk flows out of her, just as it's supposed to, and her body practically glows with relief. The only time she relaxes is when one of the twins is latched on, even though she suspects she looks like a cow. Kate keeps telling her there's "no shame" in switching to formula.

"They *need* me, Mother," Blair says. "Just let me do this."

Everyone loves the babies! Kate, David, Jessie, even Exalta. Kirby ends up being the most helpful of all. She's a natural with the babies, and she always remembers to bring Blair a tall glass of ice water and a cold bottle of beer before each feeding time. Blair gets desperately thirsty the instant the twins latch on, and beer is supposed to increase a mother's milk supply. This might be just an old wives' tale, but Blair doesn't want to find out. The beer always lightens her mood.

Kirby isn't put off by the zeppelins that Blair's breasts have become, and she offers words of encouragement, calling Blair "Mama." As soon as one twin is done feeding, Kirby takes him or her to the rocker until she gets a burp.

"Just so you know," Kirby says, "I'm singing protest songs in their ears."

"I wouldn't have it any other way," Blair says.

It's also Kirby who brings her, finally, a second telegram from Angus.

FLYING BACK TOMORROW. WILL ARRIVE NANTUCKET SAT-
URDAY AT NOON.

"Angus is coming to Nantucket," Blair says. "Saturday." Suddenly, she feels faint. "What am I going to do?"

"You're going to talk," Kirby says. "And you are going to stand up for yourself. You're a wonderful mother but you have many other talents that will go to waste if you don't use them. Angus needs to acknowledge that."

"Okay." Blair says.

"Tell you what," Kirby says. "If you think you can handle the babies by yourself for a little while, I'll get everyone out of here on Saturday. I'll plan a boat outing so that you and Angus can have some time alone."

"Thank you," Blair says. She decides not to tell Kate or Exalta that Angus is coming—in case he doesn't stay.

On Saturday, Kirby does exactly as she's promised and gets the whole family—including David, who is back again this weekend—to head out to Coatue in the Whaler. Kate doesn't want to leave Blair alone, but Blair insists she'll be fine. She'll need to learn to take care of her own children without help sooner or later.

As soon as they all troop off toward the Field and Oar Club carrying the life preservers and a picnic basket, Blair feeds and burps the babies one by one, and they barely fuss at all. Both of them look at Blair with round, watchful eyes, as though they know something important is about to happen.

"That's right," Blair says. "You're going to meet your father today." She tears up—her emotions have been unmanageable since she gave birth—and she realizes her biggest fear isn't that Angus doesn't want *her* but that he doesn't want the babies. He was the one who got her pregnant and in so doing quashed her hopes of pursuing a graduate degree, and he was the one who had the gall to conduct an affair. His behavior has been unforgivable and yet Blair wants, very badly, to forgive him. She is in love with these children, and only nine days after they arrived she can't imagine life without them.

But they need a father.

And—forget Betty Friedan!—Blair would like her husband back.

As soon as the twins fall asleep, Blair takes a long, hot shower inside, which would never be allowed if Exalta were home, and then combs out her hair and puts on a new dress, light blue gingham, maternity but still flattering. She applies makeup and perfume and puts in pearl earrings. Then she smokes a cigarette out in the backyard, and she waits.

At ten minutes past twelve, Blair hears a car pull up out front. She hears a door slam.

She hurries into the house but waits at the end of the hall until there's a knock. Then slowly, slowly, she makes her way toward the front door.

Blair opens the door to find...her husband?

"Blair!" Angus says.

He looks...different. He hasn't shaved in weeks; he has a beard, and his hair has grown out so much it's nearly shaggy. With his glasses, he looks like John Lennon or Abbie Hoffman, a revolutionary. And he's wearing jeans—Blair tries to remember if she has ever seen Angus in jeans—and a gray T-shirt that says MIT on the front in green letters. On his feet are a pair of Jesus sandals. It's almost as if Angus hasn't been at Mission Control at all but hanging out in Haight-Ashbury with Jefferson Airplane.

And yet this new look—groovy and relaxed—gives Blair hope. Maybe Angus has changed. If he'd shown up here in his suit with his hair short, Blair could only predict that things between them would have remained the same—which is to say, unsatisfactory.

Or, Blair thinks, maybe this new look is Trixie's influence. Maybe Trixie is one of these women who don't shave their legs or wash their hair; maybe she's into circle-drumming and experimenting with LSD.

Blair holds the door open. "Come in."

As Angus walks past her into the hallway, she sniffs at his clothes to see if she smells marijuana.

No, thank goodness.

Blair closes the door, then turns to face her husband, a man who stole her away from his brother with the mere mention of Edith Wharton. Blair considers asking him to sit in the formal living room or back to the kitchen for coffee or a beer, but she doesn't want him getting too comfortable.

She remains planted in the hallway at the bottom of the stairs, where she can hear the babies if they cry.

"Tell me about Trixie," Blair says. "The truth."

"Dr. Cushion introduced me to her," Angus says.

Dr. Cushion! Blair thinks. The famous professor emeritus of microbiology at MIT who hosted the ill-fated faculty potluck? Blair had suspected the "men in the den" weren't talking only about science. They were also talking about women. Leonard Cushion mentored Angus in the art of finding a mistress!

"Dr. Beatrix Scofield," Angus says. "She's an esteemed psychoanalyst. She holds a doctorate from Johns Hopkins and an endowed chair at MIT."

"I don't need her CV," Blair says. "I just want to know if you're in love with her."

"She's not my mistress, Blair. She's treating me as a patient. My episodes? They're due to clinical depression. I've been working with Trixie—Dr. Scofield—and we're having some success."

Blair is confused, but she feels a lightening across her shoulders. "She's a psychoanalyst? Like Freud? Do you lie on her couch?"

"I do, actually," Angus says. "But only half of the treatment is talk therapy. The other half is pharmaceutical." He smiles shyly. "And it's working. I feel better."

"Why didn't you just tell me this?" Blair asks.

"I was embarrassed," Angus says. "Ashamed. I didn't want you to think I was defective. I didn't want you to regret marrying me...or procreating with me." He swallows. "I didn't want you to wish you'd married Joey instead because he's easy and fun to be with. And then, when I saw the two of you together, I didn't explain because I wanted you to think I had someone else as well."

"Kissing Joey was a mistake," Blair says.

"Trixie explained that to me. She said that Joey was just trying to get even with me for past resentments."

I don't know about that, Blair thinks. She and Joey always *did* have chemistry. Blair is tempted to tell Angus the story of Joey hunting down the whipped cream for her cake, but instead she says, "There's no reason to be embarrassed about getting help."

"I've been smart my whole life," Angus says. "And I guess I was angry that I couldn't find a way to heal myself."

"Angus, no."

"Do you know when I finally made the decision to see Trixie? I would feel jealous every time I thought about the astronauts." He reaches out to caress Blair's cheek. "And no, not because you think they're so handsome or because you had their pictures pinned to your dorm-room wall." He clears his throat. "I was jealous because they got to leave this world. That's how little I wanted to be here."

"Angus!" Blair cries.

"I don't feel that way anymore," Angus says. "Trixie—Dr. Scofield—has really helped."

Thank you, Trixie, Blair thinks.

Angus seems softer now than he ever has before. But is he malleable? "Trixie isn't our only issue, Angus," Blair says. "I want to go back to school. I want to get my master's in American literature and become a professor, like you."

Angus stares at her and she thinks that he may have changed, but not *that* much. He wants Blair at home, raising the children, dusting the doodads on the shelves, mastering *poulet au porto.* "We could hire help, I suppose," he says. "And I'm sure I can learn to change a diaper."

Blair exhales in frustration. She has been a mother for only nine days, but she's already realized that her vague, prenatal sense of what children—twins!—would demand was far outpaced by the daily, hourly reality of their needs. "There's going to be a lot more to it than changing diapers," she says firmly. "And you have to know that. I'll need you to be a real partner." *Aren't you proud of me, Betty Friedan?* she thinks. Her heart is pounding and her fists are clenched; she's aware that the past months of anxiety and unhappiness are coming to a head now, in her grandmother's foyer, while Angus stands solidly before her. He takes both her hands in his and fixes her with the steady gaze that first captured her attention back in his Cambridge apartment.

"I get it, Blair," he says. "I really do. I want to be there for you and for the babies. And I want you to be able to do what makes you happy."

"I'm going to hold you to that."

"I love you, Blair."

She's not quite ready to say it back. "I'm proud of you," she says, casting her eyes skyward. "The moon landing, Angus. Truly remarkable."

"You gave birth," Angus says. "There's nothing more remarkable than that."

She happens to agree with him, but she merely shrugs.

"Can I see our babies?" he asks.

"Right after you kiss me," Blair says.

And he does and it feels both familiar and foreign. His beard scratches and Blair sinks her fingers into his long hair and tugs. Then she takes his hand and leads him up the stairs.

Both Sides Now (Reprise)

Bill Crimmins moves back to his efficiency on Pine Street. He says it's only right and Kate agrees, although she fears that now he will stop his efforts to get intelligence about Tiger. She tells him as much and he says, "Katie, don't be silly. I'm doing everything in my power to find out what I can."

It's a generous answer, especially since Bill himself has so recently lost his daughter—again—and not only Lorraine, but Pick as well. Kate asks Bill if he's heard from them and Bill offers a smile that seems to contain four decades of heartbreak.

August arrives and the household is busy. Angus and Blair are reunited and Angus has some time off before classes at MIT start up in September, and he and Blair decide they want to stay at All's Fair until Labor Day. Kate is happy for Blair, happy too to have her grandchildren under her roof, even though she has started sleeping with earplugs.

Kirby gets a job three days a week at the front desk of the Gordon Folger Hotel, filling in for a college student whose grand-mother suddenly died. Kirby tells Kate that she spent the first half of the summer thinking she wanted to be a political science major, but the Kennedy scandal has left her disenchanted. Now she's de-cided on hotel management and plans to take a semester abroad in Switzerland, which is the epicenter of luxury hospitality. She's hoping Exalta will pay for it.

The days that Kirby isn't working, she takes Jessie to the beach.

As much as Kate loves seeing her daughters spending time to-gether, she worries that Jessie will grow up too fast. "I don't want you drinking around your sister," Kate says. "Or smoking that Mary Jane. Promise me."

"Promise," Kirby says with a sly half smile that means God only knows what. "We read, we sleep, we flip over every fifteen min-utes, we swim, we take walks and collect shells. We talk."

Talk about what? Kate wonders. Jessie now knows Kate's secret and Kate supposes she should be concerned about Jessie spilling the beans, but she isn't. The secret weighs only half as much now that Kate has shared it. Some days it even feels like the secret's power has dissipated, like when you turn on the light and find out there's no monster in the closet.

Kate hasn't had a drink—or even craved one—for an entire week.

The string of bright, hot, sunny days is broken by a rogue nor'easter. Kate has always loved rainy days on the island. Nor-mally she would light a fire and suggest board games, but Kirby announces that she and Jessie are going bowling.

Kate freezes. Bowling was Tiger's thing.

Is his thing.

"Do you want to come with us, Mom?" Kirby asks.

Kate's first instinct is to say no, but what else, really, does she have to do? Exalta has been running mysterious errands lately, day and night; she claims to have made a friend who lives a few blocks away, and earlier today she set off down Fair Street with her umbrella, wearing rain boots and carrying her espadrilles in one hand so they wouldn't get wet.

Kate could stay home and help Blair and Angus with the babies but Angus has imposed a scientific method on the nursing and napping schedule that is working wonders. So why not join her two daughters? Why not bowl?

The bowling alley is in the middle of the island down a dirt road called Youngs Way. Kate hasn't been near the place since she used to drop Tiger off years ago, before he learned how to drive. The last time Kate actually went inside was for one of his tournaments—he won them all handily—and Kate remembers overhearing some of the Nantucket old-timers saying Tiger was good enough to go pro, which had made Kate chuckle. As if her only son would waste his life being a professional bowler!

Now she would accept that fate for him in an instant.

The bowling alley smells of roasted peanuts, cigarette smoke, and the damp. It's crowded today because it's raining out but it feels cozy and convivial. Kirby marches right up to the desk and secures lane 10, which is along the far wall and not, thank goodness, in the middle of the action where people might watch them. They each put on a pair of the hideous shoes that are better suited to a gangster or clown. (Kate shudders to think of the other feet that have been in these shoes, and then she flashes back on Exalta giddily walking down Fair Street in her galoshes. Most curious.) They buy a large bag of warm unshelled peanuts and three birch beers. They are ready to bowl!

It's a deceptively simple game—you just knock pins over with a heavy ball—but it takes Kate a while to figure out how to plug her fingers in the holes, take the correct number of steps, and release the ball with force and accuracy. After some gutter balls, she gets the hang of it and pins start to fall. In the first frame, Kate knocks down six, Kirby seven, and Jessie gets a spare. Kate likes the sounds of the alley, the anticipatory rumble of the ball rolling down the glossy boards and the crack of the ball against the pins. Music is playing in the background: Bill Haley and the Comets, Chuck Berry, and Chad and Jeremy. Kate drinks her birch beer and lets the shells of the peanuts fall to the floor. When it's her turn, she takes the ball that looks like a green-and-white-swirled marble and holds it up in front of her face. She *feels* Tiger then, so keenly that she nearly believes that if she turns around, she will see him sitting between his sisters. She hears his laugh. He's here. He's in the atmosphere. Kate swings her arm back and lets the ball go. It's a strike.

That evening, Kate watches Walter Cronkite alone. Blair is upstairs with the babies, one of whom is crying; Angus has run out for a pizza; Jessie and Kirby are at the Dreamland theater seeing *Butch Cassidy;* and Exalta went to bridge at the Anglers' Club with Bill Crimmins.

Exalta and Bill Crimmins, Kate thinks. She suddenly wonders if there's more to that than meets the eye. Bill Crimmins lives on Pine Street in the exact direction that Exalta walks on her mysterious errands. This might also explain why Bill moved out when he could have stayed rent-free at Little Fair. He wanted his own place so he and Exalta could be alone, away from scrutiny.

Kate is so consumed with how incredible and yet *credible* her new theory is that she misses the first part of Cronkite's report, but she tunes in when she hears him mention the Cambodian border and the Ho Chi Minh Trail.

"Earlier today, there were seventeen American casualties confirmed in an air strike in a position near the town of Svay Rieng," Cronkite says.

Seventeen casualties. Along the Cambodian border. The Ho Chi Minh Trail. Casualties meaning…dead? Or injured? Some dead, some only injured?

Tiger!

Kate calls David. She can hardly breathe. The evening newspaper has already been delivered and there was no mention of this. David says he will stay up to watch the late news. He'll call first thing in the morning.

Kate tries to explain to David about that afternoon at the bowling alley. She *felt* Tiger's spirit; when she lifted the ball, it was as if Tiger's hand were underneath her elbow, and she bowled a strike. It had seemed like a lark, but now she knows it was a sign. *That* was the moment he'd died. He was hit in an air strike, and his soul was instantly transported to Nantucket, to Mid-Island Bowl, where he helped his mother knock down all the pins.

Tiger!

Angus walks in the door with the pizza and Kate rises to turn off the TV. She follows Angus into the kitchen like a zombie.

"Would you like a slice, Kate?" he asks.

Kate shakes her head, pours herself a vodka.

When David calls in the morning, he has no further details. Seventeen American casualties along the Ho Chi Minh Trail, close to Svay Rieng.

"We don't know he was among them," David says. "Katie, we don't know."

But Kate does know. She felt him. It was different from other times she'd thought of him. It was immediate, visceral.

"Come today," she says. It's a Friday. David is booked on the six o'clock ferry along with every other attorney, doctor, and businessman in Boston. "Come right now. Skip work. Please, David." If Tiger is dead, they'll send someone to Brookline. "Leave a note on the front door. So they can find us."

"Okay," David whispers.

She can't tell the girls because she doesn't want them to overreact. Everyone else is enjoying August. Everyone else is happy. Jessie and Exalta return from their daily pilgrimage to the club. It was Jessie's last day of lessons; she received a certificate and a written note from her instructor, Suze, that says, *I have greatly enjoyed getting to know Jessica this summer. She has the makings of a fine tennis player and an even better person.* Kate smiles and says, "What a lovely note!" but her tone rings hollow.

"We should celebrate her efforts," Exalta says. "How about lunch in the garden at the Chanticleer?"

Kate says, "I couldn't possibly, Mother."

"Why not?" Exalta says.

"David is coming on the next ferry," Kate says.

"Early?" Exalta says. She does not sound pleased.

"I'll wait here for Dad," Jessie says.

"No, no, go with your grandmother," Kate says. "And take Kirby."

Kate is sitting on the edge of the bed with the picture of the family from last summer resting in her lap when David arrives. She's afraid to go down to greet him in case he has bad news. As it turns out, he meets her halfway up the stairs and says, "Nothing."

Nothing. No one came to the house last night, no one called. How long does it take? Kate wonders.

"Will you come with me to church?" Kate asks. "I need to pray."

David raises his eyebrows. "Church?"

"Please?" she says.

He nods. "Let this be proof," he says, "that I will do anything for you, Katharine Nichols."

They head outside and down Fair Street. David is Jewish, and Jewish people generally don't pray in Christian churches. Kate and David were married at the Massachusetts State House by a judge whom David knew through work. David's parents, Bud and Freda, had flown up from Florida to serve as witnesses, and afterward they took the newlyweds to dinner at Locke-Ober. Exalta refused to attend, and she would not allow Penn to go—although Penn secretly arranged for a limousine to whisk Kate and David to an inn in the Berkshires for a three-day honeymoon. It was understood by everyone that Exalta objected to the marriage because David was Jewish.

In the time that Kate and David have been married, it has never mattered that he's Jewish. Kate takes the children to church on Easter and Christmas, and once a summer they attend evensong services at St. Paul's.

Kate initially thinks of going to St. Paul's. It's a beautiful church with a pipe organ and real Tiffany windows. The Nichols family has belonged to St. Paul's for generations, although Kate acknowledges it's more of a social pursuit than a religious one. She could get down on the needlepoint kneelers, gaze at the light filtering in through the sumptuous windows, and pray—and David would pray with her. But at the last minute, she changes her mind and crosses the street to the Quaker Meeting House. David relaxes.

He pulls open the wooden plank door and they enter the simple house of worship. There are wooden pews on either side of an aisle that face a raised platform with bench seating; there are four unadorned twenty-four-pane windows. The room conveys a holiness and a purity and a luminosity that Kate craves; she knows that the Quakers value silent introspection. Church for the Quakers is when two or more people pray together; it has nothing to do with bricks and mortar.

Kate sits; David sits. Kate bows her head; David takes her hand. They are a church.

Richard Pennington Foley. Tiger. When Kate closes her eyes, she sees his chubby infant legs and round cheeks. She hears his giggle when the girls tickle him. She sees him sulking about the lima beans on his dinner plate; later, Kate would find them, flattened, under the tablecloth at Tiger's place. She remembers him chasing seagulls at the beach, skipping rocks, picking crabs up by their hind legs and waving them—snapping claw and all—at his sisters. She remembers rebuttoning his dress shirt correctly and wetting his hair down before dinner with Exalta at the Union Club. She recalls the way he smelled after football practice— sweat, grass, pride. She sees him leaping into the air for the ball, strong-arming his way into the end zone. He was such an excellent player that Kate had nearly been embarrassed. She sees him with Magee the night before he deployed, his chin resting on Magee's head, his eyes closed, as if he's memorizing how she felt in his arms. Kate had turned away, thinking the relationship wasn't real because it hadn't had enough time to steep. Magee would leave him for a boy who was available. But Kate would never leave Tiger. She would never replace him. She was his mother. She was forever.

If he's gone, Kate thinks, she will never recover. That's all there is to it.

She feels safe in the meeting house, buffered by the plain white walls. She can hear birdsong from outside, and through the window, she spies the green leaves of an oak, the piercing blue of the cloudless sky. God is up there, she supposes. She hopes.

Keep him safe, she says in her mind. This is foxhole religion at its most basic. The only person who wants the soldier to live more than the soldier himself is the soldier's mother. Kate wishes she were praying with a pure heart, with a decent past. She wishes she had been more devout, faithful, penitent. All she can say for herself is that she is self-aware. She understands her sins, acknowledges her flaws, owns her mistakes.

So many sins.

So many flaws.

So, so many mistakes.

If he's gone, it's her fault.

She stands up. "Let's go."

"You sure?" David says.

"Yes," she says. "Thank you."

As they approach All's Fair, they see Exalta and Bill Crimmins standing on the front walk.

Bill Crimmins has an envelope in his hands.

A telegram, Kate thinks. *Dear Mrs. Levin, It is with great sorrow that we inform you…*

She screams. She howls; she bends over in the middle of Fair Street and then she's choking, retching, sobbing, and David grabs her around the waist in an attempt to pull her upright.

"Katharine!" Exalta calls out. Scolding.

Kate doesn't care what she looks like. She doesn't care who sees her or what kind of scene she's making. Her son is dead.

Bill Crimmins runs down the street toward them clutching the envelope but Kate doesn't want him anywhere near her. She waves her arms and cries, "Go away! Go *away!* You promised you would help him! You promised you would *bring him home!*"

"Katie," Bill says. "I saw the news report too, but this isn't what you think. It's just a letter. A letter from Tiger. Just read it and see what it says. It's from Tiger."

Dear Ma,

By the time you get this, I will be sitting on a beach in Guam for a week of R and R. Guam is a US territory in the middle of the Pacific Ocean, which you might already know, although it came as news to me. Guess I should have paid closer attention in geography class!

I've been awarded R and R because I was in a firefight where nearly the whole platoon was killed and I collected up the pieces of my buddy Puppy's body and stayed with them until the chopper came and then I was reassigned to a special mission in Cambodia where we successfully seized twenty tons of supplies headed to VC forces. That was dangerous and exhausting—we worked mostly at night and went into hiding during the day and it was never clear which Cambodians we could trust and which were Communist sympathizers and there was no reliable source of drinking water so some of the guys gave into the temptation of drinking straight from the Mekong without even trying to purify it, and some of those guys got dysentery and some died. Then I was plucked out of that platoon for a recon mission with five other soldiers, one of whom was a guy named Banjo from Cape Girardeau, Missouri, who was at the end of his tour—basically, as soon as we completed this mission, he could go home to his wife and his three-year-

old daughter and a baby boy he'd never even met. Banjo wasn't wrapped too tight, we all knew it, but he had more time than the rest of us put together so I was hoping experience would make up for what was clearly a soft spot in his brain. We hiked across the border back into Vietnam—thirty hours over two days—and finally encountered Charlie along the trail but they didn't detect us so orders were to let them pass and ambush them from behind but Banjo just lost it and started firing his M16 and then we ended up in a full-blown firefight. We all retreated but we were in the jungle and we got disoriented and when Banjo got shot, he dropped our radio. Another guy, Romeo, stepped on a booby trap and got a bamboo spike straight through his foot so he couldn't go any farther, plus he was howling. I went out in search of the radio because without it, we were lost—and I found it. This big strapping kid named Fitz threw Romeo over his shoulder and I took Banjo and we macheted our way out of the jungle to a clearing. The clearing was actually a village that had been bombed out. The whole place was razed, black and charred, parts of it still on fire, and I shot my M16 in the air to see if anyone would materialize. That was when I heard crying. I hunted around until I found a little boy, five or six years old, sitting next to a woman, obviously the child's mother, who had been killed. I picked him up and we radioed for the chopper and the little kid came with us. I tried to figure out what his name was. The only thing he would say was "Luck, luck." So I said, "All right, your name is Luck and I'll tell you what, little buddy, the name fits."

A few days later I was called up to see one of the big guns, Colonel J. B. Neumann, and I had a private audience with him. I thought maybe I was in trouble. I hadn't done anything wrong that I knew of but even so, I was pretty nervous.

I sat down across the desk from Colonel Neumann and he said, "Well, Private Foley, looks like you have a guardian angel."

"Sir?"

He then proceeded to tell me that someone from even higher up—stratospherically high up—had called to check on me. The colonel had then done some digging and learned about my "heroic efforts" in the field—staying with the bodies of my buddies Puppy and Frog, going back for the radio and helping Banjo, and rescuing the Vietcong child from the village. Because what I forgot to tell you was that Luck's mother was wearing the black pajamas of the enemy. The colonel said to me, "Another soldier might have figured the easiest thing was to shoot him."

I said, "He was a little kid, sir, too young to understand why his country was at war. He climbed right into my arms and clung tight to my neck. I wasn't going to let anything happen to him."

The colonel said, "You're a good soldier, Foley, and a patriot besides. We need more men like you. I'm putting you in for a promotion and a full week of R and R. You deserve it. Dismissed."

I stood up and saluted and said, "Yes, sir, thank you, sir."

It wasn't until I got back outside that I wondered who had been checking in on me. I figured you used a connection or Nonny did. And I'm not going to keep this from you, Ma: In our conversation, the colonel offered me a cushier position— a job in requisitions, which would basically mean sitting at a warehouse all day keeping track of supplies. I turned the position down, Ma, and here's why.

I like being a soldier. I'm good at it. I've seen fellow

soldiers—hell, my brothers—blown to bits and I need to honor their memories by staying on the front lines and finishing what we started together. I can't just hide out in requisitions because my family is privileged and I have connections.

When I get home from Guam, I'm going to be assigned to a new platoon as a sergeant. I'm going to be a leader, Ma.

I want to say one more thing and I want you to hear me loud and clear, not like I'm shouting at you from another room or from the end of the driveway like I always used to, but like I'm standing in front of you, Ma, holding your hands, my eyes locked on yours. I plan on coming safely home to you. But the most important thing isn't whether I live or die, Ma. The most important thing is that you go to bed each night believing that you raised a hero.

Love, your son,
Tiger

Part Three

☮

November 1969

Someday We'll Be Together

It's a weekend of firsts. Magee has never been to Nantucket Island before, nor has she ever been away from her family on Thanksgiving. When Mrs. Levin called and invited her, saying, "Now that you and Tiger are engaged, you must come meet the family," Magee thought her mother would object. However, her mother had practically packed her bag and pushed her out the door.

"It's the natural way of things," Jean Johnson had said. "You're twenty years old. It's time to start your own life."

Magee knows her parents have her triplet eight-year-old brothers to feed and clothe, and besides, her mother likes Tiger. She was over the moon when Magee showed her the letter where Tiger proposed. Magee wrote back and accepted, and they'd set a date: Saturday, July 4, 1970.

Tiger will be home at the end of May, just in time to be fitted for his tuxedo.

Magee and the Levin-Foley and Whalen clans arrive on Nantucket by ferry on Wednesday afternoon. Magee worried she might get seasick—she was born and raised in the tiny hamlet of Carlisle, Massachusetts, and her experience on the water has been limited to a rowboat on Walden Pond—but the ferry is huge, like a floating building, big enough to transport forty cars. They drive off the boat caravan-style; Magee is in a station wagon with Tiger's parents and his sisters Jessie and Kirby; Tiger's other sister, Blair, her husband, and their four-month-old twins follow in a black Ford Galaxie. In the car, Tiger's mother, Kate, announces that she has a surprise.

Kirby and Jessie groan in stereo. Kirby is as pretty as a model—she's stick-thin with golden hair like Tiger's and delicate features—while Jessie is as dark and mysterious as a gypsy child. Magee has always wanted a sister. She desperately wants all three of Tiger's sisters to accept her, so she has been watching their every move.

"What *kind* of surprise?" Kirby asks.

Kate's face breaks into a grin. Magee has found Kate to be fairly reserved and proper, so her enthusiasm now is something brand-new.

"A big, big surprise. David, don't turn here."

Kate's husband, David, has been very kind and welcoming to Magee. Before they left Boston, he pulled Magee aside and said, "Don't let this family intimidate you. There are a lot of strong women. Just be yourself."

Now he says to Kate, "What do you have up your sleeve, Katie Nichols?"

"I've done something wonderful!" Kate says, clapping her hands like a child. "Just keep driving where I tell you."

Magee will be relieved if they're going to a hotel instead of the grandmother's house. In his most recent letter, Tiger told Magee that she would be expected to shower outside all weekend. That last bit had thrown Magee into a sheer panic. It was thirty-eight degrees outside; they'd been having frost for weeks. Surely Tiger was joking?

The two-car caravan rumbles up the cobblestoned main street lined with charming storefronts. Magee gazes at the pumpkins in windows, the corn shocks by doorways, the last of the orange and red leaves clinging to the trees that line the sides of the road.

"Does Blair know where we're going?" Jessie asks.

"She does not," Kate says. Kate cranks down her window and waves her arm at the car behind.

Blair says to Angus, "What is my mother *doing?* Where are we *going?*"

"It looks like she wants us to follow them," Angus says. "Maybe to look at the ocean? Is that some kind of Thanksgiving tradition you all have?"

"No," Blair says. They usually celebrate Thanksgiving at Exalta's house in Beacon Hill as they did last year, when Blair ate the cherrystone clam that didn't agree with her and then the next day discovered she was pregnant. They did come to Nantucket for Thanksgiving one year when Blair was a teenager. It had been rainy and cold and Kate lit the fireplace in the living room without remembering to open the flue and the living room filled with smoke and Exalta got in a dither about soot ruining the mural. Then it turned out that Nonny had forgotten to pick up the turkey they'd ordered from Savenor's before they left and they ended up eating Thanksgiving dinner at the Woodbox—and to protest the turn the holiday had taken, Blair ordered the beef Wellington. Blair hadn't wanted to come back to Nantucket this year. There just wasn't *room* for everyone and especially not since Kate invited Magee—but Kate insisted they would all just cram in.

"I don't know where they're going but I don't feel like a wild-goose chase right now," Blair says. "The second the babies wake up, they'll have to nurse."

"They just fell asleep," Angus says. "We have at least an hour, maybe longer. I'm going to follow them. Why not?" He reaches out to stroke Blair's leg. "It'll be an adventure."

Blair takes Angus's hand and relaxes against the seat. Angus is a new man, carefree and spontaneous. He received a whopping bonus from NASA—ten thousand dollars!—but he has declined their offer to work on the next mission. He's going to teach a normal course load, mentor his graduate students, and help out with the babies.

Blair had wondered if Angus's psychoanalysis with Trixie was any different than witchcraft, but she has to admit, he really does seem better. He hasn't suffered any episodes, and his general demeanor is looser and more relaxed. He smiles and laughs; he's present and engaged. Blair had called the graduate-school admissions office at Harvard to check on the status of her deferral and was informed that she could start her studies in January. After they get home from Nantucket, Blair will begin to wean the babies and they will interview nannies.

Kate's parents head out on the Madaket Road. If they wanted to see the water, why not drive to Cisco? It's much closer.

"Where are we going?" Blair asks.

Kirby can't believe a *surprise* has been thrown into their Thanksgiving. The whole point of Thanksgiving is tradition, sameness—although this past year has been one of enormous, unpredictable change, so why should Thanksgiving be any different?

Kirby wonders if her grandmother is in on this surprise. Exalta came up to the island on Monday, which was *completely* unheard of, and it made Kirby wonder if there was some truth to Jessie's claim that she had personally witnessed Exalta and Mr. Crimmins kissing, as in really *kissing,* on the night of the moon walk.

Kirby isn't sure that means Exalta and Mr. Crimmins are sleeping together—perish the thought!—but she will concede that Exalta has softened up. Kirby has spent a fair amount of time this fall currying favor with Exalta. She goes to lunch at the Union Club with her once a week because Exalta has agreed to pony up the three thousand dollars Kirby needs for a semester abroad in Geneva.

At their most recent lunch, Exalta ordered a bottle of champagne and they both got a little tipsy. Exalta had leaned across the table and said, "Tell me, Katharine, about your romantic life. Surely there must be a young man."

Kirby felt heat rise to her cheeks, which was a novel sensation. She wasn't sure if it was embarrassment or nerves or love. She had been seeing Darren. There was a date at Mr. Bartley's Burgers, then after that, an afternoon trip to the aquarium, then they met at the Boston Public Library to study together and went to Chinatown for noodles afterward. Kirby tried to keep things casual because she was leaving for Switzerland right after the new year and she couldn't risk a heavy romantic entanglement. But then Darren announced that he would be studying that same semester at the university in Genoa, Italy, which was only two hours away by train, and so suddenly Kirby was fantasizing about the kind of torrid affair they could conduct in cities where nobody knew them on a continent where no one would judge them.

Kirby said, "There's no one special."

"No one?" Exalta asked.

"Well," Kirby said. Exalta's gaze was unrelenting and Kirby could see she really did want to know about Kirby's life. Kirby flashed forward fifty years to 2019, when Kirby herself might have grandchildren. Wouldn't she want to know the truth about their lives? (What would being a twenty-one-year-old in 2019 look like? Kirby couldn't begin to imagine.) "There is someone I've been seeing now and again."

"I knew it," Exalta said. "You have that glow. Tell me all about him."

"Well, he goes to Harvard."

"Excellent!" Exalta said. "A Harvard man like your grandfather!"

Nothing like Gramps, Kirby thought. "His mother is a doctor and his father is a judge," Kirby said. "He has a house on Martha's Vineyard. That's where I met him."

"This all sounds marvelous," Exalta said. "Why have you been keeping this boy a secret? He sounds divine. Tell me, is he handsome?"

"Very," Kirby said.

"Of *course* he's handsome!" Exalta said. She poured more champagne into both of their glasses. Kirby watched the bubbles fizz, pop, and evaporate. Which was exactly what would happen to Exalta's enthusiasm about Kirby's mystery man. "Why don't you invite him for Thanksgiving?"

"He has a family," Kirby said. "His parents and aunts, uncles, cousins." She took a sip of her champagne. They would need another bottle if Kirby told the whole truth about Darren.

But why not just come right out and say it? Kirby wondered. She thought of Senator Kennedy, who had gone on television on July 25 and made a speech of explanation and apology about the Chappaquiddick incident. The Commonwealth of Massachusetts had not spontaneously combusted, nor had its citizens called for Kennedy's head, thrown him in jail, or stripped him of his Senate seat. If the country could accept Kennedy's story of being confused, discombobulated, and in a state of shock following the accident—so much so that he didn't even *call the police*—then Exalta could accept Kirby's relationship with Darren Frazier.

Or at least, she hoped so.

"Darren's black," Kirby said. She laid her hands on either side of her silverware on top of the linen tablecloth and forced herself to deliver the words right to Exalta's face. "He's Negro."

Exalta blinked and then said, "I've learned a lot in my seventy-five years, Katharine." She'd lowered her voice into what Kirby thought of as her serious register. "Some knowledge has come to me quite recently. I'm sure it was difficult for you to tell me that, maybe because you expect me to react in a certain way. But I'll have you know, your young man—what is his name?"

"Darren," Kirby said. "Darren Frazier."

"You can feel free to bring Darren Frazier to meet me at any time. I would be honored."

Inexplicably, this caused Kirby to tear up. "Really?"

"Of course," Exalta said. "People are people."

People are people. Her grandmother couldn't have said anything to make Kirby happier.

Now Kirby turns her attention back to her mother. "So...did Nonny drive up here by *herself* on Monday?" This seems unlikely. Exalta has a license and a car but she has never, to Kirby's knowledge, driven all the way to the Cape.

"No," Kate says. "Bill Crimmins came and fetched her."

Jessie pinches Kirby's leg. "I *told* you so," she whispers.

Her grandmother and Mr. Crimmins. The society matron and the caretaker.

People are people, Kirby thinks.

They are headed out to the end of the earth, Jessie thinks. When they are nearly at Madaket Beach, the best place to see the sunset, Kate tells David to turn left. They go down a winding sand-and-gravel road that's bordered on both sides by scrub pine and Spanish olives. They cross a battered one-lane wooden bridge and then the land opens up. There are fields on either side of the road and a steel gray stripe on the horizon—the Atlantic Ocean.

Jessie is awestruck. This part of the island is natural and wild; it's a far cry from the manicured streetscapes of town. She tries to memorize every detail so she can write about it to Tiger and to her new pen pal, Pick.

Jessie received a letter from Pick in early September, right after school started. He's living in a sustainable community outside of Pottstown, Pennsylvania. His mother did end up taking him to Woodstock, and the way he described it in his letter made Jessie glad she hadn't gone. Pick and Lorraine drove to the concert in a VW bus with a couple from their community. The bus got a flat tire right before Eldred, New York, and Pick said it was easier to abandon the bus and hitch a ride than to track down another tire; the bus didn't have a spare. Pick and Lorraine had to hitch rides in separate cars. The road was a logjam of vehicles headed to the Yasgur farm, and some cars were so crowded that people sat on the roofs and hoods. Pick worried he would never find his mother again.

Needle in a haystack, he wrote to Jessie. *Four hundred thousand people, half of them women, and all of them looked and acted just like Lavender.*

Pick hooked up with a couple who had brought their seven-year-old son, Denny, and in exchange for Pick keeping an eye on the little guy, they included Pick in their family unit and shared the food they'd brought.

The concert had good moments. Pick's favorite band, Creedence, had played after midnight on Saturday night, but he fell fast asleep before Janis Joplin went on. He woke back up to hear Jefferson Airplane. *I'd forgotten where I was,* he wrote, *then I heard Grace Slick's voice. There were times when I was bored and tired and hungry but there were other times when I was part of this teeming, gyrating, smoking, singing mass of humanity. I felt proud to live in this country.*

When Monday morning rolled around and Jimi Hendrix, the final performer, played a psychedelic version of "The Star-Spangled Banner," Pick still hadn't located his mother. He figured she would have wanted to stay and see Hendrix, but he decided if he didn't find her, he would hitch a ride with someone heading back to Cape Cod and return to his grandfather on Nantucket.

But then this amazing thing happened. Denny saw a kid who had a balloon animal and he declared that he wanted one. Pick somehow, through asking one person and then another, found the man who was making the balloon animals. He was clearly strung out—he wore only a pair of red satin shorts and a red bow tie—and Pick was hesitant to approach him. It was Denny who charged forward toward the balloon man, and thank goodness, because Pick saw that the woman who was collecting the money for him—the animals were a dime apiece—was Lavender.

We got back to the community in time for me to start at a regular high school, Pick wrote. *They had to put me back a grade, but nobody here knows me so it's not too bad. I miss you, Jessie. Write back. Your friend, Pick.*

Jessie won't lie; she loved receiving the letter from Pick and she hurried to respond. She considered telling Pick that they were, in a way, related. They were both half siblings to Blair, Kirby, and Tiger. But that was a family secret and Jessie felt a certain power in guarding it. If she were to release that secret into the world, who knew what kinds of awful dramas would unfold?

So instead, Jessie wrote to Pick about the two astonishing things that had happened since she'd started seventh grade. The first was that she had been invited to Miss Flowers's wedding to Mr. Barstow. The invitation was printed on fine stock, ivory with black lettering, in a script so fancy it was difficult to read. The envelope was addressed to Miss Jessica Levin, and it had impressed even Jessie's parents. Kate had scrutinized the invitation as though it contained a secret message from the Russians. "Do you suppose she invited every student in the school? That would be only fair and yet, one would think, impossible."

Jessie did some quiet trawling to see if this was the case. She asked Doris, "What are you doing on Saturday the twentieth?"

Doris had scowled. Over the summer she had developed a bad case of acne, probably from eating so many McDonald's French fries. "I don't know," she said. "Sleeping in?"

Jessie decided she would attend the service at the Church of the Advent in Beacon Hill but not the reception at the Hampshire House; that way, Kate could drop Jessie off, have a quick visit with Nonny on Mt. Vernon Street, then come back and pick Jessie up.

Jessie was seated in the middle of the church on the bride's side among a sea of unfamiliar faces; not only was she the only kid from school there, she was the only child, period, aside from one baby who cried until the organ music started and everyone stood up as Miss Flowers walked down the aisle.

Miss Flowers as a bride was the most beautiful woman Jessie had ever seen in real life. She had her dark hair swept back in a sleek chignon and she wore a satin column dress and a long sheer silk veil. The most extraordinary thing was that when she passed by Jessie's row, she reached out to Jessie and gave her a soulful smile; her eyes brimmed with tears as she squeezed Jessie's hand.

Dear Pick,

This past Saturday I was invited to the wedding of my school guidance counselor and the boys' gym teacher. Miss Flowers looked elegant in her white dress and veil. She was crying a little as she walked down the aisle. At first, I thought she was sad because Miss Flowers was meant to be married last year to a man named Rex Rothman, who was killed during the Tet Offensive. But then I realized her tears were tears of hope and of gratitude because she had been given a second chance at love with Mr. Barstow.

The second astonishing thing that happened was that Jessie found a new boyfriend, Andy Pearlstein. He was in Jessie's English class. During roll call, their teacher, Miss Malantantas, had mispronounced Jessie's last name as "Le*vin*," rhyming it with "the pin," and Jessie had surprised herself by speaking up and saying, "It's *Lev*in, rhymes with 'heaven.'"

"*Lev*in, rhymes with 'heaven,'" Miss Malantantas said. "Thank you, I love that."

Andy, who sat three seats up and one row to the left, turned around and winked at Jessie.

Later that week, when they were discussing their summer reading, *Anne Frank: The Diary of a Young Girl,* Andy had raised his hand and said, "I think it stinks that she dies in the end. The book would have been way better if she had lived."

Shane Harris then argued that the point of the book was that Anne had died. If she had lived, Shane said, no one would care about this diary.

"You're only saying that because you're not Jewish," Andy said.

Jessie's hand flew to her Tree of Life necklace, and Miss Malantantas jumped in to redirect the discussion.

After class, Jessie sought out Andy. He was a few inches taller than her; he must have been one of the boys who sprouted up over the summer. Jessie looked up at him and said, "I agree with you. I think it stinks that Anne died. I actually cried."

"You did?" Andy said. He seemed on the verge of confessing that he had shed a tear too—but there wasn't a seventh-grade boy in the world who would admit to that.

That weekend, Pammy Pope called to see if Jessie wanted to play tennis at the Chestnut Hill reservoir. (Pammy Pope had overheard Jessie telling Doris about Miss Flowers's wedding in the girls' locker room, and this gave Jessie a social boost she hadn't predicted.) Jessie put on her whites and her visor and stuck her autographed Jack Kramer racket in her basket and biked to the park to meet Pammy. She saw Andy and a couple of other boys from school kicking a soccer ball. He jogged right over to Jessie and asked what she was doing and she said, "I'm playing tennis with Pammy Pope." It wasn't as glamorous as saying she was a fourth in a mixed-doubles match at a house party on Hilton Head, but it had had the same effect on Andy. He looked *impressed* and said, "I'll wait for you, and when you're done, let's bike to Brigham's for ice cream."

He was asking her on a date.

Jessie shrugged. "Okay."

Pammy showed up and they agreed to play one set and Jessie won, six games to two. Pammy invited Jessie to sleep over—she said she had just gotten the new Beatles album, *Abbey Road,* if Jessie wanted to listen to it—and Jessie said, "Let's do it next weekend. I have plans tonight." This was the exact right response because Pammy said, "Okay, let's *definitely* do it next weekend." She biked off and Andy loped over, soccer ball under his arm, his dark bangs sweaty at the hairline, which made him look kind of cute.

"Who won?" Andy asked.

Jessie zipped up her racket case. "We weren't really keeping score. Pammy is a good player."

"Really?" Andy said. "Because it looked like you were cream-ing her."

"Oh," Jessie said. "Were you watching?"

Like Miss Flowers, I've gotten my own second chance at love.

Jessie crosses this out. She doesn't want Pick to know he was her first chance at love; he'll become conceited.

I have a new boyfriend. His name is Andy. He plays soccer and likes the Beatles. He took me to see Goodbye, Mr. Chips, *and next weekend his parents are taking us to the Boston College football game against the Naval Academy and we're having a tailgate picnic. I miss you too. Write soon.*

Your friend, Jessie

David slows down when the road curves to the left and Jessie sees a dilapidated barn with its roof caving in.

"This is Red Barn Road," Kate says. "And that's the barn."

Is this the surprise? Jessie wonders. Because if so, it stinks.

"Do I keep going?" David asks. He sounds wary. What are they *doing* out here?

"Up ahead," Kate says. "Pull into that driveway."

David turns to her. "Katie Nichols, what have you done?"

"Welcome home," Kate says.

There's one other house up ahead. It's *huge*—bigger than All's Fair and Little Fair put together, bigger than their house in Brook-line, bigger than Exalta's house on Mt. Vernon Street.

"Holy moly!" Kirby yells. "Did you buy this? Is this ours?"

"We did," Kate says. "It's ours."

Kirby pushes Jessie out the door. "Go, go!"

Jessie climbs out and stands in front of the house, taking it in. She starts another letter in her head, this time to Tiger.

We have a new house on Nantucket. Wait until you see it.

"Holy moly!" Kirby cries out. "Did you buy this? Is this ours?"

"We did," Kate says. "It's ours."

Blair and Angus pull up behind them in the Galaxie. Blair gets out of the car and closes the door gently so as not to wake the babies. "What is this?"

"This," Kate says, "is our new house."

"What?" Blair says. "Our new house?"

David looks at Kate the exact same way he looked at her the first time he saw her—when Kate, newly a widow, had opened the door to welcome in the lawyer who was going to defend her late husband's life insurance claim. David had later confessed that his knees buckled at the sight of her. *I didn't know God made women as beautiful as you.*

"Katie?" he says.

"I bought it," she says. It's intoxicating to know that she has done the right thing—not only for herself, but for David, for the children, for her grandchildren.

Jessie says, "Can I pick out my room?"

"Go ahead," Kate says. Her heart is filling her chest; it's hard to breathe.

"Wait," David says. He leads Kate up the walk by the hand and then he scoops her up in his arms and carries her across the threshold like they're newlyweds. It feels like a fresh start.

How many do you get in one life? Kate wonders.

David kisses her cheek. "Thank you," he whispers.

* * *

The dynamics of Tiger's family are a lot to learn, but by the time Thanksgiving dinner rolls around, Magee has them figured out. She thinks.

Kate prepares the turkey and assigns Kirby, Jessie, and Magee to tasks in the kitchen but everyone is on an equal footing because no one knows which cabinet holds the plates or whether or not they have a potato masher or which drawer holds the silverware. Kate bought the house furnished, but they're going to replace what's here with new things, hopefully by summer.

When they all first arrived here, Kate led Magee upstairs and informed her that the bright, spacious room with two windows overlooking the water would be hers and Tiger's.

"Think about what color you'd like to paint it," Kate said.

Magee felt like a newly crowned princess. She lay down across the big white bed and imagined sleeping there with Tiger, maybe even conceiving a child there. Both Tiger and Magee want a passel of kids—four or five.

The dinner menu for Thanksgiving:

Turkey with dressing made from day-old Portuguese bread, which Kate bought from a bakery downtown.

Mashed potatoes. Kate adds sour cream and tops them with snipped green onions. Magee must remember to tell her mother about this. Her mother's cooking needs some updating.

Scalloped corn.

Carrots boiled in orange juice and topped with brown butter and cinnamon.

Brussels sprouts, roasted in the oven.

Cranberry sauce out of a can, just like at Magee's house. The pies, pumpkin and apple, Kate bought at the bakery as well. They will be topped with Brigham's ice cream—vanilla and butter brickle, Tiger's favorite.

Kate brought linens from home, along with silver candlesticks and ivory tapers. Jessie makes a centerpiece out of gourds and apples. Kate turns the transistor radio to WBUR, which broadcasts classical music. All of this is a far cry from Thanksgiving at Magee's house. Jean Johnson makes sweet potatoes topped with marshmallows and green-bean casserole with crispy onions and turkey with store-bought stuffing, and because no one likes pie, she serves a Sara Lee chocolate cake. Magee's brothers always complain about the beans; they skim the marshmallows off the top of the sweet potatoes. The Johnsons eat at the kitchen table just like every other meal, and Magee's father, Al Johnson, drinks his usual Budweiser from a can. Magee wouldn't say she dreads Thanksgiving, but neither does it feel like a *holiday* the way it does here. With three little boys in her house, Magee's family Christmas is far more festive.

Kate asks Magee to set the table for ten and Magee worries that she will make a mistake. In her studies to become a dental hygienist, she has proved to be good at memorizing—incisors, cuspids, molars—and now she wishes she'd taken a book about table settings out of the library. Wine goblet, water goblet, fork, knife, spoon, dessert fork—all of those Magee can handle. (She actually isn't sure which goblet is which, so she quietly asks Kirby, who says, "Water goblet is bigger. It goes here." She places it to the side of the wine goblet. "It's pathetic that I know that, but Nonny is a Brahmin.") Magee is glad there aren't fish forks or soupspoons or cordial glasses.

There is a moment of confusion, however, because Magee counts only nine people who are eating and yet Kate clearly told her to set the table for ten. Is there a guest Magee doesn't know about? A family member she's forgotten?

She asks Kate, who says, "We're setting an honorary place for Tiger, so the chair next to yours will be empty. And look, I got this."

She shows Magee a small American flag on a stand, the same kind that rested on teachers' desks when Magee was in grade school. "Tiger's seat will be on the left side, second from the head."

Magee has a lump in her throat as she sets the flag at the place Kate specified.

At five o'clock, Exalta Nichols—"Nonny," as she's known, Tiger's grandmother—arrives with a man whom Kate calls Bill. Magee isn't sure who Bill is; she knows Tiger's grandfather has passed, and Tiger said that Exalta doesn't have a new husband or a boyfriend, "unless you count Rod Laver." But it's quite clear that Exalta and Bill are a couple. He holds her arm as they enter and he helps her off with her coat and he offers to fetch her cocktail. Magee herself enjoyed a glass of champagne in the kitchen as she helped get everything ready; Kate had popped the cork off a bottle and poured glasses for Magee and Kirby and Blair.

We drank champagne as we prepared dinner, Magee imagines telling her mother.

The champagne has also eased Magee's nerves about meeting Exalta. Once Exalta has been relieved of her coat and handed her cocktail—a gin and tonic served in a highball glass with an artful twist of lime—Magee is ushered forward to be presented to her.

My nonny, Tiger had said before he left, *can be intimidating.*

But the woman Magee meets is tiny in stature with a silver bobbed haircut held back from her face by a black velvet headband. She wears a soft red turtleneck sweater and pearl earrings. Her eyes widen as she takes stock of Magee.

"Aren't you *lovely?*" Exalta says, reaching for Magee's hand. "And you're wearing Penn's class ring. How divine that it fits."

It doesn't fit; Magee has wound tape around the back, but she won't show Exalta that. "It's a pleasure to meet you," she says.

Exalta turns to Bill. "Isn't she just beautiful?"

What interests Magee at that point isn't Bill's response (he be-nignly agrees, although really, what else could he do?) but the glowing expression on Exalta's face as she looks at Bill. Magee rec-ognizes that she and Exalta are members of the same tribe. They are women in love.

They all sit down to eat. The turkey is golden brown, fragrant, and steaming in the center of the table, just like in a Norman Rockwell painting. David is at the head of the table with Exalta at the other end. Magee is in the middle, between Kirby and the empty chair, and on the other side of the empty chair is Jessie. This is Magee's spot. She is becoming part of this story. Pennington Nichols met Exalta at a debutante ball in 1917, just after he returned from fighting in World War I. Fifty-two years later, Magee Johnson went for driving lessons because her mother decided it was worth the thirty-dollar fee to have Magee help her drive the boys around. Magee stepped out of the Walden Pond Driving Academy office and there, leaning against the car at the curb, was her instructor.

He'd stuck out his hand with a devilish grin. Devilish, he informed her later, because after twelve weeks of working as an instructor at this school, he had finally been assigned a pretty girl his age.

"Good morning," he said. "I'm Tiger."

She had noticed his eye right away—feline, wild, mesmerizing.

David rises to offer words of thanks and then lifts his glass. Magee raises her glass, filled with a delicious red wine. The only thing that could make this moment more perfect, she thinks, would be for Tiger to walk in right now, dressed in his combat fatigues, his expression weary but grateful.

However, things like that happen only in the movies and in novels.

But incredibly...

Just as all the adult members of the Levin-Foley and Whalen clans raise their glasses and say, "Cheers!," and as baby Genevieve utters a happy cry from her wind-up swing, the front door of the house opens. They all turn. Magee's heart hovers; it's a humming-bird, wings beating so fast they can't be seen.

Kate jumps to her feet.

Tiger!

But there's no one standing at the door.

It's just the wind blowing in off the water.

Fortunate Son (Reprise)

Sergeant Richard "Tiger" Foley is eighty-seven hundred miles away from Nantucket at Landing Zone George, southeast of Pleiku, in the Central Highlands of Vietnam. To surprise the troops, the U.S. Army has flown in turkeys, mashed potatoes, and Marmite cans filled with gravy. It's not perfect—there are no candied yams, no acorn squash or pickled okra, no soft snowflake rolls, no ziti for the soldiers who grew up with Italian grand-mothers, and they're all served cranberry juice instead of cranberry sauce—but it still feels festive.

Major Freeland—aptly named—stands to say grace, and the men all bow their heads.

"Lord, we offer thanks for the meal we are about to receive. We pray that You will keep us safe on the battlefield and that You will instill in us courage, strength, forbearance, resolve, patience, and trust in our fellow soldiers so that we may continue our efforts to bring peace to this war-torn country." He pauses long enough that Tiger looks up. The major, he can see, is struggling. "We ask You to hold in the palm of Your hand the brave men we have lost..."

Puppy, Tiger thinks. *Frog.* So many others. What must their families' Thanksgivings be like today? Then he thinks of Luck, the little Vietnamese boy he carried out of the smoldering village. The life he saved.

"...and let them know we miss them and will carry on in their honor and on behalf of all the good citizens of the United States of America. In Your name we pray. Amen."

Magee, Tiger thinks. Blair, Kirby, Messie, David, Exalta, Angus, the twins Tiger has yet to meet...and his mother.

His mother, Kate, loves him more than all those other people put together. Because...well, because she's his mother.

Some folks are born made to wave the flag. And he is one. Other soldiers at this table may be wishing they were safe in their homes with their families, but Tiger knows that, right now, he's where he's supposed to be. And he will see his family again soon enough. Of this, he is certain.

"Amen," he says.

Author's Note

I'm frequently asked where I get the ideas for my books. Much of the time, I don't have a satisfying answer for this beyond "ideas come to me in the night." But the novel you've just read had a very specific genesis.

My twin brother, Eric Hilderbrand, and I were born at Boston Hospital for Women on July 17, 1969. The week we were born was one of the most eventful weeks of the twentieth century. The Apollo 11 mission launched the day before my brother and I launched. (It was always my intention to include my own birth in this book, but in the end, I decided I wanted the twins born on the day of the moon launch, so the Whalen twins, Genevieve and George, are one day older than Eric and me.) The weekend after we were born was the weekend of the Chappaquiddick incident, which was of enormous interest to the nation but even more so to residents of Massachusetts. The atmosphere of the country in the summer of 1969 was tumultuous: Nixon was a new president, the war in Vietnam was raging right along with protests against that war, civil rights and women's lib were hot topics, and Woodstock was planned as a tribute to the nation's youth, who wanted peace, love, and rock 'n' roll.

Within my own family that summer, there was also uncertainty, unrest, and excitement. My mother didn't find out she was having twins until she was seven months along. (She was, like Blair, "just so big," with only one dress that fit.) My father was gravely ill and had to undergo surgery at Mass General in mid-July, which was serious, but everyone believed he would be home and on the mend by the time the twins made their appearance. He did make it through surgery just fine...but not in time for our birth.

My mother went into labor at three in the morning on July 17—four weeks before her due date—and, as family legend goes, my grandmother, then forty-nine (and today a robust ninety-nine), ran every red light in downtown Boston to get my mother to the hospital. My mother's obstetrician was hung over (too much celebrating the moon launch), and because twin births were so rare, he was asked if a class of forty student nurses could watch the delivery. (My mother was in twilight sleep and not really in a position to protest.)

I was born first, at 10:04 a.m., and all of the student nurses bet that the second would also be a girl. When my brother entered the world at 10:10, it was to an enthusiastic round of applause. And you know what? He's a great guy, an exceptionally wonderful father, and (along with my other siblings) my best friend in all the world. He has earned that applause many, many times over. This novel is my birthday present to him. It was Eric's suggestion that I someday write about the year and circumstances of our birth.

I did the best I could. I beg my kind readers' indulgence for the places where I changed facts and circumstances—on Nantucket, on the Vineyard, and in the country as a whole—in the service of my narrative. In this novel, I strive to bring you not empirical truth, but emotional truth. I like to think Jessie would approve.

—*Elin Hilderbrand, Nantucket, Massachusetts,*
December 12, 2018

Acknowledgments

The only difference between me and every other writer (save a small group) is that I have Reagan Arthur as an editor. Reagan makes every single novel of mine better in ways I can't adequately explain. I would say our working relationship is magical, but I don't think either of us believes in magic. We believe in intelligence, generosity of spirit, and hard work. My first thanks must go to her for being the best editor I could ever hope for.

Thank you to Michael Carlisle and David Forrer of Inkwell Management, my heroes, guardians, personal cheerleaders, and dear, trusted friends.

As I mentioned in the author's note, not every detail about Nantucket and Martha's Vineyard in 1969 is historically precise, but I did a fair amount of research to try and portray the spirit of these islands in that year as accurately as possible. I read many, many books, the most helpful of which were *Nantucket Only Yesterday: An Island View of the Twentieth Century,* by Nantucket legend Robert Mooney, and Rob Kirkpatrick's *1969: The Year Everything Changed.* I am much indebted to back issues of the *Inquirer and Mirror,* as well as John Stanton's film *Last Call,* a documentary about the storied Nantucket bar Bosun's Locker. I spent many enraptured hours watching and rewatching *The Vietnam War,* the outstanding documentary by Ken Burns and Lynn Novick.

Of course, the best stories and information came from the people I talked to personally. I want to start by thanking Charles Marino (half of "the perfect couple"), who served as a staff sergeant in Vietnam in 1967 and 1968 in the First Marine Division, Hotel Company, Second Battalion, Fifth Marine Regiment (better known as the Hotel 2/5). He was awarded two Purple Hearts, a Bronze Star, the Vietnam Cross of Gallantry, and his Marine unit received a Presidential Unit Citation as the most decorated in Vietnam. (Yes, Chuck is amazing. Thank you for your service, Chuck!) Jane Silva, of Galley Beach, kindly spent a wonderful evening regaling me with tales of not only the Galley back in the day, but also the glamorous Opera House and the Straight Wharf Theater. Jay Riggs—the only person one needs to know on Nantucket— gave me more information than could fit in one book and she later told me she didn't reveal any of her scandalous stories! Brian Davis patiently answered my texts about the many details of downtown that I wanted to get right. Michael May, the executive director of the Nantucket Preservation Trust, provided historical information about several houses on Fair Street that were enormously helpful in my descriptions of All's Fair and Little Fair. The generous souls on the Facebook pages Nantucket Years of Yore and Islanders Talk (Martha's Vineyard) enthusiastically shared stories (love you, Linda Herrick; you had such vivid, detailed memories). Jeanne Casey Miller, who used to be a server at the North Shore Restaurant (though *not* in 1969) gave me details about Pick's workplace. Special thanks to Susan Lister Locke and Jeannie Diamond and everyone else who filled me in on treasures such as the Mad Hatter and the Skipper and Susie's Snack Bar.

I owe a debt to other pieces of literature that inspired this book. *Anne Frank: The Diary of a Young Girl,* obviously, but also Judy Blume's *Are You There, God? It's Me, Margaret,* Tim O'Brien's iconic story "The Things They Carried," and the gorgeous, heartbreaking Anne Sexton poem "Letter Written on a Ferry While Crossing Long Island Sound."

Acknowledgments

Warm thanks to my publishing people: Jenny Schaffer, Sareena Kamath, Ashley Marudas, Peggy Freudenthal, Jayne Yaffe Kemp, Tracy Roe, Brandon Kelly, Craig Young, Terry Adams, Michael Pietsch, and my outstanding publicist, Katharine Myers.

And to my people-people, who make my life brighter and easier in big ways and small: Chuck and Margie Marino, Rebecca Bartlett, Debbie Briggs, Wendy Hudson, Wendy Rouillard, Elizabeth and Beau Almodobar, Matthew and Evelyn MacEachern, Linda Holliday, Sue Decoste, Melissa Long, John and Martha Sargent, Richard Congdon, Manda Riggs, David Rattner and Andrew Law, West Riggs, Helaina Jones, Gwenn and Mark Snider, Anne and Whitney Gifford, Mark and Eithne Yelle, Marty and Holly McGowan, Mary Haft, Sara Underwood, Rocky Fox, Jimmy Jaksic, Jessica Hicks, Elizabeth Harris, Melissa and Angus MacVicar, Michelle Birmingham, Ali Lubin, Christina Schwefel, Eric and Lisa Hilderbrand, Randy and Steph Osteen, Doug and Jen Hilderbrand, Todd Thorpe, Heather Thorpe—my sister and my bestie, the woman in charge of my sanity and my spirit—and, for his love and patience, Timothy Field.

Finally, to my children, Maxwell, Dawson, and Shelby: Everything begins and ends with you—my superstars, my bright lights, my darlings. I love you.

About the Author

Elin Hilderbrand was born on July 17, 1969, in Boston, Massachusetts. She has used her first fifty years to write twenty-three novels and raise three children on Nantucket Island.